Praise for #1 *New York Times* bestselling author

"Her stories have fueled the dreams of twenty-five million readers."

—*Chicago Tribune*

"Roberts' bestselling novels are some of the best in the romance genre. They are thoughtfully plotted, well-written stories featuring fascinating characters."

—*USA TODAY*

"When Roberts puts her expert fingers on the pulse of romance, legions of fans feel the heartbeat."

—*Publishers Weekly*

"With clear-eyed, concise vision and a sure pen, Roberts nails her characters and settings with awesome precision, drawing readers into a vividly rendered world of family-centered warmth and unquestionable magic."

—*Library Journal*

"A superb author…Ms. Roberts is an enormously gifted writer whose incredible range and intensity guarantee the very best of reading."

—*Rave Reviews*

"The publishing world might be hard-pressed to find an author with a more diverse style or fertile imagination than Roberts."

—*Publishers Weekly*

Dear Reader,

The poet Christina Rossetti once wrote, "For there is no friend like a sister." This is especially true of the Calhoun women. We are pleased to offer you *The Calhoun Women: Amanda & Lilah*, the first of two special volumes featuring three Calhoun sisters and their sister by marriage, all united by a decades-old legend and the determination to save their family home, the Towers.

Amanda is known as the responsible Calhoun sister, always coming to her family's aid. But when irresistible architect Sloan O'Riley comes to town, it's Amanda's turn to be rescued—from falling head over heels in love in *A Man for Amanda*.

Sweet sister Lilah saves a mysterious stranger from drowning, a man she discovers could touch her heart with the simplest smile. But Professor Max Quartermain is a man with secrets—what might he reveal...*For the Love of Lilah*?

The Calhoun Women: fascinating sisters, fabulous stories and fairy-tale romances you won't soon forget!

Enjoy!

The Editors

Silhouette Books

NORA ROBERTS

THE CALHOUN WOMEN:
AMANDA & LILAH

Silhouette® Books

Published by Silhouette Books

America's Publisher of Contemporary Romance

SILHOUETTE BOOKS
®

The Calhoun Women: Amanda & Lilah

ISBN-13: 978-0-373-28187-9

Copyright © 2015 by Harlequin Books S.A.

The publisher acknowledges the copyright holder
of the individual works as follows:

A Man for Amanda
Copyright © 1991 by Nora Roberts

For the Love of Lilah
Copyright © 1991 by Nora Roberts

Recycling programs
for this product may
not exist in your area.

Visit Silhouette Books at www.Harlequin.com

Printed in U.S.A.

CONTENTS

A MAN FOR AMANDA

To Joyce,
from one baby sister to another

Prologue

Bar Harbor
June 8, 1913—

In the afternoon, I walked to the cliffs. The day, our first day back in The Towers, was bright and warm. The rumble of the sea was as I had left it ten long months ago. There was a fishing boat chugging over the blue-green water, and a neat sloop gliding cheerfully along. So much was the same, and yet, one vital change dimmed the day for me.

He was not there.

It was wrong of me to wish to find him waiting where I had left him so many months ago. To find him painting as he always did, slicing the brush against canvas like a dueler in the heat of battle. It was wrong of me to wish to see him turn, look at me with those intense gray eyes—to see him smile, to hear him say my name.

Yet I did wish it.

My heart was dancing in my breast as I rushed from the house to race across the lawn, past the gardens and down the slope.

The cliffs were there, so high and proud, jutting up to the pure summer sky. The sea, almost calm today, mirrored the color so that it seemed I stood cupped in a lovely blue ball. The rocks tumbled down before me, down and down to where the waves slapped and hissed. Behind me, the towers of my summer home, my husband's home, speared up, arrogant and beautiful.

How strange that I should love the house when I have known such unhappiness inside it.

I reminded myself that I am Bianca Calhoun, wife of Fergus Calhoun, mother to Colleen and Ethan and Sean. I am a respected woman, a dutiful wife, a devoted mother. My marriage is not a warm one, but that does not alter the vows I took. There is no place in my life for romantic fancies and sinful dreams.

Still, I stood and I waited. But he did not come. Christian, the lover I have taken only with my heart, did not come. He may not even be on the island any longer. Perhaps he has packed up his canvases and brushes, moved from his cottage and gone on to paint some other sea, some other sky.

It would be best. I know it would be best. Since I met him last summer, I have hardly gone an hour without thinking of him. Yet I have a husband I respect, three children I love more than my life. It is to them I must be faithful, not to the memory of something that never was. And never could be.

The sun is setting as I sit and write by the window of my tower. In a short time I must go down and help Nanny put my babies to bed. Little Sean has grown so, and is already beginning to toddle. Soon he will be as quick as Ethan. Colleen, quite the young lady at four, wants a new pink dress.

It is of them I must think, my children, my precious loves, and not of Christian.

It will be a quiet night, one of very few we will have during our summer on Mount Desert Island. Fergus has already talked of giving a dinner dance next week. I must...

He is there. Down below on the cliffs. He is hardly more than a shadow with the distance and the dimming light. Yet I know it is he. Just as I knew, as I stood and pressed my hand to the glass, that he was looking up, looking for me. However impossible it is, I would swear I could hear him call my name. So softly.

Bianca.

Chapter One

He was a solid wall of denim and muscle. Ramming into him knocked the wind out of her lungs and the packages out of her hands. In her rush to get from one place to the next, she didn't even bother to glance at him but dove to save the flying boxes.

If he'd been looking where he'd been going, she wouldn't have run into him. Amanda managed to bite her tongue before she snapped out the thought, and scowled instead at the run-down heels of his boots. In a hurry, as usual, she knelt on the sidewalk outside the boutique where she'd been shopping, to gather up her scattered packages.

"Let me give you a hand, honey."

The slow southwestern drawl grated on her nerves. She had a million things to do, and scrambling on the sidewalk with a tourist wasn't on her schedule. "I've got it," she muttered, leaning over so that her chin-length hair drifted down to curtain her face. Everything was grating on her nerves today, she thought as she hurried to restack bags and boxes. This little irritation was the last in a long line.

"It's an awful lot for one person to carry."

"I can manage, thanks." She reached for a box just as her persistent helper did the same. The brief tug-of-war had the top slipping off and the contents spilling onto the sidewalk.

"Now, that's mighty pretty." There was amused, masculine approval in the voice as he scooped up a scrap of thin red silk that pretended to be a nightie.

Amanda snatched it from him and stuffed it into one of the bags. "Do you mind?"

"No, ma'am. I sure don't."

Amanda pushed back her tumbled hair and took her first good look at him. So far, all she'd seen were a pair of cowboy boots and the line of faded denim from knee to ankle. There was a great deal more of him. Even crouched down beside her he looked big. Shoulders, hands. Mouth, she thought nastily. Right now he was using it to grin at her. It might, under different circumstances, have been an engaging enough grin. But at the moment it was stuck in the middle of a face she'd decided to dislike on sight.

Not that it wasn't a good one, with its slashing warrior's cheekbones, velvet green eyes and deep tan. The curl of his reddish-blond hair over the collar of his denim shirt might have been charming. If he hadn't been in her way.

"I'm in a hurry," she told him.

"I noticed." He flipped a long finger through her hair

to tuck it behind her ear. "Looked like you were on the way to a fire when you plowed into me."

"If you'd moved," she began, then shook her head. Arguing would take time she simply didn't have. "Never mind." Grabbing at packages, she rose. "Excuse me."

"Hold on."

He unfolded himself as she tapped her foot and waited. Disconcerted, she frowned up at him. At five feet ten inches, she was accustomed to meeting most men almost eye to eye. With this one she had several extra inches to go. "What?"

"I can give you a ride to that fire if you need it."

Her brow arched in her frostiest look. "That won't be necessary."

Using a fingertip, he pushed a box back in place before it could slide out of her grip. "You look like you could use a little help."

"I'm perfectly capable of getting where I'm going, thank you."

He didn't doubt it for a minute. "Then maybe you can help me." He liked the way her hair kept falling into her eyes, and the impatient way she kept blowing it away again. "I just got into town this morning." His gaze lazily skimmed her face. "I thought maybe you could make some suggestions about…what I should do with myself."

At the moment, she had a pocketful of them. "Try the chamber of commerce." She started by him, then whirled when his hand came down on her arm. "Look, buster, I don't know how they do things back in Tucson—"

"Oklahoma City," he corrected.

"Wherever, but around here, cops take a dim view of men who hassle women on the streets."

"That so?"

"You bet it's so."

"Well then, I'll have to watch my step since I plan to be around awhile."

"I'll hang out a bulletin. Now, excuse me."

"Just one more thing." He held up a pair of brief black panties embroidered with red roses. "I think you forgot this."

She grabbed the bikinis, then stalked off as she balled them into her pocket.

"Nice meeting you," he called after her, and laughed when she doubled her already hurried pace.

Twenty minutes later, Amanda gathered up her packages from the backseat of her car. Balancing some under her chin, she kicked the door closed with her foot. She'd nearly forgotten about the encounter already. There was too much on her mind. Behind her, the house rose up into the sky, its gray stones staid, its towers and peaks fanciful and its porches sagging. Next to her family, there was nothing Amanda loved more than The Towers.

She raced up the steps, avoided a rotting board then struggled to free a hand enough to open the towering front door. "Aunt Coco!" The moment she stepped into the hall, an oversize black puppy raced down the stairs. On the third from the bottom, he tripped, rolled and went sprawling onto the gleaming chestnut floor. "Almost made it that time, Fred."

Pleased with himself, Fred danced around Amanda's legs as she continued to call for her aunt.

"Coming. I'm coming." Tall and stately, Cordelia Calhoun McPike hurried in from the rear of the house. She wore peach linen slacks under a splattered white apron. "I was in the kitchen. We're going to try my new recipe for cannelloni tonight."

"Is C.C. home?"

"Oh, no, dear." Coco patted the hair she'd tinted the day before to Moonlit Blonde. In an old habit, she peeked into the hall mirror to make certain the shade suited her—for the moment. "She's down at her garage. Something about rocker arms, I think—though what rocking chairs have to do with cars and engines, I can't say."

"Great. Come upstairs, I want to show you what I got."

"Looks like you bought out the shops. Here, let me help you." Coco managed to grab two bags before Amanda dashed up the stairs.

"I had the best time."

"But you hate to shop."

"For myself. This was different. Still, everything took longer than I thought it would, so I was afraid I wouldn't get back and be able to stash it all before C.C. got home." She rushed into her room to dump everything onto the big four-poster bed. "Then this stupid man got in my way and knocked everything all over the sidewalk." Amanda stripped off her jacket, folded it, then laid it neatly over the back of a chair. "Then he had the nerve to try to pick me up."

"Really?" Always interested in liaisons, romances and assignations, Coco tilted her head. "Was he attractive?"

"If you go for the Wild Bill Hickok type. Anyway, I made it—no thanks to him."

As Amanda sorted through the bags, Fred tried twice, unsuccessfully, to leap onto the bed. He ended by sitting on the rug to watch.

"I found some wonderful decorations for the bridal shower." She began to pull out white-and-silver bells, crepe paper swans, balloons. "I love this frilly parasol," she went on. "Not C.C.'s style maybe, but I thought if we hung it up over…Aunt Coco." With a sigh, Amanda sat on the bed. "Don't start crying again."

"I can't help it." Already sniffling, Coco took an embroidered hankie from her apron pocket and dabbed carefully at her eyes. "She's the baby, after all. The youngest of my four little girls."

"There's not one of the Calhoun women who could be called little," Amanda pointed out.

"You're still my babies, and have been ever since your mother and father died." Coco used the hankie expertly. She didn't want to smear her mascara. "Every time I think of her being married—and in only a matter of days, really—I just fill up. I adore Trenton, you know." Thinking of her future nephew, she blew delicately into the hankie. "He's a wonderful man, and I knew they'd be perfect together right from the start, but it's all so fast."

"You're telling me." Amanda combed a hand through her sleek cap of hair. "I've barely had time to organize. How anyone expects to put on a wedding with barely three weeks notice—or why they'd want to try—is beyond me. They'd be better off eloping."

"Don't say that." Scandalized, Coco stuck her hankie back into her pocket. "Why, I'd be furious if they cheated me out of this wedding. And if you think you can when your time comes, think again."

"My time isn't going to come for years, if ever." Meticulously Amanda tidied the decorations again. "Men are as far down on my list of priorities as they can get."

"You and your lists." Coco clucked her tongue. "Let

me tell you, Mandy, the one thing you can't plan in this life is falling in love. Your sister certainly didn't plan it, and look at her. Squeezing fittings for a wedding dress in between her carburetors and transmissions. Your time may come sooner than you think. Why just this morning when I was reading my tea leaves—"

"Oh, Aunt Coco, not the tea leaves."

Grandly Coco drew herself up to her considerable height. "I've read some very fascinating things in the tea leaves. After our last séance, I'd think you'd be a bit less cynical."

"Maybe something happened at the séance, but—"

"Maybe?"

"All right, something did happen." Letting out a deep breath, Amanda shrugged. "I know C.C. got an image—"

"A vision."

"Whatever—of Great-Grandmama Bianca's emerald necklace." And it had been spooky, she admitted to herself, the way C.C. had been able to describe it, though no one had seen the two tiers of emeralds and diamonds in decades. "And no one who's lived in this house could deny that they've felt some—some presence or something up in Bianca's tower."

"Aha!"

"But that doesn't mean I'm going to start gazing into crystal balls."

"You're just too literal minded, Mandy. I can't think where you get it from. Perhaps from my Aunt Colleen. Fred, we must not chew on the Irish lace," Coco cautioned as Fred began to gnaw on Amanda's bedspread. "In any case, we were speaking of tea leaves. When I took a reading this morning, I saw a man."

Amanda rose to hide the decorations in her closet. "You saw a man in your teacup."

"You know very well it doesn't work precisely like that. I saw a man, and I had the strongest feeling that he's very close."

"Maybe it's the plumber. He's been underfoot for days."

"No, it's not the plumber. This man—he's close, but he's not from the island." She let her eyes unfocus as she did when she practiced looking psychic. "In fact he's from some distance away. He's going to be an important part of our lives. And—I'm quite sure of this—he's going to be vitally important to one of you girls."

"Lilah can have him," Amanda decided, thinking of her free-spirited older sister. "Where is she anyway?"

"Oh, she was meeting someone after work. Rod or Tod or Dominick."

"Damn it." Amanda scooped up her jacket to hang it neatly in the closet. "We were supposed to go through more of the papers. She knew I was counting on her. We have to find some lead as to where the emeralds are hidden."

"We'll find them, dear." Distracted, Coco poked through the other packages. "When the time is right. Bianca wants us to. I believe she'll show us the next step very soon."

"We need more than blind faith and mystic visions. Bianca could have hidden them anywhere." Scowling, she plopped down onto the bed again.

She didn't care about the money—though the Calhoun emeralds were reputed to be worth a fortune. It was the publicity that had resulted when Trent, her sister's fiancé, had contracted to buy The Towers, and the old legend had become public knowledge. Amanda's idea of an ordered existence had been thrown into chaos since the first story had hit.

It certainly made good print, Amanda mused as her aunt oohed and aahed over the lingerie she had bought for her sister's shower.

Early in the second decade of the century, when the resort of Bar Harbor was in its elegant heyday, Fergus Calhoun had built The Towers as an opulent summer home. There on the cliffs overlooking Frenchman Bay, he and his wife, Bianca, and their three children had vacationed, giving elaborate parties for other members of the well-heeled society.

And there, Bianca had met a young artist. They had fallen in love. It was said that Bianca had been torn between duty and her heart. Her marriage, which had been firmly supported by her parents, had been a cold one. With her heart leading her, she had planned to leave her husband and had packed away a treasure box that had contained the emeralds Fergus had given her on the birth of their second child and first son. The whereabouts of the necklace was a mystery as, according to legend, she had thrown herself from the tower window, overwhelmed with guilt and despair.

Now, eighty years later, interest in the necklace had been revived. Even as the remaining Calhouns searched through decades of papers and ledgers for a clue, reporters and hopeful fortune hunters had become a daily nuisance.

Amanda took it personally. The legend, and the people in it, belonged to her family. The sooner the necklace was located, the better. Once a mystery was solved, interest faded quickly.

"When is Trent coming back?" she asked her aunt.

"Soon." Sighing, Coco stroked the silky red chemise. "As soon as he ties things up in Boston, he'll be on his way. He can't stand being away from C.C. There will barely be enough time to begin the renovations on the west wing before they'll be off on their honeymoon." Tears filled her eyes again. "Their honeymoon."

"Don't start, Aunt Coco. Think of what a fabulous job you'll do catering the reception. It's going to be great practice for you. This time next year you'll be starting your new career as chef for The Towers Retreat, the most intimate of the St. James hotels."

"Imagine it." Coco patted her hand at her breast.

At the knock on the front door, Fred was up and howling.

"You stay here and imagine it, Aunt Coco. I'll go answer the door."

In a race with Fred, she clattered down the steps. When the dog's four legs tangled, sending him somersaulting, she laughed and gathered him up. She was snuggling the dog against her cheek when she opened the door.

"You!"

The tone of her voice had Fred quaking. Not so the man who stood at the threshold, grinning at her. "Small world," he said in the same slow drawl he'd used when they'd knelt on the sidewalk. "I'm liking it better all the time."

"You followed me."

"No, ma'am. Though it would've been a damn good idea. The name's O'Riley. Sloan O'Riley."

"I don't care what your name is, you can turn around and start walking." She started to slam the door in his face, but he slapped a hand against it and held it wide.

"I don't think that's such a good idea. I've come a long way to get a look at the house."

Her dark blue eyes narrowed. "Oh, have you? Well, let me tell you something, this is a home, a private home. I don't care what you've read in the papers and how badly you want a shot at looking under loose stones for the emeralds. This isn't Treasure Island, and I've had my fill of people like you who think they can just come knocking at the door, or sneaking into the garden at night with a pick and shovel."

She looked just fine, Sloan thought as he waited out the tirade. Every furious inch of her. She was tall for a woman and lean with it—but not too lean. She curved out nicely in all the right places. She looked as though she could ride hard all day and still have the energy to kick up her heels at night. Stubborn chin, he decided, and approved. When she jutted it out, her warm brown hair swayed with the movement. Big blue eyes. Even while they spit fire they reminded him of cornflowers. When it wasn't scowling or swearing, he imagined her full, shapely mouth would be soft.

Soft and tasty.

"You run down yet?" he asked when she stopped to take a breath.

"No, and if you don't leave right now, I'm going to let my dog loose on you."

Taking his cue, Fred leaped out of her arms. With neck fur bristling, he bared his teeth in a growl.

"Looks pretty fierce," Sloan commented, then hunkered down to hold out the back of his hand. Fred sniffed it, then his tail began to wag joyously as Sloan scratched his ears. "Yep, pretty fierce animal you got here."

"That's it." Amanda set her hands on her hips. "I'm getting the gun."

Before she could turn inside to look for the fictitious weapon, Coco came downstairs.

"Who is it, Amanda?"

"Dead meat."

"I beg your pardon?" She stepped up to the door. The moment she spotted Sloan her ingrained vanity took over. In the blink of an eye she whipped her apron off. "Hello." Her smile was warm and feminine as she extended a hand. "I'm Cordelia McPike."

"A pleasure, ma'am." Sloan brought her fingertips to his mouth. "As I was just telling your sister here—"

"Oh, my." Coco let out a trill of delighted laughter. "Amanda's not my sister. She's my niece. The third daughter of my late brother—my much older brother."

"My mistake."

"Aunt Coco, this jerk knocked me down outside of the boutique, then followed me home. He just wants to wheedle his way into the house because of the necklace."

"Now, Mandy, you mustn't be so harsh."

"That's partially true, Mrs. McPike." Sloan gave Amanda a slow nod. "Your niece and I did have a run-in. Guess I didn't get out of her way in time. And I am trying to get into the house."

"I see." Torn between hope and doubt, Coco sighed. "I'm terribly sorry, but I don't think it would be possible to let you in. You see we have so much to do with the wedding—"

Sloan's eyes whipped back to Amanda. "You getting married?"

"My sister," she said tightly. "Not that it's any of your business. Now if you'll excuse us?"

"I wouldn't want to intrude, so I'll just be on my way. If you'll tell Trent that O'Riley was by, I'd appreciate it."

"O'Riley?" Coco repeated, then fluttered her hands. "Goodness, are you Mr. O'Riley? Please come in. Oh, I do apologize."

"Aunt Coco—"

"This is Mr. O'Riley, Amanda."

"I realize that. Why the devil have you let him in the house?"

"*The* Mr. O'Riley," Coco continued. "The one Trenton called about this morning. Don't you remember— of course you don't remember, because I didn't tell you." She patted her hands to her cheeks. "I'm afraid I'm just so flustered after keeping you standing outside that way."

"Don't you worry about it," he said to Coco. "It's an honest mistake."

"Aunt Coco." Amanda stood with her hand on the doorknob, ready to pitch the intruder out bodily if necessary. "Who is this O'Riley and why did Trent tell you to expect him?"

"Mr. O'Riley's the architect," Coco said, beaming.

Eyes narrowing, Amanda studied him from the tip of his boots to his wavy, disordered hair. "This is an architect?"

"Our architect. Mr. O'Riley will be in charge of the renovations for the retreat, and our living quarters. We'll all be working with Mr. O'Riley—"

"Sloan," he said.

"Sloan." Coco fluttered her lashes. "For quite some time."

"Terrific." Amanda let the door slam.

Sloan hooked his thumbs in his jean pockets and gave her a slow smile. "My thoughts exactly."

Chapter Two

"Where are our manners?" Coco said. "Here we are keeping you standing in the hall. Please, come in and sit down. What can I offer you? Coffee, tea?"

"Beer in a long-necked bottle," Amanda muttered.

Sloan merely smiled at her. "There you go."

"Beer?" Coco ushered him into the parlor, wishing she'd had a moment to freshen the flowers in the vase and plump the pillows. "I have some very nice beer in the kitchen that I use for my spiced shrimp. Amanda, you'll entertain Sloan, won't you?"

"Sure. Why not?" Though she wasn't feeling particularly gracious, Amanda gestured to a chair, then took one across from him in front of the fireplace. "I suppose I should apologize."

Sloan reached down to pet Fred, who had followed them in. "What for?"

"I wouldn't have been so rude if I'd realized why you were here."

"Is that so?" As Fred settled down on the rug between them, Sloan eased back in his chair to study his unwilling hostess.

After a humming ten seconds, she struggled not to fidget. "It was a natural enough mistake."

"If you say so. What exactly are these emeralds you figured I was here to dig up?"

"The Calhoun emeralds." When he only lifted a brow, she shook her head. "My great-grandmother's emerald necklace. It's been in all the papers."

"I haven't had much time to read the papers. I've been in Budapest." He reached into his pocket and pulled out a long, slim cigar. "Mind?"

"Go ahead." Automatically she rose to fetch an ashtray from across the room. Sloan considered it a pleasure to watch that out-of-my-way walk of hers. "I'm surprised Trent didn't mention it."

Sloan struck a match and took his sweet time lighting the cigar. He took an appreciative drag, then blew out a lazy stream of smoke. All the while, he was taking stock of the room, with its sagging sofa, the glistening Baccarat, the elegant old wainscoting and the peeling paint.

"I got a cable from Trent telling me about the house and his plans, and asking me to take it on."

"You agreed to take a job like this without even seeing the property first?"

"Seemed like the thing to do at the time." She sure had pretty eyes, Sloan thought. Suspicious, but pretty. He wondered how they'd look if he ever managed to get a smile out of her. "Besides, Trent wouldn't have asked if he didn't think I'd get a kick out of it."

Her foot began to tap as it did when she had sat in one place too long. "You know Trent well then?"

"We go back a few years. We were at Harvard together."

"Harvard?" Her foot stopped tapping as she gaped at him. "You went to Harvard?"

Another man might have been insulted. Sloan was amused. "Why, shucks, ma'am," he murmured, exaggerating his drawl, then watching her cheeks flush.

"I didn't mean to…it's just that you don't really seem—"

"The Ivy League type?" he suggested before he took another pull on the cigar. "Guess appearances can be deceiving. Take the house here for instance."

"The house?"

"You take your first look at it from the outside and it's hard to figure if it's supposed to be a fortress, a castle or an architect's nightmare. But you take the time to look again, and you see it's not supposed to be anything but what it is. A timeless piece of work, on the arrogant side, strong, maybe stubborn enough to hold its own, but with just enough fancy to add some charm." He grinned at her. "Some people believe that a house reflects the personality of the people who live in it."

He rose when Coco came back in wheeling a tray. "Oh, sit down, please. It's such a treat to have a man in the house. Isn't it, Mandy?"

"I'm all aflutter."

"I hope the beer's all right." She lifted a brimming pilsner glass from the tray.

"I'm sure it's fine."

"Do try some of these canapés. Mandy, I've brought us some wine." Delighted with the chance to socialize, she smiled at Sloan over the rim of her glass. "Has Amanda been telling you about the house?"

"We were just getting to it." Sloan took a long swallow of beer. "Trent wrote that it's been in the family since the early part of the century."

"Oh, yes. With Suzanna's children—Suzanna's my eldest niece—we've had five generations of Calhouns at The Towers. Fergus—" she gestured to the portrait of a dour-faced man over the mantel "—my grandfather, built The Towers in 1904, as a summer home. He and his wife, Bianca, had three children before she threw herself out of the tower window." As always, the idea of dying for love had her sighing. "I don't believe Grandpapa was ever quite right after that. He went insane later in life, but we kept him in a very nice institution."

"Aunt Coco, I'm sure Mr. O'Riley isn't interested in the family history."

"Not interested," Sloan agreed as he tapped out his cigar. "Fascinated. Don't stop now, Mrs. McPike."

"Oh, call me Coco. Everyone does." She fluffed her hair. "The house passed along to my father, Ethan. He was their second child, but the first son. Grandpapa was very adamant about the Calhoun line. His—Ethan's— elder sister, Colleen, was miffed about the arrangement. She rarely speaks to any of us to this day."

"For which we're all eternally grateful," Amanda put in.

"Well, yes. She can be a bit—overwhelming. That left Uncle Sean, my father's younger brother. He had a spot of trouble with a woman and sailed off to the West Indies before I was born. When my father was killed, the house passed to my brother, Judson. After his marriage he and his wife decided to live here year-round. They adored the place." She glanced around the parlor with its cracked walls and faded curtains. "Judson had wonderful plans for revamping the house, but tragically he and Deliah were killed before he could begin to implement them. Then I came here to care for Amanda and her three sisters. Have another canapé."

"Thanks. Can I ask why you decided to convert part of your home into a hotel?"

"That was Trent's idea. We're all so grateful to him, aren't we, Amanda?"

Since she accepted the fact that there would be no winding down Aunt Coco, Amanda smiled. "Yes, we are."

Coco sipped delicately from her glass. "To be frank, we were in some financial distress. Do you believe in fate, Sloan?"

"I'm Irish and Cherokee." He spread his long fingers. "That doesn't give me any other choice."

"Well then, you'll understand. It was fated that Trent's father would see The Towers while he was sailing in Frenchman Bay, and seeing it, develop a deep desire for it. When the St. James's corporation offered to buy the house and turn it into a resort hotel, we were torn. It was our home after all, the only home my girls have ever known, but the upkeep…"

"I understand."

"Things happen for the best," Coco put in. "And it was really very exciting and romantic. We were on the brink, the very brink, of being forced to sell, when Trent fell in love with C.C. Of course he understood how much the house meant to her, and came up with this marvelous plan of converting the west wing into hotel suites.

That way we can keep the house, and overcome the financial difficulty of maintaining it."

"Everyone gets what they want," Sloan agreed.

"Exactly." Coco leaned forward. "With your heritage, I imagine you also believe in spirits."

"Aunt Coco—"

"Now, Mandy, I know how practical minded you are. It baffles me," she said to Sloan. "All that Celtic blood and not a mystical bone in her body."

Amanda gestured with her glass. "I leave that for you and Lilah."

"Lilah's my other niece," Coco told Sloan. "She's very fey. But we were talking about the supernatural. Do you have an opinion?"

Sloan set his glass aside. "I don't think you could have a house like this without a ghost or two."

"There." Coco clapped her hands together. "I knew as soon as I saw you we'd be kindred spirits. Bianca's still here, you see. Why at our last séance I felt her so strongly." She ignored Amanda's groan. "C.C. did, too, and she's nearly as practical minded as Amanda. Bianca wants us to find the necklace."

"The Calhoun emeralds?" Sloan asked.

"Yes. We've been searching for clues, but the clutter of eight decades is daunting. And the publicity has been a bother."

"That's a mild word for it." Amanda scowled into her glass.

"It might turn up during the renovation," Sloan suggested.

"We're hoping." Coco tapped one carefully manicured finger against her lips. "I think another séance might be in order. I'm sure you're very sensitive."

Amanda choked on her wine. "Aunt Coco, Mr. O'Riley has come here to work, not to play ghosts and goblins."

"I like mixing business and pleasure." He toasted Amanda with his glass. "In fact, I make a habit of it."

A new thought jumped into Coco's mind. "You're not from the island, Sloan."

"No, Oklahoma."

"Really? That's quite a distance." She slid her gaze smugly toward Amanda. "As architect for the renovations, you'll be very important to all of us."

"I'd like to think so," he said, baffled by the arched look Coco sent her niece.

"Tea leaves," Coco murmured, then rose. "I must go check on dinner. You will join us, won't you?"

He'd planned on taking a quick look at the house then going back to the hotel to sleep for ten hours. The annoyed look on Amanda's face changed his mind. An evening with her might be a better cure for jet lag. "I'd be mighty pleased to."

"Wonderful. Mandy, why don't you show Sloan the west wing while I finish things up?"

"Tea leaves?" Sloan asked when Coco glided from the room.

"You're better off in the dark." Resigned, she rose and gestured to the doorway. "Shall we get started?"

"That's a fine idea." He followed her into the hall and up the curving staircase. "Which do you like, Amanda or Mandy?"

She shrugged. "I answer to either."

"Different images. Amanda's cool and composed. Mandy's...softer." She smelled cool, he thought. Like a quiet breeze on a hot, dusty day.

At the top of the stairs she stopped to face him. "What kind of image is Sloan?"

He stayed one step below her so that they were eye to eye. Instinct told him they'd both prefer it that way. "You tell me."

He had the cockiest grin she'd ever seen. Whenever he used it on her she felt a tremor that she was certain was annoyance. "Dodge City?" she said sweetly. "We don't get many cowboys this far east." She turned and was halfway down the hall when he took her arm.

"Are you always in such a hurry?"

"I don't like to waste time."

He kept his hand on her arm as they continued to walk. "I'll keep that in mind."

My God, the place was fabulous, Sloan thought as they started up a pie-shaped set of steps. Coffered ceilings, carved lintels, thick mahogany paneling. He stopped at an arched window to touch the wavy glass. It had to be original, he thought, like the chestnut floor and the fancy plaster work.

True, there were cracks in the walls—some of them big enough that he could slide his finger in to the first knuckle. Here and there the ceiling had given way to fist-sized holes, and portions of the molding were rotted.

It would be a challenge to bring it back to its former glory. And it would be a joy.

"We haven't used this part of the house in years." Amanda opened a carved oak door and brushed away a spider web. "It hasn't been practical to heat it during the winter."

Sloan stepped inside. The sloping floor creaked ominously as he walked across it. Somewhere along the line heavy furniture had been dragged in or out, scarring the floor with deep, jagged grooves. Two of the panes on the narrow terrace doors had been broken and replaced with plywood. Mice had had a field day with the baseboard. Above his head was a faded mural of chubby cherubs.

"This was the best guest room," Amanda explained. "Fergus kept it for people he wanted to impress. Supposedly some of the Rockefellers stayed here. It has its own bath and dressing room." She pushed open a broken door.

Ignoring her, Sloan walked to the black marble fireplace. The wall above it was papered in silk and stained from old smoke. The chip off the corner of the mantel broke his heart.

"You ought to be shot."

"I beg your pardon?"

"You ought to be shot for letting the place go like this." The look he aimed at her wasn't lazy and amused, but hot and quick as a bullet. "A mantelpiece like this is irreplaceable."

Flustered, she stared guiltily at the chipped Italian marble. "Well, I certainly didn't break it."

"And look at these walls. Plasterwork of this caliber is an art, the same way a Rembrandt is art. You'd take care of a Rembrandt, wouldn't you?"

"Of course, but—"

"At least you had the sense not to paint the molding." Moving past her, he peered into the adjoining bath. And began to swear. "These are handmade tiles, for God's sake. Look at these chips. They haven't been grouted since World War I."

"I don't see what that's—"

"No, you don't see." He turned back to her. "You haven't got a clue to what you've got here. This place is a monument to early-twentieth-century craftsmanship, and you're letting it fall apart around your ears. Those are authentic gaslight fixtures."

"I know very well what they are," Amanda snapped back. "This may be a monument to you, but to me it's home. We've done everything we could to keep the roof on. If the plaster's cracked it's because we've had to concentrate on keeping the furnace running. And if we didn't worry about regrouting tiles in a room no one uses, it's because we had to repair the plumbing in another one. You've been hired to renovate, not to philosophize."

"You get both for the same price." When he reached out toward her, she rammed back into the wall.

"What are you doing?"

"Take it easy, honey. You've got cobwebs in your hair."

"I can do it," she said, then stiffened when he combed his fingers through her hair. "And don't call me 'honey.'"

"You sure fire up quick. I had a mustang filly once that did the same thing."

She knocked his hand aside. "I'm not a horse."

"No, ma'am." In an abrupt change of mood, he smiled again. "You sure aren't. Why don't you show me what else you've got?"

Wary, she eased to the side until she felt safe again. "I don't see the point. You haven't got a notebook."

"Some things stick in your mind." His gaze lowered to her mouth, lingered, then returned to her eyes. "I like to get the lay of the land first before I start worrying about…details."

"Why don't I draw you a map?"

He grinned then. "You always so prickly?"

"No." She inclined her head. It was true, she wasn't.

She could hardly have made a success in her career as assistant manager in one of the resort's better hotels if she was. "Obviously you don't bring out the best in me."

"I'll settle for what I've got." He curled a hand around her arm. "Let's keep going."

She took him through the wing, doing her best to keep her distance. But he had a tendency to close in, blocking her in a doorway, maneuvering her into a corner, shifting unexpectedly to put them face-to-face. He had a slow and economical way of moving, wasting no gestures that would tip her off as to which way he was going to turn.

They were in the west tower the third time Amanda bumped into him. Every nerve was on edge when she stepped back. "I wish you wouldn't do that."

"Do what?"

"Be there." Annoyed, she shoved aside a cardboard box. "In my way."

"It seems to me you're in too much of a hurry to get someplace else to watch where you are."

"More homespun philosophy," she muttered, and paced to the curved window that overlooked the gardens. He bothered her, she was forced to admit, on some deep, elemental level. Maybe it was his size— those broad shoulders and wide-palmed hands. His sheer height. She was accustomed to being on a more even level with most men.

Maybe it was that drawl of his, slow and lazy and every bit as cocky as his grin. Or the way his eyes lingered on her face, persistent, with a half-amused gleam. Whatever it was, Amanda thought with a little shake, she would have to learn how to handle it.

"This is the last stop," she told him. "Trent's idea is

to convert this tower into a dining room, more intimate than the one he wants on the lower level. It should fit five tables for two comfortably, with views of the garden or the bay."

She turned as she spoke, and an early evening sunbeam shot through the window to halo her hair and pool lustrously around her. Her hands gestured with her words, a graceful flow of movement underlined by nerves. She lifted one hand to her hair to push it back. The light streamed through the honey-brown tresses, tipping them with gold. In the single shaft of light, dust motes danced around her like minute flakes of silver.

His mind wiped clean as new glass, Sloan stood and stared.

"Is something wrong?"

"No." He took a step closer. "You sure are easy on the eyes, Amanda."

She took a step back. There wasn't amusement in his eyes now, or the quick flaring anger she had seen briefly earlier. What was there was a great deal more dangerous. "If you, ah, have any questions about the tower, or the rest of the wing—"

"That was a compliment. Maybe not as smooth as you're used to, but a compliment just the same."

"Thank you." Her eyes darted around the room for a means of dignified escape as she retreated another step. "I think we could—" She ended on a gasp as his arm snaked around her waist to draw her tight against him. "What the hell do you think you're doing?"

"Keeping you from taking the same jump as your great-grandma." He nodded toward the window at her back. "If you'd kept dancing backward, you might have gone right through the glass. Those panes don't look very strong."

"I wasn't dancing anywhere." But her heart was pounding as if she had just finished a fast rumba. "Let go."

"You're a real nice armful." He leaned closer to take a sniff of her hair. "Even with all those thorns." Enjoying himself, he kept his arm where it was. "You could've said thanks, Calhoun. I probably just saved your life."

Her pulse might have been jumping, but she refused to let herself be intimidated by some slow-talking cowboy with an attitude. "If you don't let me go, now, someone's going to have to save yours."

He laughed, delighted with her, and was tempted to scoop her up there and then. The next thing he knew, he was landing on his butt five feet away. With a smug smile, Amanda inclined her head.

"That concludes our tour for this evening. Now, if you'll excuse me." When she started by him, his hand snaked out and snagged her ankle. Amanda barely had time to shriek before she landed on the floor beside him. "Why, you—oaf," she decided, and tossed the hair out of her eyes.

"What's good for the goose is good for the gander." He tipped a fingertip under her chin. "More homespun philosophy. You've got quick moves, Calhoun, but you've got to remember to keep your eye on the target."

"If I were a man—"

"This wouldn't be half as much fun." Chuckling, he gave her a quick, hard kiss, then tilted his head back to stare at her while she gaped. "Well, now," he said softly while lightning bolts went off inside his chest. "I think we'd better try that again."

She would have shoved him away. She knew she would have. Despite the heat trembling along her spine. Regardless of the thick syrupy longing that seemed to have replaced the blood churning in her veins. She would have shoved him away, had even lifted a hand to do so—certainly not to bring him closer—when footsteps clattered on the iron steps that led to the tower.

Sloan glanced up to see a tall, curvy woman in the doorway. She wore jeans that were ripped through at the knee with a plain white T-shirt tucked in the waist. Her hair was short and straight, offset by a fringe of sassy bangs. Below them her eyes registered surprise, then amusement.

"Hi." She looked at Amanda, grinning as she noted her sister's flushed face and tousled hair. The one place you didn't expect to see business-first Amanda Calhoun was on the floor with a strange and very attractive man. "What's going on?"

"We were going for the best two out of three," Sloan told her. He rose, then hauled Amanda up by the arm. With what sounded like a snarl, Amanda jerked out of his hold, then busied herself brushing the dust from her slacks.

"This is my sister, C.C."

"And you must be Sloan." C.C. walked in, offering her hand. "Trent's told me about you." Green eyes dancing, she flicked a glance at her sister, then back again. "I guess he didn't exaggerate."

Sloan held the offered hand a moment. C. C. Calhoun was exactly the opposite of the kind of woman he'd expected his old friend to be involved with. And because Trent was his friend, Sloan couldn't have been more delighted. "I can see why Trent's got himself roped and corralled."

"That's one of Sloan's whimsical compliments," Amanda pointed out.

With a laugh, C.C. threw an arm around Amanda's shoulders. "I think I figured that out. I'm glad to meet you, Sloan. Really glad. When I went up to Boston with Trent a couple of weeks ago, everyone I met was so…"

"Stuffy?" He grinned.

"Well." A little embarrassed, she moved her shoulders. "I guess it's hard for some of them to accept that Trent's going to marry a mechanic who knows more about engines than opera."

"Looks to me like Trent's getting one hell of a deal."

"We'll see." She knew with the least encouragement she would get mushy and embarrass herself. "Aunt Coco said you were staying for dinner. I was hoping you'd take one of the guest rooms here while you're on the island."

Sloan couldn't see it, but he'd have bet the pot that Amanda bit her tongue. The idea of ruffling her feathers made it tempting to change his plans. "Thanks, but I'm all taken care of. Besides…" Now he grinned at Amanda. "I'm going to be underfoot enough as it is."

"However you're most comfortable," C.C. told him. "Just so that you know you're welcome here at The Towers."

"I'll go down and see if Aunt Coco needs any help." Amanda sent Sloan a cool nod. "C.C. will show you down when you're ready."

He winked at her. "Thanks for the tour, honey."

He could almost hear her grinding her teeth as she walked away.

"That's some sister you've got there."

"Yes, she is." C.C.'s smile was warm, and warning. "Trent tells me you're quite the ladies' man."

"He's still mad because I stole a woman out from under his nose when we were both still young and foolish." Sloan took C.C.'s hand as they walked through the doorway. "You sure you're stuck on him?"

She had to laugh. "Now I see why he told me to lock up my sisters."

"If they're anything like that one, I expect they can take care of themselves."

"Oh, they can. The Calhoun women are as tough as they come." She paused at the top of the iron circular stairs. "I'd better warn you. Aunt Coco claims she saw you in the tea leaves this morning."

"In the…aah."

She gave a half apologetic, half amused shrug. "It's kind of a hobby of hers. Anyway, she might start to try to manipulate, especially if she decides the fates have linked you with one of my sisters. She means well, but…"

"O'Rileys are pretty good at handling themselves, too."

It only took one long look at him to have her believing it. C.C. tapped his shoulder. "Okay then. You're on your own."

Sloan started down behind her. "C.C., are there any men Amanda's involved with who I'm going to have to hoist out of the way?"

C.C. stopped, studying him through the opposite side of the open stairs. "No," she said after a moment. "Amanda's done all the hoisting herself."

"That's fine." He was smiling to himself as he descended the winding stairs. When they reached the second floor, he heard an echo of high-pitched screams and the frantic yapping of the dog.

"My sister Suzanna's kids," C.C. explained before he could ask. "Alex and Jenny are your typical quiet, retiring children."

"I can hear that."

A sturdy pale-haired missile zoomed up the steps. In reflex, Sloan caught it and found himself staring into a curious little face with a pouty mouth and big blue eyes.

"You're big," Jenny said.

"Nah. You're just short."

At five, she was just beginning to learn the wiles of womanhood and sent him a beaming smile. "Can I have a piggyback ride?"

"Got a quarter?" Giggling, she shook her head. "Okay," he said, "the first one's free then." When she squirmed around to his back, he started down again. At the base of the steps, Amanda had a dark-haired little boy in a headlock.

"Suzanna?" C.C. asked.

"In the kitchen. I was drafted to watch these two." She narrowed her eyes at Jenny. "The little pig-nosed one got away from me."

"Oink, oink." From the tower of Sloan's back, Jenny giggled and snorted.

"Who's he?" Alex wanted to know.

"Sloan O'Riley." Sloan offered a hand, man to man, which Alex eyed dubiously before accepting it.

"You talk funny. Are you from Texas?"

"Oklahoma."

After a moment's consideration, Alex nodded. "That's almost as good. Did you ever shoot anybody dead?"

"Not lately."

"That's enough, you ghoul." C.C. took charge. "Come on, let's go get cleaned up for dinner." She swung Jenny from Sloan's back.

"Cute kids," Sloan commented when C.C. hauled them up the stairs.

"We like them." Amanda offered him a genuine smile. Seeing him with Jenny riding his back had softened her. "They'll be in school most of the day, so they shouldn't bother you while you're working."

"I don't figure they'd be a bother one way or the other. I've got a nephew of my own back home. He's a pistol."

"Those two can be shotguns, I'm afraid." But the affection came through. "It's nice for them to be around a man now and again."

"Your sister's husband?"

The smile faded. "They're divorced. You might know him. Baxter Dumont?"

A shutter seemed to come down over Sloan's eyes. "I've heard of him."

"Well, that's history. Dinner's nearly ready. Why don't I show you where to wash up?"

"Thanks." Distracted, Sloan followed her. He was thinking that there were some points of history that had an unfortunate habit of overlapping.

Chapter Three

Anticipating the shock, Amanda dove into the cold water of the pool. She surfaced with a delicious shiver then began the first of her usual fifty laps.

There was nothing she liked better than beginning a day with a vigorous workout. It ate away the old tension to make room for the new that would develop before the workday was done.

Not that she didn't enjoy her job as assistant manager of the BayWatch Hotel. Particularly since it gave her the privilege of using the hotel pool before the guests began to crowd in. It was the end of May and the season had begun to swing. Of course it was nothing compared to what it would be by midsummer, but most of the rooms in the hotel were occupied, which meant she had her hands full. This hour, which she gave herself whenever weather permitted, was prized.

As she approached one end of the pool, she curled, tucked and pushed off.

In another year, she thought as she sent beads of water flying, she would be manager of The Towers Retreat. A St. James hotel. The goal that she had worked and struggled for since she'd taken her first part-time job as a desk clerk at sixteen was about to be realized.

It nagged at her from time to time that she would have the job only because Trent was marrying her sister. Whenever it did, she became only more determined to prove that she deserved it, that she had earned it.

She would be managing an exclusive hotel for one of the top chains in the country. And not just any hotel, she thought, cutting cleanly through the water, but The Towers. A part of her own heritage, her own history, her own family.

The ten luxurious suites Trent intended to create out of the crumbling west wing would be her responsibility. If he was right, the St. James name and the legend of The Towers would keep those suites filled year-round.

She would do a good job. An exceptional one. Every guest who traveled home from The Towers would remember the excellent service, the soothing ambience, the silky smooth organization.

It was going to happen. There would be no more slaving for a demanding and unappreciative supervisor, no more frustration at doing the work and handing over the credit. At last the credit, and the failure, would be hers alone.

It was only a matter of waiting until the remodeling was done.

And that brought her thoughts ramming headfirst into Sloan O'Riley.

She certainly hoped Trent knew what he was doing. What baffled her most was how such a smooth and polished man such as Trenton St. James III had ever become friends with a throwback like O'Riley. The man had actually knocked her down. Of course, she'd knocked him down first, but that was entirely beside the point.

Amanda kicked off again. Her leanly muscled arms sliced through the water, her long legs scissored. She didn't regret, not for a minute, that she'd had the wit and the strength to get the best of him first. He'd been pushy and overfamiliar and too full of himself from the moment she'd met him. And he'd kissed her.

She turned her head up for air then slid her face into the water again.

She hadn't given him the least bit of encouragement. In fact, just the opposite. But he'd sat there, grinning like a fool, and had kissed her. The memory of it had her gasping for air again.

Not that she'd liked it, Amanda assured herself. If C.C. hadn't walked in, she would have given the arrogant Mr. O'Riley a piece of her mind. Except that she hadn't had one left.

Because she'd been angry, that's all. She wasn't a bit attracted to the rough, outdoorsy type with callused hands and dusty boots. She wasn't fool enough to fall for a pair of dark green eyes that crinkled at the corners when they smiled. Her image of the ideal man included a certain sophistication, smooth manners, culture, a quiet aura of success. If and when she became interested in a relationship, those would be her requirements. Slow-talking cowboys need not apply.

Maybe there had been something sweet about him

when he'd talked to the children, but it wasn't enough to overcome the rest of the deficits in his personality.

She remembered the way he'd flirted and charmed Aunt Coco at dinner. He'd kept C.C. amused with stories of Trent's college days and had been tolerant and easy with Alex's and Jenny's questions about horses and Indians and six-shooters.

But he'd watched Suzanna a little too closely, a little too carefully for Amanda's liking. A woman-chaser, Amanda decided. If Lilah had been at dinner, he probably would have flirted with her, as well. But Lilah could take care of herself where men were concerned.

Suzanna was different. She was beautiful, sensitive and vulnerable. Her ex-husband had hurt her deeply, and no one, not even the cocky Sloan O'Riley, was going to get the chance to hurt Suzanna again. Amanda would make sure of it.

When she reached the edge of the pool this time, she gripped the coping and dipped her head back into the water to slick her hair out of her eyes. Surfacing, she found herself staring up into a watery image that was entirely too familiar.

"Morning." Sloan grinned down at her. The sun was at his back, bringing out the reddish tones in his untidy hair. "You got a nice form there, Calhoun."

She blinked her eyes clear. "What the hell are you doing here?"

"Here?" He glanced over his shoulder at the white-washed hotel. "You could say I'm hanging my hat here." Watching her, he jerked a thumb up and back. "Room 320."

"You're a guest at the BayWatch?" Amanda propped her elbows on the coping. "It figures."

Agreeable, Sloan crouched down. She had the clear creamy Calhoun skin, he noted, particularly striking, and vulnerable, now washed clean of any cosmetics. "Nice way to start the day."

Her full damp mouth turned down in a frown. "It was."

"Since we're asking, what are you doing here?"

"I work here."

Things were becoming more and more interesting, he thought. "No fooling?"

"No fooling," she said dryly. "I'm assistant manager."

"Well, now." He dipped an experimental finger into the water. "Checking out the water temperature for the guests? That's dedication."

"The pool doesn't open until ten."

"Don't worry." He hooked his thumbs in the front pockets of his jeans. "I wasn't planning on taking a dip just yet." What he had been planning was to take a walk, a long solitary one. But that was before he'd spotted her doing laps. "So, I guess if I have any questions about the place, you're the one I talk to."

"That's right." Amanda moved over to the steps to climb out. The one-piece sapphire-colored suit clung like a second skin as water slid from her. "Is your room satisfactory?"

"Hmm?" She had legs designed to make a man sweat, he thought, slim and shapely and a yard long.

"Your room," she repeated as she reached for her towel. "It suits you?"

"It suits me fine. Just fine." He skimmed his gaze up those damp calves and thighs, over the slim hips on a lazy journey to her face. "The view's worth the price of admission."

Amanda hooked the towel around her neck. "The view of the bay's free—like the continental breakfast now being served in The Galley. You'll want to take advantage of it."

"I've found that a couple of croissants and a cup of coffee don't do much to stanch the appetite." Because he wasn't ready for her to walk away, he reached out to take both ends of the towel in a light grip. "Why don't you join me for a real breakfast?"

"Sorry." Her heart was beginning to thud uncomfortably. "Employees are discouraged from socializing with the guests."

"I reckon we could make an exception in this case, seeing as we're…old friends."

"We're not even new friends."

There was that smile again, slow, insistent and all too knowing. And then he said, "That's something we can fix over breakfast."

"Sorry. Not interested." She started to turn away, but he tightened his grip on the towel and held her in place.

"Where I come from people are a mite more friendly."

Since he wasn't giving her a choice, she held her ground. "Where I come from people are a great deal more polite. If you have any problems with the service during your stay at the BayWatch, I'll be more than happy to accommodate you. If you have any questions about The Towers, I'll make myself available to answer them. Other than that, we have nothing to discuss."

He watched her patiently, admiring the way she could coat her husky voice with frost even while her eyes glinted. This was a woman with plenty of control. And, though he was certain she'd snarl at the term, plenty of spunk.

"What time do you go on the clock here?"

She let out a hiss of breath. Obviously the man's head was as thick as his accent. "Nine o'clock, so if you'll excuse me, I'd like to go get dressed."

Sloan squinted up at the sun. "Looks to me like you've got about an hour before you punch in. The way you move, it won't take you half that to get yourself together."

Amanda shut her eyes briefly on a prayer for patience. "Sloan, are you trying to irritate me?"

"Don't figure I have to. It seems to come natural." Casually he wound the ends of the towel around his fists and had her jerking closer. He grinned as her chin shot up. "See?"

She resented bitterly the way her pulse was dancing, and the tight, clutching sensation deep in her stomach. "What's the matter with you, O'Riley?" she demanded. "I've made it absolutely plain that I'm not interested."

"I'll tell you how it is, Calhoun." He flipped his wrists again, shortening the towel farther. The humor she was used to seeing in his eyes changed into something else in the space of a heartbeat. And that something else was dark and dangerous. And exciting. "You're one long, cool drink of water," he murmured. "Every time I'm around you I get this powerful thirst." With a last jerk, he had her tumbling against him, her hands trapped tight between their bodies. "That little sip I had yesterday wasn't nearly enough." Bending down, he nipped at her bottom lip.

He felt her tremor, but as he kept his eyes on hers, he could see it wasn't from fear. A trace of panic maybe, but not fear. Still he waited to see if she would give him

a flat-out no. That was something he would have to respect, however much the need churned through him.

But she said nothing, only stared at him with those
wide, wary eyes. Softly he brushed his lips over hers and
watched the thick lashes flutter down. "I want more,"
he murmured. And took.

Her hands curled into fists between them, but she
didn't use them to push him away. The struggle was
all inside her, a wild and violent combat that jolted her
system even as he bombarded her senses. Caught in the
crossfire, her mind simply shut down.

His mouth wasn't lazy now. Nor were his hands slow.
Hard and hot, his lips took from hers while his fingers
pressed against her damp back. The scrape of his teeth
had her gasping, then moaning when his tongue slid seductively over hers.

Her fingers uncurled to clutch at his shirt, then to
claw their way up to his shoulder, into his hair. The desperation was new, terrifying, wonderful. It drove her to
strain against him while her mouth burned with an urgency that matched his.

The change rocked him. He was used to having his
senses clouded by a woman, to having his body throb
and his blood burn. But not like this. In the instant she
went from dazed surrender to fevered urgency, he knew
a need so sharp, so jagged that it seemed to slice through
his soul.

Then all he knew was her. All he could feel was the
cool slick silk of her skin. All he could taste was the
honeyed heat of her mouth. All he could want was more.

She was certain her heart would pound its way out
of her breast. It seemed the heat from his body turned
the water on her skin to steam, and the vapors floated

through her brain. Nor did they clear when he eased her gently away.

"Amanda." He drew in a deep gulp of air but wasn't sure he'd ever get his breath back again. One look at her as she stood heavy-eyed, her swollen lips parted, had the edgy desire cutting through him again. "Come up to my room."

"Your room?" She touched unsteady fingers to her lips, then her temple. "Your room?"

Lord, that throaty voice and those dazed eyes were going to have him on his knees. One thing he'd yet to do was beg for a woman. With her, he was afraid begging was inevitable.

"Come with me." Possessively he ran his hands over her shoulders. Somewhere along the line the towel had slid to the concrete. "We need to finish this in private."

"Finish this?"

On a groan, he brought his lips back to hers again in a last, long, greedy kiss. "Woman, I think you're going to be late for work."

He had her arm and had pulled her toward the gate before she shook her head clear. His room? she thought fussily. Finish this? Oh, Lord, what had she done? What was she about to do? "No." She jerked away and took a deep, cleansing breath that did nothing to stop the tremors. "I'm not going anywhere."

He tried to steady himself and failed. "It's a little late to play games." His hand snaked out to cup the back of her neck. "I want you. And there's no way in hell you're going to convince me you don't want me right back. Not after that."

"I don't play games," she said evenly, and wondered if he could hear her over the riot of her heartbeat. She

was cold, so terribly cold. "I don't intend to start now."
She was the sensible one, she reminded herself. She
wasn't the kind of woman who raced into a hotel room
to make love with a man she barely knew. "I want you
to leave me alone."

"Not a chance." He struggled to keep his fingers light
as temper and need warred inside him. "I always finish what I start."

"You can consider this finished. It had no business
starting."

"Why?"

She turned away to snatch up her wrap. The thin terry
cloth wasn't nearly enough to warm her again. "I know
your type, O'Riley."

He reached deep for calm and rocked back on his
heels. "Do you?"

Clumsy with temper, she fought to push her arms
through the sleeves. "You swagger from town to town
and fill a few free hours with an available woman having a quick roll between the sheets." She pulled the tie
on the wrap tight. "Well, I'm not available."

"You figure you got me pegged, huh?" He didn't
touch her, but the look in his eyes was enough to have
her bracing. He didn't bother to explain that it was different with her. He hadn't yet explained it to himself. "You
can take this as a warning, Calhoun. This isn't finished
between us. I'm going to have you."

"Have me? *Have* me." Propelled by pride and fury,
she took one long stride toward him. "Why you conceited self-absorbed sonofabitch—"

"You can save the flattery for later," he interrupted.
"There will be a later, Amanda, when it's just you and
me. And I promise you, it won't be quick." Because the

idea appealed to him, he smiled. "No sir, when I make love with you, I'm going to take my time." He ran a finger down the collar of her wrap. "And I'm going to drive you crazy."

She slapped his hand away. "You already are."

"Thanks." He gave her a friendly nod. "I think I'll go see about that breakfast. You have a good day."

She would, she thought as he walked off whistling. She'd have a fine day if he was out of it.

It was bad enough that she had to work late, Amanda thought, without having to listen to one of Mr. Stenerson's droning lectures on efficiency. As manager of the BayWatch, Stenerson ruled his staff with fussy hands and whines. His preferred method of supervision was to delegate. In that way he could dole out blame when things went wrong, and gather in credit when things went right.

Amanda stood in his airy pastel office, staring at the top of his balding head as he ran through his weekly list of complaints.

"Housekeeping has been running behind by twenty minutes. In my spot check of the third floor, I discovered this cellophane wrapper under the bed of 302." He waved the tiny clear paper like a flag. "I expect you to have a better handle on things, Miss Calhoun."

"Yes, sir." *You officious little wienie.* "I'll speak to the housekeeping staff personally."

"See that you do." He lifted his ever-present clipboard. "Room service speed is off by eight percent. At this rate of deterioration, it will lower to twelve percent by the height of the season."

Unlike Stenerson, Amanda had done time in the

kitchen during the breakfast and dinner rush. "Perhaps if we hired another waiter or two," she began.

"The solution is not in adding more staff, but in culling more efficiency from those we have." He tapped a finger on the clipboard. "I expect to see room service up to maximum by the end of next week."

"Yes, sir." *You supercilious windbag.*

"I'll expect you to roll up your sleeves and pitch in whenever necessary, Miss Calhoun." He folded his soft white hands and leaned back. Before he'd opened his mouth again, Amanda knew what was coming. She could have recited the speech by rote.

"Twenty-five years ago, I was delivering trays to guests in this very hotel. It was through sheer determination and a positive outlook that I worked my way up to the position I hold today. If you expect to succeed, perhaps even take over in this office after my retirement, you must eat, sleep and drink the BayWatch. The efficiency of the staff directly reflects your efficiency, Miss Calhoun."

"Yes, sir." She wanted to tell him that in another year she would have her own staff, her own office and he could kiss his whipping boy goodbye. But she didn't tell him. Until that time, she needed the job and the weekly paycheck. "I'll have a meeting with the kitchen staff right away."

"Good, good. Now, I'll want you on call this evening, as I'll be incommunicado."

As always, she thought but murmured her agreement.

"Oh, and check the August reservations. I want a report on the ratio of Escape Weekends to Seven-Day Indulgences. Oh, and speak with the pool boy about missing towels. We're five short already this month."

"Yes, sir." Anything else? she wondered. Shine your shoes, wash your car?

"That'll be all."

Amanda opened the door and struggled to keep her unflappable professional mask in place. All she really wanted to do was knock her head against the wall for a few indulgent minutes. Before she could retreat to some private, quiet place to do so, she was called to the front desk.

Sloan took a seat in the lobby just to watch her. He was surprised to see that she was still working. He'd put in a full day at The Towers, and the scarred briefcase beside the chair was bulging with notes, measurements and sketches. He was ready for a tall beer and a rare steak.

But here she was, soothing guests, instructing desk clerks, signing papers. And looking just as cool and fresh as spring water. He watched her pull off an earring, jiggling it in her palm as she took a phone call.

It was one of life's small pleasures to watch her, he decided. All that drive and energy, the effortless control. Almost effortless, he thought with a grin. There was a line between her brows—frustration, he thought. Annoyance. Or just plain stubbornness. He had a powerful urge to go up to her and smooth it away. Instead, he gestured to a bellman.

"Yes, sir."

"Is there a florist around here?"

"Yes, sir, just down the street."

Still watching Amanda, Sloan dug out his wallet and pulled out a twenty. "Would you run down there and get me a red rose? A long-stemmed one that's still closed. And keep the change."

"Yes, *sir*. Thank you, sir."

While he waited, Sloan ordered a beer from the lobby bar and lighted a cigar. Stretching out his booted feet, he settled back to enjoy.

Amanda clipped on her earring then pressed a hand to her stomach. At least when she went down to give the kitchen staff a pep talk she could grab something to eat. A glance at her watch told her that she wouldn't have time to take her evening shift going through the paperwork, looking for a clue to the necklace. If there was any bright side to the enforced overtime, it was that Sloan wouldn't be at The Towers when she returned.

"Excuse me."

Amanda glanced up to see a trim, attractive man in a bone-colored suit. His dark hair was brushed back from a high forehead. Pale blue eyes smiled pleasantly as they looked into hers. The faint British accent added charm to his voice.

"Yes, sir. May I help you?"

"I'd like to speak with the manager."

Amanda felt her heart sink a little. "I'm sorry, Mr. Stenerson is unavailable. If there's a problem, I'll be glad to handle it for you."

"No problem, Miss—" his eyes flicked down to her name tag "—Calhoun. I'll be checking in for a few weeks. I believe I have the Island Suite."

"Of course. Mr. Livingston. We're expecting you." Quick and competent, she tapped the information into the computer herself. "Have you stayed with us before?"

"No." He smiled again. "Regrettably."

"I'm sure you'll find the suite very comfortable." She passed him a registration form as she spoke. "If there's anything we can do to make your stay more pleasant, don't hesitate to ask."

"I'm already certain it will be pleasant." He gave her another lingering look as he filled out the form. "Unfortunately, it must also be productive. I wanted to inquire about the possibility of renting a fax machine during my stay."

"We offer fax service for our guests' convenience," she said.

"I'll require my own." The diamond on his pinky winked as he slid the form across the counter. "I'm afraid I wasn't able to clear up all my business, as I had hoped. It simply wouldn't be practical for me to run down here every time I need to send or receive a document. Naturally, I'll be willing to pay whatever necessary for the convenience. If renting isn't feasible, perhaps I can purchase one."

"I'll see what I can arrange."

"I'd appreciate that." He offered her his credit card for an imprint. "Also, I'll be using the parlor in the suite as an office. I'd prefer if housekeeping left my papers and disarray undisturbed."

"Of course."

"Might I ask if you're familiar with the island?"

Smiling, she handed him his card and his keys. "I'm a native."

"Wonderful." His eyes on hers, he held her hand lightly. "Then I'll know to come to you if I have any questions. You've been very helpful, Miss Calhoun." He glanced at her name tag again. "Amanda. Thank you."

"You're quite welcome." Her pulse gave a quick jitter as she slid her hand from his to signal a bellman. "Enjoy your stay, Mr. Livingston."

"I already am."

As he walked away, the young desk clerk beside Amanda gave a low feminine sigh. "Who was that?"

"William Livingston." Amanda caught herself staring after him and pulled herself back to file the imprint.

"Gorgeous. If he had looked at me the way he looked at you, I'd have melted on the spot."

"Melting's not part of the job description, Karen."

"No." Dreamy-eyed, Karen put her hand on a ringing phone. "But it sure is part of being a woman. Front desk, Karen speaking. May I help you?"

William Livingston, Amanda thought, tapping his registration form against her palm. New York, New York. If he could afford a couple of weeks in the Island Suite, that meant he had money as well as charm, good looks and impeccable taste in clothes. If she'd been looking for a man, he would have fit the bill nicely.

Opening up the phone book, Amanda reminded herself she was looking for a fax machine, not a man.

"Hey, Calhoun."

With her finger on Office Supplies in the business section, she glanced up. Sloan, his chambray shirt rolled up to the elbows, his hair curling untidily over its collar, leaned on the counter.

"I'm busy," she said dismissively.

"Working late?"

"Good guess."

"You sure look pretty in that little suit." He reached over the counter to rub a thumb and finger down the crisp red lapel of her jacket. "Kinda prim and proper."

Unlike the little bounce her pulse had given when William Livingstone had taken her hand, it went haywire at Sloan's touch. Annoyed, she brushed it away. "Do you have a problem with your room?"

"Nope. It's pretty as a picture."

"With the service?"

"Slick as a wet rock."

"Then if you'll excuse me, I've got work to do."

"Oh, I figured that. I've been watching you tow the mark here for the last half hour."

The line appeared between her brows. "You've been watching me?"

His gaze lingered on her mouth as he remembered just how it tasted. "It made the beer go down easy."

"It must be nice to have so much free time. Now—"

"It's not how much, it's what you do with it. Since you were…tied up for breakfast, why don't we have dinner?"

Well aware that her co-workers had their ears pricked, Amanda leaned closer and kept her voice low. "Can't you get it through your head that I'm not interested?"

"No." He grinned, then sent a wink toward Karen, who was hovering as close as discretion allowed. "You said you didn't like to waste time. So I figured we could have a little supper and pick up where we left off this morning."

In his arms, she thought, lost for a moment. With her mind fuddled and her blood racing. She was staring at his mouth when it curved and snapped her back to reality. "I'm busy, and I have no desire—"

"You've got plenty of that, Amanda."

She set her teeth, wishing with all her heart she could call him a liar and mean it. "I don't want to have dinner with you. Clear?"

"As glass." He flicked a finger down her nose. "I'll be upstairs if you get hungry. Three-twenty, remember?" He lifted the rose from behind the counter and put it into her hand. "Don't work too hard."

"Two winners in one night," Karen murmured, and watched Sloan walk away. "Lord, he sure knows how to wear jeans, doesn't he?"

Indeed he did, Amanda thought, then cursed herself. "He's crude, annoying and intolerable." But she brushed the rosebud against her cheek.

"Okay, I'll take bachelor number two. You can concentrate on Mister Beautiful from New York."

Damn it, why was she so breathless? "I'm going to concentrate on my job," Amanda corrected. "And so are you. Stenerson's on the warpath, and the last thing I need is some cowboy stud interrupting my routine."

"I wish he'd offer to interrupt mine," Karen murmured, then bent over her terminal.

She wasn't going to think about him, Amanda promised herself. She set the rose aside, then picked it up again. It wasn't the flower's fault, after all. It deserved to be put in water and appreciated for what it was. Softening a bit, she sniffed at it and smiled. And it had been sweet of him to give it to her. No matter how annoying he might be, she should have thanked him.

Absently she lifted the phone as it rang. "Front desk, Amanda speaking. May I help you?"

"I just wanted to hear you say that." Sloan chuckled into the phone. "Good night, Calhoun."

Biting back an oath, Amanda banged down the receiver. For the life of her she couldn't understand why she was laughing when she took the rose back into her office to find a vase.

I ran to him. It was as if another woman burst out into the twilight to race over the lawn, down the slope, over the rocks. In that moment there was no right or wrong, no duty but to my own heart. Indeed, it was my heart that guided my legs, my eyes, my voice.

He had turned back to the sea. The first time I had seen him he had been facing the sea, fighting his own personal war with paint and canvas. Now he only stared out at the water.

When I called to him, he spun around. In his face I could see the mirror of my own joy. There was laughter, mine and his, as he rushed toward me.

His arms went around me, so tightly. My dreams had known what it would be like to finally be held by them. His mouth fitted truly to mine, so sweet, so urgent.

Time does not stop. As I sit here and write this, I know that. But then, oh then, it did. There was only the wind and the sound of the sea and the sheer and simple glory of being in his arms. It was as if I had waited my entire life, sleeping, eating, breathing, all for the purpose of that single precious window of time. If I have another hundred years left to me, I will never forget an instant of it.

He drew away, his hands sliding down my arms to grip mine, then to bring them to his lips. His eyes were so dark, like gray smoke.

"I'd packed," he said. "I'd made arrangements to sail to England. Staying here without you was hell. Thinking you would come back, and that I'd never be able to touch you nearly drove me mad. Every day, every night, Bianca, I've ached for you."

My hands moved over his face, tracing it as I'd often longed to. "I thought I'd never see you again. I tried to pray that I wouldn't." As shame crept through my joy, I tried to turn away. "Oh, what you must think of me. I'm another man's wife, the mother of his children."

*"Not here." His voice was rough, even as his hands
were gentle. "Here you belong to me. Here, where I first
saw you a year ago. Don't think of him."*

*He kissed me again, and I could not think, could
not care.*

*"I've waited for you, Bianca, through the chill of win-
ter, the warmth of spring. When I tried to paint, it was
your image that haunted me. I could see you standing
here, with the wind in your hair, the sunlight turning it
copper, then gold, then flame. I tried to forget you." His
hands were on my shoulders, holding me back while his
eyes seemed to devour my face. "I tried to tell myself it
was wrong, that for your sake if not my own, I should
leave here. I would think of you, with him, dancing at a
ball, attending the theater, taking him into your bed."
His fingers tightened on my shoulders. "She is his wife,
I would tell myself. You have no right to want her, to
wish that she would come to you. That she could belong to you."*

*I lifted my fingers to his lips. His pain was my pain.
I think it will always be so. "I have come to you," I told
him. "I do belong to you."*

*He turned away from me, the struggle between con-
science and love as strong in him as it was in me. "I
have nothing to offer you."*

"Your love. There is nothing else I want."

*"It's already yours, has been yours from the first mo-
ment I looked at you." He came back to me to touch my
cheek. I could see the regret, and the longing, in those
beautiful eyes. "Bianca, there is no future for us. I cannot and will not ask you to give up what you have."*

"Christian—"

"No. Whatever wrongs I do, I will not do that. I know

you would give me what I ask, what I have no right to ask, then come to hate me for it."

"No." Tears came to my eyes then, bitter in the cooling wind. "I could never hate you."

"Then I would hate myself." He crushed my fingers against his lips again. "But I'll ask you for the summer, for a few hours when you can come here and we can pretend winter will never be." He smiled and kissed me softly. "Come here and meet me, Bianca, in the sunlight. Let me paint you. I'll be content with that."

And so tomorrow, and every day during this sweet, endless summer I will go to him. On the cliffs above the sea we will take what happiness we can.

Chapter Four

"Well, hello."

At the husky greeting, Sloan looked up from his notes on the billiard room to see a willowy gypsy in a flowing flowered robe. Long cables of red hair streamed down her shoulders and back. Dreamy green eyes assessed him before she glided into the room like a woman who had all the time in the world and was willing to spend it generously.

"Hi." Sloan caught the elusive scent—like crushed wildflowers—before she offered a hand.

"I'm Lilah." Her voice was as lazily flirtatious as her eyes. "We've missed each other the past couple of days."

If there was a man who didn't get a jolt from this one, Sloan thought, he was dead and buried. "I'm real sorry about that."

She laughed then gave his hand a companionable

squeeze. First impressions ranked high with Lilah, and she'd already decided to like him. "Me, too. Especially now. What have you been up to?"

"Getting a feel for the place, and the people in it. How about you?"

"I've been busy trying to figure out if I was in love."

"And?"

"Nope." She moved her shoulders gently, but he caught the wistful look in her eyes before she turned to move around the room. "So, what's the plan here, Sloan O'Riley?"

"Elegant dining in a turn-of-the-century atmosphere." He kicked back in the Windsor armchair he'd been using and gestured toward the papers spread over the library table. "We take out part of that wall there, open up into the adjoining study, add a couple of glass pocket doors, and we've got a lounge."

"Just like that?"

"Just like that—after we deal with the structural hassles. I'll have some preliminary sketches for your family and Trent to look over in a couple of days."

"It seems strange," she murmured, running a finger along the old, dusty chair rail. "Thinking about this place being fresh and new again, having people in it." But if she closed her eyes, she could see it perfectly, the way it had once been. "They used to give huge parties, very elaborate, very chic. I can imagine my great-grandfather standing here beside a billiard table sipping Scotch, and wheeling and dealing." She turned back to Sloan. "Do you think about those things when you make your sketches and calculate stress and space?"

"As a matter of fact, I do. There's a burn mark on the floor right over there." He tipped his pencil toward the spot. "I imagine some fat guy in a dinner suit dropped his cigar while he was discussing the war in Europe. A couple of others were standing by the window, stripped down to their shirtsleeves and swirling brandy while they talked about the stock market."

Laughing, Lilah crossed back to him. "And the ladies were down in the parlor."

"Listening to piano music and gossiping about the latest fashions from Paris."

Lilah tilted her head. "Or discussing the possibility of being given the vote."

"There you go."

"I think you're just what The Towers needs," she decided. "Can I take a look at your drawings, or are you temperamental?"

"I make it a policy never to turn down a beautiful woman."

"Astute and clever." She went to lean over his shoulder and push through his papers. "Why, it's the Emperor's Room."

"The what?"

"The Emperor's Room, that's what I call the best guest room. Must be the harps and cherubs on the ceiling." Sliding her hair behind her shoulder, she leaned closer. "This is great."

The dressing room would be a cozy parlor, she noted, complete with a wet bar and an entertainment center that would be hidden behind the original paneling. The bath would remain almost as it was, with the addition of a private whirlpool tucked away in what had been an old storage closet.

"Both ends of one century," Lilah murmured. "You've hardly changed any of the original layout."

"Trent indicated he wanted to keep the luxury and convenience without altering the mood. We'll save most of the original materials, duplicate what's beyond hope."

"You're going to do it." And because she could see that as well, quite clearly, her eyes filled as she laid a hand on his shoulder. "My father wanted to. My mother and he used to talk about it all the time. I wish they could have seen this."

Touched, Sloan laid his hand over hers. Their fingers had linked when Amanda came to the door. Her first reaction was shock at seeing her sister with her cheek all but brushing Sloan's. Then came the spear of jealousy. There was no denying there was something private, even intimate passing between them. On the heels of that sharp green shaft, pride stepped in.

Hadn't she told herself he was a woman-chaser?

"Excuse me." Her voice was a thin sheet of ice as she stepped into the room. "I've been looking for you, Lilah."

"You found me." She blinked back the tears but didn't bother to straighten. "I thought I'd come by and meet Sloan."

"I see you have." Determined to be casual if it killed her, Amanda jammed her hands into the pockets of her sweats. "It's your turn for a shift in the storeroom."

"That's what I get for having the day off." She wrinkled her nose, then sent Sloan a smile. "The Calhouns have become detectives, searching for clues to the hiding place of the elusive emeralds."

"So I've heard."

"Maybe you'll take a hack at one of the walls, and they'll fall out, looking as fabulous and glittery as the day Bianca hid them." With a sigh, she drew away. "Well, since duty calls, I'd better get dressed for it. Mandy, you ought to take a look at some of Sloan's sketches. They're great."

"I'll bet."

The tone would have been a direct tip-off, even if Lilah hadn't known her sister so well. So, Lilah thought with a lifted brow. That's the way it was. Since she'd never been able to resist teasing her sister, she leaned down to kiss Sloan's cheek. "Welcome to The Towers."

He didn't have a doubt as to what she was up to. The eyes might be dreamy, he thought, but there was a shrewd and devilish brain behind them. "Thanks. I'm feeling more at home every day."

"I'll meet you in the sweatshop in fifteen minutes," she said to Amanda, then grinned to herself as she went out.

"Is that your new uniform?" he asked Amanda as she stood scowling in the center of the room, her hands still fisted in the pockets of baggy gray sweats.

"I don't go in until two today."

"That's nice." He crossed his outstretched legs at the ankles. "I like your sister."

"That was obvious."

He only grinned. "What does she do, anyway?"

"If you mean professionally, she's a naturalist at Acadia National Park."

"Wildflowers and stuff. It suits."

As if the admiration in his voice didn't bother her in the least, she shrugged and walked to the terrace doors. "I thought you'd be taking measurements or something." Glancing over her shoulder, she shot him a narrow look. "Of the rooms, that is."

This time he laughed outright. "You're mighty cute when you're jealous, Calhoun."

Now she turned to look deliberately down her nose. "I don't know what you're talking about."

"Sure you do, but you can relax. I've already set my sights on you."

Did he expect her to be flattered? she wondered. The hell of it was that, in a odd way, she was. "Do I look like a target?"

"I'd say more like the grand prize." In a gesture of peace, he held up a hand as she sucked in her breath to swear at him. "Before you get more fired up, why don't we deal with business?"

"I am not fired up," she lied. "And I don't see what business we could have."

"Trent said you were the one I should...collaborate with, until he got back. Seeing as you're the one who handles most of the family business, and you've got a firsthand knowledge of hotels."

Because it was logical, she calmed enough to consider it. "What do you want to know?"

How long it's going to take me to knock down that wall around you, he thought. "I figured you'd want to take a look at what I've started. I'd like to get to the drawing board soon."

Actually she was dying to see, but kept her agreement grudgingly cool. "All right, but I only have a few minutes."

"I'll take what I can get."

He waited as she crossed the room. She didn't trust him worth spit, Sloan decided. And that was just fine for now.

"I've got two of the suites mapped out," he told her,

shuffling papers. "Plus the tower and most of the dining room here."

She leaned closer, squinting a bit to focus without her reading glasses. As Lilah had been, she was impressed with the sketches. Not only were they competent, but they showed a quick understanding of mood, tone and the practicality necessary for smooth service.

"You work fast," she said, surprised.

"When it's called for." He enjoyed watching the way she lifted a hand to tuck back the swing of hair, not with the sinuous movements of her redheaded sister, but with a quick, absent flick. She smelled of soap and some cool sprinkle of scent.

"What's this?"

"What's what?" He was too busy with the way the sunlight showered on her hair to pay attention to anything else.

"This." She tapped a finger on a sketch.

"Hmm. That's an old servants' stairway. We bring this wall out here, to box it in." He took her finger to slide it along the sketch, the rough side of his palm fitting over the smooth skin of her hand. "It makes this suite two levels—the sitting room and bath down here, two bedrooms and a master bath up here. Since the stairs are already open, it gives us a separation of functions without closing off the flow of space."

"It's nice." Vaguely uneasy with the contact, she flexed her hand but only succeeded in tangling her fingers with his. "I suppose you're going to get estimates and bids."

"I've made some calls."

Something seemed to be happening to her legs from the knees down. They'd gone weak on her, as if she'd run a very long, very fast race. "Well, you…" She braced and turned her head to face him. His eyes were very close, very quiet, very calm. "Obviously you know what you're doing."

"Yeah, I do."

Oh, yeah, he did, she thought as she felt herself pulled toward him—not by his hand, but by something soft and warm and needy inside her. She had only to give in to it, to lean a little closer. Her mouth could be on his, and she would know, as she had known the day before, a kind of whippy excitement and dazzling pleasure. He was waiting, watching her, with those dark green eyes going from calm to intense, willing her to make that slight and significant move. As she began to slide toward him, she heard herself sigh.

Then she remembered.

He had been in almost this same position with Lilah just moments before. Faces close, fingers linked. Only a fool let herself be manipulated by a man who was that casual with a woman's feelings. And Amanda Kelly Calhoun was no fool.

She jerked back, tugging her hand from under his. Sloan felt the knots already winding through his stomach yank tighter.

"Did I miss something?" he asked with a casualness that cost him dearly.

"I don't know what you mean."

"The hell you don't. You were a hairsbreadth away from kissing me, Mandy. Your eyes were full of it. Now you've got them frosted up again."

She wished it was as easy to put the ice back into her blood. "You're letting your ego get the best of you. But then, that's probably typical. If you want to take time out to flirt and snuggle with a woman, try Lilah again."

He was used to holding on to his temper. When a man had a dangerous one, he learned early to keep it chained down. But it wasn't easy, not with her, not with the way she so consistently racked his system. "Are you telling me that Lilah's available to any man who asks?"

She went from frost to fire so quickly he could only stare in amazed appreciation. "You don't know anything about my sister, O'Riley. Watch what you say or you'll find yourself on your butt again."

"I was asking what you said," he reminded her.

"I can say what I like, you can't. Lilah has a warm, generous heart. If you do anything to hurt her, I'll—"

"Hold on." Chuckling, he threw up both hands, palms out. "I don't mind you taking a chunk out of me, Calhoun, but I'd rather it be for something I did—or was at least planning to do. First, I'm not quite the tomcat you seem to think I am. And second, I'm not interested in—what was it—snuggling with Lilah."

Amanda's chin lifted a fraction higher. "What's the matter with her?"

Exasperated, he let his hands fall again. "Not a damn thing. Tell me, has your great-granddaddy's insanity trickled down or are you just being plain obstinate?"

"Take your pick." Now she was as embarrassed as she was angry and stalked over to the window to stare out. Whether he was a tomcat—as he'd put it—or not, it was no concerns of hers. It was her problem that she had overreacted to his meeting with Lilah. She was getting herself wound up over nothing, Amanda told herself. If she kept snapping at him every time they spent five minutes together, their business relationship would suffer. And business was, after all, her strongest suit. She gave herself another moment to be sure she'd regained some balance, then turned back.

"We seem to have gotten off track. Let's put this back on a professional level, and keep it there."

"You do that real well," he observed.

"What?"

"Pull yourself in. It can't be easy if being around me churns you up half as much as I get being around you." Then he grinned and recrossed his ankles. "Go ahead, be professional. I got real admiration for that side of you."

She wasn't sure whether to scream or laugh or just throw her hands up in defeat. Instead she shook her head and tried again. "I like your work."

"Thanks."

"Trent and I have discussed the budget for the project. He and C.C. may still be on their honeymoon when the bids start coming in. If that's the case, you and I will have to go over them. As far as the hotel section goes, you have a free hand. As to the other part of the house, the family part, we're only interested in essential repairs."

"Why? The place deserves a decent face-lift."

"Because the hotel is a business, and the Calhouns and St. Jameses will be partners. We have the property, he has the funds. We've all agreed that we won't take advantage of his generosity, or the fact that he's marrying C.C."

Sloan considered a moment. "Trent seems to have other ideas. And I've never known him to let anyone take advantage."

The smile softened her face. "I know, and we, all of us, appreciate that he's willing to help, but we feel strongly about this. The Towers, our part of it, is a Calhoun problem. Our position is that we'll accept the needed repairs to the plumbing, the wiring and other immediate necessities, then we'll pay him back from our share of the retreat. If business is good, we'll be able to take care of the rest ourselves within the next few years."

There was pride at stake here, he noted. And more, integrity. He nodded. "You work things out with Trent. Meanwhile, I'll concentrate on the west wing."

"Fine. If your schedule allows, you can take a look at the rest. It would be helpful if we had an idea what the budget will be on the family areas."

He started to point out that he was an architect not a contractor, then shrugged. It wouldn't hurt him to take a look. "Sure. I'll work up an estimate."

"I'd appreciate it. Once you do, I'd prefer if you gave it to me. Just me."

"You're the boss."

She lifted a brow. Odd, but she hadn't thought about it quite that way before. Her lips curved as she digested it. "Then we understand each other. One more thing."

He linked his hands behind his head. "We can have as many things as you want."

"Only one," she said, though her lips quivered. "When I was finalizing some of the wedding plans, I realized you were down as best man. I left your list with Aunt Coco."

"My list?"

"Yes, of the timetable, the duties you're responsible for, that sort of thing. There's also a copy of the necessary information—the name and phone number of the photographer, the contact for the musicians, the bartender we hired…oh, and I jotted down the names of three shops where you can rent a tux." Once again she took in the sheer size of him. "You really should get in for a fitting right away."

"I've got it covered." Impressed, he shook his head. "You're damn efficient, Calhoun."

"Yes, I am. Well then, I'll let you get back to work. I'll be in the third-floor storeroom in the other wing until about one. After that you can reach me at the BayWatch if you have any questions."

"Oh, I know where to find you, Calhoun. Good hunting."

He watched her walk away, and thought of her sitting in the storeroom, surrounded by dusty boxes and mounds of yellowing papers. She'd probably already found a way to put things in their tidy place, he thought with a grin. He wondered if she realized what a sweet contrast it was. She would stack and catalogue and file in the most practical way possible, while she searched through pieces of the past for an old dream.

Amanda found no dreams that morning. By the time she arrived at the BayWatch, she had already put in a five-hour day. When she had started the quest for the necklace weeks before, she had promised herself she wouldn't become discouraged, no matter how long it took or how little she found.

Thus far, they had come across the original receipt for the emeralds, and a date book where Bianca had mentioned them. It was enough, Amanda had decided, to prove the necklace had indeed existed, and to keep hope alive that it would be found again.

She often wondered about it, about what it had meant to Bianca Calhoun and why she had secreted it away.

If indeed she had. Another old rumor was that Fergus had tossed the necklace into the sea. After all the stories Amanda had heard about Fergus Calhoun's abiding love of a dollar, it was hard to believe that he had willfully thrown away a quarter of a million in jewels.

Besides, she didn't want to believe it, Amanda admitted as she pinned on her name tag. Though she wouldn't have cared for anyone to know it, she had a strong streak of the romantic, and that part of her held tight to the notion that Bianca had hidden away the emeralds, like a gift or promise, waiting for the time they would be needed again.

It embarrassed her a little to know she felt that way. Amanda preferred the outward, and the logical, routine of sorting through papers and organizing them in the practical pursuit of a valuable heirloom.

Bianca herself remained as much a mystery to Amanda as the necklace. Her ingrained pragmatism made it impossible to understand a woman who had risked everything for, and ultimately had died for, love. Feelings that intense and that desperate seemed unlikely to her, unless they were in the pages of a book.

What would it be like to love that strongly? she wondered. To feel as though your life were so completely bound to another's that it was impossible to survive without him. Inconvenient, she decided. Uncomfortable and unwise. She could only be grateful that she hadn't inherited that dangerous kind of passion. Feeling smug about her own unbattered heart, she settled down to work.

"Amanda?"

She was halfway through the August reservations and held up a hand. "Minute," she murmured, and totaled her calculations to that point. "What is it, Karen? Wow."

She pushed her glasses back up her nose and studied the luxurious spray of roses in the desk clerk's arms. "What did you do, win a beauty pageant?"

"They're not mine." Karen buried her face in them. "Don't I wish. They just came in, for you."

"Me?"

"You're still Amanda Calhoun," Karen pointed out as she offered the florist's card. "Though if you want to trade places until these three dozen long-stemmed beauties fade, I'm game."

"Three dozen?"

"I counted." Grinning, Karen laid them on the desk. "Three dozen and one," she added, nodded toward the single rose that stood beside them.

Sloan, Amanda thought, and felt her heart give a quick, catchy sigh. How was she supposed to get a handle on a man who did sweet, unexpected things every time she thought she'd made up her mind about him? How could he have known about her secret weakness for red roses? She hadn't even thanked him for the first one.

"Aren't you going to read the card?" Karen demanded. "If I have to go back to the desk without knowing who sent them, I'll be distracted and my work will suffer. The evil Albert Stenerson'll fire me, and it'll be your fault."

"I already know who they're from," she began, unaware of the softness in her eyes. "It was really so sweet of him to—oh." Baffled, she studied the name on the card. Not Sloan, she realized, with a cutting edge of disappointment that surprised her. They weren't from Sloan.

"Well? Do you want me to beg?"

Still puzzled, Amanda handed the card over.

"With my appreciation. William Livingston. Whew." Karen tossed back her long, dark hair. "What did you have to do to deserve this kind of gratitude?"

"I got him a fax machine."

"You got him a fax machine," Karen repeated, handing the card back to Amanda. "Last Sunday I cooked a pot roast with all the trimmings and all I got was a bottle of cheap wine."

Amanda continued to frown and tapped the card on the edge of her desk. "I guess I'd better thank him."

"I guess you'd better." Karen picked up one of the roses and sniffed. "Unless you'd rather delegate. I'd be glad to go up and express your appreciation to Mr. Eyes-To-Die-For Livingston."

"Thanks, but I'll handle it." She picked up the phone, then sent Karen an arched look. "Scram."

"Spoilsport." Laughing, she went out, discreetly shutting the door at her back as Amanda dialed the extension for the Island Suite.

"Livingston."

"Mr. Livingston, this is Amanda Calhoun."

"Ah, the efficient Miss Calhoun." There was a laugh in his voice, a pleasant and flattering one. "What can I do for you?"

"I wanted to thank you for the flowers. They're beautiful. It was very thoughtful of you."

"Just a small way of showing you that I appreciate your help, and the quick work."

"That's my job. Please let me know if I can be of any further assistance during your stay."

"As a matter of fact, there is something you could help me with."

"Of course." Automatically she picked up a pen and prepared to write.

"I'd like you to have dinner with me."

"Excuse me?"

"I'd like to take you to dinner. Eating alone is unappetizing."

"I'm sorry, Mr. Livingston, it's against hotel policy for the staff to socialize with the guests. It's kind of you to ask."

"Kindness has nothing to do with it. Can I ask if you'd consider it if hotel policy could be…bent?"

There was no chance of that, Amanda thought. Not with Stenerson. "I'd be happy to consider it," she said tactfully. "Unfortunately, as long as you're a guest at the BayWatch—"

"Yes, yes. I'll get back to you shortly."

Amanda blinked at the dead receiver, shrugged, then replaced it to get back to work. Ten minutes later, Stenerson was opening her door.

"Miss Calhoun, Mr. Livingston would like to have dinner with you." His mouth primmed up even more than usual. "You're free to go. Naturally, I'll expect you to conduct yourself in a manner that will reflect properly on the hotel."

"But—"

"Don't make a habit of it."

"I—" But he was already shutting the door. Amanda was still staring at it when her phone rang. "Miss Calhoun."

"Shall we say eight o'clock?"

On a long breath, she sat back in her chair. She was on the point of refusing when she caught herself stroking the single rosebud Sloan had given her. Amanda snatched back her hand and balled it in her lap.

"I'm sorry, I'm on until ten tonight."

"Tomorrow then. Where shall I pick you up?"

"Tomorrow's fine," she said on impulse. "Let me give you directions."

Chapter Five

Sloan knew the minute Trent returned to The Towers. Even in the library at the end of a long corridor he could hear the high happy yaps of the dog, the shouts of children and the mix of laughter. Setting aside his notebook, he strolled out to see his old friend.

Trent had gotten no farther than the foyer. Jenny was hanging on his legs as Fred circled and danced. Alex was jumping up and down in a bid for attention while Coco, Suzanna and Lilah all fired questions at once. C.C. only stood beaming, held snug against Trent's side. At a shout from above, Sloan looked up to see Amanda bolting down the stairs. Her laughter glowed in her face as he'd never seen it before. Squeezing through her sisters, she took her turn at a hug.

"If you hadn't come back today, I was sending out a team of mercenaries," she told Trent. "Four days before the wedding and you're down in Boston."

"I knew you could handle the details."

"She has miles of lists," Coco put in. "It's frightening."

"There, you see?" Trent gave Amanda a quick kiss.

"What did you bring me? What did you bring me?" Jenny demanded.

"Talk about mercenary." Laughing, Suzanna scooped her daughter up. When she spotted Sloan in the hallway, her easy smile faded. She tried to tell herself that it was her imagination that his eyes changed whenever he looked at her. It had to be. What possible reason would he have for disliking her on sight?

Sloan studied her another moment, a tall, slender woman with pale blond hair pulled back in a ponytail, a face blessed with classical beauty and sad blue eyes. Dismissing her, he looked back at Trent. His smile came naturally again.

"I hate to interrupt when you're surrounded by beautiful women, but time's wasting."

"Sloan." His arm still around C.C., Trent stepped forward to grip Sloan's hand. In all of his varied groups of acquaintances, associates and colleagues, this was the only man he considered a genuine friend. "On the job already?"

"Getting started."

"You look like you've just gotten back from a long vacation in the tropics instead of six weeks in Budapest. It's good to see you."

"Same here." Sloan sent a quick wink at C.C. "It's really good to see that you're finally developing some taste."

"I like him," C.C. said.

"Women tend to," Trent said. "How's your family?"

Sloan's gaze flicked to Suzanna again. "They're fine."

"You two must have a lot to catch up on." Feeling awkward, Suzanna took her son's hand. "We're going to take a walk before dinner."

Amanda waited until Coco had urged everyone along toward the parlor before she put a hand on Sloan's arm. "Wait."

He grinned at her. "I've been waiting, Calhoun."

She wasn't even tempted to rise to the bait. "I want to know why you look at Suzanna that way."

The humor faded from his eyes. "What way is that?"

"Like you detest her."

It annoyed him that those particular and very private feelings showed so clearly. "You've got more imagination than I gave you credit for."

"It's not my imagination." Baffled, she shook her head. "What could you possibly have against Suzanna? She's the kindest, most good-hearted person I know."

It was difficult not to sneer, but he kept his face bland. "I didn't say I had anything against her. You did."

"You didn't have to say it. Obviously I can't make you talk about it, but—"

"Maybe that's because I'd rather talk about us." Casually he set both hands on the banister behind her, caging her between.

"There is no us."

"Sure there is. There's you and there's me. That makes us. That's real basic grammar."

"If you're trying to change the subject—"

"You're getting that line between your eyebrows again." He lifted a thumb to rub at it. "That Calhoun line. How come you never smile at me the way you smiled at Trent?"

"Because I like Trent."

"It's funny, most people figure I'm an amiable sort of guy."

"Not from where I'm standing."

"Why don't you stand a little closer?"

She had to laugh. If there had been a contest for persistence, Sloan O'Riley would have won hands down. "This is close enough, thanks." More than close enough, she added silently when she had to fight back an urge to run her fingers through that untidy mane of reddish-blond hair. *"Amiable* isn't the word I would use. Now, *cocky, annoying, tenacious,* those might suit."

"I kind of like tenacious." He leaned closer to breathe in her scent. "A man doesn't get very far if he caves in every time he runs into a wall. You climb over, tunnel under, or just knock the whole damn thing down."

She put a hand to his chest before he could close that last inch of distance. "Or he keeps beating his head against it until he has a concussion."

"That's a calculated risk, and worth it if there's a woman behind the wall looking at him the way you look at me."

"I don't look at you any particular way."

"When you forget that you want to be professional, you look at me with those big blue eyes of yours all soft, and a little scared. A lot curious. Makes me want to scoop you up right there and carry you off to someplace real quiet so I can satisfy that curiosity."

She could imagine it all too clearly, feel it all too sharply. There was only one solution. Escape. "Well, this has been fun, but I've got to go change."

"Are you going back to work?"

"No." Agile, she swooped under his arm and swung up the steps. "I've got a date."

"A date?" he repeated, but she was already racing across the second floor.

He told himself he wasn't waiting for her, though he'd been pacing the foyer for a good twenty minutes. He wasn't going to hang around like an idiot and watch her go strolling off with some other man—after she'd tied him into knots by just standing there and looking at him. There was plenty for him to do, including enjoying the dinner Coco had invited him to, talking over old times and new plans with Trent, even sitting down at his drawing board. He wasn't about to spend the evening mooning over the fact that some obstinate woman preferred someone else's company to his.

After all, Sloan reminded himself as he paced the foyer, she was free to come and go as she pleased. The same as he was. Neither one of them was branded. Just because he had a hankering for her didn't mean he was going to get riled up when she spent a couple of hours with another man.

The hell it didn't.

Turning, he took the steps two at a time.

"Calhoun?" He strode down the corridor, banging on doors. "Damn it, Calhoun, I want to talk to you." He was at the far end of the hall and starting back when Amanda opened her door.

"What's going on?" she demanded.

He stared a moment as she stood in the stream of light that spilled out of the room behind her. She'd done something fancy to her hair, he noted, so that it looked sexily rumpled. Played with her face, too, in that damnably sultry way some women have a talent for. Her dress was a pale icy blue, full at the skirt, nipped at the waist with two skinny straps slinking over her shoulders. Chunky stones in a deeper blue glittered at her ears and throat.

She didn't look efficient, he thought furiously. She didn't look competent. She looked as delectable as a pretty white cake on a fancy tray. And he was damned if any other man was going to take even one small nibble.

Her foot was already tapping when he started toward her.

Amiable? she thought, and had to resist the urge to bolt back into her room and lock the door. No one would call him amiable now. He looked as though he'd just finished chewing a mountain of glass and was raring for the second course.

"What kind of date?" he snapped at her, and found himself further incensed by the fact that her skin smelled like glory.

Amanda inclined her head slowly. The hands she had fisted on her hips slid carefully to her sides. When you were facing a raging bull you didn't wave a red flag but tried to ease yourself over the fence. "The usual kind."

"Is that the way you dress for the usual kind?"

Irked, she glanced down and smoothed her skirts. "What's wrong with the way I'm dressed?"

For an answer, he took her arm and swung her around. He'd been right, he thought as his stomach clutched up. Those two little straps were all that were covering her back. Right down to the waist. "Where's the rest of it?"

"Rest of what?"

"The dress."

She turned back, still cautious, and examined his face. "Sloan, I think you've gone around the bend."

She didn't know how right she was, he thought. "I've got as much sense as any man can hang on to after ten minutes with you. Cancel."

"Cancel?" she repeated.

"The date, damn it." He nudged her none too gently toward her bedroom. "Go in and call him up and tell him you can't make it. Ever."

"You really are crazy." She forgot about bulls and red flags and cut loose. "I go where I please and with whom I please. If you think I'm going to break a date with an attractive, charming and intelligent man because some overbearing baboon tells me to, then think again."

"It's the date," he warned, "or that pretty stiff neck of yours."

Her eyes narrowed down to two slits of righteous blue fire. "Don't you threaten me, you pinhead. I have a dinner date with your antithesis. A gentleman." She elbowed him aside. "Now get out of my way."

"I'll get out of your way," he promised. "After I give you something to think about."

He had her back against the wall with his mouth covering hers before she could blink. She could taste the anger. That, she would have fought against to the last breath. But she could also taste the need, and that, she surrendered to. It was such a perfect echo of her own.

He didn't care if it was unreasonable. He didn't care if it was wrong or stupid or any of the other terms that could so easily apply to his actions. He wanted to curse her for making him behave like some reckless teenager. But he could only taste her, drowning in the flavor that he was coming to understand he would always crave. He could only pull her closer against him so that he could feel the instant heat that pumped from her body into his.

He could sense each change as it flowed through her.

First the anger that kept her rigid and aloof. Then the surrender, reluctant then melting so that her bones seemed to dissolve. And the passion overlapping so quickly it stole his breath. It was that he understood he couldn't live without.

Her arms went around him as if they belonged there. Strained against his, her body throbbed until it was one sweet ache. This was an ache that once felt could never be forgotten, would always be craved. Eager, she nipped at his mouth, knowing in another moment delirium could overtake her. Wanting it, wanting that liberating mindless whirl of desire only he could ignite inside her.

Only he.

In one long possessive stroke his hands ran from her shoulders to her wrists, holding there a moment while her pulse scrambled under his palms. When he lifted his head, she leaned back limply against the wall, watching him while she struggled to catch her breath. While she fought to break through the torrent of sensations and understand the feelings beneath them.

The thought of another man touching her, of looking into her face and seeing it flushed with passion as it was now, of seeing her eyes clouded with it, terrified him. Because he preferred good clean anger to fear, he gripped her shoulders again, all but lifting her off her feet.

"Think about that," he told her in a low dangerous voice. "You think about that good and hard."

What had he done to her to make her need so terribly? He had to know, just by looking at her, that he had only to pull her inside her room to take everything he claimed to want. He had only to touch her again to have her desperate to give. He wouldn't even have to ask. It shamed her to realize it, destroyed her to understand that anyone would have such complete power over her pride and her will.

"You made your point," she said unsteadily, infuriated that tears were stinging the back of her eyes and throat. "Do you want to hear me say that you can make me want you? Fine. You can."

The sparkle of tears in her eyes did what her fury couldn't. It beat him soundly. There was regret in his voice when he lifted a hand to her face. "Amanda—"

She stiffened and shut her eyes. If he was gentle—she knew if he showed her even a scrap of tenderness, she would crumble. "You've got your conquest, Sloan. Now I'd appreciate it if you'd let me go."

He let his hand slide to his side before he stepped back. "I'm not going to tell you I'm sorry." But the way she looked at him made him feel as though he had just shattered something small and fragile.

"That's all right. I'm sorry enough for both of us."

"Amanda." Lilah stood at the top of the stairs, watching them both with her sleepy-eyed curiosity. "Your date's here."

"Thanks." Frantic for escape, she turned into her room to grab her jacket and purse. Being careful not to look at Sloan, she hurried out again to rush downstairs. Lilah glanced after her, then walked down the hall to rest her hands on Sloan's shoulders.

"You know, big guy, you look like you could use a friend."

He couldn't begin to put a name to any of the emotions currently running riot through him. "Maybe I'll just go downstairs and throw him out a window."

"You could," Lilah agreed after a moment, "but Mandy's always been a sucker for the underdog."

Sloan swore, then decided to work off some of the frustration by pacing the corridor. "So, who is he anyway?"

"I've never met him before. His name's William Livingston."

"And?"

Lilah gave a gentle shrug. "Tall, dark and handsome as the saying goes. Very faint, very charming British accent, Italian suit, upper-class manners. That patina of wealth and breeding without being ostentatious."

Sloan swore and considered punching a hole in the wall. "He sounds just dandy."

"Sounds," she agreed, but her look was troubled.

"What is it?"

"Bad vibes." Absently she ran a hand up and down her arm. "And he had a very muddy aura."

"Give me a break, Lilah."

With a little smile, she glanced back at him. "Don't knock it, Sloan. Remember, I'm on your side. I happen to think you're just what my take-it-all-too-seriously sister needs." In her easy way, she hooked a friendly arm through his. "Relax, Mr. William Livingston doesn't have a chance. Not her type." She laughed as she walked with him to the steps. "She thinks he is, but he's not. So let's go eat. There's nothing like Aunt Coco's Trout Amandine to put you in a good mood."

Pretending she had an appetite, Amanda studied her menu. The restaurant William had chosen was a lovely little place overlooking Frenchman Bay. Since the night was warm, they could enjoy the terrace service with candlelight flickering in the gentle sea breeze, and the fragile scent of spring flowers.

Amanda left the choice of wine up to him and tried to convince herself that she was about to have a delightful evening.

"Are you enjoying Bar Harbor?" she asked.

"Very much. I'm hoping to get some sailing in soon, but in the meantime, I've been content to enjoy the scenery."

"Have you been to the park?"

"Not yet." He glanced over at the bottle the waiter offered, perused the label, then nodded.

"You shouldn't miss it. The view from Cadillac Mountain is stupendous."

"So I'm told." He tasted the wine, approved, then waited for Amanda's to be poured. "Perhaps you'll find some time and act as my guide."

"I don't think—"

"Hotel policy's already been bent," he interrupted, and touched his glass lightly to hers.

"I wanted to ask you how you managed it."

"Very simply. I gave your Mr. Stenerson a choice. Either he could make an exception to his policy, or I could move to another hotel where it wouldn't be an issue."

"I see." She took a thoughtful sip of wine. "That seems a bit drastic just for a dinner."

"A very delightful dinner. I wanted to get to know you better. I hope you don't mind."

What woman could? she asked herself, and only smiled.

It was impossible not to relax, not to be charmed by his stories, flattered by his attentiveness. He did not, as so many successful men did, talk constantly of his business. As an antique dealer he'd traveled all over the world and, throughout the meal, gave Amanda glimpses of Paris and Rome, London and Rio.

When her thoughts drifted now and again to another man, she doubled her determination to enjoy herself where she was, and with whom.

"The rosewood chiffonier in your foyer," he commented as they lingered over coffee and dessert. "It's a beautiful piece."

"Thank you. It's Regency period—I think."

He smiled. "You think correctly. If I had run into it at an auction, I would have considered myself very fortunate."

"My great-grandfather had it shipped over from England when he built the house."

"Ah, the house." William's lips curved as he lifted his cup. "Very imposing. I half expected to see medieval maidens drifting about on the lawn."

"Or bats swooping out of the tower."

On a delighted laugh, he squeezed her hand. "No, but perhaps Rapunzel letting down her hair."

The image appealed and made her smile. "We love it, and always have. Maybe the next time you visit the island you'll stay at The Towers Retreat."

"The Towers Retreat," he murmured, tapping a finger thoughtfully against his lips. "Where have I heard that before?"

"A projected St. James hotel?"

His eyes cleared. "Of course. I read something a few weeks ago. You don't mean to say that your home is The Towers?"

"Yes, it is. We hope to have the retreat ready for occupancy in about a year."

"That is fascinating. But wasn't there some legend attached to the place? Something about ghosts and missing jewelry?"

"The Calhoun emeralds. They were my great-grandmother's."

With a half smile, he tilted his head. "They're real? I thought it was just a clever publicity gimmick. Stay in a haunted house and search for missing treasure. That sort of thing."

"No, in fact we're not at all pleased that the whole business leaked out." Even thinking about it annoyed her so that she began to drum her fingers on the table. "The necklace is real—was real in any event. We don't know where it might have been hidden. In the meantime we're forever bothered by reporters or having to chase erstwhile treasure hunters off the grounds."

"I'm sorry. That's very intrusive."

"We hope to find it soon, and put an end to all the nonsense. Once renovations start, it might turn up under a floorboard."

"Or behind the ubiquitous secret panel," he offered with a smile and made her laugh.

"We don't have any of those—at least that I know of."

"Then your ancestor was remiss. A place like that deserves at least one secret panel." He laid a hand over hers again. "Perhaps you'll let me help you look for it… or at least let me use it as an excuse to see you again."

"I'm sorry, but at least for the next few days I'm tied up. My sister's getting married on Saturday."

He smiled over their joined hands. "There's always Sunday. I would like to see you again, Amanda. Very much." He let the subject and her hand slip gently away.

On the drive home he kept the topics general. No

pressure, Amanda thought, grateful. No arrogant assumptions or cocky grins. This was the kind of man who knew how to treat a woman with the proper respect and attention. William wouldn't knock her to the ground and laugh in her face. He wouldn't stalk her down like a gunslinger and fire out demands.

So why was she so let down when they stopped in front of the house and Sloan's car was nowhere in sight? Shaking off the mood, she waited for William to come around and open her door.

"Thank you for tonight," she told him. "It was lovely."

"Yes, it was. And so are you." Very gently he placed his hands on her shoulders before touching his lips to hers. The kiss was very warm, very soft—an expert caress of lips and hands. And to her disappointment, it left her completely unmoved.

"Are you really going to make me wait until Sunday to see you again?"

His eyes told her that he had not been unmoved. Amanda waited for the banked desire in them to strike some chord. But there was nothing.

"William, I—"

"Lunch," he said, adding a charming smile. "Something very casual at the hotel. You can tell me more about the house."

"All right. If I can swing it." She eased away before he could kiss her again. "Thanks again."

"My pleasure, Amanda." He waited, as was proper, for her to go inside. As the door shut behind her, his smile changed ever so slightly, hardened, cooled. "Believe me, it will be my pleasure."

He walked back to his car. He would drive it well out of sight of The Towers. And then he would come back to do a quick and quiet tour of the grounds, to note down the most practical entrances.

If Amanda Calhoun could be his entryway into The Towers, that was all well and good—with the side benefit of romancing a beautiful woman. If she didn't provide him with a way in, he would simply find a different route.

One way or the other, he didn't intend to leave Mount Desert Island without the Calhoun emeralds.

"Did you have a good time?" Suzanna asked when Amanda came in the front door.

"Suze." Amused but not surprised, Amanda shook her head. "You waited up again."

"No, I didn't." To prove it, Suzanna gestured with the mug in her hand. "I just came down to make myself some tea."

Amanda laughed as she walked over to rest her hands on her sister's shoulders. "Why is it that we Irish-as-Paddy's-pig Calhouns can't tell a decent lie?"

Suzanna gave up. "I don't know. We should practice more."

"Honey, you look tired."

"Mmm." Exhausted was the word, but she didn't care for it. Suzanna sipped the tea as they started up the stairs together. "Springtime. Everybody wants their flowers done yesterday. I'm not complaining. It looks like the business is finally going to turn a real profit."

"I still think you should hire on some more help. Between the business and the kids you run yourself ragged."

"Now who's playing mama? Anyway, Island Gardens needs one more good season before I can afford anything but one part-time helper. Plus I like to be busy." Even though fatigue was dragging at her, she paused outside of Amanda's door. "Mandy, can I talk to you for a minute before you go to bed?"

"Sure. Come on in." Amanda left the door slightly ajar as she slipped out of her shoes. "Is something wrong?"

"No. At least nothing I can put my finger on. Can I ask you what you think of Sloan?"

"Think of him?" Stalling, Amanda set her shoes neatly in the closet.

"Impressions, I guess. He seems like a very nice man. Both kids are already crazy about him, and that's an almost foolproof barometer for me."

"He's good with them." Amanda took off her earrings to replace them in her jewelry box.

"I know." Troubled, she wandered the room. "Aunt Coco's set to adopt him. He's slipped right into an easy relationship with Lilah. C.C.'s already fond of him, and not just because he's a friend of Trent's."

Pouting a little, Amanda unclasped her necklace. "His type always gets along beautifully with women."

Distracted, Suzanna merely shook her head. "No, it's not a man-woman kind of thing at all. Just a kind of innate relaxation."

Amanda had no comment for that as she recalled the fevered tension in him a few hours earlier.

"He seems like an easygoing, friendly man."

"But?"

"It's probably my imagination, but whenever he looks at me, I get this wave of hostility." With a half laugh, she shrugged. "Now I sound like Lilah."

Amanda's eyes met her sister's in the mirror. "No,

I sensed something myself. I can't explain it. I even called him on it."

"Did he say anything? I don't expect everyone to like me, but when I feel a dislike this strong, at least I want to know why."

"He denied it. I don't know what to say, Suzanna, except that I don't think he's the kind of man who would react that way to someone he doesn't even know." She made a helpless gesture with her hands. "He can certainly be annoying, but I don't think he's a man to be deliberately unfair. Maybe we're both being over-sensitive."

"Maybe." Suzanna pushed the uncomfortable feelings away. "We're all a little crazed with C.C.'s wedding, and the renovations. Well, I won't lose any sleep over him." She kissed Amanda's cheek. "Good night."

"Night." As she eased down onto the bed, Amanda let out a long sigh. It was unfortunate, she thought. It was infuriating. But she already knew she'd be losing sleep over him.

Chapter Six

She was right on schedule. If there was one thing you could count on about Amanda Calhoun, Sloan thought, it was that she'd be on time. She was moving fast—typically—so he lengthened his stride and crossed the hotel patio to waylay her by the gate leading to the pool. His hand covered hers on the latch.

She jerked away, which was no less than he'd expected. "Don't you have anything better to do?" she asked.

"I want to talk to you."

"This is my time." She shoved open the gate, strode through then whirled around. "My personal time. I don't have to talk to you." To prove it, she slammed the gate smartly in his face.

Sloan took a long, slow breath, then opened the gate. "Okay, you can just listen." He caught up with her as she heaved her towel onto a deck chair.

"I'm not going to talk, and I'm not going to listen. There's absolutely nothing you have to say that could interest me." She stripped off her terry wrap, tossed it aside, then dove into the pool.

Sloan watched her through the first lap. She was mad enough to spit, he thought, then moved his shoulders. So, they'd do it the hard way.

With each kick and stroke, Amanda cursed him. She'd spent half the night replaying their last scene together over and over in her mind. It had made her miserable. It had made her furious. When she'd awakened that morning, she'd promised herself that he would never get the chance to touch her again. Certainly he would never get the chance to make her feel helpless and needy again.

Her life was just beginning to move along as she wanted. There was no way, no way in hell that Sloan O'Riley or anyone else was going to block her path.

She ran straight into him, a dud torpedo into a battleship. Sputtering, she surfaced to see him standing chest high in the water. Bare-chest high.

"What are you doing?"

"I figured I'd have a better chance of getting you to listen in here than I would if I stood on the side and yelled at you."

Eyes narrowed, she slicked the hair back from her face. There was a laugh bubbling in her throat that she refused to acknowledge. "The pool isn't open to guests until ten."

"Yeah, I think you mentioned that. What you didn't mention is that this water is freezing."

"Yeah." Now she did smile, and there was as much humor as smugness in the curve of her lips. "I know. That's why I like to keep moving."

She started off, slicing cleanly through the water. Less than a foot away, he was matching her stroke for stroke. He'd stripped off more than his shirt, she noted. The only thing covering that very long body was a pair of brief navy briefs. Each time her face went into the water, her eyes slid over to take another look.

His broad shoulders and chest tapered down to a narrow waist and hips. The skin was stretched taut over the bones there, without an ounce of excess flesh. His stomach was board flat, and…oh my. When she nearly sucked in water instead of air, Amanda forced her gaze to skip down several strategic inches to the hard, muscled thighs and calves.

The tough, weathered tan was over every inch of exposed flesh. His skin gleamed like wet copper. And what would it feel like to run her hands over it now? To feel those sleek, smooth muscles under her fingers? How could their bodies fit together now, if slick as otters, they slid against each other through the chill water?

Chill? she thought. The pool was beginning to feel like a sauna. Deliberately she pushed off hard and increased her pace. If she could outrace him, maybe she could outrace her own wayward thoughts.

He was still beside her, matching speed and stroke so that they crossed the pool in a kind of unstudied and effortless harmony. It was lovely, almost sensuous, the way their arms lifted and pulled at the same moment, the way their legs scissored and their bodies stretched… like making love, she thought dreamily, then shook herself to knock that hot image from her brain.

Amanda kicked in and put all that frustrated passion into speed. Still, their hands slapped the wall in unison.

She began to enjoy it for what it was, an unstated competition between two people who were evenly matched. She'd lost track of the laps and didn't care. When her lungs were straining and her muscles weak, she gripped the edge of the pool to surface, laughing.

He knew she'd never looked more beautiful, with her hair and face drenched with water and her eyes filled with delight. More than anything he'd ever wanted, he wanted to pull her against him then, just to hold her while her laughter danced on the morning air. But he'd made a promise to himself sometime during his own sleepless night. He intended to keep it.

He sent her a friendly grin. "That warmed things up."

"You're pretty good. For an Okie."

"You're not bad yourself, for a female."

She laughed again and rested her head on the side of the pool to look at him. His hair was dark with water, curling over his brow and neck in a way that had her fingers itching to play with it. "I like to race."

"Race? Is that what we were doing? I thought we were just taking a nice, leisurely swim."

She tossed water into his eyes, then stood. "I have to get in."

"Are you going to let me talk to you now?"

The laughter faded from her eyes. "Let's just leave it," she suggested, and hitched herself up on the side of the pool.

He laid a hand on her leg. "Mandy—"

"I don't want to argue with you again. Since we've actually managed to get along for five minutes, why can't we just leave it at that?"

"Because I want to apologize."

"If you'd just—" She broke off to stare at him. "You what?"

"I want to apologize." He stood to put his hands lightly on her arms just beneath her shoulders. "I was out of line last night, way out, and I'm sorry."

"Oh." Disconcerted, she looked down and began to rub at the beads of water on her thigh.

"Now you're supposed to say, all right, Sloan, I accept your apology."

She looked up through wet, spiky lashes, then smiled. Things were suddenly too comfortable to cling to anger. "I guess I do. You acted like such a jerk."

He grimaced. "Thanks a lot."

"You did. Spouting off threats and orders. Then there was all that steam coming out of your ears."

"Want to know why?"

She shook her head and started to rise, but he held her in place. "You brought it up," he pointed out. "I couldn't stand the idea of you being with someone else. Look at me." Gently he cupped her chin, turning her face back to his. "You triggered something in me right off. I can't shake it. I don't much want to."

"I don't think—"

"Thinking has nothing to do with it. I know how I feel when I look at you."

She was losing fast. The quick skip of panic couldn't compete with the flood of pleasure. "I have to think," she murmured. "I'm made that way."

"Okay, well here's something new for you to think about. I'm falling in love with you."

Panic was more than a skip now, but a hard slap. It darted into her eyes as she stared at him. "You don't mean that."

"Yes, I do. And you know it or you wouldn't be sitting there looking like a rabbit caught in the high beams."

"I don't—"

"I'm not asking how you feel," he cut in. "I'm giving you my side of it, so you can get used to it."

She didn't think she would, ever, any more than she would get used to him. Certainly it would be impossible to get used to the feelings shooting off inside her. Is this what love was? she wondered. This edgy and bright sensation that could turn warm and soft without warning? "I don't—I'm not sure how…" She let out a huff of breath. "Did you do this just to make me crazy?"

It helped to be able to smile. "Yep. Give me a kiss, Calhoun."

She twisted and slid wetly out of his hold. "I'm not kissing you again, because it erases every intelligent thought from my head."

Now he grinned. "Honey, that's the nicest thing you've ever said to me." When he rose smoothly from the pool, Amanda snatched up her towel. She snapped it once, hard enough to make the air crack.

"Keep back. I mean it. You either give me time to figure all this out or I aim and fire. And I aim below the belt." There was both amusement and challenge in her eyes when she tilted her chin. "You don't have a lot of protection at the moment."

He ran his tongue around his teeth. "You've got me there. How about a drive after you get off work?"

It would be nice, she thought, to go driving with him up into the hills, with the windows open and the air streaming. But, regretfully, duty came first.

"I can't. C.C.'s shower's tonight. We're surprising her

when she gets home from work." She frowned a little. "It's on your list."

"Guess it slipped my mind. Tomorrow then."

"I have the final meeting with the photographer, then I have to help Suzanna with the flowers. Not the next night, either," she said before he could ask. "Most of the out-of-town guests will be arriving, plus we've got the rehearsal dinner."

"Then the wedding," he said with a nod. "After the wedding, Calhoun."

"After the wedding, I'll…" She smiled, realizing she was enjoying herself. "I'll let you know." Grabbing her wrap, she headed for the gate.

"Hey. I haven't got a towel."

She tossed a laugh over her shoulder. "I know."

Late that afternoon, Sloan stood out on the lower terrace, making sketches of the exterior of The Towers. He wanted to add another outside stairway without disturbing the integrity of the building. He stopped when Suzanna came out carrying two wicker baskets pregnant with spring flowers.

"I'm sorry." She hesitated, then tried a smile. "I didn't know you were out here. I'm going to set things up for the shower."

"I'll be out of your way in a minute."

"That's all right." She set the basket down and went back inside.

Over the next few minutes, she went back and forth, carrying out chairs and paper decorations. They passed the time in nerve-racking silence until she finally set aside one of Amanda's swans and looked at him.

"Mr. O'Riley, have we met before?"

He kept right on sketching. "No."

"I wondered because you seemed to know me, and have a poor opinion of me."

His gaze lifted coldly to hers. "I don't know you— Mrs. Dumont."

"Then why—" She broke off. She hated confrontations, the way they tightened up her stomach muscles. Turning away, she started back inside. She could feel his eyes on her, icy and resentful. After bracing a hand on the jamb, she forced herself to turn back. "No, I'm not going to do this. You're in my home, Mr. O'Riley, and I refuse to walk on eggshells in my own home ever again. Now I want to know what your problem is."

He tossed his sketch pad onto a small glass-topped table. "The name doesn't ring any bells with you, Mrs. Dumont? O'Riley doesn't strike a chord?"

"No, why should it?"

His mouth tightened. "Maybe if I add a name to it. Megan. Megan O'Riley. Hear any bells now?"

"No." Frustrated, she pushed a hand through her hair. "Will you get to the point?"

"I guess it's easy for someone like you to forget. She wasn't anyone to you but a slight inconvenience."

"Who?"

"Megan. My sister, Megan."

Completely lost, Suzanna shook her head. "I don't know your sister."

The fact that the name meant nothing to her only infuriated him. Sloan stepped toward her, ignoring the quick fear in her eyes. "No, you never met her face-to-face. Why bother? You managed to see that she was pushed aside easily enough. Not that you ended up with any prize. Baxter Dumont was always a bastard, but she loved him."

"Your sister?" Suzanna lifted an unsteady hand to rub at her temple. "Your sister and Bax."

"Starting to get through?" When she started to turn away, he grabbed her arm and whirled her back. "Was it for love or money?" he demanded. "Either way, you could have shown some compassion. Damn it, she was seventeen and pregnant. Couldn't you have stood back far enough to let the spineless sonofabitch see his son?"

She'd gone a translucent shade of white. Under his hand, her arm seemed to turn to water. "Son," she whispered.

"She was just a kid, a terrified kid who'd believed every lie he'd told her. I wanted to kill him, but it would only have made it worse for Meg. But you, you couldn't even find it in your heart to give her the scraps from the table. You went right ahead with your fancy life as if she and the boy didn't exist. And when she called and begged you just to let him see the boy once or twice a year, you called her a whore and threatened to have her son taken away if she ever contacted your precious husband again."

She couldn't get her breath. Not since her last hideous argument with Bax had she found it so difficult to breathe. Weakly she batted at the hand that held her arm. "Please. Please, I need to sit down."

But he was staring at her. As the impetus of his own rage ebbed he could see that it wasn't shame in her eyes, it wasn't derision or even anger. It was pure shock. "My God," he said quietly, "you didn't know."

All she could do was shake her head. When his grip loosened, she turned and bolted into the house. Sloan stood for a moment, pressing his fingers against his eyes.

All the disgust he had felt for Suzanna turned sharply on himself. He started after her and ran into a furious Amanda in the doorway.

"What did you do to her?" With both hands she shoved him back. "What the hell did you say to her to make her cry like that?"

The fist in his stomach squeezed tighter. "Where did she go?"

"You're not getting near her again. When I think that I'd begun to believe I could—damn you, O'Riley."

"There's nothing you can say to me that's worse than what I'm already thinking about myself. Now where is she?"

"You go to hell." She slammed the terrace door and flipped the lock.

Sloan gave brief thought to kicking it in, then, swearing, went around to the stone steps on the side of the house. He found Suzanna standing on the second-floor balcony, looking out at the cliffs. He'd taken his first step toward her when Amanda burst out of the doors.

"You keep away from her." She already had a protective arm around her sister. "Just turn around and start walking. Don't stop until you get back to Oklahoma."

"This isn't any of your concern," Sloan told her, and Suzanna had to grab hold before Amanda sprang at him.

"It's all right." Suzanna squeezed Amanda's hand. "I need to talk to him, Mandy. Alone."

"But—"

"Please. It's important. Go down and finish setting up, will you?"

Reluctant, Amanda stepped back. "If it's what you want." She aimed a killing look at Sloan. "Watch your step."

When they were alone, Sloan struggled for the right words. "Mrs. Dumont. Suzanna—"

"What's his name?" she asked.

"What?"

"The boy. What's his name?"

"I don't—"

"Damn it, what's his name?" She whirled away from the wall. Shock had been replaced by angry tears. "He's half brother to my children. I want to know his name."

"Kevin. Kevin O'Riley."

"How old is he?"

"Seven."

Turning back to the sea, she shut her eyes. Seven years before, she had been a new bride, full of hope and dreams and blind love. "And Baxter knew? He knew that she'd had his child?"

"Yes, he knew. Megan wouldn't tell anyone at first who the father was. But after she'd called and spoken to you...but she didn't speak to you, did she?"

"No." Suzanna continued to stare straight ahead. "Baxter's mother perhaps."

"I want to apologize."

"There's no need. If it had been one of my sisters, I would have struck out with more than a few hard words." To warm herself she cupped her elbows with her hands. "Go on."

She was tougher than she looked, Sloan thought, but it didn't ease his conscience. "After she'd called, she fell apart. That's when she finally told me everything. How she'd met Dumont when she'd gone to New York to visit some friends. He was there on some business and he started showing her around. She'd never been to New York before, and it—and he dazzled her. She was just a kid."

"Seventeen," Suzanna murmured.

"And naive with it. Well, she got over that quick enough." The bitterness came though. "He gave her all the usual bull about getting married, about how he'd come out to Oklahoma and meet her family. Once she got home, he never contacted her. She got through to him on the phone once or twice. He made excuses and more promises. Then she found out she was pregnant."

He steadied himself, trying not to remember how angry and frightened he'd been when he'd learned his baby sister was going to have a baby of her own.

"When she told him, he changed tactics fast. He said some pretty awful things to her, and she grew up fast. Too fast."

Suzanna understood that, more than he could know. "It must have been terribly difficult for her, having the child without having the father."

"She handled herself. I have a very supportive family. Well, you'd know about that."

"Yes."

"Luckily, money wasn't a problem, either, so she could get all the care she and the baby needed. She never wanted his money, Suzanna."

"No, I understand that, too."

He nodded slowly, seeing that she did. "And when Kevin was born…well, Meg was great. It was for his sake that she tried to contact Dumont again, and eventually decided to appeal to his wife. All she wanted was for her son to have some contact with his father."

"I understand." Steadier, she turned around to look at him. "Sloan, if I had any influence with Bax I'd use it." She lifted her hands and let them fall. "But I don't, not even when it concerns the children he's chosen to acknowledge."

"I figure Kevin's better off the way things are. Suzanna—" he dragged a hand through his disordered hair "—how the hell did a woman like you end up with Dumont?"

She smiled a little. "Once I was a young, naive girl who believed in happy ever after."

He wanted to take her hand but wasn't certain she'd accept it. "I know you said you didn't want an apology, but I'd feel a hell of a lot better if you'd take it just the same."

It was she who offered her hand. "It's easy to do when it's family. I guess in an odd way, that's what we are." She pressed her free hand to their joined ones. Later, she promised herself, she would find a few minutes alone to let the grief come. And to let it go. "I want to ask you a favor. I'd like for my children to know about Kevin, and unless it would upset your sister, for them to have a chance to meet each other."

"When I take a wrong turn, I take it big. It would mean a lot to her."

"Jenny and Alex are going to be thrilled." She looked at her watch. "Speaking of which, they're probably already home from school and driving Aunt Coco crazy. I'd better go."

He looked down the steps toward the terrace. And thought of Amanda. "Me, too. I've got other fences to mend."

Suzanna lifted a brow. "Good luck."

He had a feeling he was going to need it. By the time he'd reached the terrace, he was sure of it. Amanda was there, fastening streamers while Lilah leisurely tied balloons to the back of chairs. A long table was already covered with a frilly white cloth.

Amanda heard the scrape of boot heels on stone and turned to aim one deadly glare. Lilah didn't need another hint.

"Well." She flicked a balloon with a fingertip to send it dancing. "I think I'll go see if Aunt Coco's got any of those chocolate pastries ready." As she walked by Sloan, she paused. Unlike Amanda's, her eyes were cool, but the meaning was clear. "I'd hate to think I was wrong about you." She walked through the terrace doors and, after a brief hesitation, shut them to give her sister privacy.

Amanda didn't wait to pounce. "You've got a nerve, or maybe you're just plain stupid, showing your face here after what you did."

"You don't know anything about it. Suzanna and I worked it out."

"Oh, you think so?" Ready to joust, she slammed down a package of pretty pink-and-silver plates. "Not by a long shot. When I think that just a few hours ago you'd nearly convinced me you were the kind of man I could care about, then I come home and find my sister running away from you looking devastated. I want to know what you did."

"I ran with the wrong information. And I'm sorry about it."

"That's not good enough."

His own emotions were a bit too raw for reason. "Well, it's going to have to be. If you want to know more, you're just going to have to ask Suzanna."

"I'm asking you."

"And I'm telling you that what happened was between her and me. It doesn't have anything to do with you."

"That's where you're wrong." She crossed the terrace until they were toe-to-toe. "You mess with one Calhoun, you mess with them all. I may have to put up with you until after the wedding, since you're supposed to be best man. But when it's over, I'm going to do whatever I have to do to see to it that you go back where you came from."

Pushed to the end of his chain, he took her by the lapels. "I told you before, I finish what I start."

"You are finished, O'Riley. The Towers doesn't need you, and neither do I."

He was just about to prove her wrong when Trent opened the terrace doors. Trent took one look at his friend and future sister-in-law glaring daggers at each other and cleared his throat.

"Looks like I'm going to have to work on my timing."

"Your timing's perfect." Amanda rammed an elbow into Sloan's stomach before she pulled away. "We've got no time for men around here tonight. Why don't you take this jerk you've sicced on us and go do something manly." She shoved by Trent and stalked into the house.

"Well." Trent let out a long breath. "I don't think I mentioned the Calhoun temperament when I asked you to take on the job."

"No, you didn't." Scowling at the empty doorway, Sloan rubbed his stomach. "Is there a dark, noisy bar anywhere in this town?"

"I guess we could find one."

"Good. Let's go get drunk."

He found the bar, and he found the bottle. Sloan slumped in the corner booth and hissed through his teeth as the whiskey stung his throat. Over the first drink, and the second, he told Trent about his altercation with Suzanna.

"Baxter Dumont is Kevin's father? You never told me."

"I gave Meg my word I wouldn't tell anybody. Even our folks don't know."

Trent was silent a moment, sipping thoughtfully at his club soda. "It's hard to figure out how such a selfish bastard managed to father three terrific kids."

"It's a puzzle, all right." Sloan signaled for another round. "Then I go off and unload both barrels on Suzanna." He broke off and swore. "Damn it, Trent, I'm never going to forget the way she looked when I cut loose on her."

"She'll handle it. From what C.C.'s told me, she's dealt with worse."

"Yeah, maybe. Maybe. But I don't care much for slapping down women. I was already feeling like something you scrape off your shoe when Amanda lit into me."

"These women stick together."

"Yeah." Scowling, Sloan drank again. "Like a dirt clod."

"Why didn't you explain things to her?"

Sloan shrugged and knocked back more whiskey. He had his own share of pride. "It wasn't any of her business."

"You just explained it to me."

"That's different."

"Okay. Do you want some pretzels to go with that?"

"No."

They sat for a moment, nursing drinks, two dynamically different men, one in battered jeans, the other in tailored slacks; one slumped comfortably, the other comfortably alert. They'd both come from money—Trent from real estate, Sloan from oil, but their backgrounds and family lives had been opposites. Trent's first experience with real family ties had come through the Calhouns, and Sloan had known them always. They had almost nothing in common, and yet in their first semester in college they had become friends and had remained so for more than ten years.

Because he was feeling sorry for himself, Sloan enjoyed the sensation of getting steadily drunk. Because he recognized the symptoms, Trent stayed meticulously sober.

Over yet another drink, Sloan eyed his friend. "When'd you start wearing basketball shoes?"

Trent glanced down at his own feet and grinned to himself. They were a symbol of sorts of the way one hot-tempered brunette had changed his life. "They're not basketball shoes, they're running shoes."

"What's the difference?" Sloan narrowed his eyes. "And you're not wearing a tie. How come you're not wearing a tie?"

"Because I'm in love."

"Yeah." With a short oath, Sloan sat back. "See what it's doing to you? It makes you nuts."

"You hate ties."

"Exactly. Damn woman's been driving me crazy since the first time I saw her."

"C.C.?"

"No, damn it. We were talking about Amanda."

"Right." Settling back in the seat, Trent smiled. "Well, some woman's always driving you crazy. I've never seen anyone with a more…admirable affection for the gentler sex."

"Gentler my ass. First she runs into me, then she knocks me on my butt. I can hardly say two words without having her claw at me." After calling for another drink, he leaned across the table. "You've known me for over ten years. Wouldn't y'say that I was a kind of even-tempered, affable sort of man?"

"Absolutely." Trent grinned. "Except when you're not."

Sloan slapped a hand on the table. "There you go." Nodding agreement, he pulled out a cigar. "So what the hell's wrong with her?"

"You tell me."

"I'll tell you." He jabbed the cigar toward Trent's face. "She's got the devil's own temper and a mule's stubbornness to go with it. If a man can keep his eyes off her legs, it's plain enough to see." He picked up his fresh whiskey and scowled into it. "She sure enough has first-class legs."

"I've noticed. They run in the family." As Sloan downed the liquor, Trent winced. "Am I going to have to carry you home?"

"More'n likely." He settled back to let the whiskey spin in his head. "What you want to go and get yourself married for, Trent? We'd both be better off hightailing it outta here."

"Because I love her."

"Yeah." On a sigh, Sloan let out a lazy stream of smoke. "That's how they get you. They get you all tangled up so you can't think straight. Used to be I thought women were God's own pleasure, but I know better now. They've only got one reason for being here, and that's to make a man's life misery." He squinted over at

Trent. "Have you seen the way her skirt jiggles when she walks—especially when she's in a hurry, like she always is."

On a chuckle, Trent lifted his glass again. "I take the Fifth on that one."

"And the sassy way her hair moves when she's yelling at you. Her eyes get all snappy. Then you grab ahold of her to shut her up, and God Almighty." He took another quick slug of whiskey, but it did nothing to put out the fire. "You ever missed your step and gone down on an electric fence?"

"Can't say I have."

"It burns," Sloan murmured. "Burns like fire and knocks you senseless for a minute. When you get your senses back, you're kind of numb and shaky."

Carefully Trent set down his drink and leaned closer to study his friend. "Sloan, is this leading where I think it's leading, or are you just drunk?"

"Not drunk enough." Annoyed, he shoved the glass aside. "I haven't had a decent night's sleep since I set eyes on her. And since I set eyes on her it's like there was never anyone else. Like there's never going to be anyone else." With his elbows propped on the table, he rubbed his hands over his face. "I'm crazy in love with her, Trent, and if I could get my hands on her right now, I'd strangle her."

"Calhoun women have a talent for that." He grinned at Sloan. "Welcome to the club."

It rained all day so I could not go down to the cliffs to see Christian. For most of the morning I played games with the children to keep them from becoming fussy about being kept indoors. They squabbled, of course, but Nanny distracted them with cookies. Even the boys enjoyed the tea party we had with Colleen's little china dishes. For me, it was one of those sweet, insular days that a mother always remembers—the way her children laugh, the funny questions they ask, the way they lay their heads on your lap when nap time approaches.

The memory of this single day is as precious to me as any I have had, or will have. They will not be my babies very long. Already Colleen is talking about balls and dresses.

It makes me wonder what my life would be like if it could be Christian who would stroll into the parlor. He would not nod absently as he opened the brandy decanter. He would not forget to ask about his children.

No, my Christian would come to me first, his hands outstretched to meet mine as I rose to kiss him. He would laugh, as I hear him laugh during our stolen hours at the cliff.

And I would be happy. Without this bittersweet pain in my heart. Without this guilt. There would be no need then for me to seek the quiet and solitude of my tower, or to sit alone watching the gray rain as I write my dreams in this book.

I would be living my dreams.

But it is all just a fancy, like one of the stories I tell the children at bedtime. A happy-ever-after story with handsome princes and beautiful maidens. My life is not a fairy tale. But perhaps, someday someone will open these pages and read my story. I hope they will have a kind and generous heart, condemn me not for my disloyalty to a husband I have never loved, but rejoice for me in my joy in those few short hours with a man I will love even after death.

Chapter Seven

Sloan's head was filled with tiny little men wielding pickaxes. To quiet them, he tried rolling over. A definite mistake, he realized, as the slight movement sent a signal to the army-navy band waiting in the wings to punch up the percussions. Gingerly he pulled a pillow over his face, hoping to smother the sound or—if that didn't work—himself.

But the noise kept booming until his abused system told him it was the door, not just the hangover. Giving up, he stumbled out of bed, grateful there was no one around to hear him whimper. With the road gang working away inside his temples, he turned the air between the bedroom and the parlor door a ribald shade of blue.

When he wrenched it open, Amanda took one look, noting the bloodshot eyes, night stubble and curled lip.

He was wearing the jeans, unclasped, that he'd fallen asleep in, and nothing else.

"Well," she said primly, "you look like you had a delightful time last night."

And she looked as neat and crisp as a freshly starched shirt. It was, he was sure, reason enough for homicide. "If you came up here to ruin my day, you're too late." He started to swing the door shut, but she held it open and stepped inside.

"I have something to say to you."

"You've said it." Instantly he regretted turning sharply away. As his head throbbed nastily, he vowed to hold on to what was left of his dignity. He would not crawl away, but walk.

Because he looked so pitiful, she decided to help him out. "I guess you feel pretty lousy."

"Lousy?" He narrowed his eyes to keep them from dropping out of his head. "No, I feel dandy. Just dandy. I live for hangovers."

"What you need is a cold shower, a couple of aspirin and a decent breakfast."

After making an inarticulate sound in his throat, he groped his way toward the bedroom. "Calhoun, you're on dangerous ground."

"I won't be in your way long." Determined to accomplish her mission, she followed him. "I just want to talk to you about—" She broke off when he slammed the bathroom door in her face. "Well." Blowing out a huffy breath, she set her hands on her hips.

Inside, Sloan stripped off his jeans then stepped into the shower. With one hand braced on the tile, he turned the water on full cold. His single vicious curse bounced along the walls then slammed right back into his head.

Still, he was a little steadier when he stepped out again, fought with the cap on the aspirin bottle and downed three.

His hangover hadn't gone away, he thought, but at least he was now fully awake to enjoy it. Wrapping a towel around his waist, he walked back into the parlor.

He'd thought she would have gotten the message, but there she was, hunched over his drawing board with glasses perched on her nose. She'd tidied up, too, he noted, emptying ashtrays, piling cups on the room-service tray, picking up discarded clothes. In fact, she had her hands full of his clothes while she studied his drawings.

"What the hell are you doing?"

She glanced up and, determined to be cheerful, smiled. "Oh, you're back." The sight of him in nothing but a damp towel had her careful to keep her eyes strictly on his face. "I was just taking a look at your work."

"I don't mean that, I mean what are you doing picking up after me? It's not part of your job to play Sally Domestic."

"I didn't see how you could work in a sty," she shot back, "so I straightened up a little while I was waiting for you."

"I like working in a sty. If I didn't, I would've picked the damn stuff up myself."

"Fine." Incensed, she hurled his clothes into the air so that they scattered over the room. "Better?"

Slowly he pulled off the T-shirt that had landed on his head. "Calhoun, do you know what's more dangerous than a man with a hangover?"

"No."

"Nothing." He took one measured step toward her when there was another knock at the door.

"That's your breakfast." Amanda's voice was clipped as she strode toward the door. "I had them put a rush on it."

Defeated, Sloan sank onto the couch and put his head in his hands so that he could catch it easily when it fell off. "I don't want any damn breakfast."

"Well, you'll eat it and stop feeling sorry for yourself." She signed the check, then took the tray herself to place it on the table in front of him. "Whole wheat toast, black coffee and a Virgin Mary, heavy on the hot sauce. It'll take the edge off."

"An electric planer couldn't take the edge off." But he reached for the coffee.

Satisfied that she had made a good start, Amanda took off her glasses and slipped them into her pocket. He really did look pathetic, she thought. His wet hair was dripping down his face. She had a strong urge to kneel down beside him and stroke those damp curls back. But he'd probably have snapped her hand off at the wrist, and she had an equally strong urge to survive.

"Trent mentioned that you did quite a bit of drinking last night."

After trying the spiced-up tomato juice, he eyed her narrowly. "So you came by to see the morning-after in person."

"Not exactly." Her fingers toyed with her name tag, then the top button on her jacket. "I thought since it was my fault you got into this condition, I should—"

"Hold it. If I get drunk, it's because my hand reaches for the bottle."

"Yes, but—"

"I don't want your sympathy, Calhoun, or your guilt any more than I want your maid service."

"Fine." Pride and temper went to war. Pride won. "I merely came by this morning to apologize."

He bit off another piece of toast. It did soothing things to the rocky sea of his belly. "What for?"

"For what I said, and the way I acted yesterday." Unable to stand still, she walked over to the window and pulled the shades open, ignoring Sloan's quick hiss of pain. "Although I still think I was perfectly justified. After all, I only knew that you'd said something to hurt Suzanna badly." But there was regret in her eyes when she turned back. "When she told me about your sister—about Bax—I realized how you must have been feeling. Damn it, Sloan, you could have told me yourself."

"Maybe. Maybe you could have trusted me."

She took her glasses out again, playing with the earpieces to keep her hands busy. "It wasn't really a matter of trust, but of automatic reflex. You don't know what Suzanna went through, how deeply she was hurt. Or if you do, because of your own sister, then you should understand why I couldn't bear to see her look like that again." She shoved the glasses away. When she looked at him, her eyes were damp. "And it was worse, because I have feelings for you."

If there was one thing he had no defense against, it was tears. Wanting to ward them off as much as he wanted to make peace, he rose to take her hands. "I made my share of mistakes yesterday." Smiling, he rubbed her knuckles over his cheek. It felt good—damn good. "I guess it's as hard for you to apologize as it is for me."

"If you mean it's like swallowing a lump of coal, then you're right."

"Why don't we call it even, all around?" But when he lowered his head to kiss her, she stepped back.

"I really need to think straight for a while."

He caught her hand again. "I really need to make love with you."

Her heart took a quick leap into her throat. For someone who moved so slowly, how did he get from one point to the next so fast? "I'm, ah, on duty. I'm already over my break, and Stenerson—"

"Why don't I give him a call?" Still smiling, he began to kiss her fingers. The hangover was down to a dull ache, not nearly as noticeable as another, more pleasant one in the pit of his stomach. "Tell him I need the assistant manager for a couple hours."

"I think—"

"There you go again," he murmured, brushing his lips lightly over hers.

"No, really, I have to…" Her mind clouded as he trailed those lips down her throat. "I really have to get back to my desk. And I—" She took a big, shuddering gasp of air. "I need to be sure." Scrambling for survival, she pulled away. "I have to know what I'm doing."

Sloan pressed a hand to the familiar burn that spread inside his gut. He had a feeling he was just going to have to live with it for a while longer. "Tell you what, Calhoun. You think about it, and think hard, until after the wedding. Like we said before." Before she could relax, he had her chin cupped firmly in his hand. "And after the wedding, if you don't come to me, you'd better run fast."

The line appeared between her brows. "That sounds like an ultimatum."

"No, that's a fact. If I were you, I'd get out that door now, while I still had the chance."

All dignity, she marched to it before turning back with a smile that should have tipped him off. "Enjoy your breakfast," she told him, then slammed the door with a vengeance. She could almost see him holding his battered head.

"I didn't think I'd be nervous." C.C. stared at the wedding dress of snowy silk and lace that hung on the back of her closet door. "Maybe it'd be better if I just wore regular clothes."

"Don't be ridiculous. And stop fidgeting." Amanda bent close to her sister to add a bit more blusher to her cheeks. "You're supposed to be nervous."

"Why?" Annoyed with herself, C.C. pressed a hand to her fluttery stomach. "I love Trent and want to get married. Why should I be nervous now that it's going to happen?" She looked back at the dress and swallowed. "Less than an hour from now."

Amanda grinned. "Maybe I should call Aunt Coco and have her give you a booster-shot course on the birds and the bees."

"Very funny." But the idea did amuse her enough to make her smile. "When's Suzanna coming back?"

"I told you, as soon as she has the kids dressed. Jenny might love the idea of being flower girl, but Alex is a most reluctant ring bearer. He'd rather be carrying a machine gun down the aisle than a satin pillow. And before you ask, again, Lilah is supposed to be downstairs making sure all the last-minute details go off properly. Though why we think we can trust her is beyond me."

"She'll be fine. She always handles things when it's important." C.C. laid a hand on Amanda's. "And it is important, Mandy."

"I know, honey. It's the most important day of your life." Misty-eyed, she laid her cheek against C.C.'s. "Oh, I feel as though I should say something profound, but I can only say be happy."

"I will be, and it's not as if I'll be really going away. We'll be living here most of the time, except when… when we're in Boston." Her throat filled up.

"Don't start," Amanda warned. "I mean it. After all the work I put in making you beautiful, you're not going out in the garden with red eyes and a runny nose." Blowing her own, she stepped back. "Now, let me help you get dressed."

When Suzanna came in a short time later, a child's hand in each of hers, she had to struggle with her own tears. "Oh, C.C., you look wonderful."

"Are you sure?" Fretting, she plucked at the lace at her throat. The dress was a slim column, elegantly simple with only that whisper of lace at the neck, and another whisper at the hem to adorn it. "Maybe I should have gone for something less formal."

"No, it's perfect." Suzanna bent down to her son, her own dress rustling with the movement. "Alex, stand still for five minutes, please."

He tried out the sneer he'd been practicing in the mirror. "I hate cummerbunds."

"I know, but if you don't want me to strap it around your mouth, you'll stand still." Tweaking his nose, she straightened. "I have something for you." She offered C.C. a small box. Inside was a single teardrop sapphire on a braided gold chain.

"Mama's necklace," C.C. whispered.

"Aunt Coco gave it to me when I—on my wedding

day." She took it out to fasten around her sister's neck. "I want you to have it and wear it on yours."

C.C. lifted a hand to it, closing her fingers around the stone. "I'm not nervous anymore."

"Then that's my cue to panic." Afraid to say more, Amanda gave her a quick kiss. "I'll run downstairs and make sure everything's on schedule."

"Mandy—"

Amanda smiled over her shoulder. "Yes, I'll send Lilah up." She went out, hurrying downstairs while she ticked off duties in her mind. Taking a moment, she stopped by the hall mirror to adjust the spray of baby's breath over her ear.

"You look great." She glanced over and saw Sloan. "Just great."

"Thanks." They stood awkwardly a moment, a man in a tuxedo and a woman in a tea-length gown the color of ripe peaches. "I, uh, where's Trent?"

"He needed a couple of minutes to himself. His father came by with some advice." Relaxing slowly, Sloan grinned. "When a man's been married as many times as Mr. S.J., he comes up with some interesting viewpoints." He had to laugh at the expression on Amanda's face. "Don't worry, I nudged him along outside with a glass of champagne and Coco. Seems like they're old friends."

"I think she met him a long time ago." When Sloan took a step toward her, she began to talk rapidly. "You look terrific. I didn't expect you to look good in a tuxedo." Before he'd finished laughing, she was rambling on. "What I mean is I didn't expect it to suit you. I mean—"

"You're cute when you're flustered."

She ended up smiling at him. As far as she could

recall, he was the only person who had ever accused her of being cute. "I really have to go." Before she gave in to the urge to fuss with his tie or something equally mushy. "We'll be starting in a few minutes. Guests need to be seen to."

"Most everybody's already in the garden."

"The photographer."

"All set up."

"The champagne."

"On ice." He took the last step toward her and tilted up her chin with a fingertip. "Weddings make you nervous, Calhoun?"

"This one does."

"Going to save a dance for me?"

"Of course."

He toyed with the flowers in her hair. "And later?"

"I…"

"C.C.'s ready!" Alex bellowed from the top of the stairs. "Can we get this dumb thing over with?"

With a laugh, Sloan kissed her fingers. "Don't worry, I'll make sure the groom's in place."

"All right, and—damn!" She swore, then snatched up the ringing phone. "Hello? Oh, William, I really can't talk. We're about to start the wedding…. Tomorrow?" She lifted a distracted hand to her hair. "No, of course. Umm…yes, that's fine. Late afternoon would be best. Three o'clock? I'll see you then." Still off balance, she turned to find Sloan watching her with very cool, measuring green eyes.

"You take big chances, Calhoun."

"That wasn't what it sounded like." She caught herself trying to explain and frowned. "What do you mean, 'chances'?"

"That's something we'd better discuss later. We've got a wedding to get to."

"You're absolutely right." They strode off in opposite directions.

Moments later, the Calhoun women took their turns walking down the garden path. First Suzanna, then Lilah, then Amanda, followed by a beaming Jenny and a thoroughly embarrassed Alex. They took their places with Amanda doing her best not to glance in Sloan's direction. Then she forgot everything as she watched C.C. come forward, a wispy veil over her hair. Beside her, prepared to give her youngest niece away, Coco held her arm and wept.

She watched her sister marry under an arbor of delicately fragrant wisteria. Through a mist of tears she looked on as the man who was now her brother-in-law slipped the circle of emeralds onto C.C.'s finger. The look that passed between them spoke more eloquently of promises than any of the vows exchanged. With her hands clasped with her sisters', she saw C.C.'s face lift to Trent's as they shared their first kiss as husband and wife.

"Is it finally over?" Alex wanted to know.

"No," Amanda heard herself say as her gaze drifted to Sloan's. "It's just beginning."

"Beautiful wedding." After Amanda was thoroughly kissed by Trent's father, she managed to nod in agreement. "Trent tells me you put most of it together."

"I'm good with details," she said, and offered him a plate for the buffet.

"So I hear." Trim, tanned and expansive, St. James

smiled at her. "I've also heard that all of the Calhoun sisters are lovely. I can now corroborate that myself."

He was quite the elegant old flirt, Amanda mused but smiled back as he arranged food on his plate. "We're delighted to welcome you to the family."

"It's odd the way things have worked out," he said. "A year ago I looked up from my boat in the bay and saw this house. I simply had to have it. Now, not only is part of it a portion of my business, but it's a part of my family." He glanced over to see Trent and C.C. dancing on the terrace. "She's made him happy," he said quietly. "I never quite had the knack for that myself." With a vague movement of his shoulders, he brushed the thought aside. "Would you care to dance?"

"I'd love to."

They'd hardly taken three steps on the dance floor, when Sloan swung Coco around and smoothly switched partners.

"You might have asked," Amanda muttered as his arms slid around her.

"I did, before. Anyway, she'll flirt with him the way he wants instead of treating him like a distant relation."

"He is a distant relation." But she glanced over and saw that Coco already had St. James laughing. "Everything's going well, I think."

"Smooth as glass." Just as smoothly, he noted, as she fit into his arms. "You did a good job."

"Thanks, but I hope it's the last wedding I have to plan for quite a while."

"Don't you think about getting married yourself?"

She missed a step and nearly stumbled over his feet. "No—that is, yes, but not really."

"That's a definitive answer."

"What I mean is it's not in my short-range plans." No matter what longings had tugged at her when her gaze had locked with Sloan's under the arbor. "I'm going to be busy over the next few years with the retreat. I've always wanted to manage a first-class hotel, to make policy instead of just carrying it out. It's what I've been working for, and now that Trent's giving me the chance, I can't afford to divide my loyalties."

"An interesting way of seeing it. With me it's always been a matter of getting tied down with one person in one place, then finding out I made a mistake."

"There's that, too." Relieved that they weren't arguing, she smiled. "I never asked, but I guess you do a lot of traveling."

"Here and there. A drawing board's portable. You might like to do some traveling yourself, check out the hotel competition. Why don't we go somewhere quiet and talk about it?"

"Sorry, I'm on call. And if you want to be helpful, you'll play best man and go get a few more bottles of champagne from the kitchen." She tucked her arm through his. "I've got to run up and get the streamers anyway."

"Streamers?"

"To decorate the car. They're up in my room."

"Tell you what," Sloan began when they reached the kitchen. "Why don't I come up to your room and help you get the streamers?"

"Because I want to decorate the car before they get back from their honeymoon." With a laugh, she dashed away. Amanda was halfway down the hall on the second floor when the creak of a board overhead had her stopping. Tuned to the moans and groans of the old house, she frowned. Footsteps, she realized. Definitely footsteps. Wondering if one of the wedding guests had decided to take an impromptu tour, she started back toward the stairway. On the third-floor landing, she spotted Fred, curled up and sleeping.

"Fine watchdog," she muttered, bending down to shake him. He only rolled over with a groggy snore. "Fred?" Alarmed, she shook him again, but instead of bouncing up, ready to play, he lay still. When she picked him up, his head lolled onto her hand. Even as she gathered him up, someone shoved her from behind and sent her headfirst into the wall.

Stunned and sprawled on the dog, she struggled up to her knees. Someone was running down the stairs. With the wrath of the Calhouns filling her, she jumped up, Fred tucked under her arm like a furry football, and gave chase. She turned sharply on the second-floor landing, ears straining. On an oath she headed down to the main floor, heels clattering on wood. Sloan caught her as she stumbled on the last step.

"Whoa. What's the hurry?" Grinning, he scanned her tumbled hair and the spray of baby's breath now hanging to her shoulder. "What did you do, Calhoun, trip over the dog?"

"Did you see him?" she demanded, and broke out of Sloan's hold to rush to the door.

"See who?"

"There was somebody upstairs." Her heart was pumping fast and hard. She hadn't noticed it before. Or the fact that her legs were shaky. "Someone was sneaking around on the third floor. I don't know what they did to Fred."

"Hold on." Gently now, he guided her back to the stairs and eased her down. "Let's have a look." He took the dog, then pulling up an eyelid, swore. When he looked back at Amanda, there was a flat grimness in his eyes she'd never seen before. "Somebody drugged him."

"Drugged him?" Amanda gathered Fred back to her breast. "Who would drug a poor little dog?"

"Someone who didn't want him to bark, I imagine. Tell me what happened."

"I heard someone on the third floor and went up to see. I found Fred, just lying there." She nuzzled the puppy. "When I started to pick him up, someone pushed me into the wall."

"Are you hurt?" His hands were instantly on her face.

"No." She let out a disgusted breath. "If it hadn't stunned me for a minute, I would have caught him."

Eyes narrowed, Sloan sat back on his heels. "Didn't it occur to you to call for help?"

"No." The baby's breath was tickling her shoulder, so she pulled it away.

"Idiot."

"Look, O'Riley, nobody's going to poke around in my house, and hurt my dog and get away with it. If he hadn't had a start on me, I'd have caught him."

"And then what?" he demanded. "God Almighty, Amanda, don't you realize he would have given you more than a push."

Actually she hadn't thought of it. But that didn't change the bottom line. "I can take care of myself. It's bad enough when people come to the door, or sneak around the grounds, but when they start breaking into the house, they're going to answer for it." She gave a nod of satisfaction as she rose. "I scared him good, anyway. The way he was running, he's halfway to the village by now. I don't think he'll be coming back. What about Fred?"

"I'll take care of him." He took the sleeping puppy from her. "He just needs to sleep it off. And you need to call the police."

"After the wedding." She shook her head before he could object. "I'm not spoiling this for C.C. and Trent just because some jerk decided to do some treasure hunting. What I will do is check the third floor and see if anything's missing. Then I'm going to go back out and make sure everything runs smoothly until it's time to throw rice at the bride and groom. After that, I'll call the police."

"Got it all figured out, nice and tidy, as usual." The hot edge of his temper seeped into his voice. "Things don't always work that way."

"I'll make it work."

"Sure you will. Can't have something like attempted robbery and a little assault mess up all your short-term plans. Just like you can't have someone like me messing up your long-term ones."

"I don't see what you're so upset about."

"You wouldn't," he said tightly. "You hear somebody in the house where they shouldn't be, get hit in the head, but you don't even think about calling for me. You don't think about asking somebody for help, not even when that somebody's in love with you."

The tightness in her chest returned, making her voice clipped. "I was just doing what I had to do."

"Yeah," he agreed with a slow nod. "You go ahead and do what you have to do now. I'll get out of your way."

Chapter Eight

And he'd stay out of her way, Sloan promised himself. The woman had fuddled his brain long enough.

He stood out on the terrace off his bedroom, trying to enjoy the balmy May evening. He'd left The Towers as soon as it had been possible. Oh, he'd done his duty, he thought. Amanda wasn't the only one who could do what was expected of her. With the help of Suzanna and the children, he'd decorated the newlyweds' car. A smile plastered on his face, he'd tossed the rice. He'd even given Coco his handkerchief when her own proved inadequate for her happy tears. He'd waited with a worried Lilah until Fred had given his first groggy bark.

Then he'd gotten the hell out of there.

She didn't need him. The fact that he hadn't realized until now just how much he needed her to need him didn't make it any easier. Here he was, waiting to sweep her off her feet, and she was chasing after thieves or making dates with guys named William. Well, he was through making a fool of himself over her.

She had a job to do, and so did he. She had a life to live, and so did he. It was time he put things back in perspective. A man had to be crazy to think about saddling himself with an ornery, my-way-or-nothing female. A sane man wanted a nice, calm woman who'd give him some peace after a long day, not one who riled him up every time he took a breath.

So, he'd put Amanda Calhoun out of his mind and be a happier man for it.

"Sloan."

With one hand still braced on the railing, he turned. She was in the doorway, her fingers linked tight together. She'd changed the silk dress for a crisp cotton blouse and slacks. Very streamlined, very simple and certainly not sexy enough to make his heart start jumping as it was now.

"I knocked," she began, then with an uneasy movement of her shoulders, stepped onto the terrace. "I was afraid you wouldn't let me in, so I got a pass key."

"Isn't that against the rules?"

"Yes. I'm sorry, but I couldn't talk to you at home. I didn't even think I wanted to. Then after the police came and went, and everything was as close to normal as it gets, I couldn't settle down." She let out a long breath. Obviously he wasn't going to say anything to make it easier. He was just going to stand there, his white dress shirt unbuttoned and pulled out of the tuxedo pants, his feet bare and his eyes watchful. "I guess I'm not comfortable with unfinished business."

"All right." After lighting a cigar, he leaned back on the railing. "Finish it."

"It isn't as simple as that." A wayward breeze fluttered her hair. She shook it back impatiently. "I was upset and angry before—about there being someone in the house. My house. I know you were concerned and I was very abrupt with you. And after I'd calmed down some I realized you were hurt that I hadn't asked you to help."

He blew out smoke. "I'll get over it."

"It's just that—" She broke off to pace the narrow width of the balcony. No, he wasn't going to make it easier. "I'm used to handling things myself. I've always been the one who's been able to find the logical solution, or the straightest route. It's part of my makeup. When something needs to be done, I do it. I have to, I guess. It's not as though I don't ever want help. It's just…it's just that I'm more used to being asked for it, than asking for it myself."

"One of the things I admire about you, Amanda, is the way you get things done." His eyes stayed on hers as he took a long, contemplative drag. "Why don't you tell me what you're going to do about me?"

"I don't know what to do." When her voice rose, she struggled to calm it and started moving again. "I don't like that. I always know what to do if I reason it out long enough. But no matter how much I think it all through, I can't find an answer."

"Maybe that's because two and two don't always make four."

"But they should," she insisted. "They always have for me. All I know is that you make me feel…different than I've ever felt before. It scares me." When she whirled back, her eyes were wide and dark with anger. "I know it's easy for you, but not for me."

"Easy for me?" he repeated. "You think this is easy for me?" In two furious motions, he tossed the cigar onto the terrace and ground it out. "I've been on slow burn since the minute I laid eyes on you. That isn't easy on a man, Amanda, believe me."

Because she found it hard to breathe, her voice came out in a whisper. "No one's ever wanted me the way you do. That frightens me." She pressed her lips together. "I've never wanted anyone the way I want you. That terrifies me."

He reached out to snag her hand by the wrist. "Don't expect to say that to me, or look at me the way you look right now, then ask me to let you go."

While panic and excitement warred inside her, she shook her head. "That's not what I'm asking."

"Then spell it out."

"Damn it, Sloan, I don't want you to be reasonable. I don't want to think. I want you to make me stop thinking, right now." On a moan, she threw her arms around him, pressed her lips to his and took exactly what she wanted.

There was fear. She was afraid she was taking a giant step off the edge of a very steep cliff.

There was exhilaration. She was taking that step with her eyes wide open.

And he was with her, all the way. His body was free-falling with hers, caught in the crosswinds, soaring on the current.

"Sloan—"

"Don't say a word." His arms locked tight around her as he pressed his mouth to her throat. The pulse hammering there matched exactly the rhythm of his own. That was what he wanted. That unity. He realized he'd never found it with another woman. "Not a word. Just come inside."

He led her from the balcony to the bedroom, leaving the door open to let in the sunset and the scent of water and flowers. He touched her hair first, watching his own fingers tangle and stroke. Then softly, a whispering touch, his lips on hers. No, he didn't want words from her, because he wasn't certain he could ever find the right ones to tell her what was in his heart. But he could show her.

Unsteady, she braced her hands on his chest. She didn't want to be weak now, but strong. Yet as those lips roamed over her face, she trembled.

Very slowly, barely touching her, he unbuttoned her blouse and slid it from her shoulders. Beneath was a white cotton chemise that made him smile. He should have known that beneath her practical clothes his Amanda would have more practicality. Watching her, he unhooked her slacks so that they slipped to the floor. When she reached out, he took her hands.

"No, just let me touch you. Let me see what it does to you."

Helpless, she closed her eyes as his fingers skimmed, lightly tracing the curve of her breasts. As if she were fashioned of the most delicate glass, he swept those fingertips over her. Elegantly erotic, the fragile caress had the blood rushing under skin, heating it, sensitizing it until she thought she might die from sheer pleasure.

Her head fell back, a shuddering moan escaped as he continued those lazy explorations with patient, gentle hands. He saw the dark delight flicker over her face, felt it shivering through her body. As excitement rioted through him, he circled his thumbs in a whispering touch over the nipples that strained against the cotton. Then his tongue replaced his hands and she gripped frantically at his shoulders for balance.

"Please…I can't…"

Now she was falling fast and hard, but he was there to catch her. When her knees gave way, he lifted her, cradling her in his arms, covering her mouth with his before laying her on the bed.

"Nobody," she murmured against his lips. "Nobody's ever made love to me like this."

"I'm just getting started."

He was true to his word. With a leisurely pace he took her places she had never been, had her lingering there before gently urging her on. With each touch he opened doors always firmly locked, then left them wide so that light and wind tunneled through. Each time she arched against him, shuddering, he soothed her until she floated down again.

Her taste was enough. Honey here, whiskey there, then as delicate as spun sugar. He filled himself with it, nibbling her skin. Down her arms, her throat, those long, lovely legs. Whenever he was tempted to hurry, to take his own release, he found himself greedy for one more taste.

He skimmed his hands up her ribs, pushing her shirt up, then over her head. At last, at long last, he sampled the smooth skin of her breast. Her hands were in his hair, pressing him closer as colors seemed to shatter behind her eyes.

Slow burn. Is that what he'd said? she wondered frantically as his clever mouth inched lower, still lower. She

understood now, now when her body was on fire from
the inside, heating degree by degree. The sparks were
shooting through her, little pinpoints of unspeakable
pleasure as ancient as the first stars that winked to life
in the sky beyond the window.

He was tugging the last barrier aside, and she could
do nothing but writhe under his hands, the breath sobbing in her lungs.

When he flicked his tongue over her, she arched
against him, her hands grabbing at the bedspread in
taut fists. Sensations hammered her, too fast, too sharp.
She struggled to separate them, but they were one wild
maze without beginning or end.

Did she know she was calling out his name over and
over? he wondered. Did she know that her body was
moving in that slow, sinuous rhythm, as if he were already inside her? He slid up her gradually, savoring each
instant, absorbing each ache, each need, each longing.
Her eyes fluttered open, dark and dazed.

She could only see his face, so close to hers—his eyes
so intense. Gracefully her arms lifted to brush his shirt
aside, to touch as thoroughly as she had been touched.
She rose to him, to press her lips to his chest, to glide
them up to his throat.

The light grew dimmer, softer. The breeze quieted.
In an easy dance she moved over him, undressing him,
needing to show him what he had done to her heart as
well as her body. Her lips curved against his flesh as she
felt him tremble as she had trembled. The glory flowed
through her like water, clear and bright, so that when her
arms came around him, when her mouth opened will-
ingly beneath his, she let it pour into the kiss.

With a murmuring sigh, he slid into her. Her breath

caught, then released gently. They moved together, the pace deliberately slow, deliciously easy. The sweetness brought tears to her eyes that he kissed away.

Gradually sweetness became heat, and heat a fresh burning. As passion misted her vision, she felt his fingers link with hers, holding tight as she rode to the top of the crest. His name tumbled from her lips as he swept to the peak with her.

He lay with his lips pressed against her throat, still haunted by the taste of her. Beneath him she was quiet, her breathing deep and steady. He wondered if she slept, and started to ease his weight aside. But her arms slid up and around him again.

"Don't." Her voice was a husky whisper that sent his blood singing again. "I don't want it to end yet."

To satisfy them both, he rolled, reversing positions. Her hair brushed his cheek, a small thing that gave him tremendous happiness. "How's that?"

"Nice." She nuzzled her cheek against his. "It was all really, really nice."

"Is that the best you can do?"

"Umm. For right now. I don't think I've ever been this relaxed in my life."

"Good." Taking her hair in his hand, he pulled her head back to study her face. "It's getting too dark to see." Reaching over, he switched on the light.

Amanda brought up a hand to shield her eyes. "Why'd you do that?"

"Because I want to see you when we make love again."

"Again?" Chuckling, she dropped her head onto his shoulder. "You've got to be kidding."

"No, ma'am. I figure I might just get my fill of you by sunup."

Feeling deliciously lazy, she snuggled against him. "I can't stay the night."

"Wanna bet?"

"No, really." She arched like a cat when he stroked her back. "I wish I could, but I've got a whole list of things to do in the morning. Oh…" She shivered under his touch. "You've got such wonderful hands. Wonderful," she murmured as she lost herself in a long, dreamy kiss.

"Stay."

Her body shuddered as she felt him harden inside her. "Maybe for just a little while longer."

Drifting awake, she shifted. On a contented sigh, she reached out. Reluctantly she opened her eyes. Bright sunlight flooded the room, and she was alone in bed. Pushing her tumbled hair back, she sat up.

He'd gotten his way, she thought with a half smile. She had stayed the night, and he hadn't gotten enough of her—or she of him—until sunup.

It had been, she admitted freely, the most magnificent night of her life.

And where the hell was Sloan?

On cue, he walked in, pushing a room-service cart. "Morning."

"Good morning." She smiled, though she felt awkward with him dressed and her still naked and in bed.

"I ordered us some breakfast." Sensing her dilemma, he plucked up a white terry-cloth robe from a chair. "Compliments of the BayWatch," he said as he handed it to her, then leaned over a bit farther to give her a leisurely kiss. "Why don't we eat on the terrace?"

"That'd be nice. Give me a minute."

When she joined him outside, there were plates set on the pale azure cloth, and a single rose in a clear vase. It touched her deeply that he would take as much care with the morning as he had with the night.

"You think of everything."

"Just of you." He grinned as he sat across from her. "We can look at this like a first date, since I never could convince you to have a meal with me before."

"No." Her gaze lowered as she poured coffee for both of them. "I guess you couldn't." Picking up her napkin, she began to pleat it with her fingers. They were having breakfast, she thought, after a long night of feasting. And they'd never even ridden in the same car, shared a pizza, talked on the phone.

It was idiotic, she told herself. It was scary.

"Sloan, I realize this might sound stupid at this stage, but I…I don't make a habit of spending the night with men in hotel rooms. I'm not usually intimate with someone I've known such a short time."

"You don't have to tell me that." He closed a hand over hers until she looked at him. "It's been a fast trip for both of us. Maybe it's because what happened between us is special. I'm in love with you, Amanda. No, don't pull away." He tightened his grip. "Normally I'm a patient man, but I have to work hard on it with you. I'm going to do my best to give you time."

"If I said I was in love with you—" she let out a cleansing breath "—what would happen next?"

In his eyes, something flickered and sent her already unsteady pulse jumping. "Sometimes you can't work out the answers first. You've got to be willing to gamble."

"I've never been much of a gambler." She bit her lip,

determined to get over that last skip of fear. "I wouldn't have come here last night if I hadn't been in love with you."

He lifted her hand to press his lips to the palm. Over it, he smiled at her. "I know."

The laugh was as much from relief as amusement. "You knew, but you just had to hear me say it."

"That's right." His eyes were suddenly very sober. "I had to hear you say it. Women aren't the only ones who need words, Amanda."

No, she thought, they weren't. "I love you, but I'm still a little scared of it. I'd like to take it slow, one step at a time."

"Fair enough. We can start by having our first date before the eggs get cold."

At ease, she buttered a piece of toast and split it with him. "You know, as long as I've worked here, I've never sat on one of these terraces and looked out at the bay."

"Never snuck into an empty room and played guest?" He laughed. "No, you wouldn't. You wouldn't even think about it. So, how does it feel, seeing it from the other side of the desk?"

"Well, the bed's comfortable, the hotel robes are roomy and the view's wonderful." There was laughter in her eyes, contented, easy laughter. "However, at The Towers Retreat, we'll offer all that and more. Private spas, romantic fireplaces, complimentary champagne with each reservation—I have to run that by Trent— *cordon bleu* meals prepared by Coco, world-renowned chef, all in a turn-of-the-century setting, complete with ghosts and a legendary hidden treasure." She rested her chin on her hand. "Unless we manage to get our hands on the emeralds before we open."

"Do you really believe they still exist?"

"Yes. Oh, not with any of the mystic business Aunt Coco or Lilah subscribe to. It's simple logic. They did exist. If anyone in the family had sold them, it would have come out. Therefore, they still exist. A quarter of a million in jewels doesn't just disappear."

His brow lifted. "They're that valuable?"

"Oh, probably more so by now—that's not even counting the aesthetic or intrigue value."

It changed the complexion of things for him entirely. "So what we've got is five women and two kids, who've been living alone in a house loaded with antiques, plus a fortune in jewels. And no security system."

She frowned a little. "It's not exactly loaded with antiques since we've had to sell off a lot over the years. And there's never been a problem. It's not as though any of us are helpless."

"I know. Calhoun women can take care of themselves. I'm beginning to think that besides being tough, they're stupid."

"Now, wait a minute—"

"No, you wait." To emphasize the point, he poked his fork at her. "First thing in the morning, we're going to see about an alarm system."

She'd already decided the same thing herself after yesterday's incident. But that didn't mean he could tell her to. "You're not going to start taking over my life."

"So, to be stubborn, you'll ignore the obvious, because I brought it up, and take a chance that someone might break in and hurt one of the kids."

"Don't put words in my mouth," she tossed back. "I've been checking into alarms for the past two weeks."

"Why didn't you just say so?"

"Because you were too busy handing out orders." She might have said more, but the horn on one of the tourist boats distracted her. "What time is it?"

"About one."

"One?" Her eyes went huge. "In the afternoon? That's not possible, we just got up."

"It's real possible when you don't get to sleep until morning."

"I've got a million things to do." She was already pushing back from the table. "All that mess from the wedding has to be cleaned up. Trent's father was coming for brunch two hours ago, and William's coming by at three."

"Hold it." That brought him out of his chair. "You're not still going to see him?"

"Mr. St. James? He'll be gone by now. I can't believe I was so rude."

"William," he corrected, snagging her arm. "The attractive, intelligent man you had dinner with the other night."

"William? Well, of course I'm going to see him."

"No." He tugged her closer. "You're not."

The dangerous light in his eyes set off one in her own. "I just told you you weren't going to take over my life."

"I don't give a damn what you told me. There's no way in hell I'm going to let you waltz out of my bed and on to a date with another man."

With a little huff, she pulled her arm free. "You don't *let* me do anything. Get that straight. Next, it isn't a date. William Livingston is an antique dealer and I promised him I would show him through The Towers. He gets a busman's holiday, and I get a free assessment. Now move." She shoved past and headed for the shower. Muttering all the way, she slipped off the robe. She'd just finished adjusting the water temperature, stepping in and shutting the curtain when it was yanked open again.

"Damn it, Sloan!" She slicked the wet hair out of her eyes and glared.

"He's an antique dealer?"

"That's what I said."

"And he wants to look at furniture?"

"Exactly."

He hooked his thumbs in his belt loops. "I'm going with you."

"Fine." With a careless shrug, she picked up the soap and began to lather her shoulders. "Be a possessive bubblehead."

"Okay."

Telling herself she wasn't amused, she glanced over to see him pulling off his shirt. "What are you doing?"

Grinning, he tossed it aside. "I'll give you three guesses. A sharp lady like you should get it in one."

She bit back a chuckle as he unsnapped his jeans. "I don't have time for water games right now."

"Oh, I think we can sneak it in just under the wire."

"Maybe." She squeezed the wet soap between her hands and shot it at him, nodding approval when he caught it, chest high. "If you wash my back first."

Before stepping from his car, Livingston checked his microrecorder and the tiny camera in his pocket. He was very fond of technology and felt that the sophisticated equipment lent an air of elegance to the job. Since the moment he'd read about the Calhoun emeralds, he'd been obsessed by them, more than any other jewels he'd stolen in his long career. He was considered by Interpol, and indeed by himself, to be one of the most clever and elusive thieves on two continents.

The emeralds presented a challenge he couldn't resist. They weren't tucked in a vault or displayed in a museum. They weren't adorning some rich matron's neck. They were lying in wait somewhere in the odd old house, daring someone to find them. He intended to be that someone.

Though he wasn't opposed to employing violence in his work, he used it sparingly. He was sorry he'd had to use it on Amanda the day before, but he was much sorrier that she'd interrupted his search.

His own fault, he chided himself as he walked to the front door of The Towers. He'd been impatient and had decided that the wedding would be the perfect diversion, giving him the time and the privacy he required to case the interior of the house. Today, however, he would wander those rooms as a guest.

He might have been a thief from the South Side of Chicago, but when he put on a two-thousand-dollar suit, a trace of a British accent and polished manners, even the most discriminating invited him into their parlors.

He knocked and waited. The barking of the dog answered first, and Livingston's eyes hardened. He detested dogs, and the little bugger inside had nearly nipped before he'd managed to give it a dose of phenobarbital.

When Coco answered the door, Livingston's eyes were clear and his charming smile already in place.

"Mr. Livingston, how nice to see you again." Coco started to offer a hand, then found it more judicious to grasp Fred's collar before the dog could leap at the man's calf. "Fred, stop that now. Mind your manners."

Holding the snarling dog at bay, Coco offered a weak smile. "He really is a very gentle animal. He never acts like this, but he had an incident yesterday and isn't himself." After gathering Fred into her arms, she called for Lilah. "Let's go into the parlor, shall we?"

"I hope I'm not intruding on your Sunday, Mrs. McPike. I couldn't resist persuading Amanda to show me through your fascinating house."

"We're delighted to have you." Though she was becoming more disconcerted by the moment as Fred continued to snarl and snap. "Amanda's not here yet, though I can't think what's keeping her. She's always so prompt."

Lilah gave a half laugh as she came down the steps. "I can think exactly what's keeping her." There was no humor in her eyes as she studied their guest. "Hello again, Mr. Livingston."

"Miss Calhoun." He didn't care for the way she looked at him, as though she could see straight through the slick outer trappings to the ruthlessness inside.

"Fred's a bit high-strung today." With a quick pleading look, Coco passed the growling pup to Lilah. "Why don't you take him in the kitchen?" Her hands fluttered before she patted her hair. "Perhaps some herbal tea would soothe him."

"I'll take care of him." Lilah started down the hall, murmuring to the puppy, "I don't like him, either, Fred. Why do you suppose that is?"

"Well then." Relieved, Coco smiled again. "How about some sherry? You can enjoy it while I show you a particularly nice japanned cabinet. It's Charles II, I believe."

"I'd be delighted." He was also delighted to note that

she was wearing an excellent set of pearls with matching earrings.

When Amanda arrived twenty minutes later, with Sloan stubbornly at her side, she found her aunt telling Livingston the family history while they admired an eighteenth-century credenza.

"William, I'm so sorry I'm late."

"Don't be." Livingston took one look at Sloan and concluded his entryway to The Towers wouldn't be Amanda after all. "Your aunt has been the most charming and informative of hostesses."

"Aunt Coco knows more about the furnishings than any of us," she told him. "This is Sloan O'Riley. Sloan is the architect who's designing the renovations."

"Mr. O'Riley." The handshake was brief. Sloan had already taken a dislike to the three-piece-suited, sherry-sipping antique dealer. "The work here must present quite a challenge."

"Oh, I'm getting by."

"I was just telling William how slow and tedious the job of sifting through all those old papers is. Not at all the exciting treasure the press makes it out to be." Coco beamed. "But I've decided to hold another séance. Tomorrow night, the first night of the new moon."

Amanda struggled not to groan. "Aunt Coco, I'm sure William isn't interested."

"On the contrary." He turned all his charm on Coco while a plan formed in his mind. "I'd love to attend myself, if I didn't have pressing business."

"The next time then. Perhaps you'd like to go upstairs—"

Before she could finish, Alex burst through the terrace doors, followed by a speeding Jenny and a laughing Suzanna. All three had dirt streaked on their hands and jeans. Eyes narrowed, Alex skidded to a halt in front of Livingston.

"Who's that?" he demanded.

"Alex, don't be a brat." Suzanna snagged his hand before he could spread any of his dirt over the buff-colored tailored pants. "I'm sorry," she began. "We've been in the garden. I made the mistake of mentioning ice cream."

"Don't apologize." Livingston forced his lips to curve. If he disliked anything more than dogs, it was small, grubby children. "They're…lovely."

Suzanna squeezed her son's hand before he could resort to violence at the term. "No, they're not," she said cheerfully. "But we're stuck with them. We'll just get out of your way." As she dragged them off to the kitchen, Alex shot a last look over his shoulder.

"He has mean eyes," he told his mother.

"Don't be silly." She tousled his hair. "He was just annoyed because you almost ran into him."

But Alex looked solemnly at Jenny, who nodded. "Like the snake on Rikki-Tikki-Tavi."

"You move, I strike," Alex said in a fair imitation of the evil cartoon voice.

"Okay, guys, you're giving me the creeps." She laughed off the quick shiver. "The last one in the kitchen has to wash the bowls." She gave them a head start while she rubbed the chill from her arms.

Chapter Nine

"There, you see." Amanda gave Sloan a quick kiss on the cheek. "That wasn't so bad."

He wasn't quite ready to be placated. "He hung around for five hours. I don't see why Coco had to invite him for dinner."

"Because he's a charming, and single man." She laughed and slipped her arms around his neck. "Remember the tea leaves."

They stood at the seawall, inside an ornate pergola. Sloan decided it was as good a time as any to nibble on her neck. "What tea leaves?"

"The ones that...mmm. The ones that told Aunt Coco that there would be a man coming along who'd be important to us."

He switched to her ear. "I thought that was me."

"Maybe." She gave a surprised yip when he bit her. "Savage."

"Sometimes the Cherokee in me takes over."

She leaned back to study his face. In the bleeding lights of sunset, his skin was almost copper, his eyes so dark a green they were nearly black. Yes, she could see both sides of his heritage, the Celtic and the Cherokee, both warriors, in those knife-edged cheekbones, the sculpted mouth, the wild reddish hair.

"I really don't know anything about you." Yet it hadn't been like making love to a stranger. When he had touched her, she'd known everything. "Just that you're an architect from Oklahoma who went to Harvard."

"You know I like beer and long-legged women."

"There's that."

Because he could see it was important to her, he sat on the wall, his back to the sea. "Okay, Calhoun, what do you want to know?"

"I don't want to interrogate you." The old nerves resurfaced, making it impossible for her to settle. "It's just that you know everything about me, really. My family, my background, my ambitions."

Because he enjoyed watching her move, he took out a cigar, lighted it, then began to speak. "My great-great-grandfather left Ireland for the New World, and headed west to trap beaver. A genuine mountain man. He married a Cherokee woman, and hung around long enough to get three sons. One day he went off trapping and never came back. The sons started a trading post, did pretty well. One of them sent for a mail-order bride, a nice Irish girl. They had a passel of kids, including my grandfather. He was, and is, a wily old devil who bought up land while it was cheap enough, then hung on until he could sell it at a profit. Keeping up family tradition, he married Irish, a redheaded spitfire who supposedly drove him crazy. He must have loved her a lot, because he named the first oil well after her."

Amanda, who had been charmed thus far, blinked. "Oil well?"

"He called it Maggie," Sloan said with a grin as he blew out smoke. "She got such a kick out of it, he gave names to the rest of them, too."

"The rest of them," Amanda said faintly.

"My father took over the company in the sixties, but the old man hasn't stopped putting his two cents in. He's still ticked that I didn't go into the company, but I wanted to build, and I figured Sun Industries didn't need me."

"Sun Industries?" She nearly choked. It was one of the biggest conglomerates in the country. "You—I had no idea that you had money."

"My family does, anyway. Problem?"

"No. I just wouldn't want you to think that I…" She trailed off helplessly.

"That you were after the family fortune?" He let out a hoot of laughter. "Honey, I know you were after my body."

He had the uncanny ability to make her want to swear and laugh at the same time. "You really are a conceited jerk."

He tossed the cigar aside before making a grab for her. "But you love me."

"Maybe I do." With pretended reluctance, she slipped her arms around him. "A little." On a laugh, she lifted her lips to his. His mouth started off teasing, then heated with demands. His hands were light, then impatient, until she was wrapped tight around him, pouring herself mindlessly into the kiss.

"How do you do that to me?" she murmured as he nipped at her moist, parted lips.

"Do what?"

"Make me want you until it hurts."

On an unsteady moan, he pressed his lips to her throat. "Let's go inside. You can show me my room."

She tilted her head to give his busy mouth more freedom. "What room?"

"The room where we'll pretend I'm going to sleep when I'm sleeping with you."

"What are you talking about?"

"I'm talking about making love with you until we both need oxygen." Because he knew he was on the point of dragging her down on the hard, cold tiles, he set her away from him. "And I'm talking about the fact that I'm staying here until the alarm system's operational."

"But you don't need—"

"Oh, I need." He crushed his mouth to hers again to show her how much.

She waited for him, chiding herself for being as nervous as a new bride on her wedding night. Perhaps the waiting was more intense because she knew what they would bring to each other.

She slipped on a thin blue chemise, an impulsive extravagance that had been folded away for months. Unable to settle, she turned down the bed. There were candles she'd kept at the bedside and on the bureau for emergencies. But when she lighted them now, their glow was soft, romantic, and anything but practical. Suzanna had placed flowers in the room, as she always did. This time they were fragile lilies of the valley that added a haunting fragrance. Though there was no moonlight, she opened the terrace doors to let in the steady roar of the water on rocks.

Then he came to her, as she stood in the open doorway with the black night at her back.

The quick joke he'd meant to make melted from his mind. He could only stare, his hand growing damp on the knob, his heart bounding up to block his throat. To have her waiting for him, looking so desirable in the flicker of candlelight, to see that smile of welcome, was everything he'd ever wanted.

He wanted to be gentle with her, as he'd been so carefully gentle the night before. But when he crossed to her, the slow burn had already turned to fire. There was challenge instead of nerves in her eyes as she lifted her arms to take him in.

"I thought you'd never get here," she said, and, led by her own needs, crushed her mouth to his.

How could there be gentleness when there was such heat? How could there be patience when there was such urgency? Her body was already vibrating—Lord, he could feel each wild beat—as it fit itself to his. The flimsy material of her chemise teased the bare flesh of his chest, daring him to rip it aside and plunder. Her scent had wrapped itself around his system, taunting with dark secrets, seducing with fevered promises.

In that moment he was so full of her, he couldn't find himself.

Breathless, disoriented, he lifted his head. He knew his hands were big and could be rough if his heart didn't guide them. He knew his needs were huge and could be ruthless if he didn't retain control.

"Wait." He needed a moment to get back his breath and his sanity, but she was shaking her head.

"No." Her hands clutched in his hair, and she pulled him back to her.

She didn't know when the recklessness had burst through her, but it held sway now, as she fell with him onto the bed. Aggressive and desperate, her hands streaked over him. No weakness this time. No submission. She wanted the power, the power of knowing she could make him careless, make him as mindless and vulnerable as he made her.

In a tangle of arms and legs they rolled over the bed. Each time he tried to pull back, she was there, her mouth greedy, her low, sultry laughter pounding in his blood.

Her busy fingers rushed to unsnap his jeans, then tugged the denim over his hips. His muscles jumped and quivered when she danced those fingertips across his stomach. He swore, snatching her hands before she could drag him over that last jagged edge.

Breath heaving, he stared down at her, her wrists trapped in his hand. Her eyes were like cobalt, glistening dark in the shifting light. He could hear, over his own ragged breaths, the steady ticking of the bedside clock.

Then she smiled, a slow, lazy smile full of knowledge. And he heard nothing but the roar of his own needs.

Hot with hunger, his mouth fused with hers. Reckless with passion, his hands sought and took. She answered, demand for demand, pleasure for pleasure. Control snapped—he could almost hear the chain break as he sated himself with her. This was liberation, a world without reason. Desperate to feel her, he tore the chemise aside. Her quick gasp of surprise only fueled the fires.

Tossed in the whirlwind, she gave herself over to the speed, surrendered herself to the fury. No thought. No question. Only hot, damp flesh, ravenous, searching lips, quick, greedy hands.

His eyes open, fixed on hers, he drove himself into her, letting the shock of pleasure fill them both. Then she was rising up to meet him so that they drove each other into the dark.

"Yes, Mr. Stenerson." Amanda hummed a tune in her head as her supervisor droned on. And on. Ten more minutes, and she was off duty. Even the upcoming séance didn't dim her pleasure.

She would be with Sloan soon. Maybe there would be time for a walk before dinner.

"You don't seem to have your mind on your work, Miss Calhoun."

That brought her back with a jolt of guilt. "You were concerned about Mr. and Mrs. Wicken's complaint."

Glaring, he tapped his pencil on the desk. "I'm very concerned that one of our waiters spilled an entire tray of drinks in Mrs. Wicken's lap."

"Yes, sir. I arranged to have her slacks cleaned, and for a complimentary dinner for them any evening during their stay. They were satisfied."

"And you've fired the waiter?"

"No, sir."

His eyebrows rose up, wiggling like worms. "May I ask why not, when I specifically requested you do so?"

"Because Tim has been with us for three years, and could hardly be blamed for spilling the tray when the little Wicken boy stuck out his foot and tripped him. Several other waiters, and several of the guests saw it happen."

"Be that as it may, I gave you a specific order."

"Yes, sir." The cheerful little tune in her head became a throbbing headache. She'd meant to go over all of this with Stenerson before. "And after a closer review of the circumstances, I chose to handle it differently."

"Need I remind you who is in charge of this hotel, Miss Calhoun?"

"No, sir, but I would think after all the years I've worked at the BayWatch, you would trust my judgment." She took a deep breath, and a big risk. "If you don't, it might be best if I turned in my resignation."

He blinked three times, then cleared his throat. "Don't you feel that's a bit rash?"

"No, sir. If you don't feel I'm competent to make certain decisions, it undermines the system."

"It isn't your competence, but your lack of experience. However," he added, holding up a hand, "I'm sure you did what you felt was best in this case."

"Yes, sir."

By the time she left his office, her jaw was clenched. Amanda forced it to relax when William stopped her in the lobby.

"I just wanted to tell you again how much I enjoyed the tour of your home, and the wonderful meal."

"It was our pleasure."

"I have the feeling if I asked you to dinner again, you would have a different reason than hotel policy for saying no."

"William, I—"

"No, no." He patted her hand. "I understand. I'm disappointed, but I understand. I suppose Mr. O'Riley will attend the séance tonight?"

She laughed. "Whether he wants to or not."

"I really am sorry I'll miss it." He gave her hand a final squeeze. "It's at eight, did you say?"

"No, nine, sharp. Aunt Coco will have us all gathered around the dining table holding hands and sending out alpha waves or whatever."

"I hope you'll let me know if you receive any messages from…the other side."

"It's a deal. Good night."

"Good night." He glanced at his watch as she left. He had more than enough time to get ready.

"I thought I'd find you here." Amanda stepped into the large circular room the family called Bianca's tower. Lilah was curled on the window seat, as she often was, looking out to the cliffs.

"Yeah, just me and fierce Fred." Coming out of a private dream, she ruffled the dozing dog's fur. "We're getting in tune for tonight's séance."

"Spare me." Amanda plopped onto the seat beside her.

"Well, what's wiped off that satisfied smile you had on your face this morning? Did you fight with Sloan?"

"No."

"Then it must be the dastardly Stenerson." At Amanda's brief oath, Lilah grinned. "Right the second time. Why do you put up with him, Mandy? The man's a weasel."

"Because I work for him."

"So quit."

"Easy for you to say." She shot Lilah an impatient look. "We can't all drift around from day to day like dreamy forest sprites." She cut herself off, letting out a disgusted breath. "Sorry."

Lilah only shrugged. "It sounds like you've got more needling you than Stenerson."

"He started it. He said I didn't have my mind on my work, and he was right."

"So your mind was wandering. Big deal."

"It is a big deal. Damn it, I like my job, and I'm good at it. But I haven't been concentrating, not on that or the necklace, or anything, since…"

"Since the big gun swaggered in from the West."

"It's not funny."

"Sure it is." Lilah wrapped her arms around her knees and rested her chin on them. "So you lose a little concentration, misplace one of your lists or miss an appointment by five minutes. So what?"

"I'll tell you so what. He's changing me and I don't know what to do about it. I have responsibilities, obligations. Damn it, I have goals. I have to think about tomorrow, and five years from tomorrow." The trouble was, when she did, she thought of Sloan. "What if he's just a glitch? A wonderful, exciting glitch that throws off everything I've planned out? A few weeks from now, he finishes up here and heads back to Oklahoma, and my life's a mess."

"What if he asks you to go with him?"

"That's worse." Flustered, Amanda rose to wander in distracted circles. "What am I supposed to do? Throw away everything I've worked for, everything I've hoped for just because he says saddle up?"

"Would you?"

Amanda shut her eyes. "I'm afraid I would."

"Then why don't you talk to him?"

"I can't." She sat again. "We haven't talked about the

future. I guess neither of us wants to think about it. It was just that today, I started thinking—"

"You would get back to it."

"I started thinking," Amanda repeated, "that a month ago I didn't even know him. It's crazy to start planning my life around someone I've only known such a short time."

"And you've always been the sensible one," Lilah put in.

"Well, yes."

"Then relax." For encouragement she patted Amanda's shoulder. "When the time comes, you're bound to do the sensible thing."

"I hope you're right," Amanda murmured, then forced herself to add a decisive nod. "Of course you're right. I'm going to work in the storeroom until dinner."

"See you're back on track already." Lilah chuckled to herself when Amanda strode out. "Come on, Fred." She nuzzled his nose. "Let's go see if we can derail her."

Sloan walked into the storeroom, armed with a bottle of champagne, a wicker basket and some of Lilah's sisterly advice. *Keep her off balance, big guy. The one thing you can't let her do is get logical on you.*

Though he wasn't exactly sure what had prompted Lilah's visit, he approved the spirit of it. Just as he approved the way Amanda looked, hunched over a desk in the storeroom, glasses on her nose, hair clipped back. There were neatly labeled file boxes stacked behind her, dozens of dusty cardboard boxes scattered alongside her and several fat piles of paper in front of her.

"Hey, Calhoun, ready for a break?"

"What?" Her head came up quickly, but it took a

moment for her eyes to focus. "Oh, hi. I didn't hear you come in."

"Where were you?"

She lifted a ledger. "Back in 1929. It seems my illustrious great-grandpapa made a little pin money running liquor in from Canada during Prohibition."

"Good old Fergus."

"Greedy old Fergus," she corrected. "But a businessman through and through. If he kept such meticulous books of his illegal activities, he certainly would have a record of sale if he sold the emeralds."

"I thought Bianca hid them."

"That's the legend." She leaned back to rub her tired eyes. "I'd rather have the facts. I had this thought that maybe he put them in a safe-deposit box he didn't tell anyone about. But I can't find any record of that, either."

"Maybe you're looking in the wrong place." He set the bottle and basket down as he stood behind her. Gently he began to massage her neck muscles. "Maybe you should concentrate on Bianca. It was her necklace after all."

"We don't have a lot of information about Bianca." When her eyes started to drift closed, she popped them open again. "Great-Grandpapa destroyed all of her pictures, her letters, just about everything concerning her. We've only come across one of her date books so far."

"He must have been crazy mad."

"Crazy, anyway. Grieving, I'd think."

"No." Bending, he kissed the top of her head. "If he'd been grieving, he would have kept everything."

"Maybe it hurt to remember."

"If he'd loved her, he would have wanted to remember. He would have needed to. When you love someone, everything about them's precious." He felt her muscles knot under his fingers. "What's the problem, Amanda? You're all tied up."

"I've been sitting too long, that's all."

"Then my timing's perfect." He stepped back to pick up the champagne.

"What's that for?"

"Most people drink it." Sloan released the cork. After the pop came the seductive hiss. "I don't know about you, but I worked my butt off today. I thought we'd take a first-class coffee break."

She didn't need champagne to cloud her brain. He did that all by himself. And that, she reminded herself as she rose, was exactly what she needed to avoid. "It's a nice thought, but I should go help Aunt Coco with dinner."

"Lilah's helping her."

"Lilah?" Amanda's brows shot up. "You've got to be kidding."

"Nope." He opened the basket to take out two fluted glasses. "Suzanna's doing homework with the kids, and you and I are having dinner alone."

"Sloan, I'm really not dressed to go out."

"I like you in sweats." He poured the wine and, setting the bottle aside, lifted both glasses. "And we're not going anywhere."

"You just said—"

"I said we were having dinner alone, and we are. Right here."

"Here?" She gestured. "In the storeroom?"

"Yep. I got some of your aunt's pâté, some cold chicken and asparagus, and fresh strawberries." He tapped his glass against hers before drinking. "I've been thinking about you all day."

He didn't even have to try to make her knees weak. When he did sweet things, said sweet things, she dissolved into a puddle of love. "Sloan, we have to talk."

"Sure." But he bent down to rub his lips lazily over hers. "Why don't we get comfortable first?"

"What?" Already dizzy, she stared at him as he took out a blanket and spread it over the floor.

"Come on."

"I really think it would be better if we…" But he was already pulling her down to the blanket.

He took the glass from her hand, setting it on the floor before nuzzling her mouth. "This is better," he murmured. "Much better."

"The children are home," she managed as his hands slid under her shirt. "If someone came in—"

"I locked the door." Gently he skimmed the rough pad of his thumb over her nipples. "Pay attention, Calhoun, I'm going to show you how to relax."

She was so relaxed, she didn't think she could move. Heavy, her eyes fluttered partway open when Sloan laid a smidgen of pâté on her tongue.

"It's good," he told her, then spread a dab on her bare shoulder so he could lick it off. "Here." He lifted her, cradling her against his chest before he handed her the glass of champagne. "We were supposed to drink this first, but I got distracted."

It tasted like sin on her tongue. She sipped again, then opened her mouth obediently when he fed her more pâté, this time on a conventional cracker.

"More?"

She sighed her assent. They began to feed each other tidbits from the basket between kisses. Replete, she watched him pour the last of the champagne. "We're going to be late for the séance."

"Nope." He drew her back more comfortably against his chest. "Coco decided that the vibes weren't right. Something about interference from a dark presence."

"Sounds just like my levelheaded aunt."

"Now she wants to wait until the last night of the new moon." He nuzzled her neck. "We can stay in here all night."

She was beginning to believe that with him, anything was possible. "That would make it my first all-night picnic."

"After we're married, we'll make it a regular event."

Champagne slopped over her hand and onto his leg as she jolted straight.

"Easy, Calhoun, don't waste it."

She struggled around to face him. "What do you mean, married?"

"You know, like man and wife, that kind of thing."

With deliberate care, she set the glass down. Just like that, she thought, both panicked and angry. Just as she'd expected. With him it was *saddle up, Calhoun. We're getting hitched.* "What gave you the idea that we were getting married?"

He didn't like the fact that the line was back between her brows. "I love you, you love me. You're the logical one, Amanda. The next step's marriage from my point of view."

"It may be a step from your point of view, but it's a big leap from mine. You can't just assume I'm going to take it."

"Why not?"

"Because you can't. In the first place, I'm not planning on marriage for years yet. I've got my career to think about."

"What's one got to do with the other?"

"Everything. You've already messed up my concentration, had me shuffling around my priorities." Knowing it sounded foolish, she stopped to drag a hand through her hair. "Look at me," she demanded. "Just look at me. I'm sitting on the storeroom floor, naked, and arguing with a man I've only known for two weeks. This isn't me."

With deceptive laziness, he skimmed his gaze down, then up again. "Then who the hell is it?"

"I don't know." Frantic, she snatched up her sweats and began to pull them on. "I don't know who I am anymore, and it's your fault. Nothing's made sense since you ran into me on the sidewalk."

"You ran into me."

"That's beside the point." Shaken to the core, she yanked the sweatshirt over her head. "I'm daydreaming when I'm supposed to be working. I'm making love with you when I should be keeping appointments. I'm having naked picnics when I should be filing papers. It's got to stop."

"Maybe I should've just hit you over the head with the bottle of champagne instead of letting you drink it." Baffled, he scratched his head. "Why don't you sit down, Calhoun, and we'll talk this thing out?"

"No, I will not sit down. You'll start on me again, and I won't be able to think. You're not going to make plans for the rest of my life without consulting me, without even having the courtesy to ask. I'm taking back control of my life."

He rose then, naked and furious. "You're mad because I want you to marry me."

The breath hissed out between her clenched teeth. "You're just stupid." She grabbed the closest thing handy and ended up hurling her glasses at him. "Too stupid for words." With this she strode to the door, fought with and cursed the lock until she managed to open it. "You can take your incredibly romantic proposal and stuff it."

The hot and hazy afternoon was perfect for pleasure. Christian surprised me with a little basket of wine and cold ham. Together we sat in the wild grass beyond the rock and watched the boats glide by below. The light was so golden, like something poured out of a gilded pitcher. But it is always so when I'm with him. In this lovely fantasy of afternoons, there is nothing but sunlight and warm, fragrant air.

We talked of everything and nothing as he sketched me. He has already done two paintings of me since the summer began. Without risking modesty I can say he made me look beautiful. What woman is not when she is in love? And it was his eyes that studied me, his hands that drew my face, my hair. His feelings that guided his brush.

If I had not believed before how deep and true his love is for me, I would have seen it in the portraits he painted.

Will someone buy my portrait from him? It saddens me to think of it. Yet it makes me proud. That would be one way I could at last declare my feelings. Hanging on some pretty wall, the portrait of a woman whose eyes are filled with love for the man who painted her.

I say we talked of everything and nothing. We do not mention how quickly the days fly into weeks. There are so little of those weeks left before I must leave the island, and Christian. I think something in me will die this time.

Fergus and I attended a dinner dance tonight. He was very jolly, though there was much talk of war. He said that clever men know that there will always be war, and money to be made from it. I was stunned to hear him speak so, but he only brushed aside my concern.

"It's for you to think of how to spend the money, and for me to make it," he told me.

It upset me because it was not for money I married him, nor is it for money I stay with him. Both were for duty. Yet I have lived under his roof, eaten his food, taken his gifts without a thought.

It scrapes at my conscience to know that I appreciated the little picnic Christian brought to me so much more than I have ever appreciated all the sumptuous dinners Fergus's money has paid for.

Because it always pleases him, I wore the emeralds, and I have not yet put them away. They lie in the shadowed light, glinting at me, reminding me of both my grief and my joy.

If it were not for the children...but I can't think of it. There are the children. Whatever sins I commit, I will never desert them. They have needs that neither Christian nor I have a right to ignore. I know, in the loneliness ahead of me, they will be solace. Being blessed with them, it is not right to grieve for the child Christian and I must never conceive.

Yet, I do.

Tonight when I turn off the lamp I'll try to sleep quickly. For then it will be morning, and morning will become the golden afternoon, when I can see Christian again.

Chapter Ten

The only thing that prevented Amanda from slamming the door was the fact that Suzanna would have already put the children to bed. But she did kick it.

Limping and muttering and occasionally sending a furious look over her shoulder, she started down the hallway. At that point, she wasn't certain if she was more angry with Sloan for taking her assent for granted, or with herself for wanting to give it to him. Marriage hadn't been in her plans, but damn it, she was good at taking the unexpected and making it work. But if he thought she would give him the satisfaction of just hopping on board because he said so, then he didn't know Amanda Kelly Calhoun.

When we get married, she fumed. Not if, not will you or would you. And the problem, the big problem was that under the instant panic and anger had been a thrill. She paused outside of her bedroom door as her own soft sigh caught up with her. Oh, Lord, she did want to marry him. Despite all the good, solid, sensible reasons against it, marrying him was exactly what she wanted. Living with him would mean living with the constant threat of upheaval. She smiled to herself. And what more satisfying life could there be for a woman so skilled at putting things back in place?

With her hand on the doorknob, she hesitated, debating whether she would go back, give in to the urge to throw herself laughing into his arms and say…yes!

No. Resolute, Amanda pushed open the door. She wasn't about to make it that easy for him. If he wanted her, really wanted her, then he was going to have to work a little harder. When he got it right—if he got it right—she corrected as she shut the door behind her, she would smile, slide her arms around him and say—

An arm whipped around her throat and cut off her breath. Instinctively she struggled, throwing both hands up to the barrier to yank and scratch as she fought to drag in the air to scream. Until the hard, cold barrel of a gun pressed against her temple.

"Don't." The voice was only a harsh whisper at her ear. "Be very still, and very quiet, and I won't have to hurt you."

Obediently she let her arms fall limply to her sides, but her mind was speeding. The children were just down the hall. Their safety came first. And Sloan…Sloan could come along at any moment, furiously demanding a showdown.

"That's better." The pressure on her windpipe eased slightly. "If you scream, people are going to get hurt—starting with you. I don't think you want that." She shook her head. "Good. Now—" He swore and tightened his grip again as Sloan bellowed in the corridor.

"Calhoun. I'm not finished with you."

"Be absolutely quiet," the man warned as he dragged her back. "Or I'll kill him."

Amanda shut her eyes and prayed.

Sloan shoved open the door of her room, but it was pitch-dark and silent inside. While he stood in the doorway, swearing, Amanda was pressed back into the corner, knowing the gun was now aimed in Sloan's direction. Her stomach seemed to be packed with ice as she stood, not even daring to breathe, willing him to turn and go. And when he did, when she heard his boots clanging on the stairs, she wondered if she would ever see him again.

"Now that we have a little privacy, we can talk." But the arm stayed around her throat and the gun at her temple. "About the emeralds."

"I don't know where they are."

"Yes. Initially I had trouble believing that, but now I'm sure you don't. So we'll play this a different way. We'll have to move quickly. First the storeroom. I'll take the papers you've yet to sort through. Then, to add a little flare to the trip, we'll fetch Coco's pearls, and a few of the smaller, more portable items."

"You'll never get out of the house."

"You just leave that up to me." There was a faint lilt of pleasure in the voice now, as if he would enjoy the challenge. "Now we're going to move quietly, and very quickly to the storeroom. If you try anything heroic, I'll regret shooting you."

She didn't dare, not with the children so close. But

the storeroom, she thought, as she started out with him
directly behind her. That was a different matter.

Sloan had left the lights on. The remnants of their
picnic were spread over the floor. The air smelled, ever
so lightly, of strawberries and champagne.

"Very sweet," Livingston murmured, then shut the
door behind them. "It would have been more convenient
for me if you had had the séance instead of a tryst." He
loosened his hold so that she could step away, but kept
his gun level.

Amanda stared at the man she knew as William Livingston. He was all in black with a soft leather pouch
worn crosswise over his chest. On his hands were thin
surgical gloves. The gun he carried was small, but she
didn't doubt it was lethal, not when she looked into his
eyes.

"No recriminations, Amanda?" His brow lifted when
she said nothing. "I'd hoped you and I could enjoy each
other while I was conducting business, but…let's not
waste time." From his pouch he pulled out a denim duffel bag. "Just the papers from those boxes there. I'm sure
you're too efficient to have filed away anything useful."

She bent to pick up the bag he'd tossed at her. "You've
lost your accent."

"It's lost its purpose. Be quick, Amanda." His eyes
narrowed as he gestured with the gun. "Very quick."

She began to stuff papers into the bag. He was stealing her history, she thought furiously. Her family. "These
won't do you any good."

"I doubt you believe that, or you wouldn't be wasting your time with them." His posture seemed almost
relaxed now as he stood between Amanda and the door.
"You're much too practical. In my profession, it pays

to do your homework. I know your family quite well."
To hurry her along, he waved the gun. "Which is why
I chose to concentrate on you, the most efficient and
straightforward of the Calhoun women."

If his ego was the only thing she could strike at, she'd
take her best shot. "I hope you weren't expecting me to
fall for you." She flicked a coolly dismissive glance over
him. "You're not my type—then or now."

It hit the mark. His vanity was as huge as his ambition. "It's a pity that the lack of time prevents me from
testing that. Perhaps when I come back, we'll pick up
where we left off."

"Even if you get away tonight, you'll never get back
in this house again."

He only smiled. "We'll see. Running into you like
this complicates my plans, but it doesn't alter the final
goal. The necklace. I want it very badly. Some jewels
have power, and I have a feeling about this necklace. A
strong feeling."

The air in the room was suddenly cold, bone-chill-
ing cold. The expression in Livingston's eyes changed.
"Drafts," he muttered uneasily. "The place is full of
drafts."

But Amanda felt it, too, and was Calhoun enough to
recognize it.

"It's Bianca," she said, and despite the gun, despite
the odds, felt completely safe. "If you've done your
homework, then you'll know she's still here." The dart-
ing nerves in his eyes made her smile. "I don't think she
wants you to have the papers, or the necklace."

"Ghosts?" he laughed, but the sound was strained.
Though he could see with his own eyes that nothing had

changed, he was no longer sure he was alone in the room with Amanda. "That's unworthy of you."

"Then why are you frightened?"

"I'm not frightened, I'm in a hurry. That's enough." He found himself desperate to get out of the room, out of the house. Despite the eerie chill, a line of sweat dribbled down his back. "You carry the bag. Since this has taken longer than expected, we'll have to forgo Coco's pearls, for now." Impatient, he waved the gun at her. "Out the terrace doors."

Amanda debated heaving the duffel bag at him and running. But then he would have the papers. Instead, she struggled with it, then fumbled at the door. "It's stuck."

She was braced when he came up behind her to fight with the old latch. The minute the door opened, she stuck a foot behind him, threw her weight against him, then ran.

Wanting to lead him away from her family, she headed toward the west wing. As she hit the first set of stone stairs, she shouted for Sloan. The heavy bag bumped each step as she dragged it with her. She could hear him behind her, closing in, and zigged around a corner as the first bullet pinged off granite.

She didn't stop to catch her breath, though her lungs were beginning to burn. The May night was warm, oppressively warm after the cold of the storeroom. The air was heavy with the threat of rain.

The sensation of safety she had felt in the storeroom had vanished. There was no protection now, except for her knowledge of the complex layout of the terraces and stairs. But she was straining, fighting her way through the dark and through the sudden certainty that she could not handle this alone.

Then she saw Sloan, heading toward her from the opposite direction. The relief lasted only an instant before she heard another shot.

Lights were flashing everywhere inside the house. Sloan shouted at her before he came forward like a charging bull. Unarmed, Amanda realized, blind with fury, and straight into a loaded gun.

Without hesitation, she whirled away from Sloan and heaved the bag of papers at Livingston. As he snatched it up, she could hear raised voices from inside, Jenny's crying, the dog's frantic barks. Wanting to protect as much as be protected, Amanda raced toward Sloan. When she reached him, arms outstretched, he shoved her aside.

"Get in the house."

"He's got a gun," she said, desperately clinging to his arm. "Just let him go."

"I said get inside." He shook her off, then before her astonished eyes, leaped over the wall.

With her heart in her throat, she raced to it, to see him scrambling up from the terrace below. Even as Lilah burst through a door, Amanda was giving chase.

"What the hell's going on?" Lilah shouted after her.

"Call the police." After the single order, Amanda saved her breath for running, following the sound of stampeding feet and Fred's furious barks.

There was no moonlight to guide her, but she plunged heedlessly into the dark, screaming for Sloan when she heard the explosion of gunfire. She flew down the steps, tearing around the house in a dead run. Over her own ragged gasps, she heard a shouted curse, then the sound of tires squealing on asphalt.

In her hurry, she stumbled once, scrambling back up from the driveway with gravel stinging her palms.

Then for an instant, a terrifying instant, there was only the sound of the sea and the wind and her own thundering pulse.

Her legs trembled as she dashed down the slope, so blind with fear that she didn't see Sloan until she rammed into him.

"Oh, God." Her hands were instantly on his face. "I thought he'd killed you."

He was too infuriated at having lost his quarry to appreciate her concern. "Not for lack of trying. Are you all right?"

"Yes, yes, I'm fine. It was—"

"You're bleeding." Every other thought in his head vanished. "There's blood on your hands."

"I fell." She dropped her head onto his shoulder. "It was so dark, and I couldn't see." Fighting tears, she held on to him as Fred whined at their feet. In an abrupt change of mood, she pulled back, pushing at his chest with her sore hands. Her damp eyes sizzled. "Are you crazy, chasing after him that way? I told you he had a gun. He could have shot you."

"He damn near shot you," Sloan retorted. "And didn't I tell you to stay inside?"

"I don't take orders from you," she began.

"You're both alive," Lilah commented. Flashlight in hand, she strolled toward them. "I could hear you arguing from the end of the driveway." The light shot across papers scattered in the road. "What's all this?"

"Oh, God, he must have dropped some." Amanda was already down on her hands and knees, gathering them up.

"Must've been when Fred bit his leg." Far from pacified, Sloan bent to snatch up a paper before it blew away.

"Fred bit him?" Amanda and Lilah said in unison.

"Good and hard from the sound of it." It was a small but sweet satisfaction. "We might have had him, too, but he had a car stashed down the road."

"And he might have shot both of you," Amanda retorted.

"Excuse me." Lilah felt she was doing her part by shining the light so they could see to find papers. "Who is he?"

"Livingston," Sloan told her, then added a string of curses. "You'll have to get the details from your sister."

"Inside," Lilah suggested. "The rest of the family is in an uproar."

"You called the police?"

"Yes." Right before she'd rushed out of the house, barefoot, to chase her sister down the graveled driveway. When Fred stopped to perk his ears then give a long, ululant howl, she laughed. "And I'd say they're on the way. Fred already hears the sirens."

Because her arms were full, Amanda pushed the papers into Lilah's arms, then began to pick up more as they started back. "He didn't get everything," she muttered, then thought of that moment in the storeroom when the air had changed. "I knew he wouldn't."

At the door of the house Suzanna stood, a slim gladiator, armed with a fireplace poker. "Is everyone all right?"

"Fine." Amanda let out an exhausted breath. "The kids?"

"In the parlor with Aunt Coco. Oh, honey, your hands."

"I just scraped them."

"I'll get some antiseptic."

"And some brandy," Lilah added, before laying the papers on a table in the hallway.

Twenty minutes later, the story had been related to the police, and the family was left alone to absorb it. Sloan paced behind the sofa while the Calhoun women huddled together.

"We had that—that thief to dinner." Coco glared into her brandy. "I baked a chocolate soufflé. And all the time he was plotting to steal from us."

"The police will shoot him," Alex piped up. "Bang! Between the eyes."

"I think we've had enough excitement for one night." Suzanna kissed the top of his head. Less sure of himself than he wanted to be, Alex slipped a hand into hers and held tight.

"He got most of the papers." With a sigh, Amanda reached for the pile she'd tossed onto the coffee table. "I hope Fred took a good chunk out of him."

"Good boy, Fred." Lilah cuddled the dog in her lap. "I don't think they'll do Livingston—or whoever he is— any good. He's not meant to find the emeralds. We are."

"He won't get the chance," Sloan said grimly. "Not with the security system I'm putting in." He shot a look at Amanda, daring her to argue, but she was staring at one of the papers.

"It's a letter," she murmured. "A letter from Bianca to Christian."

"Oh, my dear." Coco leaned forward. "What does it say?"

Amanda read,

"My love,
I'm writing this as the rain continues to fall and keeps me from you. I wonder what you are doing, if you paint today in the gloomy light and think of me. When I'm alone like this in my tower, sepa-

rated from the reality of my duties, I let the memories sweep over me. Of the first time I saw you, standing on the cliffs. Of the last time I touched you. I'm praying for the sun, Christian, so that we can make more memories. I cannot tell you how you have changed me, how much more my eyes see, now that they see with my heart. I can't imagine how empty my life would have been without this time we had together. I know now that love is very rare, very precious. It is something to be cherished and held on to tightly while too often it is smothered, or brushed carelessly away. Remember, even when our time together ends, I will hold your love. It will live in my heart long after that heart stops beating.

Bianca."

Coco let out a long, dreamy sigh. "Oh, how much they must have loved each other."

"Yucky," Alex said sleepily, and rested his head on his mother's breast.

Amanda smoothed the letter out, hating the fact that it had become crumpled. "I guess she never got the chance to send it to him. All these years it's been mixed up with receipts and account sheets."

"And tonight *we* found it, not Livingston," Lilah reminded her.

"Luck," Amanda murmured.

"Fate," her sister insisted.

When the phone rang, Amanda was the first up to answer. "It's the police," she said, then settled back to listen. "I see. Yes, thank you for letting us know." She hung up, blowing out a disgusted breath. "Looks like he got away. He didn't go back to the BayWatch for any of his things, or he slipped in and took what he wanted and left the rest."

"Do they think he'll come back?" Alarmed, Coco patted her chest.

"No, but they're going to keep an eye on the house until they're sure he's left the island."

"I imagine he's halfway to New York by now." Suzanna shifted the drowsy children on her lap. "And if he comes back, we'll be ready for him."

"More than ready," Amanda agreed. "They have an APB out, but…I guess that's all that can be done for tonight."

"No." Sloan crossed the room to her. "There's a little more that has to be done." He nodded to the rest of the room as he pulled her toward the doorway. "You'll excuse us."

"They might, but I don't," Amanda told him. "Let go of my arm."

"Okay." He did, then nipping her by the waist, hauled her over his shoulder. "It's always the hard way with you."

"I will not be slung around like a sack of potatoes." As he climbed the stairs, she wriggled, trying for one clear shot with her foot.

"We left some loose ends before you stormed off to go tangle with an armed robber. Now we're damn well going to tie them up. You like straight talk, Calhoun, and you're about to get some."

"You don't know what I like." She slammed a fist into his back. "You don't know anything."

"Then it's time I found out." He kicked open the door

of her room, stalked over and dumped her onto the bed. When she scrambled up, fists raised, he shoved her down again. "You sit where I put you. So help me, we're going to have this out once and for all."

Amanda stunned them both by covering her face with her hands and bursting into tears. She couldn't stop them. Everything that had happened in the past few hours reared up to set off an emotional jag that knocked her flat. On an oath, Sloan stepped toward her, then away, then dragged a helpless hand through his hair.

"Don't do that, Mandy."

She only shook her head and continued to sob.

"Come on now, please." His voice gentled as he crouched in front of her. "I didn't mean to make you cry." Lost, he stroked her hair, patted her shoulder. "I'm sorry, honey. I know you've been through hell tonight. I should have waited to start on this." Cursing himself, he rubbed her arm. "Look, you can hit me if it'd make you feel better."

She sniffled, drew in a hitching breath, then clipped him hard enough to send him sprawling. Through a veil of tears, she studied him as he dabbed at his mouth with the back of his hand.

"I forgot how literal minded you were." He sat where he was as they watched each other. "You finished crying?"

"I think so." Sniffling again, she dug into her pocket for a tissue. "Your lip's bleeding."

"Yeah." He started to reach for the tissue, but she was wiping her face with it. Laughing, he sat back again. "God Almighty, you're a piece of work."

"I'm glad you think this whole thing is a big joke. Men breaking into the house, waving guns around.

You're lucky I didn't find you facedown in the road with a hole in your head."

He saw the tears welling again and took her hands. "Is that what this is about?" He pressed a kiss to her freshly bandaged palms. "You're upset because I went after him?"

"I told you not to."

"Hey." His gaze fixed on hers, he raised a hand to cup her chin. "Do you think I could stand around after he'd taken a potshot at you? The only thing I regret is that I didn't catch up with him, so I could rearrange that pretty face of his."

"That's just stupid machismo," she said, but turned her cheek into his hand.

"That's the second time tonight you've called me stupid. I'd like to get back to the first time."

Instantly she pulled back and pokered up. "I don't want to talk about it."

"Too bad. That little chase was quite a diversion, but it's done now. We're not. How come you jumped all over me when I mentioned marriage?"

"Mentioned it? You ordered it."

"I just said that—"

"You just assumed," she interrupted, then pushed by him to stand up. "Just because I love you, just because I've made love with you, doesn't give you any right to take me for granted. I told you before that I make my own plans."

"I've had it with your plans, Calhoun." He took her arm to hold her still. "I've got plans, too, and needs. It so happens they all include you. I love you, damn it." He emphasized the point with a quick, frustrated shake. "You're the only woman I've ever needed, really needed.

The only woman I've ever wanted to spend my life with, have children with, make a home with. God knows why when you're as ornery as a mule with two heads, but that's the way it is."

"Then why didn't you just ask?"

Baffled, he shook his head. "Ask what?"

She made a strangled sound and began to pace again. "It's not like I'm asking for Byron or Shelley. I don't expect you to get down on your knees with a hand over your heart. Maybe a little violin music wouldn't have hurt," she muttered. "Or some candlelight."

"Violin music?"

"Forget it." She stopped, hands on her hips, to face him down. "Do you think just because I'm sensible and organized that I don't need any trappings, any romance? You come here, change my entire life, make me love you so much I can't see straight, then you don't even have the good sense to do it right."

"Hold on." He held up a hand before she could stride by him again. "Are you saying you're mad because I didn't ask you fancy enough?"

The sound came again, louder this time. Her face was flushed with temper, her eyes glowing with it. "You didn't ask at all, but why should you? You already know the answer."

Trying to figure women, he thought while he rubbed his hands over his face, was like…trying to figure women. "You wait here," he told her, and strode out.

"Typical," Amanda called after him, then plopped down onto the bed. She was still stewing, her chin on her hand, when he came back in. "Now what?" she demanded.

"Just shut up a minute." He set the tape recorder

he'd borrowed on her dresser, then pulled out a pack of matches. Systematically he began to light candles, moving from one part of the room to another while she scowled at him. When he was satisfied, he turned off the lights.

"What are you doing?"

"I'm getting things ready so I can ask you to marry me without having you throw something at me again."

Chin up, she jumped out of bed. "Now you're making fun of me."

"No, I'm not. Damn it, woman, are you going to argue with me all night or let me try to do this right?"

There was enough exasperation in his voice to make her stop and consider him. He didn't look terribly comfortable, she noted. And because he didn't, she wanted to smile. He was doing it for her, she realized. Because he loved her.

"I guess I'll let you try. What's that?" she asked, gesturing to the tape recorder.

"It's Lilah's." He punched the Play button. The soft, weeping sound of violins flowed into the room. Now she did smile, though her heart was beginning to thud.

"It's lovely."

"So are you. I should have made a point of telling you that more often." Stepping toward her, he held out a hand.

"Now's a good time to start." She placed her hand in his.

"I love you, Amanda." Very gently, he touched his lips to hers. "I love everything about you. The woman who makes lists and lines up her shoes in the closet. The woman who goes swimming in freezing water, just so she can be alone for a while. I love the incredibly sexy woman I found in bed, and the tough one, who knows her own mind. It's all the things you are I don't want to live without."

"I love you, too." She lifted a hand to his face. "I meant it when I said you'd changed my life. Tonight, when I read Bianca's letter, I understood how she felt. I'll never feel about anyone the way I feel about you. I'll never want to."

Smiling, he caught her wrist, turning it so that he could brush a kiss over her hand. "Then you're going to marry me?"

She laughed as she threw her arms around him. "I thought you'd never ask."

* * * * *

FOR THE LOVE OF LILAH

For my great-great-grandmother Selina MacGruder,
who fell in love unwisely and well.

Prologue

Bar Harbor, 1913—

The cliffs call to me. High and fierce and dangerously
beautiful, they stand and beckon as seductively as a
lover. In the morning, the air was as soft as the clouds
that rode the sky to the west. Gulls wheeled and called,
a lonely sound, like the distant ring of a buoy that carried up on the wind. It brought an image of a church
bell tolling a birth. Or a death.

Like a mirage, other islands glinted and winked
through the faint mist the sun had yet to burn from the
water. Fishermen piloted their sturdy boats from the
bay and out to the rolling sea.

Even knowing he would not be there, I couldn't stay
away.

I took the children. It can't be wrong to want to share

with them some of the happiness that I always feel when I walk in the wild grass that leads to the tumbled rocks. I held Ethan's hand on one side, and Colleen's on the other. Nanny gripped little Sean's as he toddled through the grass after a yellow butterfly that fluttered just beyond his questing fingers.

The sound of their laughter—the sweetest sound a mother can hear—lifted through the air. They have such bright and depthless curiosity, such unquestioning trust. As yet, they are untouched by the worries of the world, of uprisings in Mexico, of unrest in Europe. Their world does not include betrayals or guilt or passions that sting the heart. Their needs, so simple, are immediate and have nothing to do with tomorrow. If I could keep them so innocent, so safe and so free, I would. Yet I know that one day they will face all of those churning adult emotions and worries.

But today there were wildflowers to be picked, questions to be answered. And for me, dreams to be dreamed.

There is no doubt that Nanny understands why I walk here. She knows me too well not to see into my heart. She loves me too well to criticize. No one would be more aware than she that there is no love in my marriage. It is, as it has always been, a convenience to Fergus, a duty to me. If not for the children, we would have nothing in common. Even then, I fear he considers them worthwhile possessions, symbols of his success, such as our home in New York, or The Towers, the castlelike house he built for summers on the island. Or myself, the woman he took as wife, one whom he considers attractive enough, well-bred enough to share the Calhoun name, to grace his dinner table or adorn his arm when we walk into the society that is so important to him.

It sounds cold when I write it, yet I cannot pretend there has been warmth in my marriage to Fergus. Certainly there is no passion. I had hoped, when I followed my parents' wishes and married him, that there would be affection, which would deepen into love. But I was very young. There is courtesy, a hollow substitute for emotion.

A year ago perhaps, I could convince myself that I was content. I have a prosperous husband, children I adore, an enviable place in society and a circle of elegant friends. My wardrobe is crowded with beautiful clothes and jewelry. The emeralds Fergus gave me when Ethan was born are fit for a queen. My summer home is magnificent, again suited to royalty with its towers and turrets, its lofty walls papered in silk, its floors gleaming beneath the richest of carpets.

What woman would not be content with all of this? What more could a dutiful wife ask for? Unless she asked for love.

It was love I found along these cliffs, in the artist who stood there, facing the sea, slicing those rocks and raging water onto canvas. Christian, his dark hair blowing in the wind, his gray eyes so dark, so intense, as they studied me. Perhaps if I had not met him I could have gone on pretending to be content. I could have gone on convincing myself that I did not yearn for love or sweet words or a quiet touch in the middle of the night.

Yet I did meet him, and my life has changed. I would not go back to that false contentment for a hundred emerald necklaces. With Christian I have found something so much more precious than all the gold Fergus so cleverly accumulates. It is not something I can hold in my hand or wear around my throat, but something I hold in my heart.

When I meet him on the cliffs, as I will this afternoon, I will not grieve for what we can't have, what we dare not take, but treasure the hours we've been given. When I feel his arms around me, taste his lips against mine, I'll know that Bianca is the luckiest woman in the world to have been loved so well.

Chapter One

A storm was waiting to happen. From the high curving window of the tower, Lilah could see the silver tongue of lightning licking at the black sky to the east. Thunder bellowed, bursting through the gathering clouds to send its drumbeat along the teeth of rock. An answering shudder coursed through her—not of fear, but of excitement.

Something was coming. She could feel it, not just in the thickening of the air but in the primitive beating of her own blood.

When she pressed her hand to the glass, she almost expected her fingers to sizzle, snapped with the power of the building electricity. But the glass was cool and smooth, and as black as the sky.

She smiled a little at the distant rumble of thunder and thought of her great-grandmother. Had Bianca ever stood here, watching a storm build, waiting for it to crash over the house and fill the tower with eerie light? Had she wished that her lover had stood beside her to share the power and the unleashed passion? Of course she had, Lilah thought. What woman wouldn't?

But Bianca had stood here alone, Lilah knew, just as she herself was standing alone now. Perhaps it had been the loneliness, the sheer ache of it, that had driven Bianca to throw herself out of that very window and onto the unforgiving rocks below.

Shaking her head, Lilah took her hand from the glass. She was letting herself get moody again, and it had to stop. Depression and dark thoughts were out of character for a woman who preferred to take life as it came—and who made it a policy to avoid its more strenuous burdens.

Lilah wasn't ashamed of the fact that she would rather sit than stand, would certainly rather walk than run and saw the value of long naps as opposed to exercise for keeping the body and mind in tune.

Not that she wasn't ambitious. It was simply that her ambitions ran to the notion that physical comfort had priority over physical accomplishments.

She didn't care for brooding and was annoyed with herself for falling into the habit over the past few weeks. If anything she should be happy. Her life was moving along at a steady if unhurried pace. Her home and her family, equally important as her own comfort, were safe and whole. In fact, both were expanding along very satisfactory lines.

Her youngest sister, C.C., was back from her honeymoon and glowing like a rose. Amanda, the most practical of the Calhoun sisters, was madly in love and planning her own wedding.

The two men in her sisters' lives met with Lilah's

complete approval. Trenton St. James, her new brother-in-law, was a crafty businessman with a soft heart under a meticulously tailored suit. Sloan O'Riley, with his cowboy boots and Oklahoma drawl, had her admiration for digging beneath Amanda's prickly exterior.

Of course, having two of her beloved nieces attached to wonderful men made Aunt Coco delirious with happiness. Lilah laughed a little, thinking how her aunt was certain she'd all but arranged the love affairs herself. Now, naturally, the Calhoun sisters' longtime guardian was itching to provide the same service for Lilah and her older sister Suzanna.

Good luck, Lilah wished her aunt. After a traumatic divorce, and with two young children to care for—not to mention a business to run—Suzanna wasn't likely to cooperate. She'd been badly burned once, and a smart woman didn't let herself get pushed into the fire.

For herself, Lilah had been doing her best to fall in love, to hear that vibrant inner click that came when you knew you'd found the one person in the world who was fated for you. So far, that particular chamber of her heart had been stubbornly silent.

There was time for that, she reminded herself. She was twenty-seven, happy enough in her work, surrounded by family. A few months before, they had nearly lost The Towers, the Calhoun's crumbling and eccentric home that stood on the cliffs overlooking the sea. If it hadn't been for Trent, Lilah might not have been able to stand in the tower room she loved so much and look out at the gathering storm.

So she had her home, her family, a job that interested her and, she reminded herself, a mystery to solve. Great-Grandmama Bianca's emeralds, she thought. Though she had never seen them, she was able to visualize them perfectly just by closing her eyes.

Two dramatic tiers of grass-green stones accented with icy diamonds. The glint of gold in the fancy filigree work. And dripping from the bottom strand, that rich and glowing teardrop emerald. More than its financial or even aesthetic value, it represented to Lilah a direct link with an ancestor who fascinated her, and the hope of eternal love.

The legend said that Bianca, determined to end a loveless marriage, had packed a few of her treasured belongings, including the necklace, into a box. Hoping to find a way to join her lover, she had hidden it. Before she had been able to take it out and start a life with Christian, she had despaired and leaped from the tower window to her death.

A tragic end to a romance, Lilah thought, yet she didn't always feel sad when she thought of it. Bianca's spirit remained in The Towers, and in that high room where Bianca had spent so many hours longing for her lover, Lilah felt close to her.

They would find the emeralds, she promised herself. They were meant to.

It was true enough that the necklace had already caused its problems. The press had learned of its existence and had played endlessly on the hidden-treasure angle. So successfully, Lilah thought now, that the annoyance had gone beyond curious tourists and amateur treasure hunters, and had brought a ruthless thief into their home.

When she thought of how Amanda might have been killed protecting the family's papers, the risk she had taken trying to keep any clue to the emeralds out of the wrong hands, Lilah shuddered. Despite Amanda's heroics, the man who had called himself William Livingston had gotten away with a sackful. Lilah sincerely hoped he found nothing but old recipes and unpaid bills.

William Livingston, alias Peter Mitchell, alias a dozen other names wasn't going to get his greedy hands on the emeralds. Not if the Calhoun women had anything to do about it. As far as Lilah was concerned, that included Bianca, who was as much a part of The Towers as the cracked plaster and creaky boards.

Restless, she moved away from the window. She couldn't say why the emeralds and the woman who had owned them preyed so heavily on her mind tonight. But Lilah was a woman who believed in instinct, in premonition, as naturally as she believed the sun rose in the east.

Tonight, something was coming.

She glanced back toward the window. The storm was rolling closer, gathering force. She felt a driving need to be outside to meet it.

Max felt his stomach lurch along with the boat. Yacht, he reminded himself. A twenty-six-foot beauty with all the comforts of home. Certainly more than his own home, which consisted of a cramped apartment, carelessly furnished, near the campus of Cornell University. The trouble was, the twenty-six-foot beauty was sitting on top of a very cranky Atlantic, and the two seasickness pills in Max's system were no match for it.

He brushed the dark lock of hair away from his brow where, as always, it fell untidily back again. The reeling of the boat sent the brass lamp above his desk dancing. Max did his best to ignore it. He really had to concentrate on his job. American history professors weren't offered fascinating and lucrative summer employment every day. And there was a very good chance he could get a book out of it.

Being hired as researcher for an eccentric millionaire was the fodder of fiction. In this case, it was fact.

As the ship pitched, Max pressed a hand to his queasy stomach and tried three deep breaths. When that didn't work, he tried concentrating on his good fortune.

The letter from Ellis Caufield had come at a perfect time, just before Max had committed himself to a summer assignment. The offer had been both irresistible and flattering.

In the day-to-day scheme of things, Max didn't consider that he had a reputation. Some well-received articles, a few awards—but that was all within the tight world of academia that Max had happily buried himself in. If he was a good teacher, he felt it was because he received such pleasure from giving both information and appreciation of the past to students so mired in the present.

It had come as a surprise that Caufield, a layman, would have heard of him and would respect him enough to offer him such interesting work.

What was even more exciting than the yacht, the salary and the idea of summering in Bar Harbor, to a man with Maxwell Quartermain's mind-set, was the history in every scrap of paper he'd been assigned to catalogue.

A receipt for a lady's hat, dated 1932. The guest list for a party from 1911. A copy of a repair bill on a 1935 Ford. The handwritten instructions for an herbal remedy for the croup. There were letters written before World War I, newspaper clippings with names like Carnegie and Kennedy, shipping receipts for

Chippendale armoires, a Waterford chandelier. Old dance cards, faded recipes.

For a man who spent most of his intellectual life in the past, it was a treasure trove. He would have shifted through each scrap happily for nothing, but Ellis Caufield had contacted him, offering Max more than he made teaching two full semesters.

It was a dream come true. Instead of spending the summer struggling to interest bored students in the cultural and political status of America before the Great War, he was living it. With the money, half of which was already deposited, Max could afford to take a year off from teaching to start the book he'd been longing to write.

Max felt he owed Caufield an enormous debt. A year to indulge himself. It was more than he had ever dared to dream of. Brains had gotten him into Cornell on a scholarship. Brains and hard work had earned him a Ph.D. by the time he'd been twenty-five. For the eight years since then, he'd been slaving, teaching classes, preparing lectures, grading papers, taking the time only to write a few articles.

Now, thanks to Caufield, he would be able to take the time he had never dared to take. He would be able to begin the project he kept secret inside his head and heart.

He wanted to write a novel set in the second decade of the twentieth century. Not just a history lesson or an oratory on the cause and effect of war, but a story of people swept along by history. The kind of people he was growing to know and understand by reading through their old papers.

Caufield had given him that time, the research and the opportunity. And it was all gilded by a summer spent luxuriously on a yacht. It was a pity Max hadn't realized how much his system would resent the motion of the sea.

Particularly a stormy one, he thought, rubbing a hand over his clammy face. He struggled to concentrate, but the faded and tiny print on the papers swam then doubled in front of his eyes and added a vicious headache to the grinding nausea. What he needed was some air, he told himself. A good blast of fresh air. Though he knew Caufield preferred him to stay below with his research during the evenings, Max figured his employer would prefer him healthy rather than curled up moaning on his bed.

Rising, he did moan a little, his stomach heaving with the next wave. He could almost feel his skin turn green. Air, definitely. Max stumbled from the cabin, wondering if he would ever find his sea legs. After a week, he'd thought he'd been doing fairly well, but with the first taste of rough weather, he was wobbly.

It was a good thing he hadn't—as he sometimes liked to imagine—sailed on the *Mayflower*. He never would have made it to Plymouth Rock.

Bracing a hand on the mahogany paneling, he hobbled down the pitching corridor toward the stairs that led above deck.

Caufield's cabin door was open. Max, who would never stoop to eavesdropping, paused only to give his stomach a moment to settle. He heard his employer speaking to the captain. As the dizziness cleared from Max's head, he realized they were not speaking about the weather or plotting a course.

"I don't intend to lose the necklace," Caufield said impatiently. "I've gone to a lot of trouble, and expense, already."

The captain's answer was equally taut. "I don't see why you brought Quartermain in. If he realizes why you want those papers, and how you got them, he'll be trouble."

"He won't find out. As far as the good professor is concerned, they belong to my family. And I am rich enough, eccentric enough, to want them preserved."

"If he hears something—"

"Hears something?" Caufield interrupted with a laugh. "He's so buried in the past he doesn't hear his own name. Why do you think I chose him? I do my homework, Hawkins, and I researched Quartermain thoroughly. He's an academic fossil with more brains than wit, and is curious only about what happened in the past. Current events, such as armed robbery and the Calhoun emeralds are beyond him."

In the corridor, Max remained still and silent, the physical illness warring with sick suspicion. *Armed robbery.* The two words reeled in his head.

"We'd be better off in New York," Hawkins complained. "I cased out the Wallingford job while you were kicking your heels last month. We could have the old lady's diamonds inside of a week."

"The diamonds will wait." Caufield's voice hardened. "I want the emeralds, and I intend to have them. I've been twenty years in the business of stealing, Hawkins, and I know that only once in a lifetime does a man have the chance for something this big."

"The diamonds—"

"Are stones." Now the voice was caressing and perhaps a little mad. "The emeralds are a legend. They're going to be mine. Whatever it takes."

Max stood frozen outside the stateroom. The clammy

illness roiling inside of his stomach was iced with shock. He hadn't a clue what they were talking about or how to put it together. But one thing was obvious—he was being used by a thief, and there was something other than history in the papers he'd been hired to research.

The fanaticism in Caufield's voice hadn't escaped him, nor had the suppressed violence in Hawkins's. And fanaticism had proved itself throughout history to be a most dangerous weapon. His only defense against it was knowledge.

He had to get the papers, get them and find a way off the boat and to the police. Though whatever he could tell them wouldn't make sense. He stepped back, hoping he could clear his thoughts by the time he got to his stateroom. A wicked wave had the boat lurching and Max pitching through the open doorway.

"Dr. Quartermain." Gripping the sides of his desk, Caufield lifted a brow. "Well, it seems as though you're in the wrong place at the wrong time."

Max grasped the doorjamb as he stumbled back, cursing the unsteady deck beneath his feet. "I—wanted some air."

"He heard every damn word," the captain muttered.

"I'm aware of that, Hawkins. The professor isn't blessed with a poker face. Well then," he began as he slid a drawer open, "we'll simply alter the plans a bit. I'm afraid you won't be granted any shore leave during our stay in Bar Harbor, Doctor." He pulled out a chrome-plated revolver. "An inconvenience, I know, but I'm sure you'll find your cabin more than adequate for your needs while you work. Hawkins, take him back and lock him in."

A crash of thunder vibrated the boat. It was all Max

needed to uproot his legs. As the boat swayed, he rushed back into the corridor. Pulling himself along by the handrail, he fought the motion of the boat. The shouts behind him were lost as he came above deck into the howl of the wind.

A spray of saltwater dashed across his face, blinding him for a moment as he frantically looked for a means of escape. Lightning cracked the black sky, showing him the single stab of light, the pitching seas, the distant, angry rocks and the vague shadow of land. The next roll nearly felled him, but he managed through a combination of luck and sheer will to stay upright. Driven by instinct, he ran, feet sliding on the wet deck. In the next flash of lightning he saw one of the mates glance over from his post. The man called something and gestured, but Max spun around on the slippery deck and ran on.

He tried to think, but his head was too crowded, too jumbled. The storm, the pitching boat, the image of that glinting gun. It was like being caught in someone else's nightmare. He was a history professor, a man who lived in books, rarely surfacing long enough to remember if he'd eaten or picked up his cleaning. He was, he knew, terminally boring, calmly pacing himself on the academic treadmill as he had done all of his life. Surely he couldn't be on a yacht in the Atlantic being chased by armed thieves.

"Doctor."

His erstwhile employer's voice was close enough to cause Max to turn around. The gun being held less than five feet away reminded Max that some nightmares were real. Slowly he backed up until he rammed into the guardrail. There was nowhere left to run.

"I know this is an inconvenience," Caufield said, "but

I think it would be wise if you went back to your cabin."
A bolt of lightning emphasized the point. "The storm
should be short, but quite severe. We wouldn't want you
to…fall overboard."

"You're a thief."

"Yes." Legs braced against the rolling deck, Caufield
smiled. He was enjoying himself—the wind, the electric
air, the white face of the prey he had cornered. "And now
that I can be more frank about just what I want you to
look for, our work should go much more quickly. Come
now, Doctor, use that celebrated brain of yours."

From the corner of his eye, Max saw that Hawkins
was closing in from the other side, as steady on the
heeling deck as a mountain goat on a beaten path. In a
moment, they would have him. Once they did, he was
quite certain he would never see the inside of a classroom again.

With an instinct for survival that had never been
tested, he swung over the rail. He heard another crack
of thunder, felt a burning along his temple, then plunged
blindly beneath the dark, swirling water.

Lilah had driven down, following the winding road
to the base of the cliff. The wind had picked up, was
shrieking now as she stepped out of her car and let it
stream through her hair. She didn't know why she'd felt
compelled to come here, to stand alone on this narrow
and rocky stretch of beach to face the storm.

But she had come, and the exhilaration streamed into
her, racing just under her skin, speeding up her heart.
When she laughed, the sound hung on the wind then
echoed away. Power and passion exploded around her
in a war she could delight in.

Water fumed against the rock, spouting up, spraying her. There was an icy feel to it that made her shiver, but she didn't draw back. Instead she closed her eyes for a moment, lifted her face and absorbed it.

The noise was huge, wildly primitive. Above, closer now, the storm threatened. Big and bad and boisterous. The rain, so heavy in the air you could taste it, held up, but the lightning took command, spearing the sky, ripping through the dark while the boom of thunder competed with the crash of water and wind.

She felt as though she were alone in a violent painting, but there was no sense of loneliness and certainly none of fear. It was anticipation that prickled along her skin, just as a passion as dark as the storm's beat in her blood.

Something, she thought again as she lifted her face to the wind, was coming.

If it hadn't been for the lightning, she wouldn't have seen him. At first she watched the dark shape in the darker water and wondered if a dolphin had swum too close to the rocks. Curious, she walked over the shale, dragging her hair away from the greedy fingers of wind.

Not a dolphin, she realized with a clutch of panic. A man. Too stunned to move, she watched him go under. Surely she'd imagined it, she told herself. She was just caught up in the storm, the mystery of it, the sense of immediacy. It was crazy to think she'd seen someone fighting the waves in this lonely and violent span of water.

But when the figure appeared again, floundering, Lilah was kicking off her sandals and racing into the icy black water.

His energy was flagging. Though he'd managed to pry off his shoes, his legs felt abominably heavy. He'd always been a strong swimmer. It was the only sport he had had any talent for. But the sea was a great deal stronger. It carried him along now rather than his own arms and legs. It dragged him under as it chose, then teasingly released him as he struggled to break free for one more gulp of air.

He couldn't even remember why he was fighting. The cold that had long since numbed his body granted the same favor to his brain. His thrashing movements were merely automatic now and growing steadily weaker. It was the sea that guided him, that trapped him, that would, he was coming to accept, kill him.

The next wave battered him, and exhausted, he let it take him under. He only hoped he would drown before he bashed into the rocks.

He felt something wrap around his neck and, with the last of his strength, pushed at it. Some wild thought of sea snakes or grasping weeds had him struggling. Then his face was above the surface again, his burning lungs sucking air. Dimly he saw a face close to his own. Pale, stunningly beautiful. A glory of dark, wet hair floated around him.

"Just hang on," she shouted at him. "We'll be all right."

She was pulling him toward shore, fighting the backwash of wave. Hallucinating, Max thought. He had to be hallucinating to imagine a beautiful woman coming to his aid a moment before he died. But the possibility of a miracle kicked into his fading sense of survival, and he began to work with her.

The waves slammed into them, dragging them back a foot for every two exhausting feet of progress they made. Overhead the sky opened to pour out a lashing rain. She was shouting something again, but all he could hear was the dull buzzing in his own head.

He decided he must already be dead. There certainly was no more pain. All he could see was her face, the glow of her eyes, the water-slicked lashes. A man could do worse than to die with that image in his mind.

But her eyes were bright with anger, electric with it. She wanted help, he realized. She needed help. Instinctively he put an arm around her waist so that they were towing each other.

He lost track of the times they went under, of the times one would pull the other up again. When he saw the jutting rocks, fangs spearing up through the swirling black, he turned his weary body without thought to shield hers. An angry wave flicked them waist high out of the water, as easily as a finger flicks an ant from a stone.

His shoulder slammed against rock, but he barely felt it. Then there was the grit of sand beneath his knees, biting into flesh. The water fought to suck them back, but they crawled onto the rocky shore.

The initial sickness was hideous, racking through him until he was certain his body would simply break apart. When the worst of it passed, he rolled, coughing, onto his back. The sky wheeled overhead, black, then brilliant. The face was above his again, close. A hand moved gently over his brow.

"You made it, sailor."

He only stared. She was eerily beautiful, like something he might have conjured if he'd had enough imagination. In the flickering lightning he could see her hair was a rich, golden red. She had acres of it. It flowed around her face, down her shoulders, onto his chest. Her eyes were the mystical green of a calm sea. As the water ran from her onto him, he reached up to touch her face, certain they would pass through the image. But he felt her skin, cold, wet and soft as spring rain.

"Real." His voice was a husky croak. "You're real."

"Damn right." She smiled, then cupping his face in her hands, laughed. "You're alive. We're both alive." And kissed him. Deeply, lavishly, until his head spun with it. There was more laughter beneath the kiss. He heard the joy in it, but not the simple relief.

When he looked at her again, she was blurring, that ethereal face fading until all he could see were those incredible, glowing eyes.

"I never believed in mermaids," he murmured before he lost consciousness.

Chapter Two

"Poor man." Coco, splendid in a flowing purple caftan, hovered beside the bed. She kept her voice low and watched, eagle eyed, as Lilah bandaged the shallow crease on their unconscious guest's temple. "What in the world could have happened to him?"

"We'll have to wait and ask." Her fingers gentle, Lilah studied the pale face on the pillow. Early thirties, she guessed. No tan, though it was mid-June. The indoor type, she decided, despite the fact that he had fairly good muscles. His body was well toned, if a bit on the lanky side—the weight of it had given her more than a little trouble when she'd dragged him to the car. His face was lean, a little long, nicely bony. Intellectual, she thought. The mouth was certainly engaging. Rather poetic, like the pallor. Though his eyes were closed now, she knew they were blue. His hair, nearly dry, was full of sand and long and thick. It was dark and straight, like his lashes.

"I called the doctor," Amanda said as she hurried into the bedroom. Her fingers tapped on the footboard as she frowned down at the patient. "He says we should bring him into Emergency."

Lilah looked up as the lightning struck close to the house and the rain slashed against the windows. "I don't want to take him out in this unless we have to."

"I think she's right." Suzanna stood on the other side of the bed. "I also think Lilah should have a hot bath and lie down."

"I'm fine." At the moment she was wrapped in a chenille robe, warmed by that and a healthy dose of brandy. In any case, she was feeling much too proprietary about her charge to turn him over.

"Crazy is what you are." C.C. massaged Lilah's neck as she lectured her. "Diving into the ocean in the middle of a storm."

"I guess I could've let him drown." Lilah patted C.C.'s hand. "Where's Trent?"

C.C. sighed as she thought of her new husband. "He and Sloan are making sure the new construction's protected. The rain's coming down pretty hard and they were worried about water damage."

"I think I should make some chicken soup." Coco, maternal instincts humming, studied the patient again. "That's just what he needs when he wakes up."

He was already waking up, groggily. He heard the distant and lovely sound of women's voices. Low pitched, smooth, soothing. Like music, it lulled him in and out of dreams. When he turned his head, Max felt the gentle feminine touch on his brow. Slowly, he opened eyes still burning from salt water. The dimly lit room blurred, tilted, then slid into soft focus.

There were five of them, he noted dreamily. Five stupendous examples of womanhood. On one side of the bed was a blonde, poetically lovely, eyes filled with concern. At the foot was a tall, trim brunette who seemed both impatient and sympathetic. An older woman with smoky-blond hair and a regal figure beamed at him. A green-eyed, raven-haired Amazon tilted her head and smiled more cautiously.

Then there was his mermaid, sitting beside him in a white robe, her fabulous hair falling in wild curls to her waist. He must have made some gesture, for they all came a little closer, as if to offer comfort. The mermaid's hand covered his.

"I guess this is heaven," he managed through a dry throat. "It's worth dying for."

With a laugh, Lilah squeezed his fingers. "Nice thought, but this is Maine," she corrected. Lifting a cup, she eased brandy-laced tea through his lips. "You're not dead, just tired."

"Chicken soup." Coco stepped forward to tidy the blanket over him. She was vain enough to take an instant liking to him for his waking statement. "Doesn't that sound good, dear?"

"Yes." The thought of something warm sliding down his aching throat sounded glorious. Though it hurt to swallow, he took another greedy gulp of tea. "Who are you?"

"We're the Calhouns," Amanda said from the foot of the bed. "Welcome to The Towers."

Calhouns. There was something familiar about the name, but it drifted away, like the dream of drowning. "I'm sorry, I don't know how I got here."

"Lilah brought you," C.C. told him. "She—"

"You had an accident," Lilah interrupted her sister, and smiled at him. "Don't worry about it right now. You should rest."

It wasn't a question of should, but must. He could already feel himself drifting away. "You're Lilah," he said groggily. As he drifted to sleep, he repeated the name, finding it lyrical enough to dream on.

"How's the lifeguard this morning?"

Lilah turned from the stove to look at Sloan, Amanda's fiancé. At six-four, he filled the doorway, was so blatantly male—and relaxed with it—she had to smile.

"I guess I earned my first merit badge."

"Next time try making a pot holder." After crossing the room, he kissed the top of her head. "We wouldn't want to lose you."

"I figure jumping into a stormy sea once in my life is enough." With a little sigh, she leaned against him. "I was petrified."

"What the hell were you doing down there with a storm coming?"

"Just one of those things." She shrugged, then went back to fixing tea. For now, she preferred to keep the sensation of being sent to the beach to herself.

"Did you find out who he is?"

"No, not yet. He didn't have a wallet on him, and since he was in pretty rough shape last night, I didn't want to badger him." She glanced up, caught Sloan's expression and shook her head. "Come on, big guy, he's hardly dangerous. If he was looking for a way into the house to have a shot at finding the necklace, he could have taken an easier route than drowning."

He was forced to agree, but after having Amanda

shot at, he didn't want to take chances. "Whoever he is, I think you should move him to the hospital."

"Let me worry about it." She began to arrange plates and cups on a tray. "He's all right, Sloan. Trust me?"

Frowning, he put a hand on hers before she could lift the tray. "Vibes?"

"Absolutely." With a laugh, she tossed back her hair. "Now, I'm going to take Mr. X some breakfast. Why don't you get back to knocking down walls in the west wing?"

"We're putting a few up today." And because he did trust her, he relaxed a little. "Aren't you going to be late for work?"

"I took the day off to play Florence Nightingale." She slapped his hand away from the saucer of toast. "Go be an architect."

Balancing the tray, she left Sloan to start down the hallway. The main floor of The Towers was a hodge-podge of rooms with towering ceilings and cracked plaster. In its heyday, it had been a showplace, an elaborate summer home built by Fergus Calhoun in 1904. It had been his symbol of status with gleaming paneling, crystal doorknobs, intricate murals.

Now the roof leaked in too many places to count, the plumbing rattled and the plaster flaked. Like her sisters, Lilah adored every inch of chipped molding. It had been her home, her only home, and held memories of the parents she had lost fifteen years before.

At the top of the curving stairs, she paused. Muffled with distance came the energetic sound of hammering. The west wing was getting a much needed face-lift. Between Sloan and Trent, The Towers would recapture at least part of its former glory. Lilah liked the idea and, as a woman who considered napping a favored pastime, enjoyed the sound of busy hands.

He was still sleeping when she walked into the room. She knew he had barely stirred through the night because she had stretched out on the foot of the bed, reluctant to leave him, and had slept there, patchily, until morning.

Quietly Lilah set the tray on the bureau and moved over to open the terrace doors. Warm and fragrant air glided in. Unable to resist, she stepped out to let it revitalize her. The sunlight sparkled on the wet grass, glittered on the petals of shell-pink peonies still heavy-headed from rain. Clematis, their saucer-sized blossoms royally blue, spiraled on one of the white trellises in a race with the climbing roses.

From the waist-high terrace wall, she could see the glint of the deep blue water of the bay and the greener, less serene, surface of the Atlantic. It hardly seemed possible that she had been in the water just last night, grasping a stranger and fighting for life. But muscles, unaccustomed to the exercise, ached enough to bring the moment, and the terror, back.

She preferred concentrating on the morning, the generous laziness of it. Made tiny as a toy by the distance, one of the tourist boats streamed by, filled with people clutching cameras and children, hoping to see a whale.

It was June, and the summer people poured into Bar Harbor to sail, to shop, to sun. They would gobble up lobster rolls, haunt the ice cream and T-shirt shops and pack the streets, searching for the perfect souvenir. To them it was a resort. To Lilah, it was home.

She watched a three-masted schooner head out to sea and allowed herself to dream a little before going back inside.

* * *

He was dreaming. Part of his mind recognized it as a dream, but his stomach muscles still fisted, and his pulse rate increased. He was alone in an angry black sea, fighting to make his arms and legs swim through the rising waves. They dragged at him, pulling him under into that blind, airless world. His lungs strained. His own heartbeat roared in his head.

His disorientation was complete—black sea below, black sky above. There was a hideous throbbing in his temple, a terrifying numbness in his limbs. He sank, floating down, fathoms deep. Then she was there, her red hair flowing around her, twining around lovely white breasts, down a slender torso. Her eyes were a soft, mystical green. She spoke his name, and there was a laugh in her voice—and an invitation in the laugh. Slowly, gracefully as a dancer, she held out her arms to him, folding him in. He tasted salt and sex on her lips as she closed them over his.

With a groan, he came regretfully awake. There was pain now, ripe and throbbing in his shoulder, sharp and horrible in his head. His thought patterns skidded away from him. Concentrating, he worked his way above the pain, focusing first on a high, coffered ceiling laced with cracks. He shifted a little, acutely aware that every muscle in his body hurt.

The room was enormous—or perhaps it seemed so because it was so scantily furnished. But what furnishings. There was a huge antique armoire with intricately carved doors. The single chair was undoubtedly Louis Quinze, and the dusty nightstand Hepplewhite. The mattress he lay on sagged, but the footboard was Georgian.

Struggling up to brace on his elbows, he saw Lilah

standing in the open terrace doors. The breeze was fluttering those long cables of hair. He swallowed. At least he knew she wasn't a mermaid. She had legs. Lord, she had legs—right up to her eyes. She wore flowered shorts, a plain blue T-shirt and a smile.

"So, you're awake." She came to him and, competent as a mother, laid a hand on his brow. His tongue dried up. "No fever. You're lucky."

"Yeah."

Her smile widened. "Hungry?"

There was definitely a hole in the pit of his stomach. "Yeah." He wondered if he'd ever be able to get more than one word out around her. At the moment he was lecturing himself for having imagined her naked when she'd risked her life to save his. "Your name's Lilah."

"That's right." She walked over to fetch the tray. "I wasn't sure you'd remember anything from last night."

Pain capered through him so that he gritted his teeth against it and struggled to keep his voice even. "I remember five beautiful women. I thought I was in heaven."

She laughed and, setting the tray at the foot of the bed, came to rearrange his pillows. "My three sisters and my aunt. Here, can you sit up a little?"

When her hand slid down his back to brace him, he realized he was naked. Completely. "Ah…"

"Don't worry, I won't peek. Yet." She laughed again, leaving him flustered. "Your clothes were drenched—I think the shirt's a lost cause. Relax," she told him as she set the tray on his lap. "My brother-in-law and future brother-in-law got you into bed."

"Oh." It looked as though he was back to single syllables.

"Try the tea," she suggested. "You probably swallowed a gallon of sea water, so I'll bet your throat's raw." She saw the intense concentration in his eyes and the nagging pain behind it. "Headache?"

"Vicious."

"I'll be back." She left him, trailing some potently exotic scent in her wake.

Max used the time alone to build back what little strength he had. He hated being weak—a leftover obsession from childhood when he'd been puny and asthmatic. His father had given up in disgust on building his only and disappointing son into a football star. Though he knew it was illogical, sickness brought back unhappy memories of childhood.

Because he'd always considered his mind stronger than his body, he used it now to block the pain.

Moments later, she was back with an aspirin and witch hazel. "Take a couple of these. After you eat, I can drive you into the hospital."

"Hospital?"

"You might want to have a doctor take a look."

"No." He swallowed the pills. "I don't think so."

"Up to you." She sat on the bed to study him, one leg lazily swinging to some inner tune.

Never in his life had he been so sexually aware of a woman—of the texture of her skin, the subtle tones of it, the shape of her body, her eyes, her mouth. The assault on his senses left him uneasy and baffled. He'd nearly drowned, he reminded himself. Now all he could think about was getting his hands on the woman who'd saved him. Saved his life, he remembered.

"I haven't even thanked you."

"I figured you'd get around to it. Try those eggs before they get any colder. You need food."

Obediently he scooped some up. "Can you tell me what happened?"

"From the time I came into it." Relaxed, she brushed her hair behind her shoulder and settled more comfortably on the bed. "I drove down to the beach. Impulse," she said with a lazy movement of her shoulders. "I'd been watching the storm build from the tower."

"The tower?"

"Here, in the house," she explained. "I got the urge to go down, watch it roll in from sea. Then I saw you." In a careless gesture, she brushed the hair back from his brow. "You were in trouble, so I went in. We sort of pulled each other to shore."

"I remember. You kissed me."

Her lips curved. "I figured we both deserved it." She touched a gentle hand to the bruise spreading on his shoulder. "You hit the rocks. What were you doing out there?"

"I…" He closed his eyes to try to clear his fuzzy brain. The effort had sweat pearling on his brow. "I'm not sure."

"Okay, why don't we start with your name?"

"My name?" He opened his eyes to give her a blank look. "Don't you know?"

"We didn't have the chance to introduce ourselves formally. Lilah Calhoun," she said, and offered a hand.

"Quartermain." He accepted her hand, relieved that much was clear. "Maxwell Quartermain."

"Drink some more tea, Max. Ginseng's good for you." Taking the witch hazel, she began to rub it gently over the bruise. "What do you do?"

"I'm, ah, a history professor at Cornell." Her fingers

eased the ache in his shoulder and cajoled him into relaxing.

"Tell me about Maxwell Quartermain." She wanted to take his mind off the pain, to see him relax into sleep again. "Where are you from?"

"I grew up in Indiana…" Her fingers slid up to his neck to unknot muscles.

"Farm boy?"

"No." He sighed as the tension eased and made her smile. "My parents ran a market. I used to help out after school and over the summer."

"Did you like it?"

His eyes were growing heavy. "It was all right. It gave me plenty of time to study. Annoyed my father—always had my face in a book. He didn't understand. I skipped a couple grades and got into Cornell."

"Scholarship?" she assumed.

"Hmm. Got my doctorate." The words were slurred and weighty. "Do you know how much man accomplished between 1870 and 1970?"

"Amazing."

"Absolutely." He was nearly asleep, coaxed into comfort by her quiet voice and gentle hands. "I'd like to have been alive in 1910."

"Maybe you were." She smiled, amused and charmed. "Take a nap, Max."

When he awakened again, he was alone. But he had a dozen throbbing aches to keep him company. He noted that she had left the aspirin and a carafe of water beside the bed, and gratefully swallowed pills.

When that small chore exhausted him, he leaned back to catch his breath. The sunlight was bright, streaming through the open terrace doors with fresh sea air. He'd lost his sense of time, and though it was tempting just to lie back and shut his eyes again, he needed to take back some sort of control.

Maybe she'd read his mind, he thought as he saw his pants and someone else's shirt neatly folded at the foot of the bed. He rose creakily, like an old man with brittle bones and aching muscles. His body sang a melody of pain as he picked up the clothes and peeked through a side door. He eyed the claw-footed tub and chrome shower works with pleasure.

The pipes thudded when he turned on the spray, and so did his muscles as the water beat against his skin. But ten minutes later, he felt almost alive.

It wasn't easy to dry off—even that simple task had his limbs singing. Not sure the news would be good, he wiped the mist from the mirror to study his face.

Beneath the stubble of beard, his skin was white and drawn. Flowering out from the bandage at his temple was a purpling bruise. He already knew there were plenty more blooming on his body. As a result of salt water, his eyes were a patriotic red, white and blue. Though he'd never considered himself a vain man— his looks had always struck him as dead average—he turned away from the mirror.

Wincing and groaning and swearing under his breath, he struggled into the clothes.

The shirt fit fairly well. Better, in fact, than many of his own. Shopping intimidated him—rather salesclerks intimidated him with their bright, impatient smiles. Most of the time Max shopped out of catalogues and took what came.

Glancing down at his bare feet, Max admitted that he'd have to go shopping for shoes—and soon.

Moving slowly, he walked out onto the terrace. The sunlight stung his eyes, but the breezy, moist air felt like heaven. And the view… For a moment he could only stop and stare, hardly even breathing. Water and rock and flowers. It was like being on top of the world and looking down at a small and perfect slice of the planet. The colors were vibrant—sapphire, emerald, the ruby red of roses, the pristine white of sails pregnant with wind. There was no sound but the rumble of the sea and then, far off, the musical gong of a buoy. He could smell hot summer flowers and the cool tang of the ocean.

With his hand braced on the wall, he began to walk. He didn't know which direction he should take, so wandered aimlessly and with no little effort. Once, when dizziness overtook him, he was forced to stop, shut his eyes and breathe his way through it.

When he came to a set of stairs leading up, he opted to climb them. His legs were wobbly, and he could already feel fatigue tugging at him. It was pride as much as curiosity that had him continuing.

The house was built of granite, a sober and sturdy stone that did nothing to take away from the fancy of the architecture. Max felt as though he were exploring the circumference of a castle, some stubborn bulwark of early history that had taken its place upon the cliffs and held it for generations.

Then he heard the anachronistic buzz of a power saw and a man's casual oath. Walking closer, he recognized the busy noises of construction in progress—the slap of hammer on wood, the tinny music from a portable radio, the whirl of drills. When his path was blocked by saw-horses, lumber and tarps, he knew he'd found the source.

A man stepped out of another set of terrace doors. Reddish-blond hair was tousled around a tanned face. He squinted at Max, then hooked his thumbs in his pockets. "Up and around, I see."

"More or less."

The guy looked as if he'd been kicked by a team of mules, Sloan thought. His face was dead white, his eyes bruised, his skin sheened with the sweat of effort. He was holding himself upright through sheer stubbornness. It made it tough to hold on to suspicions.

"Sloan O'Riley," he said, and offered a hand.

"Maxwell Quartermain."

"So I hear. Lilah says you're a history professor. Taking a vacation?"

"No." Max's brow furrowed. "No, I don't think so."

It wasn't evasion Sloan saw in his eyes, but puzzlement, laced with frustration. "Guess you're still a little rattled."

"I guess." Absently he reached up to touch the bandage at his temple. "I was on a boat," he murmured, straining to visualize it. "Working." On what? "The water was pretty rough. I wanted to go on deck, get some air..." Standing at the rail, deck heaving. Panic. "I think I fell—" jumped, was thrown "—I must have fallen overboard."

"Funny nobody reported it."

"Sloan, leave the man alone. Does he look like an international jewel thief?" Lilah strolled lazily up the steps, a short-haired black dog at her heels. The dog jumped at Sloan, tripped, righted himself and managed to get his front paws settled on the knees of Sloan's jeans.

"I wondered where you'd wandered off to," Lilah continued, and cupped a hand under Max's chin to examine his face. "You look a little better," she decided as the dog started to sniff at Max's bare toes. "That's Fred," she told him. "He only bites criminals."

"Oh. Good."

"Since you have his seal of approval, why don't you come down? You can sit in the sun and have some lunch."

He would dearly love to sit, he realized and let Lilah lead him away. "Is this really your house?"

"Hearth and home. My great-grandfather built it just after the turn of the century. Look out for Fred." The dog dashed between them, stepped on his own ear and yelped. Max, who'd gone through a long clumsy stage himself, felt immediate sympathy. "We're thinking of giving him ballet lessons," she said as the dog struggled back to his feet. Noting the blank look on Max's face, she patted his cheek. "I think you could use some of Aunt Coco's chicken soup."

She made him sit and kept an eye on him while he ate. Her protective instincts were usually reserved for family or small, wounded birds. But something about the man tugged at her. He seemed so out of his element, she thought. And helpless with it.

Something was going on behind those big blue eyes, she thought. Something beyond the fatigue. She could almost see him struggle to put one mental foot in front of the other.

He began to think that the soup had saved his life as surely as Lilah had. It slid warm and vital into his system. "I fell out of a boat," he said abruptly.

"That would explain it."

"I don't know what I was doing on a boat, exactly."

In the chair beside him she brought up her limber legs to settle in the lotus position. "Taking a vacation?"

"No." His brow furrowed. "No, I don't take vacations."

"Why not?" She reached over to take one of the crackers from his plate. She wore a trio of glittering rings on her hand.

"Work."

"School's out," she said with a lazy stretch.

"I always teach summer courses. Except..." Something was tapping at the edges of his brain, tauntingly. "I was going to do something else this summer. A research project. And I was going to start a book."

"A book, really?" She savored the cracker as if it were laced with caviar. He had to admire her basic, sensual enjoyment. "What kind?"

Her words jerked him back. He'd never told anyone about his plans to write. No one who knew him would have believed that studious, steady-as-she-goes Quartermain dreamed of being a novelist. "It's just something I've been thinking of for a while, but I had a chance to work on this project...a family history."

"Well, that would suit you. I was a terrible student. Lazy," she said with a smile in her eyes. "I can't imagine anyone wanting to make a career out of a classroom. Do you like it?"

It wasn't a matter of liking it. It was what he did. "I'm good at it." Yes, he realized, he was good at it. His students learned—some more than others. His lectures were well attended and well received.

"That's not the same thing. Can I see your hand?"

"My what?"

"Your hand," she repeated, and took it, turning it palm up. "Hmm."

"What are you doing?" For a heady moment, he thought she would press her lips to it.

"Looking at your palm. More intelligence than intuitiveness. Or maybe you just trust your brains more than your instincts."

Staring at the top of her bent head, he gave a nervous laugh. "You don't really believe in that sort of thing. Palm reading."

"Of course—but it's not just the lines, it's the feeling." She glanced up briefly with a smile that was at once languid and electric. "You have very nice hands. Look here." She skimmed a finger along his palm and had him swallowing. "You've got a long life ahead of you, but see this break? Near-death experience."

"You're making it up."

"They're your lines," she reminded him. "A good imagination. I think you'll write that book—but you'll have to work on that self-confidence."

She looked up again, a trace of sympathy on her face. "Rough childhood?"

"Yes—no." Embarrassed, he cleared his throat. "No more than anyone's, I imagine."

She lifted a brow, but let it pass. "Well, you're a big boy now." In one of her casual moves, she slid her hair back then studied his hand again. "Yes, see, this represents careers, and there's a branch off this way. Things have been very comfortable for you professionally—you've hoed yourself a nice little rut—but this other line spears off. Could be that literary effort. You'll have to make the choice."

"I really don't think—"

"Sure you do. You've been thinking about it for years. Now here's the Mound of Venus. Hmm. You're a very sensual man." Her gaze flicked up to his again. "And a very thorough lover."

He couldn't take his eyes off her mouth. It was full, unpainted and curved teasingly. Kissing her would be like sinking into a dream—the dark and erotic kind. And if a man survived it, he would pray never to wake up.

She felt something creep in over her amusement. Something unexpected and arousing. It was the way he looked at her, she thought. With such complete absorption. As though she were the only woman in the world— certainly the only one who mattered.

There couldn't be a female alive who wouldn't weaken a bit under that look.

For the first time in her life she felt off balance with a man. She was used to having the controls, of setting the tone in her own unstudied way. From the time she'd understood that boys were different from girls, she had used the power she'd been born with to guide members of the opposite sex down a path of her own choosing.

Yet he was throwing her off with a look.

Struggling for a casualness that had always come easily, she started to release his hand. Max surprised them both by turning his over to grip hers.

"You are," he said slowly, "the most beautiful woman I've ever seen."

It was a standard line, even a cliché, and shouldn't have had her heart leaping. She made herself smile as she drew away. "Don't get out much, do you, Professor?"

There was a flicker of annoyance in his eyes before he made himself settle back. It was as much with himself as with her. He'd never been the hand-holding

Casanova type. Nor had he ever been put so neatly back in his place.

"No, but that was a simple statement of fact. Now, I guess I'm supposed to cross your palm with silver, but I'm fresh out."

"Palm reading's on the house." Because she was sorry she'd been so glib and abrupt, she smiled again. "When you're feeling better, I'll take you up for a tour of the haunted tower."

"I can't wait."

His dry response had her laughing. "I have a feeling about you, Max. I think you could be a lot of fun when you forget to be intense and thoughtful. Now I'm going downstairs so you can have some quiet. Be a good boy and get some more rest."

He might have been weak, but he wasn't a boy. Max rose as she did. Though the move surprised her, she gave him one of her slow, languid smiles. His color was coming back, she noted. His eyes were clear and, because he was only an inch or so taller than she, nearly on level with hers.

"Is there something else I can get you, Max?"

He felt steadier and took a moment to be grateful. "Just an answer. Are you involved with anyone?"

Her brow lifted as she swept her hair over her shoulder. "In what way?"

"It's a simple question, Lilah, and deserves a simple answer."

The lecturing quality of his tone had her frowning at him. "If you mean am I emotionally or sexually involved with a man, the answer is no. At the moment."

"Good." The vague irritation in her eyes pleased him. He'd wanted a response, and he'd gotten one.

"Look, Professor, I pulled you out of the drink. You strike me as being too intelligent a man to fall for that gratitude transference."

This time he smiled. "Transference to what?"

"Lust seems appropriate."

"You're right. I know the difference—especially when I'm feeling both at the same time." His own words surprised him. Maybe the near-death experience had rattled his brains. For a moment she looked as though she would swipe at him. Then abruptly, and beautifully, she laughed.

"I guess that was another simple statement of fact. You're an interesting man, Max."

And, she told herself as she carried the tray inside, harmless.

She hoped.

Chapter Three

Even after he'd arranged to have funds wired from his account in Ithaca, the Calhouns wouldn't consider Max's suggestion that he move to a hotel. In truth, he didn't put up much of a fight. He'd never been pampered before, or fussed over. More, he'd never been made to feel part of a big, boisterous family. They took him in with a casual kind of hospitality that was both irresistible and gracious.

He was coming to know them and appreciate them for their varied personalities and family unity. It was a house where something always seemed to be happening and where everyone always had something to say. For someone who had grown up an only child, in a home where his bookishness had been considered a flaw, it was a revelation to be among people who celebrated their own, and each other's, interests.

C.C. was an auto mechanic who talked about engine blocks and carried the mysterious glow of a new bride. Amanda, brisk and organized, held the assistant manager's position at a nearby hotel. Suzanna ran a gardening business and devoted herself to her children. No one mentioned their father. Coco ran the house, cooked lavish meals and appreciated male company. She'd only made Max nervous when she'd threatened to read his tea leaves.

Then there was Lilah. He discovered she worked as a naturalist at Acadia National Park. She liked long naps, classical music and her aunt's elaborate desserts. When the mood struck her, she could sit, sprawled in a chair, prodding little details of his life from him. Or she could curl up in a sunbeam like a cat, blocking him and everything else around her out of her thoughts while she drifted into one of her private daydreams. Then she would stretch and smile and let them all in again.

She remained a mystery to him, a combination of smoldering sensuality and untouched innocence—of staggering openness and unreachable solitude.

Within three days, his strength had returned and his stay at the The Towers was open-ended. He knew the sensible thing to do was leave, use his funds to purchase a one-way ticket back to New York and see if he could pick up a few summer tutoring jobs.

But he didn't feel sensible.

It was his first vacation and, however he had been thrust into it, he wanted to enjoy it. He liked waking up in the morning to the sound of the sea and the smell of it. It relieved him that his accident hadn't caused him to fear or dislike the water. There was something incredibly relaxing about standing on the terrace, looking across indigo or emerald water and seeing the distant clumps of islands.

And if his shoulder still troubled him from time to time, he could sit out and let the afternoon sun bake the ache away. There was time for books. An hour, even two, sitting in the shade gobbling up a novel or biography from the Calhoun library.

His life had been full of timetables, never timelessness. Here, in The Towers, with its whispers of the past, momentum of the present and hope for the future, he could indulge in it.

Underneath the simple pleasure of having no schedule to meet, no demands to answer, was his growing fascination with Lilah.

She glided in and out of the house. Leaving in the morning, she was neat and tidy in her park service uniform, her fabulous hair wound in a neat braid. Drifting home later, she would change into one of her flowing skirts or a pair of sexy shorts. She smiled at him, spoke to him, and kept a friendly but tangible distance.

He contented himself with scribbling in a notebook or entertaining Suzanna's two children, Alex and Jenny, who were already showing signs of summer boredom. He could walk in the gardens or along the cliffs, keep Coco company in the kitchen or watch the workmen in the west wing.

The wonder of it was, he could do as he chose.

He sat on the lawn, Alex and Jenny hunched on either side of him like eager frogs. The sun was a hazy silver disk behind a sheet of clouds. Playful and brisk, the breeze carried the scent of lavender and rosemary from a nearby rockery. There were butterflies dancing in the grass, easily eluding Fred's pursuits. Nearby a bird trilled insistently from the branch of a wind-gnarled oak.

Max was spinning a tale of a young boy caught up in the terrors and excitement of the revolutionary war. In weaving fact with fiction, he was keeping the children entertained and indulging in his love of storytelling.

"I bet he killed whole packs of dirty redcoats," Alex said gleefully. At six, he had a vivid and violent imagination.

"Packs of them," Jenny agreed. She was a year younger than her brother and only too glad to keep pace. "Single-handed."

"The Revolution wasn't all guns and bayonets, you know." It amused Max to see the young mouths pout at the lack of mayhem. "A lot of battles were won through intrigue and espionage."

Alex struggled with the words a moment then brightened. "Spies?"

"Spies," Max agreed, and ruffled the boy's dark hair. Because he had experienced the lack himself, he recognized Alex's hunger for a male bond.

Using a teenage boy as the catalyst, he took them through Patrick Henry's stirring speeches, Samuel Adams's courageous Sons of Liberty, through the politics and purpose of a rebellious young country to the Boston Tea Party.

Then as he had the young hero heaving chests of tea into the shallow water of Boston Harbor, Max saw Lilah drifting across the lawn.

She moved with languid ease over the grass, a graceful gypsy with her filmy chiffon skirt teased by the wind. Her hair was loose, tumbling free over the thin straps of a pale green blouse. Her feet were bare, her arms adorned with dozens of slim bracelets.

Fred raced over to greet her, leaped and yipped and made her laugh. As she bent to pet him, one of the straps slid down her arm. Then the dog bounded off, tripping himself up, to continue his fruitless chase of butterflies.

She straightened, lazily pushing the strap back into place as she continued across the grass. He caught her scent—wild and free—before she spoke.

"Is this a private party?"

"Max is telling a story," Jenny told her, and tugged on her aunt's skirt.

"A story?" The array of colored beads in her ears danced as she lowered to the grass. "I like stories."

"Tell Lilah, too." Jenny shifted closer to her aunt and began to play with her bracelets.

"Yes." There was laughter in her voice, an answering humor in her eyes as they met Max's. "Tell Lilah, too."

She knew exactly what effect she had on a man, he thought. Exactly. "Ah...where was I?"

"Jim had black cork all over his face and was tossing the cursed tea into the harbor," Alex reminded him. "Nobody got shot yet."

"Right." As much for his own defense against Lilah as for the children, Max put himself back on the frigate with the fictional Jim. He could feel the chill of the air and the heat of excitement. With a natural skill he considered a basic part of teaching, he drew out the suspense, deftly coloring his characters, describing an historical event in a way that had Lilah studying him with a new interest and respect.

Though it ended with the rebels outwitting the British, without firing a shot, even the bloodthirsty Alex wasn't disappointed.

"They won!" He jumped up and gave a war hoot. "I'm a Son of Liberty and you're a dirty redcoat," he told his sister.

"Uh-uh." She sprang to her feet.

"No taxation without restoration," Alex bellowed, and went flying for the house with Jenny hot on his heels and Fred lumbering after them both.

"Close enough," Max murmured.

"Pretty crafty, Professor." Lilah leaned back on her elbows to watch him through half-closed eyes. "Making history entertaining."

"It is," he told her. "It's not just dates and names, it's people."

"The way you tell it. But when I was in school you were supposed to know what happened in 1066 in the same way you were supposed to memorize the multiplication tables." Lazily she rubbed a bare foot over her calf. "I still can't remember the twelves, or what happened in 1066—unless that was when Hannibal took those elephants across the Alps."

He grinned at her. "Not exactly."

"There, you see?" She stretched, long and limber as a cat. Her head drifted back, her hair spreading over the summer grass. Her shoulders rolled so that the wayward strap slipped down again. The pleasure of the small indulgence showed on her face. "And I think I usually fell asleep by the time we got to the Continental Congress."

When he realized he was holding his breath, he released it slowly. "I've been thinking about doing some tutoring."

Her eyes slitted open. "You can take the boy out of

the classroom," she murmured, then arched a brow. "So, what do you know about flora and fauna?"

"Enough to know a rabbit from a petunia."

Delighted, she sat up again to lean toward him. "That's very good, Professor. If the mood strikes, maybe we can exchange expertise."

"Maybe."

He looked so cute, she thought, sitting on the sunny grass in borrowed jeans and T-shirt, his hair falling over his forehead. He'd been getting some sun, so that the pallor was replaced by the beginnings of a tan. The ease she felt convinced her that she'd been foolish to be unsteady around him before. He was just a nice man, a bit befuddled by circumstances, who'd aroused her sympathies and her curiosity. To prove it, she laid a hand on the side of his face.

Max saw the amusement in her eyes, the little private joke that curved her lips before she touched them to his in a light, friendly kiss. As if satisfied with the result, she smiled, leaned back and started to speak. He circled a hand around her wrist.

"I'm not half-dead this time, Lilah."

Surprise came first. He saw it register then fade into a careless acceptance. Damn it, he thought as he slid a hand behind her neck. She was so certain there would be nothing. With a combination of wounded pride and fluttery panic, he pressed his lips to hers.

She enjoyed kissing—the affection of it, the elemental physical enjoyment. And she liked him. Because of it, she leaned into the kiss, expecting a nice tingle, a comforting warmth. But she hadn't expected the jolt.

The kiss bounced through her system, starting with her lips, zipping to her stomach, vibrating into her fingertips. His mouth was very firm, very serious—and very smooth. The texture of it had a quiet sound of pleasure escaping, like a child might make after a first taste of chocolate. Before the first sensation could be fully absorbed, others were drifting through to tangle and mix.

Flowers and hot sun. The scent of soap and sweat. Smooth, damp lips and the light scrape of teeth. Her own sigh, a mere shifting of air, and the firm press of his fingers on the sensitive nape of her neck. There was something more than simple pleasure here, she realized. Something sweeter and far less tangible.

Enchanted, she lifted her hand from the carpet of grass to skim it through his hair.

He was reexperiencing the sensation of drowning, of being pulled under by something strong and dangerous. This time he had no urge to fight. Fascinated, he slid his tongue over hers, tasting those secret flavors. Rich and dark and seductive, they mirrored her scent, the scent that had already insinuated itself into his system so that he thought he would taste that as well, each time he took a breath.

He felt something shift inside him, stretch and grow and heat until it gripped him hard by the throat.

She was outrageously sexual, unabashedly erotic, and more frightening than any woman he had known. Again he had the image of a mermaid sitting on a rock, combing her hair and luring helplessly seduced men to destruction with the promise of overwhelming pleasures.

The instinct for survival kicked in, so that he drew back. Lilah stayed as she was, eyes closed, lips parted. It wasn't until that moment that he realized he still held her wrist and that her pulse was scrambling under his fingers.

Slowly, holding on to that drugging weightlessness a moment longer, she opened her eyes. She skimmed her tongue over her lips to capture the clinging flavor of his. Then she smiled.

"Well, Dr. Quartermain, it seems history's not the only thing you're good at. How about another lesson?" Wanting more, she leaned forward, but Max scrambled up. The ground, he discovered, was as unsteady as the deck of a ship.

"I think one's enough for today."

Curious, she swung her hair back to look up at him. "Why?"

"Because..." Because if he kissed her again, he'd have to touch her. And if he touched her—and he desperately wanted to touch her—he would have to make love with her, there on the sunny lawn in full sight of the house. "Because I don't want to take advantage of you."

"Advantage of me?" Touched and amused, she smiled. "That's very sweet."

"I'd appreciate it if you wouldn't make me sound like a fool," he said tightly.

"Was I?" The smile turned thoughtful. "Being a sweet man doesn't make you a fool, Max. It's just that most men I know would be more than happy to take advantage. Tell you what, before you take offense at that, why don't we go inside? I'll show you Bianca's tower."

He'd already taken offense and was about to say so when her last words struck a chord. "Bianca's tower?"

"Yes. I'd like to show you." She lifted a hand, waiting.

He was frowning at her, struggling to fit the name "Bianca" into place. Then with a shake of his head, he helped her to her feet. "Fine. Let's go."

* * *

He'd already explored some of the house, the maze of rooms, some empty, some crowded with furniture and boxes. From the outside, the house was part fortress, part manor, with sparkling windows, graceful porches married to jutting turrets and parapets. Inside, it was a rambling labyrinth of shadowed hallways, sun-washed rooms, scarred floors and gleaming banisters. It had already captivated him.

She took him up a set of circular stairs to a door at the top of the east wing.

"Give it a shove, will you, Max?" she asked, and he was forced to thud the wood hard with his good shoulder. "I keep meaning to ask Sloan to fix this." Taking his hand, she walked inside.

It was a large, circular room, ringed with curving windows. A light layer of dust lay softly on the floor, but someone had tossed a few colorful pillows onto the window seat. An old floor lamp with a stained and tassled shade stood nearby.

"I imagine she had lovely things up here once," Lilah began. "To keep her company. She used to come up here to be alone, to think."

"Who?"

"Bianca. My great-grandmother. Come look at the view." Feeling a need to share it with him, she drew him to the window. From there it was all water and rock. It should have seemed lonely, Max thought. Instead it was exhilarating and heartbreaking all at once. When he put a hand to the glass, Lilah glanced over in surprise. She had done the same countless times, as if wishing for something just out of reach.

"It's…sad." He'd meant to say beautiful or breathtaking, and frowned.

"Yes. But sometimes it's comforting, too. I always feel close to Bianca in here."

Bianca. The name was like an insistent buzz in his head.

"Has Aunt Coco told you the story yet?"

"No. Is there a story?"

"Of course." She gave him a curious look. "I just wondered if she'd given you the Calhoun version rather than what's in the press."

A faint throbbing began in his temple where the wound was healing. "I don't know either version."

After a moment, she continued. "Bianca threw herself through this window on one of the last nights of summer in 1913. But her spirit stayed behind."

"Why did she kill herself?"

"Well, it's a long story." Lilah settled on the window seat, her chin comfortably propped on her knees, and told him.

Max listened to the tale of an unhappy wife, trapped in a loveless marriage during the heady years before the Great War. Bianca had married Fergus Calhoun, a wealthy financier, and had borne him three children. While summering on Mount Desert Island, she had met a young artist. From an old date book the Calhouns had unearthed, they knew his name had been Christian, but nothing more. The rest was legend, that had been passed down to the children from their nanny who had been Bianca's confidante.

The young artist and the unhappy wife had fallen in love, deeply. Torn between duty and her heart, Bianca had agonized over her choice and had ultimately decided to leave her husband. She had taken a few personal items, known now as Bianca's treasure, and had hidden them away in preparation. Among them had been an emerald necklace, given to her on the birth of her first son and second child, Lilah's grandfather. But rather than going to her lover, Bianca had thrown herself through the tower window. The emeralds have never been found.

"We didn't know the story until a few months ago," Lilah added. "Though I'd seen the emeralds."

His mind was whirling. Nagged by the pain, he pressed his fingers to his temple. "You've seen them?"

She smiled. "I dreamed about them. Then during a séance—"

"A séance," he said weakly, and sat.

"That's right." She laughed and patted his hand. "We were having a séance, and C.C. had a vision." He made a strangled sound in his throat that had her laughing again. "You had to be there, Max. Anyway, C.C. saw the necklace, and that's when Aunt Coco decided it was time to pass on the Calhoun legend. To get where we are today, Trent fell in love with C.C. and decided not to buy The Towers. We were in pretty bad shape and were on the point of being forced to sell. He came up with the idea of turning the west wing into a hotel, with the St. James's name. You know the St. James hotels?"

Trenton St. James, Max thought. Lilah's brother-in-law owned one of the biggest hotel corporations in the country. "By reputation."

"Well, Trent hired Sloan to handle the renovations— and Sloan fell for Amanda. All in all, it couldn't have worked out better. We were able to keep the house, combine it with business, and culled two romances out of the bargain."

Annoyance flickered into her eyes, darkening them. "The downside has been that the story about the necklace leaked, and we've been plagued with hopeful treasure hunters and out-and-out thieves. Just a few weeks ago, some creep nearly killed Amanda and stole stacks of the papers we'd been sorting through to try to find a clue to the necklace."

"Papers," he repeated as a sickness welled in his stomach. It was coming back now and with such force he felt as though he were being battered on the rocks again. Calhoun, emeralds, Bianca.

"What's wrong, Max?" Concerned, Lilah leaned over to lay a hand on his brow. "You're white as a sheet. You've been up too long," she decided. "Let me take you down so you can rest."

"No, I'm fine. It's nothing." He jerked away to rise and pace the room. How was he going to tell her? How could he tell her, after she had saved his life, taken care of him? After he'd kissed her? The Calhouns had opened their home to him, without hesitation, without question. They had trusted him. How could he tell Lilah that he had, however inadvertently, been working with men who were planning to steal from her?

Yet he had to. Marrow-deep honesty wouldn't permit anything else.

"Lilah…" He turned back to see her watching him, a combination of concern and wariness in her eyes. "The boat. I remember the boat."

Relief had her smiling. "That's good. I thought it would come back to you if you stopped worrying. Why don't you sit down, Max? It's easier on the brain."

"No." The refusal was sharp as he concentrated on

her face. "The boat—the man who hired me. His name was Caufield. Ellis Caufield."

She spread her hands. "And?"

"The name doesn't mean anything?"

"No, should it?"

Maybe he was wrong, Max thought. Maybe he was letting her family story meld in his mind with his own experience. "He's about six foot, very trim. About forty. Dark-blond hair graying at the temples."

"Okay."

Max let out a frustrated breath. "He contacted me at Cornell about a month ago and offered me a job. He wanted me to sort through, catalogue and research some family papers. I'd get a generous salary, and several weeks on a yacht—plus all my expenses and time to work on my book."

"So, seeing as you're not brain damaged, you took the job."

"Yes, but damn it, Lilah, the papers—the receipts, the letters, the ledgers. They had your name on them."

"Mine?"

"Calhoun." He jammed his useless hands into his pockets. "Don't you understand? I was hired, and worked on that boat for a week, researching your family history from the papers that were stolen from you."

She only stared. It seemed a long time to Max before she unfolded herself from the window seat and stood. "You're telling me that you've been working for the man who tried to kill my sister?"

"Yes."

She never took her eyes from his. He could almost feel her trying to get into his thoughts, but when she spoke, her voice was very cool. "Why are you telling me this now?"

Frazzled, he dragged a hand through his hair. "I didn't remember it all until now, until you told me about the emeralds."

"That's odd, isn't it?"

He watched the shutter come down over her eyes and nodded. "I don't expect you to believe me, but I didn't remember. And when I took the job, I didn't know."

She continued to watch him carefully, measuring every word, every gesture, every expression. "You know, it seemed strange to me that you hadn't heard about the necklace, or the robbery. It's been in the press for weeks. You'd have to be living in a cave not to have heard."

"Or a classroom," he murmured. Caufield's mocking words about having more intelligence than wit came back to him and made him wince. "Look, I'll tell you whatever I can before I leave."

"Leave?"

"I can't imagine any of you will want me to stay after this."

She considered him, instinct warring against common sense. With a long sigh, she lifted a hand. "I think you'd better tell the whole story to the whole family, all at once. Then we'll decide what to do about it."

It was Max's first family meeting. He hadn't grown up in a democracy, but under his father's uncompromising dictatorship. The Calhouns did things differently. They gathered around the big mahogany dining room table, so completely united that Max felt like an intruder for the first time since he'd awakened upstairs. They listened, occasionally asking questions as he repeated what he had told Lilah in the tower.

"You didn't check his references?" Trent asked. "You

just contracted to do a job with a man you'd never met, and knew nothing about?"

"There didn't seem to be any reason to. I'm not a businessman," he said wearily. "I'm a teacher."

"Then you won't object if we check yours." This from Sloan.

Max met the suspicious eyes levelly. "No."

"I already have," Amanda put in. Her fingers were tapping against the wood of the table as all eyes turned to her. "It seemed the logical step, so I made a couple of calls."

"Leave it to Mandy," Lilah muttered. "I guess it never occurred to you to discuss it with the rest of us."

"No."

"Girls," Coco said from the head of the table. "Don't start."

"I think Amanda should have talked about this." The Calhoun temper edged Lilah's voice. "It concerns all of us. Besides, what business does she have poking into Max's life?"

They began to argue heatedly, all four sisters tossing in opinions and objections. Sloan kicked back to let it run its course. Trent closed his eyes. Max merely stared. They were discussing him. Didn't they realize they were arguing about him, tossing him back and forth across the table like a Ping-Pong ball?

"Excuse me," he began, and was totally ignored. He tried again and earned his first smile from Sloan. "Damn it, knock it off!" It was his annoyed professor's voice and did the trick. All of the women stopped to turn on him with irritated eyes.

"Look, buster," C.C. began, but he cut her off.

"You look. In the first place, why would I be telling

you everything if I had some ulterior motive? And since you want to corroborate who I am and what I do, why don't you stop pecking at each other long enough to find out?"

"Because we like to peck at each other," Lilah told him grandly. "And we don't like anyone getting in the way while we're at it."

"That'll do." Coco took advantage of the lull. "Since Amanda's already checked on Max—though it was a bit impolite—"

"Sensible," Amanda objected.

"Rude," Lilah corrected.

They might have been off and running again, but Suzanna held up a hand. "Whatever it was, it's done. I think we should hear what Amanda found out."

"As I was saying." Amanda flicked a glance over at Lilah. "I made a couple of calls. The dean of Cornell speaks very highly of Max. As I recall the terms were 'brilliant' and 'dedicated.' He's considered one of the foremost experts on American history in the country. He graduated magna cum laude at twenty, and had his doctorate by twenty-five."

"Egghead," Lilah said with a comforting smile when Max shifted in his seat.

"Our Dr. Quartermain," Amanda continued, "comes from Indiana, is single and has no criminal record. He's been on the staff at Cornell for over eight years, and has published several well-received articles. His most recent was an overview of the social-political atmosphere in America prior to World War I. In academic circles, he's considered a wunderkind, serious minded, unflaggingly responsible, with unlimited potential." Sensing his embarrassment, Amanda softened her tone. "I'm sorry for intruding, Max, but I didn't want to take any chances, not with my family."

"We're all sorry." Suzanna smiled at him. "We've had an unsettling couple of months."

"I understand that." And they certainly couldn't know how much he detested the term *wunderkind.* "If my academic profile eases your minds, that's fine."

"There's one more thing," Suzanna continued. "None of this explains what you were doing in the water the night Lilah found you."

Max gathered his thoughts while they waited. It was easy to take himself back now, as easy as it was for him to put himself into the Battle of Bull Run or Woodrow Wilson's White House.

"I'd been working on the papers. A storm was coming in so the sea was rough. I guess I'm not much of a sailor. I was trying to crawl out on deck, for some air, when I heard Caufield talking to Captain Hawkins."

As concisely as he could, he told them what he had heard, how he had realized what he'd gotten into.

"I don't know what I was going to do. I had some wild idea about getting the papers and getting off the boat so I could take them to the police. Not very brilliant considering the circumstances. In any case, they caught me. Caufield had a gun, but this time the storm was on my side. I got up on deck, and took my chances in the water."

"You jumped overboard, in the middle of a storm?" Lilah asked.

"It wasn't very smart."

"It was very brave," she corrected.

"Not when you consider he was shooting at me." Frowning, Max rubbed a hand over the bandage on his temple.

"The way you describe this Ellis Caufield doesn't fit." Amanda tapped her fingers again as she thought it through. "Livingston, the man who stole the papers was dark haired, only about thirty."

"So, he dyed his hair." Lilah lifted her hands. "He couldn't come back using the same name and the same appearance. The police have his description."

"I hope you're right." A slow, humorless smile spread over Sloan's face. "I hope the sonofabitch is back so I can have another go at him."

"So we all can have another go at him," C.C. corrected. "The question is, what do we do now?"

They began to argue about that, with Trent telling his wife she wasn't going to do anything—Amanda reminding him it was a Calhoun problem—Sloan suggesting hotly that she keep out of it. Coco decided it was time for brandy and was ignored.

"He thinks I'm dead," Max murmured, almost to himself. "So he feels safe. He's probably still close by, on the same boat. The *Windrider*."

"You remember the boat?" Lilah held up a hand, signaling for silence. "You can describe it?"

"In detail," Max told her with a small smile. "It was my first yacht."

"So we take that information to the police." Trent glanced around the table, then nodded. "And we do a little checking ourselves. The ladies know the island as well as they know this house. If he's on it, or around it, we'll find him."

"I'm looking forward to it." Sloan glanced over at Max and went with his instincts. "You in, Quartermain?"

Surprised, Max blinked, then found himself smiling. "Yeah, I'm in."

* * *

I went to Christian's cottage. Perhaps it was risky as I might have been seen by some acquaintance, but I wanted so badly to see where he lived, how he lived, what small things he kept around him.

It's a small place near the water, a square wooden cottage with its rooms crowded with his paintings and smelling of turpentine. Above the kitchen is a sun-drenched loft for his studio. It seemed to me like a doll's house with its pretty windows and low ceilings—old leafy trees shading the front and a narrow porch dancing along the back where we could sit and watch the water.

Christian says that at low tide the water level drops so that you can walk across the smooth rocks to the little glade of trees beyond. And at night, the air is full of sound. Musical crickets, the hoot of owls, the lap of temperate water.

I felt at home there, as quietly content as I have been in my life. It seemed to me that we had lived there together for years. When I told Christian, he gathered me close, just to hold me.

"I love you, Bianca," he said. "I wanted you to come here. I needed to see you in my house, watch you stand among my things." When he drew me away, he was smiling. "Now, I'll always see you here, and I'll never be without you."

I wanted to swear to him I would stay. God, the words leaped into my throat only to be blocked there by duty. Wretched duty. He must have sensed it for he kissed me then, as if to seal the words inside.

I had only an hour with him. We both knew I would have to go back to my husband, to my children, to the life I had chosen before I met him. I felt his arms around me, tasted his lips, sensed the straining need inside him that was such a vibrant echo of my own.

"I want you." I heard my own whisper and felt no shame. "Touch me, Christian. Let me belong to you." My heart was racing as I pressed wantonly against him. "Make love to me. Take me to your bed."

How tightly his arms gripped me, so tightly I couldn't get my breath. Then his hands were on my face, and I felt the tremor in his fingertips. His eyes were nearly black. So much could be read there. Passion, love, desperation, regret.

"Do you know how often I've dreamed of it? How many nights I've lain awake aching for you?" Then he released me to stride across the room to where my portrait hung on his wall. "I want you, Bianca, every time I take a breath. And I love you too much to take what can't be mine."

"Christian—"

"Do you think I could let you go if I'd ever touched you?" There was anger now, ripe and violent as he whirled back. "I hate knowing that we sneak like sinners just to spend an hour together, as innocent as children. If I don't have the strength to turn away from you completely, then I will have enough to keep you from taking a step you'd only regret."

"How could I regret belonging to you?"

"Because you already belong to someone else. And every time you go back to him, I dream of killing him with my bare hands if only because he can look at you when I can't. If we took this last step, I'd leave you no choice. There would be no going back to him, Bianca. No going back to your home, or your life."

*And I knew it was true, as he stood between me and
the image of me he'd created.*

*So I left him to come home, to tie a ribbon in Colleen's
hair, to chase a ball with Ethan, to dry Sean's tears when
he scraped his knee. To dine in miserable politeness with
a husband who is more and more of a stranger to me.*

*Christian's words were true, and it is a truth I must
face. The time is coming when I will no longer be able
to live in both worlds, but must choose one, only one.*

Chapter Four

"I have the most marvelous idea," Coco announced. Like a ship in full sail, she streamed into the kitchen where Lilah, Max, Suzanna and her family were having breakfast.

"Good for you," Lilah said over a bowl of chocolate-chip ice cream. "Anyone who can think at this hour deserves a medal, or should be committed."

Like a mother hen, Coco checked the herbs she had potted on the window. She clucked over the basil before she turned back. "I have no idea why I didn't think of it before. It's really so—"

"Alex is kicking me under the table."

"Alex, don't kick your sister," Suzanna said mildly. "Jenny, don't interrupt."

"I wasn't kicking her." Milk dribbled down Alex's chin. "She got her knee in the way of my foot."

"Did not."

"Did too."

"Turkey face."

"Booger head."

"Alex." Suzanna bit down on the inside of her lip to maintain the properly severe maternal disapproval. "Do you want to eat that cereal or wear it?"

"She started it," he muttered.

"Did not," Jenny said under her breath.

"Did too."

Another glance at their mother had them subsiding to eye each other with grim dislike over their cereal bowls.

"Now that that's settled." Amused, Lilah licked her spoon. "What's your marvelous idea, Aunt Coco?"

"Well." She fluffed her hair, absently checking her reflection in the toaster, approving it, then beaming. "It all has to do with Max. Really it's so obvious. But, of course, we were worried about his health, then it's so difficult to think clearly with this construction going on. Do you know one of those young men was out on the terrace this morning in nothing but a pair of jeans and a tool belt? Very distracting." She peeked out of the kitchen window, just in case.

"I'm sorry I missed it." Lilah winked at Max. "Was it the guy with the long blond hair tied back with a leather thong?"

"No, the one with dark curly hair and a mustache. I must say, he's extremely well built. I suppose one would keep fit swinging hammers or whatever all day. The noise is a bother, though. I hope it doesn't disturb you, Max."

"No." He'd learned to flow with Coco's rambling thought patterns. "Would you like some coffee?"

"Oh, that's sweet of you. I believe I will." She sat

while he got up to pour her a cup. "They've literally transformed the billiard room already. Of course, we've a long way to go—thank you, dear," she added when Max set a cup of coffee in front of her. "And all those tarps and tools and lumber make things unsightly. But it will all be worth it in the end." As she spoke, she doctored her coffee with cream and heaps of sugar. "Now, where was I?"

"A marvelous idea," Suzanna reminded her, putting a restraining hand on Alex's shoulder before he could fling any soggy cereal at his sister.

"Oh, yes." Coco set her cup down without taking a sip. "It came to me last night when I was doing the tarot cards. There were some personal matters I'd wanted to resolve, and I'd wanted to get a feel for this other business."

"What other business?" Alex wanted to know.

"Grown-up business." Lilah dug a knuckle into his ribs to make him laugh. "Boring."

"You guys better go find Fred." Suzanna checked her watch. "If you want to go with me today, you've got five minutes."

They were up and shooting out of the room like little bullets. Surreptitiously Max rubbed his shin where Alex's foot had connected.

"The cards, Aunt Coco?" Lilah said when the explosion was over.

"Yes. I learned that there was danger, past and future. Disconcerting." She cast a worried look over both her nieces. "But we're to have help dealing with it. There seemed to be two different sources of aid. One was cerebral, the other physical—potentially violent." Uneasy, she frowned a little. "I couldn't place the physical

source, though it seemed I should because it was from
someone familiar. I thought it might be from Sloan. He's
so, well, Western. But it wasn't. I'm quite sure it wasn't."
Brushing that aside, she smiled again. "But naturally the
cerebral source is Max."

"Naturally." Lilah patted his hand as he shifted uncomfortably in his chair. "Our resident genius."

"Don't tease him." Suzanna rose to take bowls to
the sink.

"Oh, he knows I don't just like him for his brain.
Don't you, Max?"

He was mortally afraid he would blush in a minute.
"If you keep interrupting your aunt, you'll be late for
work."

"And so will I," Suzanna pointed out. "What's the
idea, Aunt Coco?"

She'd started to drink again, and again set the coffee
down untouched. "That Max should do what he came
here to do." Smiling, she spread her manicured hands.
"Research the Calhouns. Find out as much as possible
about Bianca, Fergus, everyone involved. Not for that
awful Mr. Caufield or whatever his name is, but for us."

Intrigued, Lilah thought the idea over. "We've already
been through the papers."

"Not with Max's objective, and scholarly eye," Coco
pointed out. Already fond of him, she patted his shoulder. Her interpretation of the cards also had indicated
that he and Lilah would suit very well. "I'm sure if he
put his mind to it, he could come up with all kinds of
wonderful theories."

"It's a good idea." Suzanna came back to the table.
"How do you feel about it?"

Max considered. Though he didn't put any stock in

tarot cards, he didn't want to hurt Coco's feelings. Besides, however she had come up with the idea, it was sound. It would be a way of paying them back and a way to justify staying on in Bar Harbor a few more weeks.

"I'd like to do something. There's a good chance that even with the information I gave them the police won't find Caufield. While everyone's looking for him, I could be concentrating on Bianca and the necklace."

"There." Coco sat back. "I knew it."

"I'd wanted to check out the library, the newspaper, interview some of the older residents, but Caufield shut down the idea." The more he thought about it, the more Max liked the notion of working on his own. "Claimed he wanted everything to come out of the family papers, or his own sources." He moved his cup aside. "Obviously he couldn't give me a free hand or I'd find out the truth."

"Now you have a free hand," Lilah put in. It amused her that she could already see the wheels turning. "But I don't think you'll find the necklace in a library."

"But I may find a photograph of it, or a description."

Lilah simply smiled. "I've already given you that."

He didn't put much stock in dreams and visions, either, and shrugged. "All the same, I might find something tangible. And I'll certainly find something on Fergus and Bianca Calhoun."

"I suppose it'll keep you busy." Unoffended by his lack of faith in her mystical beliefs, Lilah rose. "You'll need a car to get around. Why don't you drop me off at work and use mine?"

Irked by her lack of faith in his research abilities, Max spent hours in the library. As always, he felt at home there, among stacks of books, in the center of the murmuring quiet, with a notebook at his elbow. To him, research was a quest—perhaps not as exciting as riding a white charger. It was a mystery to be solved, though the clues were less adventurous than a smoking gun or a trail of blood.

But with patience, cleverness and skill, he was a knight, or a detective, carefully working his way to an answer.

The fact that he had always been drawn to such places had disappointed his father bitterly, Max knew. Even as a boy he had preferred mental exercise over the physical. He had not picked up the torch to follow his father's blaze of glory on the high school football field. Nor had he added trophies to the shelf.

Lack of interest and a long klutzy adolescence had made him a failure in sports. He had detested hunting, and on the last outing his father had pressured him into had come up with a vicious asthma attack rather than a buck.

Even now, years later, he could remember his father's disgusted voice creeping into his hospital room.

"Damn boy's a pansy. Can't understand it. He'd rather read than eat. Every time I try to make a man out of him, he ends up wheezing like an old woman."

He'd gotten over the asthma, Max reminded himself. He'd even made something out of himself, though his father wouldn't consider it a man. And if he never felt completely adequate, at least he could feel competent.

Shrugging off the mood, he went back to his quest.

He did indeed find Fergus and Bianca. There were little gems of information peppered through the research books. In the familiar comfort of a library, Max took reams of notes and felt the excitement build.

He learned that Fergus Calhoun had been self-made, an Irish immigrant who through grit and shrewdness had become a man of wealth and influence. He'd landed in New York in 1888, young, poor and, like so many who had poured into Ellis Island, looking for his fortune. Within fifteen years, he had built an empire. And he had enjoyed flaunting it.

Perhaps to bury the impoverished youth he had been, he had surrounded himself with the opulent, muscling his way into society with wealth and will. It was in polite, exclusive society that he had met Bianca Muldoon, a young debutante of an old, established family with more gentility than money. He had built The Towers, determined to outdo the other vacationing rich, and had married Bianca the following year.

His golden touch had continued. His empire had grown, and so had his family with the birth of three children. Even the scandal of his wife's suicide in the summer of 1913 hadn't affected his monetary fortune.

Though he had become somewhat of a recluse after her death, he had continued to wield his power from The Towers. His daughter had never married and, estranged from her father, had gone to live in Paris. His youngest son had fled, after a peccadillo with a married woman, to the West Indies. Ethan, his eldest child, had married and had two children of his own, Judson, Lilah's father, and Cordelia Calhoun, now Coco McPike.

Ethan had died in a sailing accident, and Fergus had lived out the last years of his long life in an asylum, committed there by his family after several outbursts of violent and erratic behavior.

An interesting story, Max mused, but most of the details could have been gleaned from the Calhouns themselves. He wanted something else, some small tid-bit that would lead him in another direction.

He found it in a tattered and dusty volume titled *Summering in Bar Harbor.*

It was such a flighty and poorly written work that he nearly set it aside. The teacher in him had him reading on, as he would read a student's ill-prepared term paper. It deserved a C- at best, Max thought. Never in his life had he seen so many superlatives and cluttered adjectives on one page. Glamorously to gloriously, magnificent to miraculous. The author had been a wide-eyed admirer of the rich and famous, someone who saw them as royalty. Sumptuous, spectacular and splendiferous. The syntax made Max wince, but he plodded on.

There were two entire pages devoted to a ball given at The Towers in 1912. Max's weary brain perked up. The author had certainly attended, for the descriptions were in painstaking detail, from fashion to cuisine. Bianca Calhoun had worn gold silk, a flowing sheath with a beaded skirt. The color had set off the highlights in her titian hair. The scooped bodice had framed…the emeralds.

They were described in glowing and exacting detail. Once the adjectives and the romantic imagery were ed-ited, Max could see them. Scribbling notes, he turned the page. And stared.

It was an old photograph, perhaps culled from a news-paper print. It was fuzzy and blurred, but he had no trouble recognizing Fergus. The man was as rigid and stern-faced as the portrait the Calhouns kept over the mantel in the parlor. But it was the woman sitting in front of him that stopped Max's breath.

Despite the flaws of the photo, she was exquisite,

ethereally beautiful, timelessly lovely. And she was the image of Lilah. The porcelain skin, the slender neck left bare with a mass of hair swept up in the Gibson style. Oversize eyes he was certain would have been green. There was no smile in them, though her lips were curved.

Was it just the romance of the face, he wondered, or did he really see some sadness there?

She sat in an elegant lady's chair, her husband behind her, his hand on the back of the chair rather than on her shoulder. Still, it seemed to Max that there was a certain possessiveness in the stance. They were in formal wear—Fergus starched and pressed, Bianca draped and fragile. The stilted pose was captioned, Mr. and Mrs. Fergus Calhoun, 1912.

Around Bianca's neck, defying time, were the Calhoun emeralds.

The necklace was exactly as Lilah had described to him, the two glittering tiers, the lush single teardrop that dripped like emerald water. Bianca wore it with a coolness that turned its opulence into elegance and only intensified the power.

Max trailed a fingertip along each tier, almost certain he would feel the smoothness of the gems. He understood why such stones become legends, to haunt men's imaginations and fire their greed.

But it eluded him, a picture only. Hardly realizing what he was doing, he traced Bianca's face and thought of the woman who had inherited it.

There were women who haunt and inflame.

Lilah paused in her stroll down the nature path to give her latest group time to photograph and rest. They had had an excellent crowd in the park that day, with a hefty percentage of them interested enough to hike the trails and be guided by a naturalist. Lilah had been on her feet for the best part of eight hours, and had covered the same ground eight times—sixteen if she counted the return trip.

But she wasn't tired, yet. Nor did her lecture come strictly out of a guidebook.

"Many of the plants found on the island are typically northern," she began. "A few are subarctic, remaining since the retreat of the glaciers ten thousand years ago. More recent specimens were brought by Europeans within the last two hundred and fifty years."

With a patience that was a primary part of her, Lilah answered questions, distracted some of the younger crowd from trampling the wildflowers and fed information on the local flora to those who were interested. She identified the beach pea, the seaside goldenrod, the late-blooming harebell. It was her last group of the day, but she gave them as much time and attention as the first.

In any case she always enjoyed this seaside stroll, listening to the murmur of pebbles drifting in the surf or the echoing call of gulls, discovering for herself and the tourists what treasures lurked in the tide pools.

The breeze was light and balmy, carrying that ancient and mysterious scent that was the sea. Here the rocks were smooth and flat, worn to elegance by the patient ebb and flow of water. She could see the glitter of quartz running in long white rivers down the black stone. Overhead, the sky was a hard summer blue, nearly cloudless. Under it, boats glided, buoys clanged, orange markers bobbed.

She thought of the yacht, the *Windrider,* and though

she searched as she had on each tour, she saw nothing but sleek tourist boats or the sturdy crafts of lobstermen.

When she saw Max hiking the nature trail down to join the group, she smiled. He was on time, of course. She'd expected no less. She felt a slow tingle of warmth when his gaze lifted from his feet to her face. He really had wonderful eyes, she thought. Intent and serious, and just a little shy.

As always when she saw him, she had an urge to tease him and an underlying longing to touch. An interesting combination, she thought now, and one she couldn't remember experiencing with anyone else.

She looked so cool, he thought, the mannish uniform over the willowy feminine form. The military khaki and the dangle of gold and crystal at her ears. He wondered if she knew how suited she was to stand before the sea while it bubbled and swayed at her back.

"At the intertidal zone," she began, "life has acclimated to tidal change. In spring, we have the highest and lowest tides, with a rise and fall of 14.5 feet."

She went on in that easy, soothing voice, talking of intertidal creatures, survival and food chains. Even as she spoke, a gull glided to perch on a nearby rock to study the tourists with a beady, expectant eye. Cameras clicked. Lilah crouched down beside a tide pool. Fascinated by her description of life there, Max moved to see for himself.

There were long purple fans she called dulse, and she had the children in the group groaning when she told them it could be eaten raw or boiled. In the dark little pool of water, she found a wealth of living things, all waiting, she said, for the tide to come in again before they went back to business.

With a graceful fingertip she pointed out the sea anemones that looked more like flowers than animals, and the tiny slugs that preyed on them. The pretty shells that were mollusks and snails and whelks. She sounded like a marine biologist one moment and a stand-up comedian the next.

Her appreciative audience bombarded her with questions. Max caught one teenage boy staring at her with a moony kind of lust and felt instant sympathy.

Tossing her braid behind her back, she wound up the tour, explaining about the information available at the visitors' center, and the other naturalist tours. Some of the group started to meander their way back along the path, while others lingered behind to take more pictures. The teenager loitered behind his parents, asking any question his dazzled brain could form on the tide pools, the wildflowers and, though he wouldn't have looked twice at a robin, the birds. When he'd exhausted all angles, and his mother called impatiently for the second time, he trudged reluctantly off.

"This is one nature walk he won't forget anytime soon," Max commented.

She only smiled. "I like to think they'll all remember some pieces of it. Glad you could make it, Professor." She did what her instincts demanded and kissed him fully, softly on the mouth.

Looking back, the teenager experienced a flash of miserable envy. Max was simply knocked flat. Lilah's lips were still curved as she eased away.

"So," she asked him, "how was your day?"

Could a woman kiss like that then expect him to continue a normal conversation? Obviously this one could, he decided and took a long breath. "Interesting."

"Those are the best kind." She began to walk up the path that would lead back to the visitors' center. Arching a brow, she glanced over her shoulder. "Coming?"

"Yeah." With his hands in his pockets, he started after her. "You're very good."

Her laugh was light and warm. "Why, thank you."

"I meant—I was talking about your job."

"Of course you were." Companionably she tucked an arm through his. "It's too bad you missed the first twenty minutes of the last tour. We saw two slate-colored juncos, a double-crested cormorant and an osprey."

"It's always been one of my ambitions to see a slate-colored junco," he said, and made her laugh again. "Do you always do the same trail?"

"No, I move around. One of my favorites is Jordan Pond, or I might take a shift at the Nature Center, or hike up in the mountains."

"I guess that keeps it from getting boring."

"It's never boring, or I wouldn't last a day. Even on the same trail you see different things all the time. Look." She pointed to a thatch of plants with narrow leaves and faded pink blooms. "Rhodora," she told him. "A common azalea. A few weeks ago it was at peak. Stunning. Now the blooms will die off, and wait until spring." She brushed her fingertips over the leaves. "I like cycles. They're reassuring."

Though she claimed to be an unenergetic woman, she walked effortlessly along the trail, keeping an eye out for anything of interest. It might be lichen clinging to a rock, a sparrow in flight or a spray of hawkweed. She liked the scent here, the sea they were leaving behind, the green smell of trees that began to crowd in to block the view.

"I didn't realize that your job kept you on your feet most of the day."

"Which is why I prefer to stay off them at all other times." She tilted her head to look at him. "Tell you what though, the next time I have an afternoon, I'll give you a more in-depth tour. We can kill two birds with one stone, so to speak. Take in the scenery, and poke around for your friend, Caufield."

"I want you to stay out of it."

The statement took her so off guard that she walked another five feet before it registered. "You what?"

"I want you to stay out of it," he repeated. "I've been giving it a lot of thought."

"Have you?" If he had known her better, he might have recognized the hint of temper in the lazy tone. "And just how did you come to that particular conclusion?"

"He's dangerous." The voice, laced with hints of fanaticism came back clearly. "I think he might even be unbalanced. It's certain that he's violent. He's already shot at your sister, and at me. I don't want you getting in his way."

"It's not a matter of what you want. It's family business."

"It's been mine since I took a swim in a storm." Caught between sunlight and shade on the path, he stopped to put his hands on her shoulders. "You didn't hear him that night, Lilah. I did. He said nothing would stop him from getting the necklace, and he meant it. This is a job for the police, not for a bunch of women who—"

"A bunch of women who what?" she interrupted with a gleam in her eyes.

"Who are too emotionally involved to react cautiously."

"I see." She nodded slowly. "So it's up to you and Sloan and Trent, the big, brave men to protect us poor, defenseless women and save the day?"

It occurred, a bit too late, that he was on very shaky ground. "I didn't say you were defenseless."

"You implied it. Let me tell you something, Professor, there isn't one of the Calhoun women who can't handle herself and any man who comes swaggering down the road. That includes geniuses and unbalanced jewel thieves."

"There, you see?" His hands lifted from her shoulders, then settled again. "Your reaction is pure emotion without any logic or thought."

The heated eyes narrowed. "Do you want to see emotion?"

Besides brains, he prided himself on a certain amount of street smarts. Cautious, he eased back. "I don't think so."

"Fine. Then I suggest you take care with your phrasing, and think twice before you tell me to keep out of something that is wholly my concern." She brushed by him to continue toward the voices around the visitors' center.

"Damn it, I don't want you hurt."

"I don't intend to get hurt. I have a very low threshold for pain. But I'm not going to sit around with my hands folded while someone plots to steal what's mine."

"The police—"

"Haven't been a hell of a lot of help," she snapped. "Did you know that Interpol has been looking for Livingston, and his many aliases, for fifteen years? No one was able to trace him after he shot at Amanda and stole our papers. If Caufield and Livingston are one and the same, then it's up to us to protect what's ours."

"Even if it means getting your brains bashed in?"

She tossed a look over her shoulder. "I'll worry about my brains, Professor. You worry about yours."

"I'm not a genius," he muttered, and surprised a smile out of her.

The exasperation on his face took the edge off her temper. She stepped off the path. "I appreciate the concern, Max, but it's misplaced. Why don't you wait out here, sit on the wall? I've got to go in and get my things."

She left him muttering to himself. He only wanted to protect her. Was that so wrong? He cared about her. After all, she had saved his life. Scowling, he sat on the stone wall. People were milling in and out of the building. Children were whining as parents tugged, dragged or carried them to cars. Couples were strolling along hand in hand while others pored eagerly through guide books. He saw a lot of skin broiled Maine-lobster-red by the sun.

He glanced at his own forearms and was surprised to see that they were tanned. Things were changing, he realized. He was getting a tan. He had no schedule to keep, no itinerary to follow. He was involved in a mystery, and with an incredibly sexy woman.

"Well…" Lilah adjusted the strap of her purse on her arm. "You're looking very smug."

He looked up at her and smiled. "Am I?"

"As a cat with feathers in his mouth. Want to let me in on it?"

"Okay. Come here." He rose, gave her one firm yank and closed his mouth over hers. All of his new and amazed feelings poured into the kiss. If he took the kiss deeper than expected, it only added to the dawning pleasure of discovery. If kissing her made the people walking around them disappear, it only accented the newness. Starting fresh.

It was happiness rather than lust she felt from him. It confused her. Or perhaps it was the way his lips slid over hers that dimmed coherent thought. She didn't resist. The reason for her earlier irritation was already forgotten. All she knew now was that it felt wonderful, somehow perfect, to be standing with him on the sunny patio, feeling his heart thud against hers.

As his mouth slipped from hers, she let out a long, pleased sigh, opening her eyes slowly. He was grinning at her, and the delighted expression on his face had her smiling back. Because she wasn't sure what to do with the tender feelings he tugged from her, she patted his cheek.

"Not that I'm complaining," she began, "but what was that for?"

"I just felt like it."

"An excellent first step."

Laughing, he swung an arm around her shoulder as they started toward the parking lot. "You've got the sexiest mouth I've ever tasted."

He didn't see the cloud come into her eyes. If he had, she couldn't have explained it. It always came down to sex, she supposed and made an effort to shrug the vague disappointment away. Men usually saw her just that way, and there was no reason to let it start bothering her now, particularly when she'd enjoyed the moment as much as he.

"Glad I could oblige," she said lightly. "Why don't you drive?"

"All right, but first I've got something to show you." After settling into the driver's seat, he picked up a manilla envelope. "I went through a lot of books in the library. There are several mentions of your family in histories and biographies. There was one in particular I thought would interest you."

"Hmm." She was already stretched out and thinking of a nap.

"I made a copy of it. It's a picture of Bianca."

"A picture?" She straightened again. "Really? Fergus destroyed all her pictures after she died, so I've never seen her."

"Yes, you have." He drew the copy out and handed it to her. "Every time you look in the mirror."

She said nothing, but with her eyes focused on the grainy copy she lifted a hand to her own face. The same jaw, the same mouth, nose, eyes. Was this why she felt the bond so strongly? she wondered, and felt tears burn her throat.

"She was beautiful," Max said quietly.

"So young." The words came out as a sigh. "Younger than I when she died. She'd already fallen in love when this was taken. You can see it, in her eyes."

"She's wearing the emeralds."

"Yes, I know." As he had, she traced a fingertip over them. "How difficult it must have been for her, tied to one man, loving another. And the necklace—a symbol of one man's hold on her, and a reminder of her children."

"Is that how you see it, a symbol?"

"Yes. I think her feelings for it, about it, were terribly strong. Otherwise, she wouldn't have hidden it." She slipped the paper back into the envelope. "A good day's work, Professor."

"It's just a beginning."

As she looked at him, she linked her fingers with his. "I like beginnings. Everything that follows has such possibilities. We'll go home and show this to everyone, after we make a couple of stops."

"Stops?"

"It's time for another beginning. You need some new clothes."

He hated shopping. He told her, repeatedly and firmly, but she blithely ignored him and strolled from shop to shop. He held his ground on a fluorescent T-shirt, but lost it again over one depicting a lobster dressed like a maître d'.

She wasn't intimidated by clerks, but sailed through the process of selection and purchase with a languid air of pure relaxation. Most of the merchants called her by name, and during the chats that accompanied the buying and selling, she would casually ask about a man fitting Caufield's description.

"Are we finished yet?" There was a plea in his voice that made her chuckle as they stepped out onto the sidewalk again. It was teeming with people in bright summer clothes.

"Not quite." She turned to study him. Harassed, definitely. Adorable, absolutely. His arms were full of bags and his hair was falling into his eyes. Lilah brushed it back. "How are you fixed for underwear?"

"Well, I..."

"Come on, there's a shop right down here that has great stuff. Tiger prints, obscene sayings, little red hearts."

"No." He stopped dead. "Not on your life."

It was a struggle, but she kept her composure. "You're

right. Completely unsuitable. We'll just stick with those nice white briefs that come three to a package."

"For a woman with no brothers, you sure know a lot about men's underwear." He shifted the bags, and as an afterthought, shoved half of them into her arms. "But I think I can handle this one on my own."

"Okay. I'll window-shop."

She was easily diverted by a window filled with crystals of different sizes and shapes. They dangled from wire, shooting colored light behind the glass. Beneath them was a display of handmade jewelry. She was on the point of stepping inside to wrangle over a pair of earrings when someone bumped her from behind.

"Sorry." The apology was terse. Lilah glanced up at a burly man with a weathered face and graying hair. He looked a great deal more irritated than the slight bump warranted, and something about the pale eyes had her taking a step back. Still, she shrugged and smiled.

"It's all right."

Frowning after him a moment, she started to turn back into the shop. She spotted Max a few feet away, staring in shock. Then he was moving fast, and the expression on his face had her catching her breath.

"Max—"

With one hard shove, he had her in the shop. "What did he say to you?" he demanded with an edge to his voice that had her eyes widening. "Did he touch you? If the bastard put his hands on you—"

"Hold on." Since they had most of the people in the shop staring, Lilah kept her voice low. "Calm down, Max. I don't know what you're talking about."

There was a violence trembling through his blood he'd never experienced before. The echo of it in his eyes had several tourists edging back out the door. "I saw him standing next to you."

"That man?" Baffled, she glanced out the window, but he had long since moved on. "He just bumped into me. The sidewalks are crowded in the summer."

"He didn't say anything to you?" He didn't even realize that his hands had firmed into fists and that the fists were ready to do damage. "He didn't hurt you?"

"No, of course not. Come on, let's go sit down." Her tone was soothing now as she nudged him out. But instead of taking one of the benches that lined the street, Max kept Lilah behind him and searched the crowd. "If I'd known buying underwear would put you in such a state, Max, I wouldn't have brought it up."

There was fury in his eyes when he whirled around. "It was Hawkins," he said grimly. "They're still here."

Chapter Five

She didn't know what to make of him. Alone, with the lamplight glowing gold, Lilah sat in the tower room, watching night fall gently over water and rock. And thought of Max. He wasn't nearly as simple a man as she had believed at first—and as she was certain he believed of himself.

One moment he was shy and sweet and easily intimidated. The next he was as fierce as a Viking, the mild blue eyes electric, the poet's mouth grim. The metamorphosis was as fascinating as it was baffling, and left Lilah off balance. It wasn't a sensation she cared for.

After he had seen the man he called Hawkins, Max had all but dragged her to the car—muttering under his breath all the way—bundled her inside, then had driven off. Her idea about following Hawkins had been briskly and violently vetoed. Back at The Towers, he'd called the police, relating the information as calmly as he would list assigned reading for a student. Then, in a typical male move had powwowed with Sloan and Trent.

The authorities had not yet located Caufield's boat, nor, from Max's descriptions, had they identified either Caufield or Hawkins.

It was much too complicated, Lilah decided. Thieves and aliases and international police. She preferred the simple. Not the humdrum, she thought, but the simple. Life had been anything but since the press had begun their love affair with the Calhoun emeralds, and things had become only more convoluted since Max had washed up on the beach.

But she was glad he had. She wasn't sure why. Certainly she'd never considered the shy and brainy sort her type. It was true that she enjoyed men in general, simply for being men. An offshoot, she supposed, from living in a female household most of her life. But when she dated, she most often looked for fun and easy companionship. Someone to dance with or to laugh with over a meal. She'd always hoped she would fall in love with one of those carefree, uncomplicated men and start a carefree, uncomplicated life.

Sober college professors with outdated notions of chivalry and serious minds hardly met the qualifications.

Yet he was so sweet, she thought with a little smile. And when he kissed her, there was nothing sober or cerebral about it.

With a little sigh, she wondered just what she should do about Dr. Maxwell Quartermain.

"Hey." C.C. poked her head through the doorway. "I thought I'd find you in here."

"Then I must be becoming too predictable." Happy

to have company, Lilah curled up her legs to make room on the window seat. "What's going on with you, Mrs. St. James?"

"Nearly finished the reconditioning on that Mustang." She sighed as she sat. "Lord, what a honey. I had an electrical system that gave me fits today, and two tune-ups." An unaccustomed fatigue was dragging at her, making her close her eyes and think about an early night. "Then all this excitement at home. Imagine, you bumping into one of the characters the cops are after."

"The curse and blessing of small towns."

"I cruised around a little before I came home." C.C. rolled her tired shoulders. "Down to Hulls Cove and back."

"You shouldn't be poking around alone."

"Just looking." C.C. shrugged. "Anyway, I didn't see anything. Our fearless men are out right now on search and destroy."

A quick bolt of alarm shot into Lilah. "Max went with them?"

On a yawn, C.C. opened her eyes. "Sure. Suddenly, they're the Three Musketeers. Is there anything more annoying than machismo?"

"Tooth decay," Lilah said absently, but there were nerves bumping along in her system she didn't care for. "I thought Max was going to stick to the research books."

"Well, he's one of the boys now." She patted Lilah's ankle. "Don't worry, honey. They can handle themselves."

"For heaven's sake, he's a history professor. What if they actually run into trouble?"

"He already has," C.C. reminded her. "He's tougher than he looks."

"What makes you think so?" Unreasonably distressed, Lilah got up to pace. The unaccustomed show of energy had C.C. lifting a brow.

"The man jumped out of a boat in the middle of a storm and almost made it to shore, despite the fact he'd been grazed by a bullet. The next day, he was on his feet again—looking like hell, but on his feet. There's a stubborn streak behind those quiet eyes. I like him."

Restless, Lilah moved her shoulders. "Who doesn't? He's a likable man."

"Well, with everything that Amanda found out—the wonder boy stuff—you'd expect him to be conceited, or stiff-necked. But he's not. He's sweet. Aunt Coco's ready to adopt him."

"He is sweet," Lilah agreed as she sat again. "And I don't want him to get hurt because of some misguided sense of gratitude."

C.C. leaned forward to look into her sister's eyes. There was more than casual concern in them, she thought, and smiled to herself. "Lilah, I know you're the mystic in the family, but I'm getting definite vibes. Are you getting serious about Max?"

"Serious?" The word had Lilah's nerves stretching. "Of course not. I'm fond of him, and I feel a certain responsibility toward him." *And when he kisses me, I go directly to meltdown.* She frowned a little. "I enjoy him," she slowly added.

"He's very attractive."

"You're a married woman now, kiddo."

"But not blind. There's something appealing about all that intelligence, those romantic and scholarly looks." She waited a beat. "Don't you think?"

Lilah sat back. Her lips were curved again to match

the amusement in her eyes. "Are you apprenticing with Aunt Coco as matchmaker?"

"Just checking. I guess I'm so happy I want everyone I love to feel the same way."

"I am happy." She took a long, limbering stretch. "I'm too lazy not to be."

"Speaking of lazy, I feel like I could sleep for a week. Since Trent's out playing Hardy Boys, I think I'll go to bed." C.C. started to rise when a wave of dizziness had her plopping down again. Lilah was up like a shot and bending over her.

"Hey. Hey, honey. Are you all right?"

"Got up too fast, that's all." As the light grayed, she lifted a hand to her spinning head. "I feel a little…"

Moving fast, Lilah shoved C.C.'s head between her knees. "Just breathe slow. Take it easy."

"This is stupid." But she did as she was told until the faintness passed. "I'm just overtired. Maybe I'm coming down with something, damn it."

"Mmm." Because she suspected just what C.C. had come down with, Lilah's lips curved. "Tired? Have you been feeling sick?"

"Not really." Steadier, C.C. straightened. "Out of sorts, I guess. A little queasy the past couple of mornings, that's all."

"Honey." With a laugh, Lilah tapped her knuckles on her sister's head. "Wake up and smell the baby powder."

"Huh?"

"Hasn't it occurred to you that you could be pregnant?"

"Pregnant?" The dark green eyes widened like saucers. "Pregnant? Me? But we've only been married a little over a month."

Lilah laughed again and cupped C.C.'s face in her hands. "You haven't spent all that time playing pinochle, have you?"

C.C.'s mouth opened and closed before she managed to form a word. "It just never crossed my mind…. A baby." Her eyes changed, misting, softening. "Oh, Lilah."

"Could be Trenton St. James IV."

"A baby," C.C. repeated, and laid a hand over her stomach in a gesture that was filled with awe and protectiveness. "Do you really think?"

"I really think." She slid back on the seat to hug C.C. tight. "I don't have to ask you how you feel about it. It's all over your face."

"Don't say anything to anyone yet. I want to be sure." Laughing, she squeezed Lilah against her. "Suddenly I don't feel tired at all. I'll call the doctor first thing in the morning. Or maybe I should pick up one of those tests from the drugstore. I could do both."

Lilah let her ramble. Long after C.C. had gone, the echoes of her joy remained in the room.

It was what the tower needed, Lilah thought. That jolt of pure happiness. She stayed where she was, content now, watching the moon rise. Half-full, bone white, it hung in the sky and had her dreaming.

What would it be like, being with someone, smugly married, having a child growing inside you? Making a life with someone who would know you so well. Know every part of you and love you despite the flaws. Maybe because of them.

Lovely, she thought. It would be simply lovely. And if she had yet to find that for herself, she had only to look at C.C. and Amanda to know it could happen.

With some regret she switched off the light and started downstairs to her room. The house was quiet now. She imagined it must be at least midnight, and everyone had gone to bed. A wise choice, she mused, but she couldn't seem to shake the restlessness.

To comfort herself, she indulged in a long, fragrant bath before slipping into her favorite robe. Those were the little things that always pleased her—hot, scented water, cool, thin silk. Still unsettled, she walked out onto the terrace to see if the night air would lull her.

It was much too romantic, she thought. The glitter of moonlight silvering the trees, the quiet whoosh of water on rock, the scents from the garden. As she stood, a bird, as restless as she, began a lonely night song. It made her long for something. For someone. A touch, a whisper in the dark. An arm around her shoulders.

A mate.

Not just the physical, but the emotional, the spiritual partner. She had had men desire her and knew that could never be enough. There had to be someone who could look beyond the color of her hair or the shape of her face and into her heart.

Perhaps she was asking for too much, Lilah thought with a sigh. But wasn't that better than asking for too little? In the meantime she would have to concentrate on other things and leave her heart in fate's capricious hands.

She had started to turn back into her room when a movement caught her eye. In the swaying moonlight she saw two shadows bent low, moving with silent swiftness across the lawn. Before she could do more than register the shapes, they had melted into the garden.

She didn't even think about it. A home was meant to

be defended. Her bare feet were noiseless on the stone steps as she walked down them. Whoever was trespassing on Calhoun territory was about to get the scare of their lives.

Like a ghost, she slipped into the garden, the robe floating around her. There were voices, muffled and excited, a faint yellow beam of a flashlight. There was a laugh, quickly smothered, then the sound of a shovel striking earth.

That more than anything brought the Calhoun temper bubbling to the surface. With the courage of the righteous, she strode forward.

"What the hell do you think you're doing?"

The shovel clanged on stone as it was dropped. The flashlight went spiraling into the azaleas. Two teenagers, wound up with the treasure hunt, looked around wildly for the source of the voice. They saw the pale figure of a woman draped in white. Summing up her quarry, Lilah lifted her arms for effect, knowing the full sleeves would billow nicely.

"I am guardian of the emeralds." She nearly chuckled, pleased with the way her voice floated. "Do you dare to face the curse of the Calhouns? Hideous death is certain for any who defile this ground. Run, if you value your lives."

They didn't have to be told twice. The treasure map they had paid ten bucks for fluttered to the ground as they raced back down the path, shoving each other and tripping over their own scrambling feet. Chuckling to herself, Lilah picked up the map.

She'd seen its like before. Some enterprising soul was making them up and selling them to gullible tourists. After shoving it into her pocket, she decided to give her two uninvited guests a little extra boost. She dashed after them. Ready to send up a ghostly wail, she burst out of the garden.

The wail turned into a grunt as she rammed into another shadow. Stopped in a dead run, Max overbalanced, swore, then went tumbling to the ground on top of her.

"What the hell are you doing?"

"It's me," she managed, then sucked in a breath. "What the hell are you doing?"

"I saw someone. Stay here."

"No." She grabbed his arms and held on. "It was just a couple of kids with a treasure map. I scared them off."

"You—" Furious, he braced on an elbow. Despite the dark, the anger shone clearly in his eyes. "Are you out of your mind?" he demanded. "You came out here, alone, to face down two intruders?"

"Two terrified teenagers with a treasure map," she corrected. Her chin lifted. "It's my house."

"I don't give a damn whose house it is. It might have been Caufield and Hawkins. It might have been anyone. No one with an ounce of sense follows potential robbers into a dark garden alone, in the middle of the night."

She had her breath back and studied him blandly. "What were you doing?"

"I was going after them," he began, then caught her expression. "That's different."

"Why? Because I'm a woman?"

"No. Well, yes."

"That's stupid, untrue and sexist."

"That's sensible, factual and sexist." They'd been arguing in furious whispers. Now he sighed. "Lilah, you might have been hurt."

"The only one who hurt me was you, with that flying tackle."

"I didn't tackle you," he muttered. "I was watching them and didn't see you. And I certainly didn't expect to find you out here sneaking around in the dark."

"I wasn't sneaking." She blew hair out of her eyes. "I was playing ghost, and very effectively."

"Playing ghost." He shut his eyes. "Now I know you're out of your mind."

"It worked," she reminded him.

"That's beside the point."

"It's precisely the point, the other being that you knocked me down before I could finish the job."

"I've already apologized."

"No, you haven't."

"All right. I'm sorry if I…" He started to push himself off her and made the mistake of glancing down. Her robe had come loose during the fall and lay open to the waist. Like alabaster, her breasts glowed in the moonlight. "Oh, Lord," he managed to say through suddenly dry lips.

She'd lost her breath again. Lying still, she watched his eyes change. Irritation to shock, shock to wonder, wonder to a deep and dark desire. As his gaze skimmed up, came back to hers, every muscle in her body melted like hot wax.

No one had ever looked at her just that way. There was such intensity in his eyes, the same focused concentration they had held when he'd struggled to block out pain. They roamed to her mouth, lingering there until her lips trembled apart on his name.

It was like moving into a dream, he thought as he lowered himself onto her again. Everything was just one click out of focus, soft and fuzzy. His hands were in her hair, lost in it. Beneath his, her lips were warm, beautifully warm. Her arms came around him as if they had been waiting. He heard her sigh, long and deep.

His mouth was so gentle on hers, as if he were afraid she might vanish if he dared too much too soon. Yet she could feel the tension in the way he held himself, the way his hands fisted in her hair, the way his breath shuddered out as he brushed his lips over hers.

Her limbs grew heavy, her head light. Though she wanted to keep her eyes open, as his were, they drifted closed. The most pleasant of aches coursed through her as he nibbled delicately at her parted lips. Her murmur mixed with his, indecipherable.

The grass whispered as she shifted beneath him. Its cool, fresh fragrance seemed perfectly suited to him. As his fingers slid softly over her breast, she heard her own quiet moan of acceptance.

She was unbelievably perfect, he thought dizzily. Like some fantasy conjured on a lonely night. Long slender limbs, silky skin, an avid and generous mouth. The sheer physical pleasure of her was like a drug, and he was already addicted.

Murmuring her name, he skimmed his lips to her throat. There her pulse beat like thunder, heating her skin so that her scent tangled with each breath he took. Tasting her was like dining on sin. Touching her was paradise. He brought his lips back to hers to lose himself on that glorious edge between heaven and hell.

She could almost feel herself floating an inch above the cool grass. Her body felt free as air, soft as water. When his mouth met hers again, she let herself drift into the new kiss. Then it happened.

It was not the sweet click of a door opening that she

had been hoping for. It was a rushing roar, like a gust of wind sweeping through her body. Behind it, speeding in its wake, was a pain, sharp, sweet and stunning. She stiffened against it, her cry of protest muffled against his lips.

If she had slapped him, his passion wouldn't have cooled more quickly. He jerked back to see her staring at him, her eyes wide and filled with fear and confusion. Appalled by his behavior, he scrambled to his knees. He was trembling, he realized. So was she. Small wonder. He had acted like a maniac, knocking her down, pawing her.

Lord help him, he wanted to do it again.

"Lilah…" His voice was a husky rasp, and he struggled to clear it. She didn't move a muscle. Her eyes never left his. He wanted to stroke her cheek, to gather her close and hold her, but was afraid to touch her again. "I'm sorry. Very sorry. You looked so beautiful. I guess I lost my head."

She waited for a moment, for the balance and ease that was so much a part of her. But it didn't come. "Is that it?"

"I…" What did she want him to say? he wondered. He felt like a monster already. "You're an incredibly desirable woman," he said carefully. "But that's no excuse for what happened just now."

What had happened? She was afraid she had fallen in love with him, and if she had, love hurt. She didn't like it one damn bit. "You want me, physically."

He cleared his throat. *Want* wasn't the word. *Craved* was closer, but still fell pitifully short of the mark. As gently as he would for a child, he brought her robe together again. "Any man would," he said, nerves straining.

Any man, she thought and closed her eyes on the slash

of disappointment. She hadn't been waiting for any man, but for one man. "It's all right, Max." Her voice was a shade overbright as she sat up. "No harm done. It's just a matter of us finding the other physically attractive. Happens all the time."

"Yes, but—" Not to him, he thought. Not like this. He frowned down at a blade of grass. It was easier for her, he supposed. She was so open, so uninhibited. There had probably been dozens of men in her life. Dozens, he thought on a jolt of fury that had him tearing the blade in two. "What do you suggest we do about it?"

"Do about it?" Her smile was strained, but he wasn't even looking at her. "Why don't we just see if it passes. Like the flu."

He looked at her then, with something dangerous edging his eyes. "It won't. Not for me. I want you. A woman like you would know just how badly I want you."

The words brought both a thrill and an ache. "A woman like me," she repeated softly. "Yes, that's the crux of it, isn't it, Professor?"

"The crux of what?" he began, but she was already on her feet.

"A woman who enjoys men, and who's very generous with them."

"I didn't mean—"

"One who'll wrestle half-naked on the grass. A little bohemian for you, Dr. Quartermain, but you're not above experimenting a little bit here and there—with a woman like me."

"Lilah, for God's sake—" He too was on his feet, baffled.

"I wouldn't apologize again if I were you. There's certainly no need." Hurt beyond measure, she tossed back her hair. "Not when it concerns a woman like me. After all, you've got me pegged, don't you?"

Good Lord, were those tears in her eyes? He gestured helplessly. "I haven't got a clue."

"Right again. All you understand about this is your own wants." She swallowed the tears. "Well, Professor, I'll take them under consideration and let you know."

Completely lost, he watched her gather the skirts of her robe and dart up the stairs. Moments later her terrace doors closed with an audible click.

She didn't cry. Lilah reminded herself it was an exhausting experience that usually left her with a miserable headache. She couldn't think of a single man who was worth the trouble. Instead, she dragged open the drawer of her nightstand and pulled out her emergency bar of chocolate.

After plopping down onto the bed, she took a healthy bite and stared at the ceiling.

Sexy. Beautiful. Desirable. Big damn deal, she thought and bit off another hunk. For all his celebrated brains, Maxwell Quartermain was as big a jerk as any other man. All he saw was a pretty package, and once he'd unwrapped it, that would be that. He wouldn't see any substance, any of the softer needs.

Oh, he was more polite than most. A gentleman to the last, she thought in disgust. She hadn't had to untangle herself. God knew he'd been in a hurry to do that for himself.

Lost his head. At least he was honest, she thought, and brushed impatiently at a tear that sneaked past her guard.

She knew the kind of image she projected. It rarely bothered her what people thought of her. She understood herself, was comfortable with Lilah Maeve Calhoun.

There certainly was no shame in the fact that she enjoyed men. Though she hadn't enjoyed them to the extent that others, including, she supposed, her family might think.

Uninhibited? Perhaps, but that wasn't synonymous with promiscuity. Did she flirt? Yes, it came naturally to her, but it wasn't done with malice or guile.

If a man flirted with women he was suave. If a woman flirted, she was a tease. Well, as far as she was concerned the game between the sexes was a two-way street, and she enjoyed playing. And as for the good professor...

She curled up into a tight, defensive ball. Oh, God, he'd hurt her. All that stuttering, apologizing, explaining. And all the time he looked so appalled.

A woman like you. The phrase played back in her head.

Couldn't he see what he'd done to her with that careful tenderness? Hadn't he been able to feel how deeply he'd affected her? All she had wanted was for him to touch her again, to smile in that sweet, shy way of his and tell her that he cared. About who she was, what she was, how she felt inside. She'd wanted comfort and reassurance, and he'd given her excuses. She had looked up at him, with the stab of love still streaking through her, the terror of it still trembling, and he'd jerked back as if she'd clipped him on the jaw.

She wished she had. If this was love, she didn't want her share after all.

Because it was quiet, or perhaps because her ears were tuned for him, she heard Max come up the steps, sensed him hesitate near her doors. She stopped breathing, though her heart picked up a quick beat. Would he come in now, push those doors open and come to her, tell her what she wanted so badly to hear? She could almost see his hand reach for the knob. Then she heard his footsteps again as he moved on down the terrace to his own room.

Her breath came out in a sigh. It wouldn't fit his principles to enter her bedroom uninvited. Outside, on the grass, he'd been following his instincts rather than his intellect, she admitted. No one was more in favor of that than Lilah. For him, it had been the moment, the moon, the mood. It was difficult to blame him, certainly impossible to expect him to feel as she felt. Want as she wanted.

She sincerely hoped he didn't sleep a wink.

She sniffled, swallowed chocolate, then began to think. Only two months before, C.C. had come to her, hurt and infuriated because Trent had kissed her, then apologized for it.

Pursing her lips, Lilah rolled onto her back again. Maybe it was typical male stupidity. It was difficult to fault the breed for something they were born with. If Trent had apologized because he'd cared about her sister, then it could follow that Max had played the same cards.

It was an interesting theory, and one that shouldn't be too difficult to prove. Or disprove, she thought with a sigh. Either way, it was probably best to know before she got in any deeper. All she needed was a plan.

Lilah decided to do what she did best, and slept on it.

Chapter Six

It wasn't difficult in a house the size of The Towers to avoid someone for a day or two. Max noted that Lilah had effortlessly stayed out of his way for that amount of time. He couldn't blame her, not after how badly he had botched things.

Still, it irked him that she wouldn't accept a simple and sincere apology. Instead she'd turned it into… damned if he knew what she'd turned it into. The only thing he was sure of was that she'd twisted his words, and their meaning, then had stalked off in a snit.

And he missed her like crazy.

He kept busy enough, buried in his research books, poring over the old family papers that Amanda had meticulously filed according to date and content. He found what he considered the last public sighting of the necklace in a newspaper feature covering a dinner

dance in Bar Harbor, August 10, 1913. Two weeks before Bianca's death.

Though he considered it a long shot, he began a list
of every servant's name he came across who had worked
at The Towers the summer of 1913. Some of them could
conceivably be alive. Tracking them or their families
down would be difficult but not impossible. He had in-
terviewed the elderly before on their memories of their
youth. Quite often, those memories were as clear as
crystal.

The idea of talking to someone who had known Bianca, who had seen her—and the necklace—excited
him. A servant would remember The Towers as it had
been, would have knowledge of their employers' habits.
And, he had no doubt, would know their secrets.

Confident in the notion, Max bent over his lists.

"Hard at work, I see."

He glanced up, blinking, to see Lilah in the doorway of the storeroom. She didn't have to be told she'd
dragged him out of the past. The blank, owlish look he
gave her made her want to hug him. Instead she leaned
lazily against the jamb.

"Am I interrupting?"

"Yes—no." Damn it, his mouth was watering. "I was
just, ah, making a list."

"I have a sister with the same problem." She was
wearing a full-skirted sundress in sheer white cotton,
her gypsy hair like cables of flames against it. Long
chunks of malachite swung at her ears when she crossed
the room.

"Amanda." Because the pencil had gone damp in his
hand, he set it aside. "She did a terrific job of catalog-
ing all this information."

"She's a fiend for organization." Casually she rested a hip on the card table he was using. "I like your shirt."

It was the one she'd chosen for him, with the cartoon lobster. "Thanks. I thought you'd be at work."

"It's my day off." She slid off the table to round it and lean over his shoulder. "Do you ever take one?"

Though he knew it was ridiculous, he felt his muscles bunch up. "Take what?"

"A day off." Brushing her hair aside, she turned her face toward his. "To play."

She was doing it deliberately, there could be no doubt. Maybe she enjoyed watching him make a fool out of himself. "I'm busy." He managed to tear his gaze away from her mouth and stared down at the list he was making. He couldn't read a word. "Really busy," he said almost desperately. "I'm trying to note down all the names of the people who worked here the summer Bianca died."

"That's quite an undertaking." She leaned closer, delighted with his reaction to her. It had to be more than lust. A man didn't fight so hard against basic lust. "Do you want some help?"

"No, no, it's a one-man job." And he wanted her to go away before he started to whimper.

"It must have been a terrible time here, after she died. Even worse for Christian, hearing about it, reading about it, and not being able to do anything. I think he loved her very much. Have you ever been in love?"

Once again, she drew his eyes back to hers. She wasn't smiling now. There was no teasing light in her eyes. For some reason he thought it was the most serious question she had ever asked him.

"No."

"Neither have I. What do you think it's like?"

"I don't know."

"But you must have an opinion." She leaned a little closer. "A theory. A thought."

He was all but hypnotized. "It must be like having your own private world. Like a dream, where everything's intensified, a bit off balance and completely yours."

"I like that." He watched her lips curve, could almost taste them. "Would you like to take a walk, Max?"

"A walk?"

"Yes, with me. Along the cliffs."

He wasn't even sure he could stand. "A walk would be good."

Saying nothing, she offered him her hand. When he rose, she led him through the terrace doors.

The wind was up, pushing the clouds across a blue sky. It tore at Lilah's skirts and sent her hair flying. Unconcerned, she strolled into it, her hand lightly clasped in his. They crossed the lawn and left the busy sounds of building behind.

"I'm not much on hiking," she told him, "since I spend most days doing just that, but I like to go to the cliffs. There are very strong, very beautiful memories there."

He thought again of all the men who must have loved her. "Yours?"

"No, Bianca's, I think. And if you don't choose to believe in such things, the view's worth the trip."

He started down the slope beside her. It felt easy, simple, even friendly. "You're not angry with me anymore."

"Angry?" Deliberately she lifted a brow. She had no intention of making things too simple. "About what?"

"The other night. I know I upset you."

"Oh, that."

When she added nothing else, he tried again. "I've been thinking about it."

"Have you?" Her eyes, mysterious with secrets, lifted to his.

"Yes. I realize I probably didn't handle it very well."

"Would you like another chance?"

He stopped dead in his tracks and made her laugh.

"Relax, Max." She gave him a friendly kiss on the cheek. "Just give it some thought. Look, the mountain cranberry's blooming." She bent to touch a spray of pink bell-shaped flowers that clung to the rocks. Touch, but not pick, he noted. "It's a wonderful time for wildflowers up here." Straightening, she tossed her hair back. "See those?"

"The weeds?"

"Oh, and I thought you were a poet." With a shake of her head, she had her hand tucked back in his. "Lesson number one," she began.

As they walked, she pointed out tiny clumps of flowers that pushed out of crevices or thrived in the thin, rocky soil. She showed him how to recognize the wild blueberry that would be ripe and ready the following month. There was the flutter of butterfly wings and the drone of bees deep in the grass. With her, the common became exotic.

She snipped off a thin leaf, crushing it to release a pungent fragrance that reminded him of her skin.

He stood with her on a precipice thrown out over the water. Far below, spray fumed on the rock, beating them smooth in a timeless war. She helped him spot the nests, worked cleverly onto narrow ridges and clinging tenaciously to faults in the rocks.

It was what she did every day for groups of strangers, and for herself. There was a new kind of pleasure in sharing it all with him, showing him something as simple and special as the tiny white sandwort or the wild roses that grew as tall as a man. The air was like wine, freshened by the wind, so that she sat on a huddle of rock to drink it with each breath.

"It's incredible here." He couldn't sit. There was too much to see, too much to feel.

"I know." She was enjoying his pleasure as much as the sun on her face and the wind in her hair. It was in his as well, streaming through the shaggy locks. There was fascination in his eyes, darkening them to indigo as the faint smile curved his lips. The wound on his temple was healing, but she thought it would leave a slight scar that would add something rakish to the intelligent face.

As a thrush began to trill, she circled her knee with her arms. "You look good, Max."

Distracted, he glanced over his shoulder. She was sitting easily on the rocks, as relaxed as she would have been on a cushy sofa. "What?"

"I said you look good. Very good." She laughed as his jaw dropped. "Hasn't anyone ever told you you're attractive?"

What game was she playing now? he wondered, and shrugged uncomfortably. "Not that I remember."

"No star-struck undergraduate, no clever English Lit professor? That's very remiss. I imagine more than one of them tried to catch your eye—and a bit more than that—but you were too buried in books to notice."

His brows drew together. "I haven't been a monk."

"No." She smiled. "I'm already aware of that."

Her words reminded him vividly of what had happened between them two nights before. He had touched her, tasted her, had managed, barely, to pull himself back before taking her right there on the grass. And she had rushed off, he remembered, furious and hurt. Now she was taunting him, all but daring him to repeat the mistake.

"I never know what to expect from you."

"Thank you."

"That wasn't a compliment."

"Even better." Her eyes slanted, half-closed now against the sun. When she spoke, her voice was almost a purr. "But you like predictability, don't you, Professor? Knowing what happens next."

"Probably as much as you like irritating me."

Laughing, she held out a hand. "Sorry, Max, sometimes it's irresistible. Come on, sit down. I promise to behave."

Wary, he sat on the rock beside her. Her skirts fluttered teasingly around her legs. In a gesture he felt was almost maternal, she patted his thigh.

"Want to be pals?" she asked him.

"Pals?"

"Sure." Her eyes danced with amusement. "I like you. The serious mind, the honest soul." He shifted, making her laugh. "The way you shuffle around when you're embarrassed."

"I do not shuffle."

"The authoritative tone when you're annoyed. Now you're supposed to tell me what you like about me."

"I'm thinking."

"I should have added your dry wit."

He had to smile. "You're the most self-possessed person I've ever met." He glanced at her. "And you're kind, without making a fuss about it. You're smart, but you don't make a fuss about that, either. I guess you don't make a fuss about anything."

"Too tiring." But his words had a glow spreading around her heart. "It's safe to say we're friends then?"

"Safe enough."

"That's good." She gave his hand a gentle squeeze. "I think it's important for us to be friends before we're lovers."

He nearly fell off the rock. "Excuse me?"

"We both know we want to make love." When he began to stammer she gave him a patient smile. She'd thought it through very carefully and was sure—well, nearly sure—this was right for both of them. "Relax, it isn't a crime in this state."

"Lilah, I realize I've been…that is, I know I've made advances."

"Advances." Desperately in love, she laid a hand on his cheek. "Oh, Max."

"I'm not proud of my behavior," he said stiffly, and had her hand sliding away. "I don't want…" His tongue tied itself into knots.

The hurt was back, a combination of rejection and defeat she detested. "You don't want to go to bed with me?"

Now his stomach was in knots, as well. "Of course I do. Any man—"

"I'm not talking about any man." They were the poorest two words he could have chosen. It was him, only him she cared about. She needed to hear him say he wanted her, if nothing else. "Damn it, I'm talking about you and me, right here, right now." Temper pushed her off the rock. "I want to know about your feelings. If I wanted to know how any man felt, I'd pick up the phone or drive into the village and ask any man."

Keeping his seat, he considered her. "For someone who does most things slowly, you have a very quick temper."

"Don't use that professorial tone on me."

It was his turn to smile. "I thought you liked it."

"I changed my mind." Because her own attitude confused her, she turned away to look out over the water. It was important to remain calm, she reminded herself. She was always able to remain calm effortlessly. "I know what you think of me," she began.

"I don't see how you can, when I'm far from sure myself." He took a moment to gather his thoughts. "Lilah, you're a beautiful woman—"

She whirled back, eyes electric. "If you tell me that again, I swear, I'll hit you."

"What?" Completely baffled, he threw his hands up and rose. "Why? Good God, you're frustrating."

"That's much better. I don't want to hear that my hair's the color of sunset, or that my eyes are like sea foam. I've heard all that. I don't care about that."

He began to think that being a monk, completely divorced from the mysterious female, had its advantages. "What do you want to hear?"

"I'm not going to tell you what I want to hear. If I do, then what's the point?"

At wit's end, he raked both hands through his hair. "The point is, I don't know what the point is. One minute you're telling me about sandwarts—"

"Sandwort," she said between her teeth.

"Fine. We're talking about flowers and friendship, and the next you're asking me if I want to take you to bed. How am I supposed to react to that?"

Her eyes narrowed. "You tell me."

He went on a mental search for safe ground and found none. "Look, I realize you're used to having men…"

Her narrowed eyes glinted. "Having them what?"

If he was going to sink, Max decided, he might as well go down with a flourish. "Just shut up." He grabbed her arms, dragged her hard against him and crushed his mouth to hers.

She could taste the frustration, the temper, the edgy passion. It seemed that what he was feeling was a reflection of her own emotions. For the first time, she struggled against him, fighting to hold back her response. And for the first time, he ignored the protest and demanded one.

His hand was in her billowing hair, pulling her head back so that he could plunder mindlessly. Her body was arched, straining away from him, but he locked her closer, so close even the wind couldn't slip between them.

This was different, she thought. No man had ever forced her to…feel. She didn't want this ache, these needs, this desperation. Since the last time they had been together she had convinced herself that love could be painless, and simple and comfortable, if only she were clever enough.

But there was pain. No amount of passion or desire could completely coat it.

Furious with both of them, he tore his mouth from hers, but his hands dug into her shoulders. "Is that what you want?" he demanded. "Do you want me to forget every rule, every code of decency? You want to know how I feel? Every time I'm around you I itch to get my hands on you. And when I do I want to drag you off

somewhere and make love to you until you forget that
there was ever anyone else."

"Then why don't you?"

"Because I care about you, damn it. Enough to want
to show you some respect. And too much to want to be
just the next man in your bed."

The temper faded from her eyes to be replaced by a
vulnerability more poignant than tears. "You wouldn't
be." She lifted a hand to his face. "You're a first for me,
Max. There's never been anyone else like you." He said
nothing, and the doubt in his eyes had her hand slipping
to her side again. "You don't believe me."

"I've found it difficult to think clearly since I met
you." Abruptly he realized he was still gripping her
shoulders, and gentled his hold. "You could say you
dazzle me."

She looked down. How close she had come, she realized, to telling him everything that was in her heart.
And humiliating herself, embarrassing him. If it was just
to be physical between them, then she would be strong
enough to accept it. "Then we'll leave it at that for now."
She managed a smile. "We've been taking ourselves too
seriously anyway." To comfort herself, she gave him a
soft, lingering kiss. "Friends?"

He let out a long breath. "Sure."

"Walk back with me, Max." She slipped a hand into
his. "I feel like a nap."

An hour later, he sat on the sunny terrace outside of
his room, the notebook on his lap forgotten and his mind
crowded with thoughts of her.

He didn't come close to understanding her—was
certain he couldn't come closer if he had several de-

cades to consider the problem. But he did care, enough to add a good jolt of fear to the rest of the emotions she pulled out of him. What did he, a painfully middle-class college professor, have to offer a gorgeous, exotic and free-spirited woman who exuded sex like other women exuded perfume?

He was so pitifully inept that he was stuttering around her one minute and grabbing her like a Neanderthal the next.

Maybe the best thing for him was to remember that he was more comfortable and certainly more competent with his books than with women.

How could he tell her that he wanted her so badly he could hardly breathe? That he was terrified to act on his needs because, once done, he knew he'd never be free of her? An easy summer romance for her, a life-altering event for him.

He was falling in love with her, which was ridiculous. He couldn't have a place in her life, and hoped he was smart enough to get a grip on his emotions before they carried him too far. In a few weeks, he would go back to his nicely ordered routine. It was what he wanted. It had to be.

And he couldn't survive it if she haunted him.

"Max?" Trent, taking the circular route to the west wing, stopped. "Interrupting?"

"No." Max glanced down at the blank sheet on his lap. "Nothing to interrupt."

"You looked like you were trying to puzzle out a particularly difficult problem. Anything to do with the necklace?"

"No." Max looked up, squinted against the sun. "Women."

"Oh. Good luck." He lifted a brow. "Particularly if it's a Calhoun woman."

"Lilah." Weary, Max rubbed his hands over his face. "The more I think about her, the less I understand."

"A perfect start in a relationship." Because he was feeling smug about his own, Trent took a moment and sat down. "She's a fascinating woman."

"I've decided the word's *unstable*."

"Beautiful."

"You can't tell her that. She bites your head off." Intrigued, he studied Trent. "Does C.C. threaten to hit you if you tell her she's beautiful?"

"Not so far."

"I thought it might be a family trait." He began to tap his pencil against the pad. "I don't know very much about women."

"Well then, I should tell you all I know." Steepling his fingers, Trent sat back. "They're frustrating, exciting, baffling, wonderful and infuriating."

Max waited a moment. "That's it?"

"Yeah." He glanced up, lifting a hand in salute as Sloan approached.

"Coffee break?" Sloan asked, and finding the idea appealing, took out a cigar.

"A discussion on women," Trent informed him. "You might like to add something to my brief dissertation."

Sloan took his time lighting the cigar. "Stubborn as mules, mean as alley cats and the best damn game in town." He blew out smoke and grinned at Max. "You've got a thing for Lilah, don't you?"

"Well, I—"

"Don't be bashful." Sloan's grin widened as he poked out with the cigar. "You're among friends."

Max wasn't accustomed to discussing women, and certainly not his feelings toward a particular woman. "It would be difficult not to be interested."

Sloan gave a hoot of laughter and winked at Trent. "Son, you'd be dead if you weren't interested. So what's the problem?"

"I don't know what to do about her."

Trent's lips curved. "Sounds familiar. What do you want to do?"

Max slanted Trent a long, slow look that had him chuckling.

"Yeah, there is that." Sloan puffed contentedly on his cigar. "Is she, ah, interested?"

Max cleared his throat. "Well, she's indicated that she—that is, earlier we took a walk up on the cliffs, and she...yeah."

"But?" Trent prompted.

"I'm already in over my head."

"Then you might as well go under for the third time," Sloan told him, and eyed the tip of his cigar. "'Course, if you make the lady unhappy, I'd have to pound your face in." He stuck the cigar back into his mouth. "I'm right fond of her."

Max studied him a moment, then laid his head back and laughed. "There's no way to win here. I think I finally figured that out."

"That's the first step." Trent shifted. "Since we've got a minute here without the ladies I thought you both should know that I finally got a report on this Hawkins character. Jasper Hawkins, smuggler, out of Miami. He's a known associate of our old friend Livingston."

"Well, well," Sloan murmured, crushing out the cigar.

"It begins to look like Livingston and Caufield are one and the same. No sign of the boat yet."

"I've been thinking about that," Max put in. "It might be that they covered their tracks there. Even if they figured I was dead, they'd have to consider that the body would wash up eventually, be identified. Questions would be asked."

"So they ditched the boat," Trent mused.

"Or switched it." Max spread his hands. "They won't back off. I'm sure of that. Caufield, or whoever he is, is obsessed with the necklace. He'd change tactics, but he wouldn't give up."

"Neither will we," Trent murmured. The three men exchanged quiet looks. "If the necklace is in this house, we'll find it. And if that bastard—" He cut himself off as he spotted his wife racing through the doors at the far end of the terrace. "C.C." He was up quickly, starting toward her. "What's wrong? What are you doing home?"

"Nothing. Nothing's wrong." With a laugh, she threw her arms around him. "I love you."

"I love you, too." But he drew away to study her face. Her cheeks were flushed, her eyes brilliant and wet. "Well, it must be good news." He brushed her hair back, checking her brow as he did so. He knew she hadn't been feeling quite herself for the past week.

"The best." She glanced over at Sloan and Max. "Excuse us." Gripping Trent's hand, she pulled him down the terrace toward their room where she could tell him in private. Halfway there, she exploded. "Oh, I can't wait. I know I broke the sound barrier getting home after the test came in."

"What test? You're sick?"

"I'm pregnant." She held her breath, watching his face. Concern to shock, shock to wonder.

"You—pregnant?" He gaped down at her flat stomach, then back into her face. "A baby? We're having a baby?"

Even as she nodded, he was scooping her up, to swing her around and around as she clung to him.

"What the hell's with them?" Sloan wondered.

"Men." Behind Max, Lilah glided from another room. "You're all so dense." With a sigh, she laid a hand on Max's shoulder, watching her sister and Trent through misty eyes. "We're having a baby, you dummies."

"I'll be damned." After a whoop, Sloan headed down to slap Trent on the back and kiss C.C. Hearing the sniffle behind him, Max rose.

"You okay?"

"Sure." She brushed a tear from her lashes, but another fell. "She's my baby sister." She sniffed again, then gave a watery laugh when Max offered her a handkerchief. "Trust you." She dabbed her eyes, blew her nose then sighed. "I'm going to keep it awhile, okay? We're all going to cry buckets when we go down and make the announcement to the rest of the family."

"That's all right." Unsure of himself, he stuck his hands into his pockets.

"Let's go down and see if there's any champagne in the fridge."

"Well, I think I should stay up here. Out of the way."

With a shake of her head, she took his hand firmly in hers. "Don't be a jerk. Like it or not, Professor, you're part of the family."

He let her lead him away and discovered he did like it. He liked it a lot.

* * *

It was the stray puppy that started it. Such a poor, bedraggled little thing. Homeless and helpless. I have no idea how he found his way to the cliffs. Perhaps someone had disposed of an unwanted litter, or the pup had become separated from its mother. But we found him, Christian and I, on one of our golden afternoons. He was hiding in a huddle of rocks, half-starved and whimpering, a tiny black bundle of bones and scruffy black fur.

How patiently Christian lured him out, with a gentle voice and bits of bread and cheese. It touched me to see this sweetness in the man I love. With me, he is always tender, but I have seen the fierce impatience in him, for his art. I have felt the near-violent passion fighting for freedom when he holds me in his arms.

Yet with the puppy, the poor little orphan, he was instinctively kind. Perhaps sensing this, the pup licked his hand and allowed himself to be petted even after the meager meal had been gobbled down.

"A scrapper." Christian laughed as he took his beautiful artist's hands over the dirty fur. "Tough little fellow, aren't you?"

"He needs a bath," I said, but laughed as well when the dusty paws streaked my dress. "And a real meal." Delighted with the attention, the pup licked my face, his whole body trembling with delight.

Of course, I fell in love. He was such a homely little bundle, so trusting, so needy. We played with him, as charmed as children, and had a laughing argument over what to call him.

We named him Fred. He seemed to approve as he yipped and danced and tumbled in the dirt. I will never forget the sweetness of it, the simplicity. My love and

I sitting on the ground with a little lost pup, pretending that we would take him home together, care for him together.

In the end, I took Fred with me. Ethan had been asking for a pet, and I felt he was old enough now to be both appreciative and responsible. What a clamor there was when I brought the puppy to the nursery. The children were wide-eyed and excited, each taking turns holding and hugging until I'm sure young Fred felt like a king.

He was bathed and fed with a great deal of ceremony. Stroked and cuddled and tickled until he fell asleep in exhausted euphoria.

Fergus returned. The excitement over Fred had caused me to forget our plans for the evening. I'm sure my husband was right to be annoyed that I was far from ready to go out and dine. The children, unable to contain their delight, raced about, adding to his impatience. Little Ethan, proud as a new father, carried Fred into the parlor.

"What the devil have you got?" Fergus demanded.

"A puppy." Ethan held the wriggling bundle up for his father's inspection. "His name is Fred."

Noting my husband's expression, I took the puppy from my son and began to explain how it had come about. I suppose I'd hoped to appeal to Fergus's softer side, to the love, or at least the pride he felt for Ethan. But he was adamant.

"I'll not have a mongrel in my house. Do you think I have worked all my life to own such things only to have some flea-ridden mutt relieving himself on the carpets, chewing on the draperies?"

"He'll be good." Lip quivering, Colleen hugged my

skirts. "Please, Papa. We'll keep him in the nursery and watch him."

"You'll do no such thing, young lady." Fergus dismissed Colleen's tears with a glance and turned to Ethan, whose eyes were also brimming. There was a fractional softening in his expression. After all this was his first son, his heir, his immortality. "A mongrel's no pet for you, my lad. Why any fisherman's son might own a mongrel. If it's a dog you want, we'll look into it when we get back to New York. A fine dog, with a pedigree."

"I want Fred." With his sweet face crumbling, Ethan looked up at his father. Even little Sean was crying now, though I doubt he understood.

"Out of the question." With his temper obviously straining, Fergus walked to the whiskey decanter and poured. "It's completely unsuitable. Bianca, have one of the servants dispose of it."

I know I paled as quickly as the children. Even Fred whimpered, pressing his face to my breast. "Fergus, you can't be so cruel."

There was surprise in his eyes, I have no doubt of it. It had never occurred to him that I would speak to him so, and in front of the children. "Madam, do as I bid."

"Mama said we could keep him," Colleen began, her youthful temper lifting her voice. "Mama promised. You can't take him away. Mama won't let you."

"I run this home. If you don't wish a strapping, mind your tone."

I found myself clutching Colleen's shoulders, as much to suppress her as to protect. He would not lift a hand to my children. Fury at the thought of it blinded me to all else. I know I trembled as I bent to her, to shift Fred back into her arms.

"Go upstairs to Nanny now," I said quietly. "Take your brothers."

"He won't kill Fred." Is there a rage more poignant than that of a child? "I hate him, and I won't let him kill Fred."

"Shh. It will be all right, I promise you. It will be all right. Go up to Nanny."

"A poor job you've done, Bianca," Fergus began when the children had left us. "The girl is old enough to know her place."

"Her place?" The fury had my heart roaring in my head. "What is her place, Fergus? To sit quietly in some corner, her hands folded, her thoughts and feelings unspoken until you have bartered her off into a suitable marriage? They are children. Our children. How could you hurt them so?"

Never in our marriage had I used such a tone with him. Never had I thought to. For a moment I was certain that he would strike me. It was in his eyes. But he seemed to pull himself back, though his fingers were white as marble against the glass he held.

"You question me, Bianca?" His face was very pale with his rage, his eyes very dark. "Do you forget whose house you stand in, whose food you eat, whose clothes you wear?"

"No." Now I felt a new kind of grief, that our marriage should be brought down to only that. "No, I don't forget. I can't forget. I would sooner wear rags and starve than see you hurt my children so. I will not allow you to take that dog from them and have him destroyed."

"Allow?" He was no longer pale, but crimson with fury. "Now it is you who forget your place, Bianca.

Is it any wonder the children openly defy me with such a mother?"

"They want your love, your attention." I was shouting now, beyond restraint. "As I have wanted it. But you love nothing but your money, your position."

How bitterly we argued then. The names he called me I can't repeat. He dashed the glass against the wall, shattering the crystal and his own control. There was a wildness in his eyes when his hands came around my throat. I was afraid for my life, terrified for my children. He shoved me aside so that I fell into a chair. He was breathing quickly as he stared down at me.

Very slowly, with great effort, he composed himself. The violent color faded from his cheeks. "I can see now that I've been too generous with you," he said. "From this point, it will change. Don't think you will continue to go your own way as you choose. We will cancel our plans for this evening. I have business in Boston. While I'm there, I will interview governesses. It's time the children learned respect, and how to appreciate their position. Between you and their nanny, they have become spoiled and willful." He took his watch from his pocket and studied the time. "I will leave tonight and be gone two days. When I return I expect you to have remembered your duties. If the mongrel is still in my house when I return, both you and the children will be punished. Am I clear, Bianca?"

"Yes." My voice shook. "Quite clear."

"Excellent. In two days then."

He walked out of the parlor. I did not move for an hour. I heard the carriage come for him. Heard him instruct the servants. In that time my head had cleared and I knew what I had to do.

Chapter Seven

"What the hell good is messing with all these papers?" Hawkins paced the sun-washed room in the rented house. He had never been a patient man and preferred to use his fists or a weapon rather than his brain. His associate, now going by the name of Robert Marshall, sat at an oak desk, carefully leafing through the papers he had stolen from The Towers a month before. He had dyed his hair a nondescript brown and had grown a credible beard and mustache that he tinted the same shade.

If Max Quartermain had seen him, he would have called him Ellis Caufield. Whatever name he chose, whatever disguise he employed, he was a thief whose unscrupulous mind had centered on the Calhoun emeralds.

"I went through a great deal of trouble to get these papers," Caufield said mildly. "Now that we've lost the professor, I'll have to decipher them myself. It will simply take a little longer."

"This whole job stinks." Hawkins stared out the window at the thick trees that sheltered the house. It was tucked behind a grove of quaking aspen, and the cool leaves quivered continually in the breeze. With the windows of the study thrown open, the scents of pine and sweet peas wafted into the room. He could only smell his own frustration. The bright glint of blue that was the bay didn't lift his mood. He'd spent enough time in prison to feel shut in, however lovely the surroundings.

Cracking his knuckles, he turned away from the view. "We could be stuck in this place for weeks."

"You should learn to appreciate the scenery. And the room." His partner's nervous habit was an annoyance, but he tolerated it. For the time being, he needed Hawkins. After the emeralds had been found...well, that was another matter. "I certainly prefer the house to the boat for the long term. And finding the right accommodations across the bay on this island was difficult and expensive."

"That's another thing." Hawkins pulled out a cigarette. "We're spending a bundle, and all we've got to show for it is a bunch of old papers."

"I assure you, the emeralds will be more than worth any overhead."

"If the bloody things exist."

"They exist." Caufield waved the smoke away in a fussy gesture, but his eyes were intense. "They exist. Before the summer ends, I'm going to hold them in my hands." He lifted them. They were smooth and white and clever. He could all but see the glittery green stones dripping from his palms. "They're going to be mine."

"Ours," Hawkins corrected.

Caufield looked up and smiled. "Ours, of course."

After dinner, Max went back to his lists. He told himself he was being responsible, doing what needed to be done. In truth he'd needed to put some distance between himself and Lilah. He couldn't delude himself into thinking it was only desire he felt for her. That was a basic biological reaction and could be triggered by a face on a television screen, a voice on the radio.

There was nothing so simple or so easily dismissed about his reaction to Lilah.

Every day he was around her his emotions became more tangled, more unsteady and more ungovernable. It had been difficult enough when he had looked at her and wanted her. Now he looked at her and felt his needs meld with dreams that were unrealistic, foolish and impossible.

He'd never given much thought to falling in love, and none at all to marriage and family. His work had always been enough, filling the gaps nicely. He enjoyed women, and if he fell far short of being the Don Juan of Cornell, he had managed a few comfortable and satisfying relationships. Still, he'd never felt a burning need to race to the altar or to start building picket fences.

Bachelorhood had suited him, and when he had thought about the future, he had imagined himself getting crusty, perhaps taking up the pipe and buying a nice dog for companionship.

He was an uncomplicated man who lived a quiet life. At least until recently. Once he had helped the Calhouns locate the emeralds, he would go back to that quiet life. And he would go back alone. While things might never be exactly the same for him, he knew that she would forget the awkward college professor before the winter winds blew across the bay.

And he figured the sooner he finished what he had agreed to do and went away, the easier it would be to go. Gathering his lists, he decided it was time to take the next step toward ending the most incredible summer of his life.

He found Amanda in her room, going over her own lists. These were for her wedding, which would take place in three weeks.

"I'm sorry to interrupt."

"That's okay." Amanda pushed her glasses back up her nose and smiled. "I've got everything under control here except my nerves." She tapped her papers together and set them aside on the slant-top desk. "I was all for eloping, but Aunt Coco would have murdered me."

"I guess weddings take a lot of work."

"Even planning a small family ceremony is like plotting a major offensive. Or being in the circus," she decided, and laughed. "You end up juggling photographers with color schemes and fittings and floral arrangements. But I'm getting good at it. I took care of C.C.'s, I ought to be able to do the same for myself. Except..." Pulling her glasses off, she began to fold and unfold the earpieces. "The whole thing scares the good sense right out of me. So, take my mind off it, Max, and tell me what's on yours."

"I've been working on this. I don't know how complete it is." He set his list in front of her. "The names of all the servants I could find, the ones who worked here the summer Bianca died."

Lips pursed, Amanda slid her glasses back on. She

appreciated the precise handwriting and neat columns. "All of these?"

"According to the ledger I went through. I thought we could contact the families, maybe even luck out and find a few still alive."

"Anyone who worked here back then would have to be over the century mark."

"Not necessarily. A lot of the help could have been young. Some of the maids, the garden and kitchen help." When she began to tap her pencil on the desk, he shrugged. "It's a long shot, I know, but—"

"No." Her gaze still on the list, she nodded. "I like it. Even if we can't reach anyone who actually worked here then, they might have told stories to their children. It's a safe bet some of them were local—maybe still are." She looked up at him. "Good thinking, Max."

"I'd like to help you try to pin some of the names down."

"I can use all the help I can get. It's not going to be easy."

"Research is what I'm best at."

"You've got yourself a deal." She held out a hand to shake. "Why don't we split the list in half and start tomorrow? I imagine the cook, the butler, the housekeeper, Bianca's personal maid and the nanny all traveled with them from New York."

"But the day help, and the lower positions were hired locally."

"Exactly. We could divide the list in that way, then cross-reference…" She trailed off as Sloan came in through the terrace doors carrying a bottle of champagne and two glasses.

"Leave you alone for five minutes and you start entertaining other men in your room." He set the wine aside. "And talking about cross-referencing, too. Must be serious."

"We hadn't even gotten to alphabetizing," Amanda told Sloan.

"Looks like I got here just in time." He took the pencil out of her hand before drawing her to her feet. "In another minute you might have been hip deep in correlations."

They certainly didn't need him, Max decided. By the way they were kissing each other, it was apparent they'd forgotten all about him. On his way out, he cast one envious look over his shoulder. They were just smiling at each other, saying nothing. It was obvious that they were two people who knew what they wanted. Each other.

Back in his room, Max decided he would spend the rest of the evening working on notes for his book. Or, if he could gather up the courage, he could sit in front of the old manual typewriter Coco had unearthed for him. He could take that step, that big one, and begin writing the story instead of preparing to write it.

He took one look at the battered Remington and felt his stomach clutch. He wanted to sit down, to lay his fingers on those keys, just as desperately as a man wants to hold a loved and desired woman in his arms. He was as terrified of facing the single blank sheet of paper as he would have been of a firing squad. Maybe more so.

He just needed to prepare, Max told himself. His reference books needed to be positioned better. His notes had to be more easily accessible. The light had to be adjusted.

He thought of dozens of minute details to be perfected

before he could begin. Once he had accomplished that, had tried and failed to think of more, he sat.

Here he was, he realized, about to begin something he'd dreamed of doing his entire life. All he had to do was write the first sentence, and he would be committed.

His fingers curled into fists on the keys.

Why did he think he could write a book? A thesis, a lecture, yes. That's what he was trained to do. But a book, God, a novel wasn't something anyone could be taught to do. It took imagination and wit and a sense of drama. Daydreaming a story and articulating it on paper were two entirely different things.

Wasn't it foolish to begin something that was bound to lead to failure? As long as he was preparing to write the book, there was no risk and no disappointment. He could go on preparing for years without any sense of shame. If he started it, really started it, there would be no more hiding behind notes and research books. When he failed, he wouldn't even have the dream.

Wound tight, he ran his fingers over the keys while his mind jumped with dozens of excuses to postpone the moment. When the first sentence streaked from his brain to his fingers and appeared on the blank sheet of paper, he let out a long, unsteady breath.

Three hours later, he had ten full sheets. The story that had swum through his head for so long was taking shape with words. His words. He knew it was probably dreadful, but it didn't seem to matter. He was writing, actually writing. The process of it fascinated and ex-hilarated. The sound of it, the clatter and thud of the keys, delighted him.

He'd stripped off his shirt and shoes and sat bent over, his brows together, his eyes slightly unfocused.

His fingers would race over the keys then stop while he strained to find the way to take what was in his head and put it on paper.

That was how Lilah found him. He'd left his terrace doors open for the breeze, though he'd long since stopped noticing it. The room was dark but for the slant of light from the lamp on the desk. She stood watching him, aroused by his total concentration, charmed by the way his hair fell into his eyes.

Was it any wonder she had come to him? she thought. She was so completely in love with him, how could she stay away? It couldn't be wrong to want to have a night with him, to show him that love in a way he might understand and accept. She needed to belong to him, to forge a bond that would matter to both of them.

Not sex, but intimacy. It had begun the moment he had lain half-drowned on the shingle and lifted a hand to her face. There was a connection she couldn't escape. And as she had risen from her own bed to come to his, one that she no longer wanted to escape.

Her instinct had led her to his room tonight as surely as it had led her to the beach during the storm.

The decision was hers, she knew. However badly he wanted her, he wouldn't take what wasn't offered. And he would hesitate to take even that because of his rules and his codes. Perhaps if he'd loved her... But she couldn't let herself think of that. In time, he would love her. Her own feelings were too deep and too strong not to find their match.

So she would take the first step. Seduction.

His concentration was so intense that a shout wouldn't have broken it. But her scent, whispering across the room on the night breeze, shattered it. Desire pumped into his blood before he glanced up and saw her in the doorway. The white robe fluttered around her. Caught in the fanning air, her hair danced over her shoulders. Behind her the sky was a black canvas, and she had—illusion to reality—stepped out of it. She smiled and his fingers went limp on the keys.

"Lilah."

"I had a dream." It was true, and speaking the truth helped calm her nerves. "About you and me. There was moonlight. I could almost feel the light on my skin until you touched me." She stepped inside, the movement causing the silk to make a faint shushing sound, like water rippling over water. "Then I didn't feel anything but you. There were flowers, the fragrance very light, very sweet. And a nightingale, that long liquid call for a mate. It was a lovely dream, Max." She stopped beside his desk. "Then I woke up, alone."

He was certain the ball of tension in his stomach would rip free any moment and leave him helpless. She was more beautiful than any fantasy, her hair like wildfire across her shoulders, her graceful body silhouetted enticingly beneath the thin, shifting silk.

"It's late." He tried to clear the huskiness from his throat. "You shouldn't be here."

"Why?"

"Because…it's—"

"Improper?" she suggested. "Reckless?" She brushed the hair from his brow. "Dangerous?"

Max lurched to his feet to grasp the back of the chair. "Yes, all of that."

There were age-old women's secrets in her eyes. "But I feel reckless, Max. Don't you?"

Desperate was the word. Desperate for just one touch.

His fingers whitened on the chair back. "There's a matter of respect."

Her smile was suddenly very warm and very sweet. "I respect you, Max."

"No, I mean…" She looked so lovely when she smiled that way, so young, so fragile. "We decided to be friends."

"We are." With her eyes on his, she lifted her hand to smooth back her hair. Her rings glittered in the lamplight.

"And this is—"

"Something we both want," she finished. When she stepped toward him, he jerked back. The chair tumbled over. Her laughter wasn't mocking, but warm and delighted. "Do I make you nervous, Max?"

"That's a mild word for it." He could barely drag air through his dry throat. At his sides his hands were fisted, twins of the fists in the pit of his stomach. "Lilah, I don't want to ruin what we have together. Lord knows I don't want you to break my heart."

She smiled, feeling a surge of hope through her own nerves. "Could I?"

"You know you could. You've probably lost track of the hearts you've broken."

There it was again, she thought as disappointment shuddered through her. He still saw her, would likely always see her, as the careless siren who lured men, then discarded them. He didn't understand that it was her heart on the line, had been her heart on the line all along. She wouldn't let it stop her—couldn't. Tonight, being with him tonight, was meant. She felt it too strongly to be wrong.

"Tell me, Professor, do you ever dream of me?" She

stepped toward him; he backed up. Now they stood in the shadows beyond the lamplight. "Do you ever lie in the dark and wonder what it would be like?"

He was losing ground fast. His mind was so full of her there wasn't room for anything but need. "You know I do."

Another step and they were caught in a slash of moonlight as white as her robe, and as seductive. "And when you dream of it, where are we?"

"It doesn't seem to matter where." He had to touch her, couldn't resist, even if it was only to brush his fingertips over her hair. "We're alone."

"We're alone now." She slid her hands over his shoulders to link them behind his neck. "Kiss me, Max. The way you did the first time, when we were sitting on the grass in the sunlight."

His fingers were in her hair, taut as wires. "It won't end there, Lilah. Not this time."

Her lips curved as they lifted to his. "Just kiss me."

He fought to gentle his grip, to keep his mouth easy as it cruised over hers. Surely he was strong enough to hold back this clawing need to ravage. He wouldn't hurt her. He swore it. And clung to the dim hope that he could have this one night with her and emerge unscathed.

So sweet, she thought. So lovely. The tenderness of the kiss was all the more poignant as she could feel the tremble of repressed passion in both of them. Her heart, already brimming with love, overflowed. When their lips parted, there were tears glittering in her eyes.

"I don't want it to end there." She touched her lips to his again. "Neither of us do."

"No."

"Make love with me, Max," she murmured. She kept

her eyes on his as she stepped back, unbelting her robe. "I need you tonight." The robe slithered to the floor.

Beneath it her skin was as white and smooth as marble. Her long slender limbs might have been carved and polished by an artist's hands. She stood, cloaked only in moonlight, and waited.

He'd never seen anything more perfect, more elegant or fragile. Suddenly his hands felt big and clumsy, his fingers rough. His breath tore raggedly through his lips as he touched her. Though his fingers barely floated over her skin, he was terrified he would leave bruises behind. Fascinated, he watched his hand skim over her, tracing the slope of her shoulders, sliding down the graceful arms and back again. Carefully, very carefully, brushing over the water-soft skin of her breasts.

First her legs went weak. No one had ever touched her like this, with such drugging gentleness. It was as though she were the first woman he had ever seen and he was memorizing her face and form through his fingertips. She had come to seduce, yet her arms lay weighted at her sides. And she was seduced. Her head fell back in an involuntary gesture of surrender. He had no way of knowing that this surrender was her first.

That vulnerable column of her throat was impossible to resist. He pressed his mouth against it even as his palm brushed lightly over the point of her breast.

The combination had a bolt of sensation shooting through her. Stunned by it, she jolted and gasped out his name.

He retreated instantly, cursing himself. "I'm sorry." He was half-blind with needs and shook his head to clear it. "I've always been clumsy."

"Clumsy?" In a haze of longing, she swayed toward

him, running her lips over his shoulder, his throat, down his chest. "Can't you feel what you're doing to me? Don't stop." Her mouth found his and lingered. "I think I'd die if you did."

The barrage on his system nearly felled him. Her hands streaked over him, impatient and greedy. Her mouth, Lord her mouth was hot and quick, searing his skin with every breathy kiss. He couldn't think, could barely breathe. There was nothing to do but feel.

Straining for control, he lifted her face to his, calming her lips, drugging them and her as he centered all of his needs into that one endless kiss. Yes, he could feel what he was doing to her, and it amazed him. On a low, throaty groan, she went limp in a surrender more erotic than any seduction. Her body seemed to melt into his in total pliancy, total trust. When he lifted her into his arms she made a small, lazy sound of pleasure.

Her eyes were nearly closed. He could see the glint of green under the cover of her lashes. As he carried her to the bed he felt as strong as Hercules. Gently, watching her face, he laid her on the covers.

There was moonlight here, streaming through the windows like liquid silver. He could hear the wind sighing through the trees and the distant drum of water on rock. Her scent, as mysterious as Eve, reached for him as easily as her arms.

He took her hands. Struck by the romance of the night, he brought them to his lips, skimming his mouth over her knuckles, down her fingertips, over her palms. All the time, he watched her as he scraped lightly with his teeth, soothed and aroused with his tongue. He heard her breath quicken, watched her eyes cloud with dazed pleasure and confusion as he made love to her hands.

He felt the thunder of her pulse when he pressed his lips to her wrist.

He was bringing her something she hadn't prepared for. Total helplessness. Did he know how completely she was in his power? she wondered hazily. The drunk and weighty pleasure was flowing from her fingertips into every part of her. When his lips slid down her arm to nuzzle the inside of her elbow, a moan was wrenched from her.

She wasn't even aware that she was moving under him, inviting him to take anything, everything he wanted. When his mouth came to hers at last, his name was the only word she could form.

He fought back greed. It was impossible not to feel it, with her body so hot, so soft, so agile beneath his. But he refused to give in to it. Tonight, for there might only be tonight, would last. He wanted more than that fast and frantic union his body ached for. He wanted the dazzling pleasure of learning every inch of her, of discovering her secrets, her weaknesses. With patience he could brand in his brain what it was like to touch her and feel her tremble, what it was like to taste and hear her sigh. When her hands moved over him, he knew she was as lost in the night as he.

He slid down her slowly, searing her flesh with open-mouthed kisses, whispering fingertips. With torturous patience he lingered at her breasts until they were achingly full with pleasure. Down, gradually down, while her fingers clenched and unclenched in his hair. He could hear her now, soft, incoherent pleas, gasping sighs as he trailed his mouth down her torso, nipped teasing teeth across her hip. She felt his breath flutter against her thigh and cried out, rearing up as the first hot wave slammed into her. She flew over the edge then cartwheeled down as he roamed relentlessly to her knee.

He couldn't get enough. Every taste of her was more potent than the last. He sated himself on it as the tension began to roar in his temples, burn in his blood. Grasping her flailing hands, he drove himself mad by pushing her to peak again. When her body went lax, when her breath was sobbing, he brought his mouth back to hers.

She was willing to beg, but she couldn't speak. Sensation after sensation tore through her, leaving her weak and giddy and aching for more. Desperate for him, she fumbled with the catch of his jeans. She would have screamed with frustration if his mouth hadn't seduced hers into a groan.

Tugging, gasping, she dragged the denim over his hips, too delirious to know that her urgent fingers were making him shudder. Damp flesh slid over damp flesh as they pulled the jeans aside.

"Wait." The word came harshly through his lips as he fought to hold on to the last of his control. "Look at me." His fingers tightened in her hair as she opened her eyes. "Look at me," he repeated. "I want you to remember."

Muscles trembling with the effort to go slowly, he slipped into her. Her eyes went cloudy but remained on his as they set an easy rhythm. She knew as he filled her, with himself, with such perfect beauty, that she would always remember.

It was so sweet, so natural, the way his head rested between her breasts. Lilah smiled at the sensation as she stroked his hair. One hand was still linked with his as it had been when they'd slid over the crest together.

Half-dreaming now, she imagined what it would be like
to fall asleep together, just like this, night after night.

He could feel her relax beneath him, her body warm
and pliant, her skin still sheened with the dew of passion. Her heartbeat was slowing gradually. For a moment
he could pretend that this was one night among many.
That she could belong to him in that complex and intimate way a woman belonged to a man.

He knew he'd given her pleasure, and that for a time
they had been as bound together as two people could be.
But now, he hadn't an idea what he should say—because
all he wanted to say was that he loved her.

"What are you thinking?" she murmured.

He steadied himself. "My brain's not working yet."

Her laugh was low and warm. She shifted, wriggling
down until they were face-to-face. "Then I'll tell you
what I'm thinking." She brought her mouth to his in a
languid, lingering kiss. "I like your lips." Teasingly she
nipped the lower one. "And your hands. Your shoulders,
your eyes." As she spoke, she trailed a fingertip up and
down his spine. "In fact, at the moment I can't think of
anything I don't like about you."

"I'll remind you of that the next time I irritate you."
He combed her hair back because he enjoyed seeing it
spread over his sheets. "I can't believe I'm here with
you, like this."

"Didn't you feel it, Max, almost from the beginning?"

"Yes." He traced her mouth with a fingertip. "I figured it was wishful thinking."

"You don't give yourself enough credit, Professor."
She traced light, lazy kisses over his face. "You're an
attractive man with an admirable mind and a sense of
compassion that's irresistible." Her eyes didn't light with

amusement when he shifted. Instead she lay a hand on his cheek. "When you made love with me tonight, it was beautiful. The most beautiful night of my life."

She saw it in his eyes. Not embarrassment now, but plain disbelief. Because she was defenseless, stripped to the soul, nothing could have hurt her more. "Sorry," she said tightly and moved away. "I'm sure that sounds trite coming from me."

"Lilah…"

"No, it's fine." She pressed her lips together until she was certain her voice would be light and breezy again. "No use complicating things." As she sat up, she tossed her hair back. "There aren't any strings here, Professor. No trapdoors, no fine print. We're two consenting adults who enjoy each other. Agreed?"

"I'm not sure."

"Let's just say we'll take it a day at a time. Or a night at a time." She leaned over to kiss him. "Now that we've got that settled, I'd better go."

"Don't." He took her hand before she could slip off the bed. "Don't go. No strings," he said carefully as he studied her. "No complications. Just stay with me tonight."

She smiled a little. "I'll just seduce you again."

"I was hoping you'd say that." He pulled her against him. "I want you with me when the sun comes up."

Chapter Eight

When the sun came up to pour golden light through the windows and chase away the last dusky shadows, she was in his arms. It seemed incredible to him that her head would be resting on his shoulder, her hand fisted lightly over his heart. She slept like a child, deeply, curled toward him for warmth and comfort.

Though the night was over, he lay still, loath to wake her. The birds had begun their morning chorus. It was so quiet, he could hear the wind breathing through the trees. He knew that soon the sound of saws and hammers would disrupt the peace and bring reality back. So he clung to this short interlude between the mystery of the night and the bustle of day.

She sighed and settled closer as he stroked her hair. He remembered how generous she had been in those dark sleepy hours. It seemed he had only to think, to wish, and she would turn toward him. Again and again they had loved, in silence and with perfect understanding.

He wanted to believe in miracles, to believe that it had been as special and monumental a night for her as it had been for him. He was afraid to take her words at face value.

No one's ever made me feel the way you do.

Yet they had played over and over in his head, giving him hope. If he was careful and patient and weighed each step before it was taken, maybe he could make a miracle.

Though he didn't feel suited to the role of prince, he tilted her face to his to wake her with a kiss.

"Mmm." She smiled but didn't open her eyes. "Can I have another?"

Her voice, husky with sleep, sent desire shivering along his skin. He forgot to be careful. He forgot to be patient. His mouth took hers the second time with an edgy desperation that had her system churning before she was fully awake.

"Max." Throbbing, she locked herself around him. "I want you. Now. Right now."

He was already inside her, already dragging her with him where they both wanted to go. The ride was fast and furious, shooting them both to the top where they clung, breathless and giddy.

When her hands slid off his damp back, she still hadn't opened her eyes. "Good morning," she managed. "I just had the most incredible dream."

Though he was still light-headed, he braced on his forearms to look down at her. "Tell me about it."

"I was in bed with this very sexy man. He had big blue eyes, dark hair that was always falling in his face."

Smiling, she opened her eyes and brushed it back for him. "This long, streamlined body." Still watching him, she moved her hands deliberately over him. "I didn't want to wake up, but when I did, it was even better than the dream."

Afraid he was crushing her, he rolled to reverse their positions. "What are the chances of spending the rest of our lives in this bed?"

She dropped a kiss on his shoulder. "I'm game." Then she groaned when the drone of power tools cut through the morning quiet. "It can't be seven-thirty."

As reluctant as she, he glanced at the clock beside the bed. "I'm afraid it can."

"Tell me it's my day off."

"I wish I could."

"Lie," she suggested, laying her cheek on his chest.

"Will you let me take you to work?"

She winced. "Don't say that word."

"Go for a drive with me after?"

She lifted her head again. "Where?"

"Anywhere."

Tilting her head, she smiled. "My favorite place."

Max kept his mind off Lilah—or tried to—by focusing on the multilayered task of locating people to go with the names on his list. He checked court records, police records, church records and death certificates. His meticulous legwork was rewarded with a handful of addresses.

When he felt he'd exhausted all the leads for that day, he drove by C.C.'s garage. He found her buried to the waist under the hood of a black sedan.

"I'm sorry to interrupt," he shouted over the din jingling out of a portable radio.

"Then don't." There was a streak of grease over her brow, but her scowl disappeared when she looked up and saw Max. "Hi."

"I could come back."

"Why, just because I snapped your head off?" She grinned, taking a rag out of her coveralls to wipe her hands. "Buy you a drink?" She jerked her head toward a soft drink machine.

"No, thanks. I just stopped by to ask you about a car."

"You're driving Lilah's, aren't you? Is it acting up?"

"No. The thing is I might be doing a lot of driving in the next few days, and I don't feel right using her car. I thought you might know if there's anything for sale in the area."

C.C. pursed her lips. "You want to buy a car?"

"Nothing extravagant. Just some convenient transportation. Then when I get back to New York..." He trailed off. He didn't want to think about going back to New York. "I can always sell it later."

"It so happens I do know somebody with a car for sale. Me."

"You?"

Nodding, she stuffed the rag back into her pocket. "With a baby coming, I've decided to turn in my Spitfire for a family car."

"Spitfire?" He wasn't sure what that was, but it didn't sound like the kind of car a dignified college professor would drive.

"I've had her for years, and I sure would feel better selling her to someone I know." She already had his hand and was pulling him outside.

There it sat, a fire-engine-red toy with a white rag top and bucket seats. "Well, I..."

"I rebuilt the engine a couple of years ago." C.C. was busy opening the hood. "She drives like a dream. There's less than ten thousand miles on the tires. I'm the original owner, so I can guarantee she's been treated like a lady. And there's..." She glanced up and grinned. "I sound like a guy in a plaid sports jacket."

He could see his face in the shiny red paint. "I've never owned a sports car."

The wistfulness in his voice made C.C. smile. "Tell you what, leave me Lilah's car, drive her around. See how she suits you."

Max found himself behind the wheel, trying not to grin like a fool as the wind streamed through his hair. What would his students think, he wondered, if they could see sturdy old Dr. Quartermain tooling around in a flashy convertible? They'd probably think he'd gone around the bend. Maybe he had, but he was having the time of his life.

It was a car that would suit Lilah, he thought. He could already see her sitting beside him, her hair dancing as she laughed and lifted her arms to the wind. Or kicked back in the seat, her eyes closed, letting the sun warm her face.

It was a nice dream, and it could come true. At least for a while. And maybe he wouldn't sell the car when he got back to New York. There was no law that said he had to drive a practical sedan. He could keep it to remind him of a few incredible weeks that had changed his life.

Maybe he'd never be sturdy old Dr. Quartermain again.

He cruised up the winding mountain roads, then back

down again to try out the little car in traffic. Delighted with the world in general, he sat at a light, tapping his fingers against the wheel to the beat of the music on the radio.

There were people jamming the sidewalks, crowding the shops. If he'd seen a parking place, he might have whipped in, strolled into a shop himself just to test his endurance. Instead, he entertained himself by watching people scout for that perfect T-shirt.

He noticed the man with dark hair and a trim dark beard standing on the curb, staring at him. Full of himself and the spiffy car, Max grinned and waved. He was halfway down the block before it hit him. He braked, causing a bellow of bad-tempered honking. Thinking fast, he turned a sharp left, streaked down a side street and fought his way through traffic back to the intersection. The man was gone. Max searched the street but couldn't find a sign of him. He cursed low and bitterly over the lack of a parking space, over his own slow-wittedness.

The hair had been dyed, and the beard had hid part of the face. But the eyes...Max couldn't forget the eyes. It had been Caufield standing on the crowded sidewalk, looking at Max not with admiration or absent interest, but with barely controlled rage.

He had himself under control by the time he picked Lilah up at the visitors' center. He had made what he considered the logical decision not to tell her. The less she knew, the less she was involved. The less she was involved, the better chance there was that she wouldn't be hurt.

She was too impulsive, he reflected. If she knew

Caufield had been in the village, she would try to hunt him down herself. And she was too clever. If she managed to find him... The idea made Max's blood run cold. No one knew better than he how ruthless the man could be.

When he saw Lilah coming across the lot toward the car, he knew he'd risk anything, even his life, to keep her safe.

"Well, well, what's this?" Brows lifted, she tapped a finger on the fender. "My old heap wasn't good enough, so you borrowed my sister's?"

"What?" Foolishly he'd forgotten the car and everything else since he'd recognized Caufield. "Oh, the car."

"Yes, the car." She leaned over to kiss him, and was puzzled by his absent response and the pat on her shoulder.

"Actually, I'm thinking of buying it. C.C.'s in the market for a family car, so..."

"So you're going to buy yourself a snappy little toy."

"I know it's not my usual style," he began.

"I wasn't going to say that." Her brows drew together as she studied his face. Something was going on in that complicated mind of his. "I was going to say good for you. I'm glad you're giving yourself a break." She hopped in and stretched. Her lifted hand reached for his, but he only gave it a light squeeze, then released it. Telling herself she was being oversensitive, she fixed a smile in place. "So, how about that drive? I was thinking we could cruise down the coast."

"I'm a little tired." He hated lying, but he needed to get back to talk to Trent and Sloan, to feed the new description to the police. "Can I have a rain check?"

"Sure." She managed to keep her smile in place. He

was so polite, so distant. Wanting some echo of their pre-
vious intimacy, she put a hand over his when he slipped
into the car beside her. "I'm always up for a nap. Your
room or mine?"

"I'm not...I don't think that's a good idea."

His hand was tense over the gearshift, and his fingers
made no move to link with hers. He wouldn't even look
at her, hadn't really looked at her, she realized, since
she'd crossed the lot.

"I see." She lifted her hand from his and let it fall in
her lap. "Under the circumstances, I'm sure you're right."

"Lilah—"

"What?"

No, he decided. He needed to do this his way. "Nothing." Reaching for the keys, he switched on the ignition.

They didn't speak on the way home. Max continued
to convince himself that lying to her was the best way.
Maybe she was miffed because he'd put off the drive, but
he'd make it up to her. He just had to keep out of her way
until he'd handled a few details. In any case his mind
was crowded with possibilities that he needed time and
space to work through. If Caufield and Hawkins were
both still on the island, both of them bold enough to
stroll through the village, did that mean they had found
something useful in the papers? Were they still looking?
Had they, as he had, dipped into the resources at the library to find out more?

They knew he was alive now. Would they manage
to connect him with the Calhouns? If they considered
him a liability, would his relationship with Lilah put
her in danger?

That was a risk he couldn't afford to take.

He turned up the winding road that brought the peak of The Towers into view.

"I may have to go back to New York sooner than I expected," he said, thinking out loud.

To keep from protesting, she pressed her lips tight. "Really?"

He glanced over, cleared his throat. "Yes…ah, business. I could continue to do my research from there."

"That's very considerate of you, Professor. I'm sure you'd hate to leave a job half-done. And you wouldn't have any awkward relationships to interfere."

His mind was already focused on what needed to be done, and he made an absent sound of agreement.

By the time they pulled up at The Towers, Lilah had managed to turn the hurt into anger. He didn't want to be with her, and by his attitude it was plain he regretted that they'd ever been together. Fine. She wasn't about to sit around and sulk because some highbrow college professor wasn't interested in her.

She resisted slamming the car door, barely resisted biting his hand off at the wrist when he set it on her shoulder. "Maybe we can drive down the coast tomorrow."

She glanced at his hand, then at his face. "Don't hold your breath."

He jammed his hands into his pockets as she strolled up the steps. Definitely miffed, he thought.

By the time he had relayed his information to the other men and had fought his way through the pecking order at the police station, he really was tired. It might have been tension or the fact that he'd only had a couple hours' sleep the night before, but he gave in, stretched across his bed and tuned out until dinner.

Feeling better, he wandered downstairs. He thought about finding Lilah, asking her to walk in the gardens after the meal. Or maybe they'd take a drive after all, in the moonlight. It hadn't been a very big lie, and now that he'd unburdened himself to the police, he wouldn't have to dwell on it. In any case, if he decided it was best to leave, he might not have another evening with her.

Yes, a drive. Maybe he could ask her if she'd consider visiting him in New York—or just going away for a weekend somewhere. It didn't have to end, not if he started taking those careful steps.

He strolled into the parlor, found it empty and strolled out again. Just the two of them, watching the moon on the water, maybe pulling over to walk along the beach. He could begin to court her properly. He imagined she'd be amused by the term, but it was what he wanted to do.

He followed the sound of a piano into the music room. Suzanna was alone, playing for herself. The music seemed to match the expression in her eyes. There was a sadness in them, too deep for anyone else to feel. But when she saw him, she stopped and smiled.

"I didn't mean to interrupt."

"That's all right. It's time to get back to the real world anyway. Amanda took the kids into town so I was taking advantage of the lull."

"I was just looking for Lilah."

"Oh, she's gone."

"Gone?"

Suzanna was pushing back from the piano when Max barked the word and had her rising slowly. "Yes, she went out."

"Where? When?"

"Just a little while ago." Suzanna studied him as she crossed the room. "I think she had a date."

"A—a date?" He felt as though someone had just swung a sledgehammer into his solar plexus.

"I'm sorry, Max." Concerned, she laid a comforting hand on his. She didn't think she'd ever seen a man more miserably in love. "I didn't realize. She may have just gone out to meet friends, or to be by herself."

No, he thought, shaking his head. That would be worse. If she was alone, and Caufield was anywhere close… He shook off the panic. It wasn't Lilah the man was after, but the emeralds.

"It's all right, I only wanted to talk to her about something."

"Does she know how you feel?"

"No—yes. I don't know," he said lamely. He saw his romantic dreams about moonlight and courtship go up in smoke. "It doesn't matter."

"It would to her. Lilah doesn't take people or their feelings lightly, Max."

No strings, he thought. No trapdoors. Well, he'd already fallen through the trapdoor, and his feelings were the noose around his neck. But that wasn't the point. "I'm just concerned about her going out alone. The police haven't caught Hawkins or Caufield yet."

"She went out to dinner. I can't see anyone popping up in a restaurant and demanding emeralds she doesn't have." Suzanna gave his hand a friendly squeeze. "Come on, you'll feel better when you've eaten. Aunt Coco's lemon chicken should be about ready."

He sat through dinner, struggling to pretend that he had an appetite, that the empty place at the table didn't bother him. He discussed the progress of the servants list with Amanda, dodged Coco's request to read his cards and felt generally miserable. Fred, sitting on his left foot, benefited from his mood by gobbling up the morsels of chicken Max slipped to him.

He considered driving into town, casually cruising, stopping at a few clubs and restaurants. But decided that would make him look like as big a jerk as he felt. In the end he retreated to his room and lost himself in his book.

The story didn't come as easily as it had the night before. Now it was mostly fits and starts with a lot of long pauses. Still he found even the pauses constructive as an hour passed into two, and two into three. It wasn't until he glanced at his watch and saw it was after midnight that he realized he hadn't heard Lilah come home. He'd deliberately left his door ajar so that he would know when she passed down the hall.

There was a good chance he'd been engrossed in his work and hadn't noticed when she'd walked by to her room. If she'd gone out to dinner, surely she'd be home by now. No one could eat for five hours. But he had to know.

He went quietly. There was a light in Suzanna's room, but the others were dark. At Lilah's door, he hesitated, then knocked softly. Feeling awkward, he put his hand on the knob. He'd spent the night with her, he reminded himself. She could hardly be offended if he looked in to see if she was asleep.

She wasn't. She wasn't even there. The bed was made; the old iron head- and footboards that had probably belonged to a servant had been painted a gleaming white. The rest was color, so much it dazzled the eyes.

The spread was a patchwork quilt, expertly made

from scraps of fabrics. Polka dots, checks, stripes, faded reds and blues. It was piled high with pillows of varied shapes and sizes. The kind of bed, Max thought, a person could sink into and sleep the day away. It suited her.

The room was huge, as most were in The Towers, but she'd cluttered it and made it cozy. On the walls that were painted a dramatic teal were sketches of wildflowers. The bold signature in the corners told him she'd done them herself. He hadn't even known she could draw. It made him realize there was quite a bit he didn't know about the woman he was in love with.

After closing the door behind him, he wandered the room, looking for pieces of her.

A baker's rack was packed with books. Keats and Byron jumbled with grisly murder mysteries and contemporary romances. A little sitting area was grouped in front of one of her windows, a blouse tossed carelessly over the back of a Queen Anne chair, earrings and glittering bracelets scattered over a Hepplewhite table. There was a bowl of smooth gemstones beside a china penguin. When he picked the bird up, it played a jazzy rendition of "That's Entertainment."

She had candles everywhere, in everything from elegant Meissen to a tacky reproduction of a unicorn. Dozens of pictures of her family were scattered throughout. He picked up one framed snapshot of a couple, arms around each other's waists as they laughed into the camera. Her parents, he thought. Lilah's resemblance to the man, Suzanna's to the woman were strong enough to make him certain of it.

When the cuckoo in the clock on the wall jumped out, he jolted and realized it was twelve-thirty. Where the hell was she?

Now he paced, from the window where she'd hung faceted crystals to the brass urn filled with dried flowers, from bookcase to bureau. Nerves humming, he picked up an ornate cobalt bottle to sniff. And smelled her. He set it down hastily when the door opened.

She looked…incredible. Her hair windblown, her face flushed. She wore some sheer drapey dress that swirled around her legs in bleeding colors. Long multicolored columns of beads danced at her ears. She lifted a brow and closed the door.

"Well," she said. "Make yourself at home."

"Where the hell have you been?" The demand shot out, edged with frustration and worry.

"Did I miss curfew, Daddy?" She tossed a beaded bag onto the bureau. She'd lifted a hand to remove an earring when he whirled her around.

"Don't get cute with me. I've been worried sick. You've been out for hours. No one knew where you were." Or who you were with, he thought, but managed to bite that one back.

She jerked her arm free. He saw the temper flash hot into her eyes, but her voice was cool and slow and unmoved. "It may surprise you, Professor, but I've been going out on my own for a long time."

"It's different now."

"Oh?" Deliberately she turned back to the bureau. Taking her time, she unfastened an earring. "Why?"

"Because we…" Because we're lovers. "Because we don't know where Caufield is," he said with more control. "Or how dangerous he might be."

"I've also been looking out for myself for a long time." Deceptively sleepy, her eyes met his in the mirror. "Is the lecture over?"

"It's not a lecture, Lilah, I was worried. I have a right to know your plans."

Still watching him, she slid bracelets from her arms. "Just how do you figure that?"

"We're—friends."

The smile didn't reach her eyes. "Are we?"

He jammed impotent hands into his pockets. "I care about you. And after what happened last night, I thought we...I thought we meant something to each other. Now, twenty-four hours later you're out with someone else. Looking like that."

She stepped out of her shoes. "We went to bed last night, and enjoyed it." She nearly choked over the bitterness lodged in her throat. "As I recall we agreed there'd be no complications." Tilting her head, she studied him. Her easy shrug masked the fact that her hands were balled tight. "Since you're here, I suppose we could arrange a repeat performance." Her voice a purr, she stepped closer to run a finger down the front of his shirt. "That's what you want from me, isn't it, Max?"

Furious, he pushed her hand aside. "I don't care to be the second act of the evening."

The flush vanished, leaving her cheeks pale before she turned away. "Congratulations," she whispered. "Direct hit."

"What do you want me to say? That you can come and go as you please, with whomever you please, and I'll sit up and beg for the scraps from the table?"

"I don't want you to say anything. I just want you to leave me alone."

"I'm not going anywhere until we've straightened this out."

"Fine." The cuckoo chirped out again as she unzipped

her dress. "Stay as long as you like. I'm getting ready for bed."

She stepped out of the dress, tossed it aside, then walked over to her vanity in a lacy, beribboned chemise. Sitting, she picked up her brush to drag it through her hair.

"What are you so angry about?"

"Angry." She set her teeth as she slapped the bristles against her scalp. "What makes you think I'm angry? Just because you're waiting for me in my room, incensed that I had the nerve to make plans of my own when you didn't have the time or inclination to spend an hour with me. Unless it was in the sack."

"What are you talking about?" He took her arm, then yelped when she rapped the brush hard on his knuckles.

"I'll let you know when I want to be touched."

He swore, grabbed the brush and tossed it across the room. Too enraged to see the surprise in her eyes, he hauled her to her feet. "I asked you a question."

She cocked her chin. "If you've finished your temper tantrum—" He nearly lifted her off her feet.

"Don't push," he said between his teeth.

"You hurt me." The words exploded out of her. "Last night, even this morning, I was worth a little of your time and attention. As long as there was sex. Then this afternoon, you couldn't even look at me. You couldn't wait to dump me off here and get away from me."

"That's crazy."

"That's just what happened. Damn you, you made up lame excuses and practically patted me on the head. And tonight, you've got an itch and you're annoyed that I wasn't here to scratch it."

He was as pale as she now. "Is that what you think of me?"

She sighed then, and the anger dropped out of her voice. "It's what you think of me, Max. Now let me go."

His grip loosened so that she slipped away. "I had something on my mind this afternoon. It wasn't that I didn't want to spend time with you."

"I don't want excuses." She went to the terrace doors to fling them open. Maybe the wind would blow the tears away. "You've made it clear how you feel."

"Obviously I haven't. The last thing I wanted to do was hurt you, Lilah." But he'd lied to her, he thought. That had been his first mistake. "Just before I came to pick you up, I saw Caufield in the village."

She spun around. "What? You saw him? Where?"

"I was waiting at a light, and I saw him on the sidewalk. He's dyed his hair and grown a beard. By the time I'd realized, I was caught up in traffic and had to double back. He was gone."

"Why didn't you tell me you'd seen him?"

"I didn't want to worry you, and I wasn't going to have you getting some lamebrained idea about hunting him up yourself. You have a habit of acting on impulse, and I—"

"You jerk." The flush was back in her cheeks when she stepped forward to give him a shove. "That man is determined to take something from my family, and you don't have the sense to tell me you've seen him a few miles from here. If I'd known I might have been able to find him."

"Exactly my point. I'm not having you involved any more than necessary. That's why I thought it might be best if I went back to New York. They know I'm here now, and I'm not having you caught in the middle."

"You're not having?" She would have shoved him again, but he caught both her hands.

"That's right. You're going to stay out of it."

"Don't tell me—"

"I am telling you," he interrupted, pleased when she gaped at him. "What's more, you're not going to go wandering off at night until he's in custody. After I thought it over, I decided it was best if I stayed close and watched out for you. I'm going to take care of you whether you like it or not."

"I don't like it, and I don't need to be taken care of."

"Nonetheless." And he considered the argument closed.

It was her turn to stutter. "Why, you arrogant, self-important—"

"That's enough," he said in his best professor's voice and had her blinking. "There's no use arguing when the most intelligent decision's been made. Now, I think it's best if I take you to work every day. Whenever you make other plans, you'll let me know."

Her anger turned to simple shock. "I will not."

"Yes," he said mildly, "you will." He moved her hands behind her back to bring her closer. "About tonight," he began when their bodies brushed. "Clearly, you're laboring under a misconception concerning my motives, and my feelings."

She arched back, more surprised than annoyed when he didn't release her. "I don't want to talk about it."

"No, you prefer yelling about it, but that's unconstructive, and not my style." Both his hands and his voice were very firm. "To be precise, I didn't come here because I had an itch, though I certainly have every intention of making love with you."

Baffled, she stared at him. "What the devil's gotten into you?"

"I've suddenly realized that the best way to handle you is the way I handle difficult students. It takes more than patience. It requires a firm hand and a clear-cut outline of intentions and goals."

"A difficult—" She took a deep breath to hold on to her temper. "Max, I think you'd better go take some aspirin and lie down."

"As I was saying." He whispered a kiss over her cheek. "It isn't just a matter of sex, despite the fact that that aspect is incredibly satisfying. It's more of a matter of my being completely bewitched by you."

"Don't," she said weakly when he leaned close to nip at her ear.

"Maybe I've made the mistake of indicating that it's only the way you look, the way you feel under my hands, the way you taste that attracts me." He drew her bottom lip into his mouth, sucking gently until her eyes unfocused. "But it's more than that. I just don't know how to tell you." Her pulse beat fast and hard against his hands as he walked her backward. "There's never been anyone like you in my life. I intend to keep you there, Lilah."

"What are you doing?"

"I'm taking you to bed."

She struggled to clear her head as his lips skimmed down her throat. "No, you're not." She was angry with him about something. But the reason floated just out of reach as his mouth seduced her.

"I need to show you how I feel about you." Still toying with her lips, he lowered her to the mattress.

Her hands were free now and slipped under his shirt to run along the warm flesh beneath. She didn't want to think. There were so many feelings to be absorbed, and she drew him closer, eager.

"I was jealous," he murmured as he slid one lacy strap from her shoulder and replaced it with his mouth. "I don't want another man touching you."

"No." He was touching her now, long, lingering strokes up and down her trembling body. "Just you."

He sank into a kiss, spinning it out, wallowing in the flavor, the texture, until he was drunk on it. Then, like an addict, he went back for more.

This was comfort and care and romance, she thought hazily. To float together like this, with a sweet breeze blowing over heated bodies, soft murmurs muffled against clinging lips. Desire so perfectly balanced with affection. Nothing mattered so much as this—holding on to the hope of love.

She lifted his shirt over his head and let her hands roam. He was strong. It was more than the subtle ridge of muscles over his back and shoulders. It was the strength inside that aroused her. The integrity, the dedication to do what was right. He would be strong enough to be loyal and honest and gentle with those he loved.

He shifted her so that she was cocooned by pillows. Kneeling beside her, he began to untie each tiny ribbon down the center of the ivory silk. The contrast of patient fingers and hungry eyes left her breathless. He parted the material, caressing the newly exposed flesh with his lips. It amazed and humbled him that her skin should be as soft as the silk.

As patiently as he, she undressed him. Though the

need to hurry was clawing at both of them, they held back, the understanding spoken.

She rose, wrapping her arms around his neck until they were torso to torso, thigh to thigh. With the bright light showering around them, they explored each other. A shudder then a sigh, a request and an answer. Questing lips sought out new secrets. Eager hands discovered new pleasures.

When she locked herself around him, he filled her. Glorying in the sensation, she arched back, taking him deeper, gasping out his name as the first shock waves struck. He could see her, her willowy body bowed, her skin glowing in the light while her bright hair rained down her back. As she shuddered, the stunned pleasure rushed into her face.

Then his vision grayed, his own body trembled. His hands slid down to grip her hips. She was wrapped tight around him when they shot over the peak together.

Chapter Nine

Max was whistling as he poured his coffee. It was the penguin's natty little tune and suited his mood. He had plans. Big ones. A drive along the coast, dinner at some out-of-the-way spot, then a nice long walk on the beach.

He sipped, scalded his tongue and grinned.

He was having a romance.

"Well, it's nice to see someone in such a bright mood so early in the morning." Coco sailed into the kitchen. She'd dyed her hair a raven black the night before, and the result had put her in a cheerful state of mind. "How about some blueberry pancakes?"

"You look terrific."

She beamed and reached for a frilly apron. "Why, thank you, dear. A woman needs a change now and again, I always say. Keeps men on their toes." After taking a large mixing bowl from the cupboard, she glanced back at him. "I must say, Max, you're looking rather well yourself this morning. The sea air or...something must agree with you."

"It's wonderful here. I'll never be able to thank you enough for letting me stay."

"Nonsense." In her haphazard way she began dumping ingredients into the bowl. It never failed to amaze Max how anyone could cook so carelessly with such exquisite results. "It was meant, you know. I knew it the moment Lilah brought you home. She was always one for bringing things home. Wounded birds, baby rabbits. Even a snake once." The memory of that made her pat her breast. "This was the first time she brought in an unconscious man. But that's Lilah," she continued, gaily mixing as she talked. "Always the unexpected. Quite talented, too. She knows all those Latin terms for weeds and the migratory habits of birds and things. When she's in the mood, she can draw beautifully."

"I know. I saw the sketches in her room."

She slanted him a look. "Did you?"

"I..." He took a quick gulp of coffee. "Yes. Do you want a cup?"

"No, I'll have my coffee when this is done." Oh, my, my, she thought, things were moving along just beautifully. The cards didn't lie. "Yes, our Lilah's quite a fascinating girl. Headstrong like the others, but in such a casual, deceptively amiable sort of way. I've always said that the right sort of man would recognize how special she is." Keeping an eye on Max, she rinsed and drained blueberries. "He'd need to be patient, but not malleable. Strong enough to keep her from veering off course too far, and wise enough not to try to change her." Gently folding the berries into the batter she smiled.

"But then, if you love someone why would you want to change her?"

"Aunt Coco, are you pumping poor Max?" Lilah strolled in, yawning.

"What a thing to say." Coco heated the griddle and clucked her tongue. "Max and I were having a nice conversation. Weren't we, Max?"

"It certainly was a fascinating one."

"Really?" Lilah took the cup from him, and since he didn't make the move, leaned over to kiss him good morning. Watching, Coco all but rubbed her hands together. "I'll take that as a compliment, and since I see blueberry pancakes on the horizon, I won't complain."

Because the kiss had delighted her, Coco hummed as she got out dishes. "You're up early."

"It's becoming a habit of mine." Sipping Max's coffee, Lilah sent him a lazy smile. "I'll have to break it soon."

"The rest of the brood will be trooping down any minute." And Coco liked nothing better than to have all of her chicks in one place. "Lilah, why don't you set the table?"

"I'll definitely have to break it." With a sigh, she handed Max back his coffee. But she kissed Coco's cheek. "I like your hair. Very French."

With what sounded almost like a giggle, Coco began to spoon up batter. "Use the good china, dear. I feel like celebrating."

Caufield hung up the phone and went into a small, nasty rage. He pounded the desk with his fists, tore a few pamphlets to bits and ended by smashing a crystal bud vase against the wall. Because he'd seen the mood before, Hawkins hung back until it passed.

After three calming breaths, Caufield sat back. The glaze of blank violence faded from his eyes as he steepled his fingers. "We seem to be victims of fate, Hawkins. The car our good professor was driving is registered to Catherine Calhoun St. James."

On an oath, Hawkins heaved his bulk away from the wall. "I told you this job stinks. By rights he should be dead. Instead he plops right down in their laps. He'll have told them everything by now."

Caufield tapped the tips of his fingers together. "Oh, assuredly."

"And if he recognized you—"

"He didn't." Exercising control, Caufield laced his fingers then laid them on the desk. "He never would have waved in my direction. He doesn't have the wit for it." Feeling his fingers tighten, he deliberately relaxed them. "The man's a fool. I learned more in one year on the streets than he in all of his years in higher institutions. After all, we're here, not on the boat."

"But he knows," Hawkins insisted, viciously cracking his knuckles. "Now they all know. They'll take precautions."

"Which only adds spice to the game and it's time to begin playing. Since Dr. Quartermain has joined the Calhouns, I believe I'll pay one of the ladies a call."

"You're out of your mind."

"Have a care, old friend," Caufield said mildly. "If you don't like my rules, there's nothing holding you here."

"I'm the one who paid for the damn boat." Hawkins dragged a hand through his short wiry hair. "I've put over a month in this job already. I've got an investment."

"Then leave it to me to make it pay off." Thinking,

Caufield rose to go to the window. There were pretty summer flowers in neat borders just outside. It reminded him that he'd come a long way from the tenements of south Chicago. With the emeralds, he'd go even further.

Perhaps a nice villa in the South Seas where he could relax and refresh himself while Interpol ran in circles looking for him. He already had a new passport, a new background, a new name in reserve—and a tidy sum gathering interest in a discreet Swiss account.

He'd been in the business most of his life, quite successfully. He didn't need the emeralds for the percentage of their value he'd cull by fencing them. But he wanted them. He intended to have them.

As Hawkins paced and abused his knuckles, Caufield continued to gaze out of the window. "Now, as I recall, during my brief friendship with the lovely Amanda, she mentioned that her sister Lilah knew the most about Bianca. Perhaps she knows the most about the emeralds, as well."

This, at least, made some sense to Hawkins. "Are you going to grab her?"

Caufield winced. "That's your style, Hawkins. Credit me with a little more finesse. I believe I'll pay a visit to Acadia. They say the naturalist tours are very informative."

Lilah had always preferred the long, sunny days of summer. Though she felt there was something to be said for the long stormy nights of winter, as well. In truth, it was time she preferred. She didn't wear a watch. Time was something to be appreciated just for its existence, not as something to keep track of. But for the first time in her memory, she wished time would hurry.

She missed him.

It didn't matter how foolish it made her feel. She was in love and giddy with it. When the feeling was so strong, she resented every hour they weren't together.

It was stronger. She had fallen in love with his sweetness, his basic goodness. She had recognized his insecurity and, as she had with broken wings and damaged paws, had wanted to fix it.

She still loved all of those things, but now she had seen a different side of him. He'd been—masterful. She cringed at the term that entered her head and would have sworn she found it offensive. But it hadn't been offensive, not in Max. It had been illuminating.

He had taken charge. He had taken her, she thought with a quick flash of excitement. Though she still resented being compared to a difficult student, she had to admire his technique. He'd simply stated his intentions and moved on them.

She'd be the first to admit that she'd have frozen another man in his tracks with a few well-chosen words if he'd attempted the same thing. But Max wasn't any other man.

She hoped he was beginning to believe it.

While her mind wandered, she kept an eye on her group. Jordan Pond was a favored spot and she had a full load.

"Please, don't disturb the plant life. I know the flowers are tempting, but we have thousands of visitors who'll want to enjoy them, in their natural setting. The bottle-shaped flower you see in the pond is yellow cow lily, or spatterdock. The leaves floating on the surface are bladderwort, and common to most Acadia ponds. It is their tiny bladders that help the plant float, and that trap small insects."

In his ripped jeans and tattered backpack, Caufield listened to her lecture. Behind his dark glasses, his eyes were watchful. He paid attention, though the talk of bog and pond plants meant nothing to him. He held back a sneer when the group gasped as a heron glided overhead to wade in the shallows several yards away.

As if fascinated, he lifted the camera strapped around his neck and snapped pictures of the bird, the wild orchards, even of a bullfrog who had come out to bask on a floating leaf.

Most of all, he bided his time.

She continued to lecture, tirelessly answering questions as they moved along the trail beside the glassy water. She spelled a weary mother by hitching a toddler on her hip and pointing out a family of black ducks.

When the lecture was over, the group was free to follow the circular trail around the pond or retreat to their cars.

"Miss Calhoun?"

Lilah glanced around. She'd noticed the bearded hiker in the group, though he hadn't asked any questions during the lecture. There was a hint of the South in his voice.

"Yes?"

"I wanted to tell you how terrific your talk was. I teach high school geography and reward myself every summer with a trip through a national park. You're really one of the best guides I've come across."

"Thank you." She smiled, and though it was a natural gesture for her, felt reluctant to offer her hand. She didn't recognize the sweaty, bearded hiker, but she picked up something disturbing. "You'll have to visit the Nature Center while you're here. Enjoy your stay."

He put a hand on her arm. It was a casual move, far from demanding, but she disliked it intensely.

"I was hoping you could give me a little one-on-one, if you've got a minute. I like to give the kids a full-scale report when school starts in the fall. A lot of them never see the inside of a park."

She forced herself to shake off the mood. It was her job, she reminded herself, and she appreciated talking to someone with a genuine interest. "I'd be happy to answer any questions."

"Great." He pulled out a notebook he'd been careful to scribble in.

She relaxed a little, giving him a more in-depth talk than the average group required.

"This is so kind of you. I wonder, could I buy you some coffee, or a sandwich?"

"That isn't necessary."

"But it would be a pleasure."

"I have plans, but thanks."

He kept his smile in place. "Well, I'll be around for a few more weeks. Maybe some other time. I know this is going to sound strange, but I'd swear I'd seen you before. Have you ever been to Raleigh?"

Her instincts were humming, and she wanted to get away from him. "No, I haven't."

"It's the darnedest thing." As if puzzled, he shook his head. "You seem so familiar. Well, thanks again. I'd better start back to camp." He turned, then stopped. "I know. The papers. I've seen your picture. You're the woman with the emeralds."

"No. I'm afraid I'm the woman without them."

"What a story. I read about it down in Raleigh a month or two ago, and then…well, I have to confess, I'm just addicted to those supermarket tabloids. Comes from living alone and reading too many essays." He gave her a sheepish smile that would have charmed her if her senses hadn't been working overtime.

"I guess the Calhouns have been lining a lot of bird cages lately."

He rocked back on his heels and laughed. "Pays to keep a sense of humor. I guess it's a hassle, but it gives people like me a lot of vicarious excitement. Missing emeralds, jewel thieves."

"Treasure maps."

"There's a map?" His voice sharpened and he worked hard at easing it again. "I hadn't heard."

"Sure, you can pick them up in the village." She reached in her pocket and drew the latest one out. "I've been collecting them. A lot of people are spending hard-earned money only to find out too late that *x* doesn't mark the spot."

"Ah." He had to fight against clenching his jaw. "Capitalism."

"You bet. Here, a souvenir." She handed it to him, careful for reasons she couldn't quite place not to brush his fingers. "Your students might get a kick out of it."

"I'm sure they will." To give himself time, he folded it and slipped it into his pocket. "I really am fascinated by the whole thing. Maybe we can have that sandwich soon and you can give me a firsthand account of what it's like to look for buried treasure."

"Mostly, it's tedious. Enjoy your stay in the park."

Knowing there was no safe way to detain her, he

watched her go. She had a long, graceful body, he noted. He certainly hoped he wouldn't have to damage it.

"You're late." Max met her on the trail when she was still twenty yards from the parking area.

"It seems to be my day for teachers." She leaned into the kiss, pleased with how warm and solid it was. "I was detained by a Southern gentleman who wanted information on flora for his geography class."

"I hope he was bald and fat."

She didn't quite manage the laugh and rubbed the chill from her arms instead. "No, actually, he was quite trim and had an abundance of hair. But I turned down his request that I become the mother of his children."

"Did he make a pass at you?"

"No." She held a hand up before he could rush by her. And did laugh. "Max, I'm kidding—and if I wasn't, I can dodge passes all by myself."

He didn't feel as foolish as he might have even a day before. "You haven't been dodging mine."

"I can intercept them, too. Now what's behind your back?"

"My hands."

She laughed again and gave him a delighted kiss. "What else?"

He held out a clutch of painted daisies. "I didn't pick them," he said, knowing her feelings. "I bought them from Suzanna. She said you had a weakness for them."

"They're so cheerful," she murmured, absurdly touched. She buried her face in them, then lifted it to his. "Thanks."

As they began to walk, he draped an arm around her shoulders. "I bought the car from C.C. this afternoon."

"Professor, you're full of surprises."

"I thought you might like to hear about the progress Amanda and I are making on those lists. We could drive down the coast, have some dinner. Be alone."

"It sounds wonderful, but my flowers'll wilt."

He grinned down at her. "I bought a vase. It's in the car."

When the sun was setting behind the hills to the west, they walked along a cobble beach that formed a natural seawall on the southern point of the island. The water was calm, barely murmuring over the mounds of smooth stones. With the approach of dusk, the line between the sky and sea blurred until all was a soft, deep blue. A single gull, heading home, soared overhead with one long, defiant cry.

"This is a special place," Lilah told him. With her hand in his, she walked down the slope of cobbles to stand close to the verge of water. "A magic one. Even the air's different here." She closed her eyes to take a deep breath of it. "Full of stored energy."

"It's beautiful." Idly he bent to pick up a rock, just to feel the texture. In the near distance an island melted into the twilight.

"I often drive down here, just to stand and feel. I think I must have been here before."

"You just said you'd been here before."

Her eyes were soft and dreamy as she smiled. "I mean a hundred years ago, or five hundred. Don't you believe in reincarnation, Professor?"

"Actually, I do. I did a paper on it in college and after completing the research, I found it was a very viable theory. When you apply it to history—"

"Max." She framed his face with her hands. "I'm crazy about you." Her lips were curved when they met his, curved still when she drew away.

"What was that for?"

"Because I can see you, waist deep in thick books and cramped notes, your hair falling into your face and your eyebrows all drawn together the way they get when you're concentrating, doggedly pursuing truth."

Frowning, he tossed the cobble from hand to hand. "That's a pretty boring image."

"No, it's not." She tilted her head, studying him. "It's a true one, an admirable one. Even courageous."

He gave a short laugh. "Boxing yourself into a library doesn't take courage. When I was a kid, it was a handy escape. I never had an asthma attack reading a book. I used to hide there, in books," he continued. "It was fun imagining myself sailing with Magellan, or exploring with Lewis and Clark, dying at the Alamo or marching across a field at Antietam. Then my father would…"

"Would what?"

Uncomfortable, he shrugged. "He'd hoped for something different. He was a high school football star. Wide receiver. Played semipro for a while. The kind of man who's never been sick a day in his life. Likes to toss back a few beers on Saturday night and hunt on weekends during the season. I'd start wheezing as soon as he put a thirty-thirty in my hands." He tossed the cobble aside. "He wanted to make a man out of me, and never quite managed it."

"You made yourself." She took his hands, feeling a trembling anger for the man who hadn't appreciated or understood the gift he'd been given. "If he isn't proud of you, the lack is in him, not in you."

"That's a nice thought." He was more than a little embarrassed that he'd pulled those old, raw feelings out. "In any case, I went my own way. I was a lot more comfortable in a classroom than I was on a football field. And the way I figure it, if I hadn't hidden in the library all those years, I wouldn't be standing here with you right now. This is exactly where I want to be."

"Now that's a nice thought."

"If I tell you you're beautiful, are you going to hit me?"

"Not this time."

He pulled her against him, just to hold her as night fell. "I need to go to Bangor for a couple of days."

"What for?"

"I located a woman who worked as a maid at The Towers the year Bianca died. She's living in a nursing home in Bangor, and I made arrangements to interview her." He tilted Lilah's face to his. "Come with me."

"Just give me time to rearrange my schedule."

When the children were asleep, I told Nanny of my plans. I knew she was shocked that I would speak of leaving my husband. She tried to soothe. How could I explain that it wasn't poor Fred who had caused my decision. The incident had made me realize how futile it was to remain in an unhappy and stifling marriage. Had I convinced myself that it was for the children? Their father didn't see them as children who needed to be loved and coddled, but as pawns. Ethan and Sean he would strive to mold in his image, erasing every part of them he considered weak. Colleen, my sweet little girl, he would ignore until such time as he could marry her for profit or status.

I would not have it. Fergus, I knew, would soon wrench control from me. His pride would demand it. A governess of his choosing would follow his instructions and ignore mine. The children would be trapped in the middle of the mistake I had made.

For myself, he would see that I became no more than an ornament at his table. If I defied him, I would pay the price. I have no doubt that he meant to punish me for questioning his authority in front of our children. Whether it would be physical or emotional, I didn't know, but I was sure the damage would be severe. Discontent I might hide from the children, open animosity I could not.

I would take them and go, find somewhere we could disappear. But first I went to Christian.

The night was moon-washed and breezy. I kept my cloak pulled tight, the hood over my hair. The puppy was snuggled at my breast. I had the carriage take me to the village, then walked to his cottage through the quiet streets with the smell of water and flowers all around. My heart was pounding in my ears as I knocked. This was the first step, and once taken, I could never go back.

But it wasn't fear, no, it wasn't fear that trembled through me when he opened the door. It was relief. The moment I saw him I knew the choice had already been made.

"Bianca," he said. "What are you thinking of?"

"I must talk to you." He was already pulling me inside. I saw that he'd been reading in the lamplight. Its warm glow and the scent of his paints soothed me more than words. I set the pup down and he immediately began to explore, sniffing into corners and making himself at home.

Christian made me sit, and no doubt sensing my nerves, brought me a brandy. As I sipped, I told him of the scene with Fergus. Though I struggled to remain calm, I could see his face, the violence in it, as his hands had closed over my throat.

"My God!" With this, Christian was crouching beside my chair, his fingers skimming up my throat. I hadn't known there were bruises there where Fergus's thumbs had pressed.

Christian's eyes went black. His hands gripped the arms of the chair before he lunged to his feet. "I'll kill him for this."

I jumped up to stop him from storming out of the cottage. My fear was such I'm not sure what I said, though I know I told him that Fergus had left for Boston, that I couldn't bear more violence. In the end it was my tears that stopped him. He held me as though I was a child, rocking and comforting while I poured out my heart and my desperation.

Perhaps I should have been ashamed to have begged him to take me and the children away, to have thrust that kind of burden and responsibility on him. If he had refused, I know I would have gone on alone, taken my three babies to some quiet village in Ireland or England. But Christian wiped away my tears.

"Of course we'll go. I'll not see you or the children spend another night under the same roof with him. He'll never lay a hand on any of you again. It will be difficult, Bianca. You and the children won't have the kind of life you're used to. And the scandal—"

"I don't care about the scandal. The children need to feel loved and safe." I rose then, to pace. "I can't be sure what's right. Night after night I've lain in bed ask-

ing myself if I have the right to love you, to want you. I took vows, made promises, and was given three children." I covered my face with my hands. "A part of me will always suffer for breaking those vows, but I must do something. I think I'll go mad if I don't. God may never forgive me, but I can't face a lifetime of unhappiness."

He took my hands to pull them away from my face. *"We were meant to be together. We knew it, both of us, the first time we saw each other. I was content with those few hours as long as I knew you were safe. But I'll not stand by and see you give your life to a man who'll abuse you. From tonight, you're mine, and will be mine forever. Nothing and no one will change that."*

I believed him. With his face close to mine, his fine gray eyes so clear and sure, I believed. And I needed.

"Then tonight, make me yours."

I felt like a bride. The moment he touched me, I knew I had never been touched before. His eyes were on mine as he took the pins from my hair. His fingers trembled. Nothing, nothing has ever moved me more than knowing I had the power to weaken him. His lips were gentle against mine even as I felt the tension vibrating through his body. There in the lamplight he unfastened my dress, and I his shirt. And a bird began to sing in the brush.

I could see by the way he looked at me that I pleased him. Slowly, almost torturously he drew off my petticoats, my corset. Then he touched my hair, running his hands through it, and looking his fill.

"I'll paint you like this one day," he murmured. *"For myself."*

He lifted me into his arms, and I could feel his heart pounding in his chest as he carried me to the bedroom.

The light was silver, the air like wine. This was no

*hurried coupling in the dark, but a dance as graceful
as a waltz, and as exhilarating. No matter how impossible it seems, it was as though we had loved countless
times before, as though I had felt that hard, firm body
against mine night after night.*

*This was a world I had never experienced, yet it was
achingly, beautifully familiar. Each movement, each
sigh, each need was as natural as breath. Even when
the urgency stunned me, the beauty didn't lessen. As he
made me his, I knew I had found something every soul
searches for. Simple love.*

*Leaving him was the most difficult thing I have ever
done. Though we told each other it would be the last
time we were separated, we lingered and loved again.
It was nearly dawn before I returned to The Towers.
When I looked at the house, walked through it, I knew I
would miss it desperately. This, more than any place in
my life, had been home. Christian and I, with the children, would make our own, but I would always hold The
Towers in my heart.*

*There was little I would take with me. In the quiet be-
fore sunrise, I packed a small case. Nanny would help
me put together what the children would need, but this
I wanted to do alone. Perhaps it was a symbol of in-
dependence. And perhaps that is why I thought of the
emeralds. They were the only things Fergus had given
me that I considered mine. There were times I had detested them, knowing they had been given to me as a
prize for producing a proper heir.*

Yet they were mine, as my children were mine.

*I didn't think of their monetary value as I took them
out, held them in my hands and watched them gleam
in the light of the lamp. They would be a legacy for my*

children, and their children, a symbol of freedom, and of hope. And with Christian, of love.

As dawn broke, I decided to put them, together with this journal, in a safe place until I joined Christian again.

Chapter Ten

The woman seemed ancient. She sat, looking as frail and brittle as old glass, in the shade of a gnarled elm. Close by, pert young pansies basked in a square of sunlight and flirted with droning bees. Residents made use of the winding stone paths through the lawns of the Madison House. Some were wheeled by family or attendants; others walked, in pairs or alone, with the careful hesitance of age.

There were birds trilling. The woman listened, nodding to herself as she plied a crochet hook and thread with fingers that refused to surrender to arthritis. She wore bright pink slacks and a cotton blouse that had been a gift from one of her great-grandchildren. She had always loved vivid colors. Some things don't fade with age.

Her skin was nut-brown, as creased and lined as an

old map. Until two years before, she had lived on her own, tending her own garden, cooking her own meals. But a fall, a bad one that had left her helpless with pain on her kitchen floor for nearly twelve hours, had convinced her it was time to change.

Stubborn and set in her ways, she had refused offers by several members of her large family to live with them. If she couldn't have her own place, she'd be damned if she would be a burden. She'd been comfortably off, well able to afford a good home and good medical care. At the Madison House, she had her own room. And if the days of puttering in her garden were past, at least she could enjoy the flowers here.

She had company if she wanted it, privacy if she didn't. Millie Tobias figured that at ninety-eight and counting, she'd earned the right to choose.

She was pleased that she was having visitors. Yes, she thought as she worked her needle, she was right pleased. The day had already started off well. She'd awakened that morning with no more than the usual sundry aches. Her hip was twitching a bit, which meant rain on the way. No matter, she mused. It was good for the flowers.

Her hands worked, but she rarely glanced at them. They knew what to do with needle and thread. Instead, she watched the path, her eyes aided by thick, tinted lenses. She saw the young couple, the lanky young man with shaggy dark hair; the willowy girl in a thin summer dress, her hair the color of October leaves. They walked close, hand in hand. Millie had a soft spot for young lovers and decided they looked pretty as a picture.

Her fingers kept moving as they walked off the path to join her in the shade.

"Mrs. Tobias?"

She studied Max, saw earnest blue eyes and a shy smile. "Ayah," she said. "And you'd be Dr. Quartermain." Her voice was a crackle, heavy with down-east. "Making doctors young these days."

"Yes, ma'am. This is Lilah Calhoun."

Not a shy bone in this one, Millie decided, and wasn't displeased when Lilah sat on the grass at her feet to admire the crocheting.

"This is beautiful." Lilah touched a fingertip to the gossamer blue thread. "What will it be?"

"What it wants to. You're from the island."

"Yes, I was born there."

Millie let out a little sigh. "Haven't been back in thirty years. Couldn't bear to live there after I lost my Tom, but I still miss the sound of the sea."

"You were married a long time?"

"Fifty years. We had a good life. We made eight children, and saw all of them grown. Now I've got twenty-three grandchildren, fifteen great-grandchildren and seven great-great-grandchildren." She let out a wheezy laugh. "Sometimes I feel like I've propagated this old world all on my own. Take your hands out of your pockets, boy," she said to Max. "And come on down here so's I don't have to crane my neck." She waited until he was settled. "This here your sweetheart?" she asked him.

"Ah...well..."

"Well, is she or isn't she?" Millie demanded, and flashed her dentures in a grin.

"Yes, Max." Lilah sent him an amused and lazy smile. "Is she or isn't she?"

Cornered, Max let out a little huff of breath. "I suppose you could say so."

"Slow to make up his mind, is he?" she said to Lilah

and winked. "Nothing wrong with that. You've got the look of her," she said abruptly.

"Of whom?"

"Bianca Calhoun. Isn't that what you came to talk to me about?"

Lilah laid a hand on Millie's arm. The flesh was thin as paper. "You remember her."

"Ayah. She was a great lady. Beautiful with a good and kind heart. Doted on her children. A lot of the wealthy ladies who came summering on the island were happy to leave their children to nursemaids and nannies, but Mrs. Calhoun liked to see to them herself. She was always taking them for walks, or spending time in the nursery. Saw them off to bed herself, every night, unless her husband made plans that would take her out before their bedtime. A good mother she was, and nothing better can be said of a woman than that."

She gave a decisive nod and perked up when she saw that Max was taking notes. "I worked there three summers, 1912, '13 and '14." And with the odd trick of old age, she could remember them with perfect clarity.

"Do you mind?" Max took out a small tape recorder. "It would help us remember everything you tell us."

"Don't mind a bit." In fact, it pleased her enormously. She thought it was just like being on a TV talk show. Her fingers worked away as she settled more comfortably in the chair. "You live in The Towers still?" she asked Lilah.

"Yes, my family and I."

"How many times I climbed up and down those stairs. The master, he didn't like us using the main staircase, but when he wasn't about, I used to come down that way and fancy myself a lady. A-swishing my skirts and holding my nose in the air. Oh, I was a pistol in those days, and not hard to look at either. Used to flirt with one of the gardeners. Joseph was his name. But that was just to make my Tom jealous, and hurry him along a bit."

She sighed, looking back. "Never seen a house like it, before or since. The furniture, the paintings, the crystal. Once a week we'd wash every window with vinegar so they'd sparkle like diamonds. And the mistress, she'd like fresh flowers everywhere. She'd cut roses and peonies out of the garden, or pick the wild orchids and lady's slippers."

"What can you tell us about the summer she died?" Max prompted.

"She spent a lot of time in her tower room that summer, looking out the window at the cliffs, or writing in her book."

"Book?" Lilah interrupted. "Do you mean a journal, a diary?"

"I suppose that's what it was. I saw her writing in it sometimes when I brought her up some tea. She'd always thank me, too. Call me by name. 'Thank you, Millie,' she would say, 'it's a pretty day.' Or, 'You didn't have to trouble, Millie. How is your young man?' Gracious, she was." Millie's mouth thinned. "Now the master, he wouldn't say a word to you. Might as well have been a stick of wood for all he noticed."

"You didn't like him," Max put in.

"Wasn't my place to like or dislike, but a harder, colder man I've never met in all my years. We'd talk about it sometimes, me and one of the other girls. Why did such a sweet and lovely woman marry a man like that? Money, I would have said. Oh, the clothes she had, and the parties, the jewelry. But it didn't make her happy.

Her eyes were sad. She and the master would go out in the evenings, or they'd entertain at home. He'd go his own way most other times, business and politics and the like, hardly paying any mind to his wife, and less to his children. Though he was partial to the boy, the oldest boy."

"Ethan," Lilah supplied. "My grandfather."

"A fine little boy, he was, and a handful. He liked to slide down the banisters and play in the dirt. The mistress didn't mind him getting dirty, but she made certain he was all polished up when the master got home. A tight ship he ran, Fergus Calhoun. Was it any wonder the poor woman looked elsewhere for a little softness?"

Lilah closed a hand over Max's. "You knew she was seeing someone?"

"It was my job to clean the tower room. More than once I looked out that window and saw her running out to the cliffs. She met a man there. I know she was a married woman, but it wasn't for me to judge then, or now. Whenever she came back from seeing him, she looked happy. At least for a little while."

"Do you know who he was?" Max asked her.

"No. A painter, I think, because there were times he had an easel set up. But I never asked anyone, and never told what I saw. It was the mistress's secret. She deserved one."

Because her hands were tiring, she let them still in her lap. "The day before she died, she brought a little puppy home for the children. A stray she said she'd found out on the cliffs. Lord, what a commotion. The children were wild about that dog. The mistress had one of the gardeners fill up a tub on the patio, and she and the children washed the pup themselves. They were laughing, the dog was howling. The mistress ruined one of her pretty day frocks. After, I helped the nanny clean up the children. It was the last time I saw them happy."

She paused a moment to gather her thoughts while two butterflies danced toward the pansies. "There was a dreadful fight when the master came home. I'd never heard the mistress raise her voice before. They were in the parlor and I was in the hall. I could hear them plain. The master wouldn't have the dog in the house. Of course, the children were crying, but he said, just as cold, that the mistress was to give it to one of the servants and have it destroyed."

Lilah felt her own eyes fill. "But why?"

"It wasn't good enough, you see, being a mutt. The little girl, she stood right up to him, but she was only a wee thing, and it made no difference to him. I thought he might strike her—his voice had that meanness in it—but the mistress told the children to take the dog and go up to their nanny. It got worse after that. The mistress was fit to be tied. I wouldn't have said she had a temper, but she cut loose. The master said terrible things to her, vicious things. He said he was going to Boston for a few days, and that she was to get rid of the dog, and to remember her place. When he came out of the parlor, his face—I'll never forget it. He looked mad, I said to myself, then I peeked into the parlor and there was the mistress, white as a ghost, just sitting in a chair with her hand pressed to her throat. The next night, she was dead."

Max said nothing for a moment. Lilah was looking away, her eyes blind with tears. "Mrs. Tobias, had you heard anything about Bianca planning to leave her husband?"

"Later I did. The master, he dismissed the nanny, even

though those poor babies were wild with grief. She—
Mary Beals was her name—she loved the children and
the mistress like they were her own. I saw her in the village the day they were to take the mistress back to New
York for burying. She told me that her lady would never
have killed herself, that she would never have done that
to the children. She insisted that it had been an accident.
And then she told me that the mistress had decided to
leave, that she'd come to see she couldn't stay with the
master. She was going to take the children away. Mary
Beals said she was going to New York herself and that
she was going to stay with the children no matter what
Mr. Calhoun said. I heard later that she'd gotten her position back."

"Did you ever see the Calhoun emeralds, Mrs. Tobias?" Max asked.

"Oh, ayah. Once seen, you'd never forget them. She
would wear them and look like a queen. They disappeared the night she died." A faint smile moved her
mouth. "I know the legend, boy. You could say I lived it."

Composed again, Lilah looked back. "Do you have
any idea what happened to them?"

"I know Fergus Calhoun never threw them into the
sea. He wouldn't so much as flip a penny into a wishing well, so close with his money he was. If she meant
to leave him, then she meant to take them with her. But
he came back, you see."

Max's brows drew together. "Came back?"

"The master came back the afternoon of the day
she died. That's why she hid them. And the poor thing
never had a chance to take them, and her children, and
get away."

"Where?" Lilah murmured. "Where could she have put them?"

"In that house, who could say?" Millie picked up her work again. "I went back to help pack up her things. A sad day. Wasn't one of us dry-eyed. We put all her lovely dresses in tissue paper and locked them in a trunk. We were told to clear the room out, even her hair combs and perfume. He wanted nothing left of her in there. I never saw the emeralds again."

"Or her journal?" Max waited while Millie pursed her lips. "Did you find the journal in her room?"

"No." Slowly she shook her head. "There was no diary."

"How about stationery, or cards, letters?"

"Her writing paper was in the desk, and the little book she kept her appointments in, but I didn't see a diary. We put everything away, didn't even leave a hairpin. The next summer, he came back. He kept her room locked up, and there wasn't a sign of the mistress in the house. There had been photographs, and a painting, but they were gone. The children hardly laughed. Once I came across the little boy standing outside his mother's room, just staring at the door. I gave my notice in the middle of the season. I couldn't bear to work in that house, not with the master. He'd grown even colder, harder. And he took to going up to the tower room and sitting for hours. I married Tom that summer, and never went back to The Towers."

Later Lilah stood on the narrow balcony of their hotel room. Below she could see the long blue rectangle of the pool, hear the laughter and splashing of families and couples enjoying their vacation.

But her mind wasn't on the bright summer sun or the shouts and rippling water. It was on the days eighty years past, when women wore long, graceful dresses and wrote their dreams in private journals.

When Max came up quietly behind her to slip his arms around her waist, she leaned back into him, comforted.

"I always knew she was unhappy," Lilah said. "I could feel that. Just as I could feel she was hopelessly in love. But I never knew she was afraid. I never picked up on that."

"It was a long time ago, Lilah." Max pressed a kiss to her hair. "Mrs. Tobias might have exaggerated. Remember, she was a young, impressionable woman when it all happened."

Lilah turned to look quietly, deeply into his eyes. "You don't believe that."

"No." He stroked his knuckles over her cheek. "But we can't change what happened. We can't help her now."

"But we can, don't you see? By finding the necklace, and the journal. She must have written everything she felt in that book. Everything she wanted, and feared. She wouldn't have left it where Fergus would find it. If she hid the emeralds, she hid the book, too."

"Then we'll find them. If we follow Mrs. Tobias's account, Fergus came back before Bianca expected him. She didn't have the opportunity to get the emeralds out of the house. They're still there, so it's only a matter of time before we find them."

"But—"

He shook his head, cupping his hands around her face. "Aren't you the one who says to trust your feelings? Think about it. Trent comes to The Towers and falls in love with C.C. Because of his idea to renovate and turn part of the house into a retreat, the old legend comes out. Once it's made public, Livingston or Caufield or whatever we choose to call him develops an obsession. He makes a play for Amanda, but she's already hooked on Sloan—who's also there because of the house. Caufield's impatient, so he steals some of the papers. That brings me into it. You fish me out of the water, take me into your home. Since then we've been able to piece more together. We've found a photograph of the emeralds. We've located a woman who actually knew Bianca, and who's corroborated the fact that she hid the necklace in the house. It's all connected, every step. Do you think we'd have gotten this far if we weren't meant to find them?"

Her eyes softened as she linked her hands over his wrists. "You're awfully good for me, Professor. A little optimistic logic's just what I need right now."

"Then I'll give you some more. I think the next step is to start tracking down the artist."

"Christian? But how?"

"You leave it to me."

"All right." Wanting his arms around her, she laid her head on his shoulder. "There's another connection. You might think it's out of left field, but I can't help thinking about it."

"Tell me."

"A couple of months ago, Trent was walking the cliffs. He found Fred. We've never been able to figure out what the puppy was doing out there all alone. It made me think of the little dog Bianca brought to her children, the one she and Fergus argued about so bitterly only a day before she died. I wonder what happened to that dog, Max." She let out a long sigh. "Then I think about those children. It's difficult to imagine one's grandfather as a little boy. I never even knew him because he died before I was born. But I can see him, standing outside of his mother's door, grieving. And it breaks my heart."

"Shh." He tightened his arms around her. "It's better to think that Bianca had some happiness with her artist. Can't you see her running to him on the cliffs, stealing a few hours in the sun, or finding some quiet place where they could be alone?"

"Yes." Her lips curved against his throat. "Yes, I can. Maybe that's why I love sitting in the tower. She wasn't always unhappy there, not when she thought of him."

"And if there's any justice, they're together now."

Lilah tilted her head back to look at him. "Yes, you are awfully good for me. Tell you what, why don't we take advantage of that pool down there? I'd like to swim with you when it wasn't a matter of life or death."

He kissed her forehead. "You've got a deal."

She did more floating than swimming. Max had never seen anyone who could actually sleep on the water. But Lilah could—her eyes comfortably closed behind tinted glasses, her body totally relaxed. She wore two tiny scraps of leopard-print cloth that raised Max's blood pressure—and that of every other male within a hundred yards. But she drifted, hands moving gently in the water. Occasionally she would kick into a lazy sidestroke, her hair flowing out around her. Now and again, she would reach out to link her hand with his, or twine her arms around his neck, trusting him to keep her buoyant.

Then she kissed him, her lips wet and cool, her body as fluid as the water around them.

"Time for a nap," she said, and left him in the pool to stretch out on a chaise under an umbrella.

When she awoke, the shadows were long and only a few diehards were left in the water. She looked around for Max, vaguely disappointed that he hadn't stayed with her. Gathering up her wrap, she went back inside to find him.

The room was empty, but there was a note on the bed in his careful handwriting.

Had a couple of things to see to. Be back soon.

With a shrug, she tuned the radio to a classical station and went in to take a long, steamy shower.

Revived and relaxed, she toweled off, then began to cream her skin in long, lazy strokes. Maybe they could find some cozy little restaurant for dinner, she mused. Someplace where there were dim corners and music. They could linger over the meal while the candles burned down, and drink cool, sparkling wine.

Then they would come back, draw the drapes on the balcony, close themselves in. He would kiss her in that thorough, drugging way until they couldn't keep their hands off each other. She picked up her bottle of scent, spritzing it onto her softened skin. They would make love slowly or frantically, gently or desperately, until, tangled together, they slept.

They wouldn't think about Bianca or tragedies, about emeralds or thieves. Tonight they would only think about each other.

Dreaming of him, she stepped out into the bedroom.

He was waiting for her. It seemed he'd been waiting for her all of his life. She paused, her eyes darkened by the candles he'd lit, her damp hair gleaming with the delicate light. Her scent wafted into the room, mysterious, seductive, to tangle with the fragrance of the clutch of freesias he'd bought her.

Like her, he had imagined a perfect night and had tried to bring it to her.

The radio still played, low romantic strings. On the table in front of the open balcony doors two slender white tapers glowed. Champagne, just poured, frothed in tall tulip glasses. Behind the table, the sun was sinking in the sky, a scarlet ball, bleeding into the deepening blue.

"I thought we'd eat in," he said, and held out a hand for hers.

"Max." Emotion tightened her throat. "I was right all along." Her fingers linked with his. "You are a poet."

"I want to be alone with you." Taking one of the fragile blooms, he slipped it into her hair. "I'd hoped you wouldn't mind."

"No." She let out a shaky breath when he pressed his lips to her palm. "I don't mind."

He picked up the glasses, handed her one. "Restaurants are so crowded."

"And noisy," she agreed, touching her glass to his.

"And someone might object if I nibbled on you rather than the appetizers."

Watching him, she took a sip. "I wouldn't."

He slid a finger up her throat, then tilted her chin so that their lips met. "We'd better give dinner a try," he said after a long moment.

They sat, close together to watch the sun set, to feed each other little bites of lobster drenched with sweet, melted butter. She let champagne explode on her tongue, then turned her mouth to his where the flavor was just as intoxicating.

As a Chopin prelude drifted from the radio, he

pressed a light kiss to her shoulder, then skimmed more up her throat.

"The first time I saw you," he said as he slipped a bite of lobster between her lips, "I thought you were a mermaid. And I dreamed about you that first night." Gently he rubbed his lips over hers. "I've dreamed about you every night since."

"When I sit up in the tower, I think about you—the way I imagine Bianca once thought about Christian. Do you think they ever made love?"

"He couldn't have resisted her."

Her breath shuddered out between her lips. "She wouldn't have wanted him to." With her eyes on his, she began to unbutton his shirt. "She would have ached needing him, wanting to touch him." On a sigh, she ran her hands over his chest. "When they were together, alone together, nothing else could have mattered."

"He would have been half-mad for her." Taking her hands, he brought her to her feet. He left her for a moment, to draw the shades so that they were closed in with music and candlelight. "Thoughts of her would have haunted him, day and night. Her face…" He skimmed his fingers over Lilah's cheeks, over her jaw, down her throat. "Every time he closed his eyes, he would have seen it. Her taste…" He pressed his lips to hers. "Every time he took a breath it would be there to remind him what it was like to kiss her."

"And she would have lain in bed, night after night, wanting his touch." Heart racing, she pushed the shirt from his shoulders, then shivered when he reached for the belt of her robe. "Remembering how he looked at her when he undressed her."

"He couldn't have wanted her more than I want you."

The robe slithered to the floor. His arms drew her closer. "Let me show you."

The candles burned low. A single thread of moonlight slashed through the chink in the drapes. There was music, swelling with passion, and the scent of fragile flowers.

Murmured promises. Desperate answers. A low husky laugh, a sobbing gasp. From patience to urgency, from tenderness to madness, they drove each other. Through the dark, endless night they were tireless and greedy. A gentle touch could cause a tremor; a rough caress a soft sigh. They came together with generous affection, then again like warriors.

Each time they thought they were sated, they would turn to each other once more to arouse or to soothe, to cling or to stroke, until the candles gutted out and the gray light of dawn crept into the room.

Chapter Eleven

Hawkins was sick and tired of waiting around. As far as he was concerned every day on the island was a day wasted. Worse, he'd given up a tidy little job in New York that would have earned him at least ten grand. Instead, he'd invested half that much in a heist that looked more and more like a bust.

He knew Caufield was good. The fact was, there were few better at lifting locks and dancing around the police. In the ten years of their association, they had pulled off some very smooth operations. Which was why he was worried.

There was nothing smooth about this job. Damn college boy had messed things up good and proper. Hawkins resented the fact that Caufield wouldn't let him take care of Quartermain. He knew Caufield didn't think he had any finesse, but he could have arranged a nice, quiet accident.

The real problem was that Caufield was obsessed with the emeralds. He talked about them day and night—and he talked as though they were living things rather than some pretty sparklers that would bring in some good, crisp cash.

Hawkins was beginning to believe that Caufield didn't intend to fence the emeralds after all. He smelled the double cross and had been watching his partner like a hawk. Every time Caufield went out, Hawkins would pace the empty house, looking for some clue to his partner's true intentions.

Then there were the rages. Caufield was well-known for his unstable temper, but those ugly tantrums were becoming more frequent. The day before, he had stormed into the house, white-faced and wild-eyed, his body trembling with fury because the Calhoun woman hadn't been at her station in the park. He'd trashed one of the rooms, hacking away at furniture with a kitchen knife until he'd come to himself again.

Hawkins was afraid of him. Though he was a stocky man with ready fists, he had no desire to match Caufield physically. Not when the man got that gleam in his eyes.

His only hope now, if he wanted his rightful share and a clean escape, was to outwit his partner.

With Caufield out of the house again, haunting the park, Hawkins began a slow, methodical search. Though he was a big man, often considered dull-witted by his associates, he could toss a room and hardly raise the dust. He sifted through the stolen papers, then turned away in disgust. There was nothing of use there. If Caufield had found anything, he would never have left it in plain view. He decided to start with the obvious, his partner's bedroom.

He shook out the books first. He knew Caufield liked to pretend he was educated, even erudite, though he'd had no more schooling than Hawkins himself. There was nothing in the volumes of Shakespeare and Steinbeck but words.

Hawkins searched under the mattress, through the drawers in the bureau. Since Caufield's pistol wasn't around, he decided the man had tucked it into his knapsack before setting off to find Lilah. Patient, Hawkins looked behind the mirrors, behind drawers, beneath the rug. He was beginning to think he had misjudged his partner when he turned to the closet.

There, in the pocket of a pair of jeans, he found the map.

It was crudely drawn on yellowed paper. For Hawkins, there was no mistaking its meaning. The Towers was clearly depicted, along with direction and distance and a few out-of-proportion landmarks.

The map to the emeralds, Hawkins thought as he smoothed out the creases. A bitter fury filled him while he studied each line and marker. The double-dealing Caufield had found it among the stolen papers and hidden it away for himself. Well, two could play that game, he thought. He slipped out of the room as he tucked the paper into his own pocket. Wouldn't Caufield have a fine rage when he discovered his partner had snatched the emeralds out from under his nose. Hawkins thought it was almost a pity that he wouldn't be around to see it.

He found Christian. It was so much easier than Max had supposed that he could only sit and stare at the book in his hand. In less than a half day in the library, he'd stumbled across the name in a dusty volume titled

Artists and Their Art: 1900-1950. He had patiently
dug away through the As, was meticulously slogging
through the Bs, when there it was. Christian Bradford,
1884-1976. Though the given name had caused Max to
perk up, he hadn't expected it to be so easy. But it all
fell into place.

> *Though Bradford did not come to enjoy any real
> success until his last years, his early work has be-
> come valuable since his death.*

Max skimmed over the treatise on the artist's style.

> *Considered a gypsy in his day, due to his habit
> of moving from one location to another, Bradford
> often sold his work for room and board. A prolific
> artist, he would often complete a painting in a
> matter of days. It is said he would work for twenty
> hours straight when the mood was on him. It re-
> mains a mystery why he produced nothing during
> the years between 1914 and 1916.*

Oh God, Max thought, and rubbed his damp palms
on his slacks.

> *Married in 1925 to Margaret Doogan, Bradford
> had one child, a son. Little more is known about
> his personal life, as he remained an obsessively
> private man until his death. He suffered a debili-
> tating heart attack in the late sixties, but continued
> to paint. He died in Bar Harbor, Maine, where he
> had kept a cottage for more than a half century.
> He was survived by his son and a grandson.*

"I've found you," Max murmured. Turning the page, he studied the reproduction of one of Bradford's works. It was a storm, fighting its way in from the sea. Passionate, violent, frenzied. It was a view Max knew—the view from the cliffs beneath The Towers.

An hour later, a half-dozen books under his arm, he arrived home. There was still an hour before he could pick up Lilah at the park, an hour before he could tell her they had jumped the next hurdle. Giddy with success, he greeted Fred so exuberantly that the dog raced up and down the hall, running into walls and tripping on his tail.

"Goodness." Coco trotted down the stairs. "What a commotion."

"Sorry."

"No need to apologize, I wouldn't know what to do if a day went by without a commotion. Why, Max, you look positively delighted with yourself."

"Well, as it happens, I—"

He broke off when Alex and Jenny came bounding down, firing invisible laser pistols. "Dead meat!" Alex shouted. "Dead meat!"

"If you must kill something," Coco said, "please do it outside. Fred needs an airing anyway."

"Death to the invaders," Alex announced. "We'll fry them like bacon."

In total agreement, Jenny aimed her laser at Fred and sent the dog scampering down the hall again. Deciding he made a handy invader, they raced after him. Even with the distance, the sound of the back door slamming boomed through the house.

"I don't know where they get those violent imaginations," Coco commented with a relieved sigh. "Suzanna's so mild tempered, and their father..." Something dark came into her eyes when she trailed off. "Well, that's another story. So tell me, what has you so happy?"

"I was just in the library, and I—"

This time it was the phone that interrupted. Coco slipped off an earring as she picked up the receiver. "Hello. Yes. Oh, yes, he's right here." She cupped a hand over the mouthpiece. "It's your dean, dear. He'd like to speak to you."

Max set the books on the telephone stand as Coco began to straighten pictures a few discreet feet away. "Dean Hodgins? Yes, I am, thank you. It's a beautiful spot. Well, I haven't really decided when I'm coming back...Professor Blake?"

Coco glanced back at the alarm in his voice.

"When? Is it serious? I'm sorry he's ill. I hope... I beg your pardon?" Letting out a long breath, Max leaned back against the banister. "I'm very flattered, but—" He lapsed into silence again, dragging a hand through his hair. "Thank you. Yes, I understand that. If I could have a day or two to consider. I appreciate it. Yes, sir. Goodbye."

When he simply stood, staring into space, Coco cleared her throat. "I hope it wasn't bad news, dear."

"What?" He focused on her, then shook his head. "No, well, yes. That is, the head of the history department had a heart attack last week."

"Oh." Immediately sympathetic, Coco came forward. "How dreadful."

"It was mild—if you can term anything like that mild. The doctors consider it a warning. They're recommending that he cut back on his workload, and he's taken them seriously, because he's decided to retire." He gave Coco a baffled look. "It seems he's recommended me to take over his position."

"Well now." She smiled and patted his cheek, but she was watching him carefully. "That's quite an honor, isn't it?"

"I'd have to go back next week," he said to himself. "To take over as acting head of the department until a final decision's made."

"Sometimes it's difficult to know what to do, which fork in the road to take. Why don't we have a nice cup of tea?" she suggested. "Then I'll read the leaves and we'll see."

"I really don't think—" The next interruption relieved him, and Coco clucked her tongue as she went to answer the banging on the door.

"Oh, my" was all she said. With her hand pressed to her breast, she said it again. "Oh, my!"

"Don't just stand there with your mouth hanging open, Cordelia," a crisp, authoritative voice demanded. "Have someone deal with my bags."

"Aunt Colleen." Coco's hand fluttered to her side. "What a…lovely surprise."

"Ha! You'd as soon see Satan himself on the doorstep." Leaning on a glossy, gold-tipped cane, she marched across the threshold.

Max saw a tall, rail-thin woman with a mass of luxurious white hair. She wore an elegant white suit and gleaming pearls. Her skin, generously lined, was as pale as linen. She might have been a ghost but for the deep blue eyes that scanned him.

"Who the hell is this?"

"Um. Um."

"Speak up, girl. Don't stutter." Colleen tapped the

cane impatiently. "You never kept a lick of the sense God gave you."

Coco began to wring her hands. "Aunt Colleen, this is Dr. Quartermain. Max, Colleen Calhoun."

"Doctor," Colleen barked. "Who's sick? Damned if I'm going to stay in a contagious house."

"That's a Ph.D., Miss Calhoun." Max offered a cautious smile. "It's nice to meet you."

"Ha." She sniffed and glanced around the hall. "Still letting the place fall down around your ears. Best if it was struck by lightning. Burned to the ground. See to those bags, Cordelia, and have someone bring me some tea. I've had a long trip." So saying, she clumped off toward the parlor.

"Yes, ma'am." Hands still fluttering, Coco sent Max a helpless look. "I hate to ask…"

"Don't worry about it. Where should I take her luggage?"

"Oh, God." Coco pressed her hands to her cheeks. "The first room on the right on the second floor. We'll have to stall her so that I can prepare it. Oh, and she won't have paid the driver. Tightfisted old… I'll call Amanda. She can warn the others. Max—" she clutched his hands "—if you believe in prayer, use it now and pray that this is a very short visit."

"Where's the damn tea?" Colleen demanded in a bellow and thumped her cane.

"Just coming." Coco turned and raced down the hall.

Pulling all her rabbits out of her hat, Coco plied her aunt with tea and petits fours, dragged Trent and Sloan away from their work and begged Max to fall in. Arrangements were made for Amanda to pick up Lilah and for Suzanna to close early and pitch in to prepare the guest room.

It was like preparing for an invasion, Max thought as he joined the group in the parlor. Colleen sat, erect as a general, while she measured her opponents with the same steely eye.

"So, you're the one who married Catherine. Hotels, isn't it?"

"Yes, ma'am," Trent answered politely while Coco fluttered around the room.

"Never stay in 'em," Colleen said dismissively. "Got married quick, wouldn't you say?"

"I didn't want to give her a chance to change her mind."

She almost smiled, then sniffed and aimed at Sloan. "And you're the one who's after Amanda."

"That's right."

"What's that accent?" she demanded, eyes sharpening. "Where are you from?"

"Oklahoma."

"O'Riley," she mused for a moment, then pointed a long white finger. "Oil."

"There you go."

"Humph." She lifted her tea to sip. "So you've got some harebrained notion about turning the west wing into a hotel. Better off burning it down and claiming the insurance."

"Aunt Colleen." Scandalized, Coco gaped at her. "You don't mean that."

"I say what I mean. Hated this place most of my life." She shifted to brood up at the portrait of her father. "He'd have hated seeing paying guests in The Towers. It would have mortified him."

"I'm sorry, Aunt Colleen," Coco began. "But we have to make the best of things."

"Did I ask for an apology?" Colleen snapped. "Where the hell are my grandnieces? Don't they have the courtesy to pay their respects?"

"They'll be along soon." Desperate, Coco poured more tea. "This was so unexpected, and we've—"

"A home should always be prepared for guests," Colleen retaliated with relish, then frowned at the doorway when Suzanna came in. "Which one is this?"

"I'm Suzanna." Dutifully she came forward to kiss her great-aunt's cheek.

"You favor your mother," Colleen decided with a grudging nod. "I was fond of Deliah." She shot a look at Max. "You after her?"

He blinked as Sloan struggled to turn a laugh into a cough. "Ah, no. No, ma'am."

"Why not? Something wrong with your eyes?"

"No." He shifted in his chair as Suzanna grinned and settled on a hassock.

"Max is visiting for a few weeks," said Coco, coming to the rescue. "He's helping us out with a little—historical research."

"The emeralds." Eyes gleaming, Colleen sat back. "Don't take me for a fool, Cordelia. We get newspapers aboard ship. Cruise ships," she said to Trent. "Much more civilized than hotels. Now, tell me what the hell is going on around here."

"Nothing, really." Coco cleared her throat again. "You know how the press blows things out of proportion."

"Was there a thief in this house, shooting off a gun?"

"Well, yes. It was disturbing, but—"

"You." Colleen hefted her cane and poked it at Max.

"You with the Ph.D. I assume you can articulate clearly. Explain the situation, briefly."

At the pleading glance from Coco, Max set his unwanted tea aside. "The family decided, after a series of events, to investigate the veracity of the legend of the Calhoun emeralds. Unfortunately, news of the necklace leaked, causing interest and speculation among various people, some of them unsavory. The first step was to catalogue old family papers, to verify the existence of the emeralds."

"Of course they existed," Colleen said impatiently. "Haven't I seen them with my own eyes?"

"You were difficult to reach," Coco began, and was silenced with a look.

"In any case," Max continued. "The house was broken into, and a number of the papers stolen." Max skimmed over his involvement to bring her up to date.

"Hmm." Colleen frowned at him. "What do you do, write?"

Max's brow lifted in surprise. "I teach. History. At, ah, Cornell University."

Colleen sniffed again. "Well, you've made a mess of it. The lot of you. Bringing thieves under the roof, splashing our name all over the press, nearly getting yourselves killed. For all we know the old man sold the emeralds."

"He'd have kept a record," Max put in, and had Colleen studying him again.

"You're right there, Mr. Ph.D. He kept account of every penny he made, and every penny he spent." She closed her eyes a moment. "Nanny always told us she hid them away. For us." Fierce, her eyes opened again. "Fairy tales."

"I love fairy tales," Lilah said from the doorway. She stood, flanked by C.C. and Amanda.

"Come in here where I can see you."

"You first," Lilah muttered to C.C.

"Why me?"

"You're the youngest." She gave her sister a gentle shove.

"Throwing a pregnant woman to the wolves," Amanda muttered.

"You're next."

"What's that on your face?" Colleen demanded of C.C.

C.C. wiped a hand over her cheek. "Motor oil, I guess."

"What's the world coming to? You've got good bones," she decided. "You'll age well. You pregnant yet?"

Dipping her hands in her pockets, C.C. grinned. "As a matter of fact, yes. Trent and I are expecting in February."

"Good." Colleen waved her away. Steeling herself, Amanda stepped forward.

"Hello, Aunt Colleen. I'm glad you decided to come for the wedding."

"Might, might not." Lips pursed, she studied Amanda. "You know how to write a proper letter, in any case. It reached me last week, with the invitation." She was a lovely thing, Colleen thought, like her sisters. She felt a sense of pride in that, but would have bitten off her tongue before admitting it. "Any reason you couldn't marry a man from a nice Eastern family?"

"Yes. None of them annoyed me as much as Sloan."

With what might have been a laugh, Colleen waved her away.

When she focused on Lilah, her eyes burned and she had to press her lips tight to keep them from quivering. It was like looking at her mother, with all the years, and all the hurt wiped away.

"So, you're Lilah." When her voice cracked, she lowered her brows, looking so formidable that Coco trembled.

"Yes." Lilah kissed both her cheeks. "The last time I saw you I was eight, I think. And you scolded me for going barefoot."

"And just what are you doing with your life?"

"Oh, as little as possible," Lilah said blithely. "How about you?"

Colleen's lips twitched, but she rounded on Coco. "Haven't you taught these girls manners?"

"Don't blame her." Lilah sat on the floor at Max's feet. "We're incorrigible." She glanced over her shoulder, smiled at Max, then set a companionable hand on his knee.

Colleen didn't miss a trick. "So, you've got your eye on this one."

Tossing back her hair, Lilah smiled. "I certainly do. Cute, isn't he?"

"Lilah," Max muttered. "Give me a break."

"You didn't kiss me hello," she said quite clearly.

"Leave the boy alone." More amused than she would have admitted, Colleen thumped her cane. "At least he has manners." She waved a hand at the tea things. "Take this business away, Cordelia, and bring me a brandy."

"I'll get it." Lilah unfolded herself and strolled over to the liquor cabinet. She winked at Suzanna as her sister wheeled over the tea cart. "How long do you think she plans to make our lives a living hell?"

"I heard that."

Undaunted, Lilah turned with the brandy snifter. "Of course you did, Auntie. Papa always told us you had ears like a cat."

"Don't call me 'Auntie.'" She snatched the brandy. Colleen was used to deference—her personality and her money had always demanded it. Or to fear—the kind she easily instilled in Coco. But she enjoyed, tremendously, irreverence. "The trouble is your father never lifted a hand to any of you."

"No," Lilah murmured. "He didn't have to."

"No one loved him more than I," Colleen said briskly. "Now, it's time to decide what to do about this mess you've gotten yourselves into. The sooner mended, the sooner I can rejoin my cruise."

"You don't mean—" Coco caught herself and hastily rephrased. "Do you plan to stay with us until the emeralds are found?"

"I plan to stay until I'm ready to leave." Colleen aimed a look, daring disagreement.

"How lovely," Coco said between unsteady lips. "I believe I'll go in and see about dinner."

"I dine at seven-thirty. Precisely."

"Of course." Even as Coco rose, the familiar chaos could be heard racing down the hall. "Oh, dear."

Suzanna sprang to her feet. "I'll head them off." But she was a bit late as both children came barreling into the room.

"Cheat, cheat, cheat," Jenny accused, eyes brimming.

"Crybaby." But Alex was near tears himself as he gave her a brotherly shove.

"Who are these hooligans?" Colleen asked, interest perking.

"These hooligans are my children." Suzanna studied them both and saw that though she had tidied them herself less than twenty minutes before, they were both grimy and grim faced. Obviously her idea that they spend a quiet hour playing a board game had been a disaster.

Colleen swirled her brandy. "Bring them here. I'll have a look at them."

"Alex, Jenny." The warning tone worked very well. "Come meet Aunt Colleen."

"She isn't going to kiss us, is she?" Alex muttered as he dragged his feet across the room.

"I certainly will not. I don't kiss grubby little boys." She had to swallow. He looked so like her baby brother, Sean. Formally she offered a hand. "How do you do?"

"Okay." Flushing a bit, he touched the thin-boned hand.

"You're awfully old," Jenny observed.

"Quite right," Colleen agreed before Suzanna could speak. "If you're lucky, the same problem will be yours one day." She would have liked to have stroked the girl's shiny blond hair, but it would have shattered her image. "I'll expect you to refrain from shouting and clattering about while I'm in the house. Furthermore…" She trailed off when something brushed her leg. Glancing down, she saw Fred sniffing the carpet for crumbs. "What is that?"

"That's our dog." Seized with inspiration, Alex reached down to heft the fat puppy in his arms. "If you're mean to us, he'll bite you."

"He'll do no such thing." Suzanna put a hand on Alex's shoulder.

"He might." Alex pouted. "He doesn't like bad people. Do you, Fred?"

Colleen's skin went even whiter. "What is his name?"

"His name is Fred," Jenny said gaily. "Trent found him on the cliffs and brought him home for us." She struggled the dog away from her brother to hold him out. "And he doesn't bite. He's a good dog."

"Jenny, put him down before he—"

"No." Colleen waved Suzanna's warning aside. "Let me see him." Fred wriggled, smearing dirt on Colleen's pristine white suit as she sat him in her lap. Her hands shook as they stroked his fur. "I had a dog named Fred once." A single tear spilled over and down her pale cheek. "I only had him for a little while, but I loved him very much."

Saying nothing, Lilah groped for Max's hand and held tight.

"You can play with him, if you want," Alex told her, appalled that someone so old would cry. "He doesn't really bite."

"Of course he won't bite." Recovering, Colleen set the dog on the floor, then straightened painfully. "He knows I'd just bite him back. Isn't someone going to show me to my room, or do I have to sit here all day and half the damn night?"

"We'll take you up." Lilah tugged on Max's hand so that he rose to help her to her feet.

"Bring the brandy," Colleen said imperiously, and started out stumping with her cane.

"Delightful relatives you have, Calhoun," Sloan murmured.

"Too late to back out now, O'Riley." Amanda heaved

a relieved breath. "Come on, Aunt Coco, I'll help you in the kitchen."

"Which room have you stuck me in?" Only slightly breathless, Colleen paused on the second-floor landing.

"The first one, here." Max opened the door, then stepped back.

The terrace doors had been opened to let in the breeze. The furniture had been hastily polished, a few extra pieces dragged in from storage. Fresh flowers sat atop the rosewood bureau. The wallpaper was peeling, but paintings had been culled from other rooms to hide the worst of it. A delicate lace spread had been unfolded from a cedar chest and adorned the heavy four-poster.

"It'll do," Colleen muttered, determined to fight the nostalgia. "Make sure there are fresh towels, girl. And you, Quartermain, is it? Pour me another dose of that brandy and don't be stingy."

Lilah peeked into the adjoining bath and saw all was as it should be. "Is there anything else, Auntie?"

"Mind your tone, and don't call me 'Auntie.' You can send a maid up when it's time for dinner."

Lilah stuck her tongue in her cheek. "I'm afraid it's the staff's year off."

"Unconscionable." Colleen leaned heavily on her cane. "Are you telling me you haven't even day help?"

"You know very well we've been under the financial gun for some time."

"And you'll still not get a penny from me to put into this cursed place." She walked stiffly to the open doors and looked out. God, the view, she thought. It never changed. How many times over how many years had she envisioned it? "Who has my mother's room?"

"I do," Lilah said, lifting her chin.

Very slowly, Colleen turned. "Of course, you would." Her voice had softened. "Do you know how much you favor her?"

"Yes. Max found a picture in a book."

"A picture in a book." Now the bitterness. "That's all that's left of her."

"No. No, there's much more. A part of her is still here, will always be here."

"Don't talk nonsense. Ghosts, spirits—that's Cordelia's influence, and it's a load of hogwash. Dead's dead, girl. When you're as close to it as I am, you'll know that."

"If you'd felt her as I've felt her, you'd know differently."

Colleen closed herself in. "Shut the door behind you. I like my privacy."

Lilah waited until they were out in the hall to swear. "Rude, bad-tempered old bat." Then with a lazy shrug, she tucked her arm through Max's. "Let's go get some air. To think I'd actually felt something for her downstairs when she held Fred."

"She's not so bad, Lilah." They passed through his room and onto the terrace. "You may be just as crotchety when you're eighty-something."

"I'll never be crotchety." She closed her eyes, tossed back her hair and smiled. "I'll have a nice rocking chair set in the sun and sleep old age away." She ran a hand up his arm. "Are you ever going to kiss me hello?"

"Yes." He cupped her face and did so thoroughly. "Hello. How was your day?"

"Hot and busy." But now she felt delightfully cool

and relaxed. "That teacher I told you about was back. He seems overly earnest to me. Gives me the willies."

Max's smile disappeared. "You should report him to one of the rangers."

"What, for sending off bad vibrations?" She laughed and hugged him. "No, there's just something about him that hits me wrong. He's always wearing dark glasses, as if I might see something he didn't want seen if he took them off."

"You're letting your..." His grip tightened. "What does he look like?"

"Nothing special. Why don't we take a nap before dinner? Aunt Colleen exhausted me."

"What," Max said very precisely, "does he look like?"

"He's about your height, trim. Somewhere around thirty, I'd guess. Wears the hiker's uniform of T-shirt and ripped jeans. He doesn't have a tan," she said, frowning suddenly. "Which is odd seeing as he said he'd been camping for a couple of weeks. Average sort of brown hair, well over the collar. A very neat beard and mustache."

"It could be him." His fingers dug in as the possibility iced through him. "My God, he's been with you."

"You think—you think it's Caufield." The idea left her shaken so that she leaned back against the wall. "What an idiot I've been. I had the same feeling, the same feeling with this man as I did when Livingston came to take Amanda out for dinner." She ran both hands through her hair. "I must be losing my touch."

Max's eyes were dark as he stared out at the cliffs. "If he comes back, I'll be ready for him."

"Don't start playing hero." Alarmed, she grabbed his arms. "He's dangerous."

"He's not getting near you again." The complete and focused intensity was back on his face. "I'll be taking your shift with you tomorrow."

Chapter Twelve

He never let her out of his sight. Though they had given the authorities the description, Max took no chances. By the time the day was over, he knew more about the intertidal zone than anyone could want to know. He could recognize Irish moss from rockweed—though he still grimaced at Lilah's claim that the moss made excellent ice cream.

But there hadn't been a sign of Caufield.

On the off chance that he had been speaking the truth about camping in the park, the rangers had made a quiet and thorough search but had found no trace of him.

No one had seen the bearded man watching the fruitless search through field glasses. No one had seen the rage come into his eyes when he realized his cover had been blown.

As they drove home, Lilah unwound her braid. "Feel better?" she asked Max.

"No."

She pushed her hands under her hair to let the wind catch it. "Well, you should. It was sweet of you to worry about me, though."

"It has nothing to do with sweetness."

"I think you're disappointed that you didn't get to go into hand-to-hand combat."

"Maybe I am."

"Okay." She leaned over to nip at his ear. "Want to rumble?"

"It's not a joke," he muttered. "I'm not going to feel right until he's taken care of."

Lilah snuggled back in the seat. "If he had any sense he'd give up and go away. We live in the house and we've hardly made any progress."

"That's not true. We verified the existence of the emeralds. We found a photograph of them. We located Mrs. Tobias, and have her eyewitness account of what happened the day before Bianca died. And we've identified Christian."

"We've what?" She sprang up straight. "When did we identify Christian?"

Max grimaced as he glanced over at her. "I forgot to tell you. Don't look like that. First your great-aunt invades the house and sets everyone on their ears. Then you tell me about the man in the park. I thought I had told you."

She inhaled, then exhaled deeply to keep her patience. "Why don't you tell me now?"

"It was in the library yesterday," he began, and filled her in on what he'd found.

"Christian Bradford," Lilah said, trying out the name to see how it fit. "There's something familiar about it.

I wonder if I've seen some of his paintings. It wouldn't be surprising if there were some in this area, since he lived here on and off. Died here."

"Didn't you study art in college?"

"I didn't study at all unless I was boxed in. Mostly I drifted through, and art was always more a hobby than anything else. I didn't want to work at it because I liked playing at it better. And I wanted to be a naturalist all along."

"An ambition?" He grinned. "Lilah, you'll ruin your image."

"Well, it was my only one. Everybody's entitled. Bradford, Bradford," she repeated, gnawing at the word. "I'd swear it rings a bell." She closed her eyes on it, opening them again when they pulled up at The Towers. "Got it. We knew a Bradford. He grew up on the island. Holt, Holt Bradford. The dark, broody, surly sort. He was a few years older—probably in his early thirties now. He left ten or twelve years ago, but it seems to me I heard he was back. He owns a cottage in the village. My God, Max, if he's Christian's grandson, it would be the same cottage."

"Don't get ahead of yourself. We'll look into it, one step at a time."

"If you have to be logical, I'll talk to Suzanna. She knew him a little better. I remember that she knocked him off his motorcycle the first week she had her license."

"I did not knock him off his motorcycle," Suzanna denied, and sank her aching body into a hot, frothy tub. "He fell off his motorcycle when he failed to yield. I had the right-of-way."

"Whatever." Lilah sat on the edge of the tub. "What do we know about him?"

"He has a nasty temper. I thought he was going to murder me that day. He wouldn't have scraped himself all up if he'd been wearing protective gear."

"I mean his background, not his personality."

Weary, Suzanna opened her eyes. Ordinarily the bathroom was the only place she could find true peace and privacy. Now even that had been invaded. "Why?"

"I'll tell you after. Come on, Suze."

"All right, let me think. He was ahead of me in school. Three or four years, I think. Most of the girls were crazy about him because he looked dangerous. His mother was very nice."

"I remember," Lilah murmured. "She came to the house after…"

"Yes, after Mom and Dad were killed. She used to do handwork. She'd done some lovely pieces for Mom. We still have some of them, I think. And her husband was a lobsterman. He was lost at sea when we were teenagers. I really don't remember that much."

"Did you ever talk to him?"

"Who, Holt? Not really. He'd sort of swagger around and glare. When we had that little accident he mostly swore at me. Then he went off somewhere—Portland. I remember because Mrs. Marsley was talking about him just the other day when I was selling her some climbing roses. He was a cop for a while, but there was some kind of incident, and he gave it up."

"What kind of incident?"

"I don't know. Whenever she starts I just let it flow in one ear and on out. I think he's repairing boats or something."

"He never talked about his family with you?"

"Why in the world should he? And why would you care?"

"Because Christian's last name was Bradford, and he had a cottage on the island."

"Oh." Suzanna let out a long breath as she absorbed the information. "Isn't that just our luck?"

Lilah left her sister to soak, and set off to find Max. Before she could go into his room, Coco waylaid her.

"Oh, there you are."

"Darling, you look frazzled." Lilah kissed her cheek.

"And who wouldn't be? That woman…" Coco took a deep calming breath. "I'm doing twenty minutes of yoga every morning just to cope. Be a dear and take this in to her."

"What is it?"

"Tonight's menu." Coco set her teeth. "She insists on treating this as though it's one of her cruises."

"As long as we don't have to play shuffleboard."

"Thank you, dear. Oh, did Max tell you his news?"

"Hmm? Oh, yes, belatedly."

"Has he decided? I know it's a wonderful opportunity, but I hate to think he'll be leaving so soon."

"Leaving?"

"If he takes the position, he'll have to go back to Cornell next week. I was going to read the cards last night, but with Aunt Colleen, I just couldn't concentrate."

"What position, Aunt Coco?"

"Head of the history department." She gave Lilah a baffled look. "I thought he'd told you."

"I was thinking of something else." She struggled to keep her voice even. "He's going to leave in a few days?"

"He'll have to decide." Coco cupped a hand under Lilah's chin. "You'll both have to decide."

"He hasn't chosen to bring me in on this one." She stared down at the menu until the words blurred. "It's a terrific opportunity, one I'm sure he's hoped for."

"There are a lot of opportunities in life, Lilah."

She only shook her head. "I couldn't do anything to discourage him from doing something he wants. Not if I loved him. It has to be his decision."

"Who the hell is jabbering out there?" Colleen thumped her cane on the floor.

"I'd like to take that cane and—"

"More yoga," Lilah suggested, forcing a smile. "I'll deal with her."

"Good luck."

"You bellowed, Auntie," Lilah said as she breezed through the door.

"You didn't knock."

"No, I didn't. Tonight's menu, Miss Calhoun. We hope it meets with your approval."

"Little snip." Colleen snatched the paper away, then frowned up at her grandniece. "What's wrong with you, girl? You're white as a sheet."

"Pale skin runs in the family. It's the Irish."

"It's temper that runs in the family." She'd seen eyes that had looked like that before, she thought. Hurt, confused. But then she had been only a child, unable to understand. "Trouble with your young man."

"What makes you say so?"

"Just because I never tied myself down with a man doesn't mean I don't know them. I dallied in my day."

"Dallied." This time the smile came more easily. "A nice word. I suppose some of us are meant to dally through life." She ran a finger down the bedpost. "Just as there are some women men love but don't fall in love with."

"You're jabbering."

"No, I'm trying to be realistic. I'm not usually."

"Realism is cold comfort."

Lilah's brow lifted. "Oh, Lord, I'm afraid I'm more like you than I realized. What a scary thought."

Colleen disguised a chuckle. "Get out of here. You give me a headache. Girl," she said, and Lilah paused at the door, "any man who puts that look into your eyes is worth everything or nothing at all."

Lilah gave a short laugh. "Why, Auntie, you're absolutely right."

She went to his room, but he wasn't there. She'd yet to decide whether to confront Max about his plans or to wait until he told her himself. For better or worse, she thought she would follow her instincts. Idly she picked up a shirt he'd left at the foot of his bed. It was the silly screenprint she'd talked him into on that first shopping trip. The shirt, and the memory, still made her smile. Setting it aside, she crossed to his desk.

He had it piled with books—thick volumes on World War I, a history of Maine, a treatment on the Industrial Revolution. She lifted a brow over a book on fashion in the 1900s. He'd picked up one of the pamphlets from the park that gave a detailed map of the island.

In another pile were the art books. Lilah picked up the top one and opened it to where Max had marked it. As he had, she felt the quick thrill of discovery on reading Christian Bradford's name. Lowering into the chair in front of the typewriter, she read the brief biography twice.

Fascinated, excited, she set the book down to reach for another. It was then she noticed the typed pages, neatly stacked. More reports, she thought with a faint smile. She remembered how tidily he had typed up their interview with Millie Tobias.

From the top of the high tower of rock, she faced the sea.

Curious, Lilah settled more comfortably and read on. She was midway through the second chapter when Max came in. Her emotions were so ragged she had to brace before she could speak.

"Your book. You started your book."

"Yeah." He shoved his hands into his pockets. "I was looking for you."

"It's Bianca, isn't it?" Lilah set down the page she was holding. "Laura—she's Bianca."

"Parts of her." He couldn't have explained how it felt to know that she had read his words—words that had come not so much from his head as from his heart.

"You've set it here, on the island."

"It seemed right." He didn't move toward her, he didn't smile, but only stood looking uncomfortable.

"I'm sorry." The apology was stiff and overly polite. "I shouldn't have read it without asking, but it caught my eye."

"It's all right." With his hands still balled in his pockets, he shrugged. She hated it, he thought. "It doesn't matter."

"Why didn't you tell me?"

"There wasn't really anything to tell. I only have about fifty pages, and it's rough. I thought—"

"It's beautiful." She fought back the hurt as she rose. "What?"

"It's beautiful," she repeated, and found that hurt turned quickly to anger. "You've got enough sense to know that. You've read thousands of books in your life, and know good work from bad. If you didn't want to share it with me, that's your business."

Still stunned, he shook his head. "It wasn't that I—"

"What was it then? I'm important enough to share your bed, but not to be in on any of the major decisions in your life."

"You're being ridiculous."

"Fine." Rolling easily with her temper, she tossed back her hair. "I'm being ridiculous. Apparently I've been ridiculous for some time now."

The tears crowding her voice confused as much as unnerved him. "Why don't we sit down and talk this through?"

She went with her instincts and shoved the chair at him. "Go ahead. Have a seat. But there's no need to talk anything through. You've started your book, but didn't think it was necessary to mention it. You've been offered a promotion, but didn't consider it worth bringing up. Not to me. You've got your life, Professor, and I've got mine. That's what we said right from the beginning. It's just my bad luck that I fell in love with you."

"If you'd just—" Her last words sank in, dazzling him, dazing him, delighting him. "Oh, God, Lilah." He started to rush forward, but she threw up both hands.

"Don't touch me," she said so fiercely, he stopped, baffled.

"What do you expect me to do?"

"I don't expect anything. If I had stuck to that from the beginning, you wouldn't have been able to hurt me like this. As it is, it's my problem. Now, if you'll excuse me."

He grabbed her arm before she reached the door. "You can't say things like this, you can't tell me you're in love with me then just walk away."

"I'll do exactly as I please." Eyes cold, she jerked her arm free. "I don't have anything more to say to you, and there's nothing you can say I want to hear right now."

She walked out of his room into her own and locked the door behind her.

Hours later, she sat in her room, cursing herself for losing her pride and her temper so completely. All she had succeeded in accomplishing was embarrassing herself and Max, and giving herself a vicious headache.

She'd slashed at him, and that had been wrong. She'd pushed him, and that had been stupid. Any hope she'd had of steering him gently into love had been smashed because she'd demanded things he hadn't wanted to give. Now, more than likely, she had ruined a friendship that had been vitally important to her.

There could be no apologizing. No matter how miserable she felt, she couldn't apologize for speaking the truth. And she could never claim to be sorry to have fallen in love.

Restless, she walked out on the terrace. There were clouds over the moon. The wind shoved them across the sky so that the light glimmered for a moment then was smothered. The heat of the day was trapped; the night almost sultry. Fireflies danced over the black carpet of lawn like sparks from a dying fire.

In the distance thunder rumbled, but there was no freshening scent of rain. The storm was out at sea, and even if the capricious wind blew it to land, it might be hours before it hit and relieved the hazy heat. She could smell the flowers, hot and heady, and glanced toward the garden. Her thoughts were so involved that she stared at the glimmer of light for a full minute before it registered.

Not again, she thought, and was almost depressed enough to let the amateur treasure hunters have their thrill. But Suzanna worked too hard on the gardens to have some idiot with a map dig up her perennials. In any case, at least chasing off a trespasser was constructive.

She moved quietly down the steps and into the deeper gloom of the garden. It was simple enough to follow the beam of light. As she walked toward it, Lilah debated whether to use the Calhoun curse or the old The Police Are On Their Way. Both were reliable ways of sending trespassers scurrying. Any other time the prospect might have amused her.

When the light blinked out, she stopped, frowning, to listen. There was only the sound of her own breathing. Not a leaf stirred, and no bird sang in the brush. With a shrug, she moved on. Perhaps they had heard her and had already retreated, but she wanted to be certain.

In the dark, she nearly fell over the pile of dirt. All amusement vanished when her eyes adjusted and she saw the destruction of Suzanna's lovely bed of dahlias.

"Jerks," she muttered, and kicked at the dirt with a sandaled foot. "What the hell is wrong with them?" On a little moan, she bent down to pick up a trampled bloom. Her fingers clenched over it when a hand slapped against her mouth.

"Not a sound." The voice hissed at her ear. Reacting to it, she started to struggle, then froze when she felt the point of the knife at her throat. "Do exactly what I say, and I won't cut you. Try to yell, and I'll slice this across your throat. Understand?"

She nodded and let out a long careful breath when his hand slid away from her mouth. It would have been foolish to ask what he wanted. She knew the answer. But this wasn't some adventure-seeking tourist out for a late-night lark.

"You're wasting your time. The emeralds aren't here."

"Don't play games with me. I've got a map."

Lilah closed her eyes and bit back a hysterical and dangerous laugh.

Max paced his room, scowled at the floor and wished he had something handy to kick. He'd messed things up beautifully. He wasn't exactly sure how he'd managed it, but he'd hurt Lilah, infuriated her and alienated her all in one swoop. He'd never seen a woman go through so many emotions in such a short time. From unhappiness to fury, from fury to frost—hardly letting him get in a single word.

He could have defended himself—if he'd been totally certain of the offense. How could he have known that she'd be offended he hadn't mentioned the book? He hadn't wanted to bore her. No, that was a lie, he admitted. He hadn't told her because he'd been afraid. Plain and simple.

As far as the promotion went, he'd meant to tell her, but it had slipped his mind. How could she believe that he'd have accepted the position and left without telling her?

"What the hell was she supposed to think, you jerk?" he muttered, and plopped down into a chair.

So much for all his careful plans, his step-by-step

courtship. His tidy little itinerary for making her fall in love with him had blown up in his face. She'd been in love with him all along.

She loved him. He dragged a hand through his hair. Lilah Calhoun was in love with him, and he hadn't had to wave a magic wand or implement any complicated plan. All he'd had to do was be himself.

She'd been in love with him all along, but he'd been too stupid to believe it even when she'd tried to tell him. Now she'd locked herself in her room and wouldn't listen to him.

As far as he could see, he had two choices. He could sit here and wait until she cooled off, then he could beg. Or he could get up right now, beat down her door and demand that she hear him out.

He liked the second idea. In fact, he thought it was inspired.

Without taking the time to debate with himself, he went through the terrace doors. Since it was two in the morning, it made more sense to rattle the glass than beat on the inside door and wake up the household. And it was more romantic. He'd shove open those doors, stride across the room and drag her into his arms until she...

His erotic dream veered off as he caught a glimpse of her just before she disappeared into the garden.

Fine, he thought. Maybe better. A sultry garden in the middle of the night. Perfumed air and passion. She wasn't going to know what hit her.

"You know where they are." Hawkins dragged her head back by the hair and she nearly cried out.

"If I knew where they were, I'd have them."

"It's a publicity stunt." He whirled her around, laying the edge of the knife against her cheek. "I figured it out. You've just been playing games to get your names in the paper. I've put time and money into this deal, and it's going to pay off tonight."

She was too terrified to move. Even a tremor might have the blade slicing over her skin. She recognized rage in his eyes, just as she recognized him. This was the man Max had called Hawkins. "The map," she began, then heard Max call her name. Before she could take a breath, the knife was at her throat again.

"Make a sound and I kill you, then him."

He'd kill them both anyway, she thought frantically. It had been in his eyes. "The map," she said in a whisper. "It's a fake." She gasped when the blade pricked her skin. "I'll show you. I can show you where they are."

She had to get him away, away from Max. He was calling her again, and the frustration in his voice had tears welling in her eyes.

"Down that way." She gestured on impulse and let Hawkins drag her down the path until Max's voice faded. At the side edge, the garden gave way to the rocks where the smell and sound of the sea grew stronger. "Over there." She stumbled as he pulled her over the uneven ground. Beside her, the slope ran almost gently to a ridge. Below that, dizzying feet below, were the jagged teeth of rocks and the temperamental sea.

When the first flash of lightning struck, she jolted, then looked desperately over her shoulder. The wind had come up, but she hadn't noticed. The clouds still hid the moon and smothered the light.

Was she far enough away? she wondered. Had Max given up looking for her and gone back inside? Where it was safe.

"If you're trying to pull something on me—"

"No. They're here." She tripped on a jumble of rocks and went down hard. "Under here. In a box under the rocks."

She would inch away slowly, she told herself as every instinct screamed for her to run. While he was involved, she would inch away, then spring up and race to the house. He grabbed the hem of her skirt, ripping it.

"One wrong move, and you're dead." She saw the gleam of his eyes as he bent close. "If I don't find the box, you're dead."

Then his head went up, like a wolf scenting. Out of the dark with a vicious oath, Max leaped.

She screamed then as she saw the wicked edge of the knife glint in the flash of lightning. They hit the ground beside her, rolling over dirt and rock. She was still screaming when she jumped on Hawkins's back to grope for his knife hand. The blade sliced into the ground an inch from Max's face before she was bucked off.

"Damn it, run!" Max shouted at her, gripping Hawkins's beefy wrist with both hands. Then he grunted as a fist grazed his temple.

They were rolling again, the impetus taking them down the slope and onto the ridge. She did run, but toward them, sliding along the loose dirt and sending a shower of pebbles to rain over the struggling bodies. Panting for breath, she grabbed a rock. Her next scream sliced the air as Max's leg dangled over the edge into space.

All he could see was the contorted face above his. All he could hear was Lilah shouting his name. Then he saw stars when Hawkins rammed his head against the rock. For an instant, Max teetered on the edge, the brink between sky and sea. His hand slipped down the sweaty forearm. When the knife came down, he smelled the blood and heard Hawkins's grunt of triumph.

There was something else in the air—something passionate and pleading—as insubstantial as the wind but as strong as bedrock. It slammed into him like a fist. The understanding went through him that he wasn't only fighting for his life, but for Lilah's and the life they would make together.

He wouldn't lose it. With every ounce of strength, he smashed his fist into the face grinning over his. Blood spouted out of Hawkins's nose, then they were grappling again with the knife wedged between them.

Lilah lifted the rock in both hands, started to bring it down when the men at her feet reversed positions. Sobbing, she scrambled back. There were shouts behind her and wild barking. She held tight to the only weapon she had and prayed that she would have the chance to use it.

Then the struggling stopped, and both men went still. With a grunt, Max pushed Hawkins aside and managed to gain his knees. His face was streaked with dirt and blood, his clothes splattered with it. Weakly he shook his head to clear it and looked up at Lilah. She stood like an avenging angel, hair flying, the rock gripped in her hands.

"He rolled on the knife," Max said in a distant voice. "I think he's dead." Dazed, he stared down at his hand, at the dark smear that was the blood of the man he'd killed. Then he looked up at her again. "Are you hurt?"

"Oh, Max. Oh, God." The rock slipped from her fingers as she tumbled to her knees beside him.

"It's okay." He patted her shoulder, stroked her hair.

"It's okay," he repeated though he was deathly afraid he would faint.

The dog got there first, then the others came thundering down the slope in nightgowns or robes and hastily pulled-on jeans.

"Lilah." Amanda was there, desperate hands running over her sister's body in a search for wounds. "Are you all right? Are you hurt?"

"No." But her teeth were starting to chatter in the sultry night. "No, he was—Max came." She looked over to see Trent crouched beside him, examining a long gash down his arm. "You're bleeding."

"Not much."

"It's shallow," Trent said between his teeth. "I imagine it hurts like hell."

"Not yet," Max murmured.

Trent looked over as Sloan walked back from the man sprawled on the ridge. Tight-lipped, Sloan shook his head. "It's done," he said briefly.

"It was Hawkins." Max struggled to his feet and stood, swaying. "He had Lilah."

"We'll discuss this later." Her voice uncharacteristically crisp, Coco took Max's good arm. "They're both in shock. Let's get them inside."

"Come on, baby." Sloan reached down to gather Lilah into his arms. "I'll give you a ride home."

"I'm not hurt." From the cradle of his arms she swiveled her head around to look for Max. "He's bleeding. He needs help."

"We'll fix him up," Sloan promised her as they started across the lawn. "Don't you worry, sweetie, the teacher's tougher than you think."

Up ahead, The Towers was ablaze with lights. Another roll of thunder walked the sky above its peaks, then echoed into silence. Abruptly, a tall, thin figure appeared on the second-floor terrace, a cane in one hand, a glinty chrome revolver in the other.

"What the hell is going on around here?" Colleen shouted. "How is a body supposed to get a decent night's sleep with all this hoopla?"

Coco sent one weary glance upward. "Oh, be quiet and go back to bed."

For some reason, Lilah laid her head on Sloan's shoulder and began to laugh.

It was nearly dawn when things settled. The police had come and gone, taking away their grisly package. Questions had been asked and answered—asked and answered again. Lilah had been plied with brandy, fussed over and ordered into a hot bath.

They hadn't let her tend Max's wound. Which might have been for the best, she thought now. Her hands hadn't been steady.

He'd bounced back from the incident remarkably well, she mused as she curled on the window seat in the tower room. While she had still been numb and shaky, he had stood in the parlor, his arm freshly bandaged, and given the investigating officer a clear and concise report of the whole event.

He might have been lecturing one of his classes on the cause and effect of the German economy on World War I, she thought with the ghost of a smile. It had been obvious that Lieutenant Koogar had appreciated the precision and clarity.

Lilah liked to think that her own account had been calm enough, though she hadn't been able to control the trembling very well even when her sisters had joined ranks around her.

Suzanna had finally told the lieutenant enough was enough and had bundled Lilah upstairs.

But despite the bath and brandy, she hadn't been able to sleep. She was afraid if she closed her eyes that she would see it unfolding again, see Max teetering on the edge of the ridge. They'd hardly spoken since the whole horrible business had happened. They would have to, of course, she reflected. She wanted to clear her thoughts and find just the right words.

But then he walked in, while the sky behind her was being gilded with sunrise, and she was afraid she would never find them.

He stood awkwardly, favoring his left arm, his face shadowed by fatigue. "I couldn't sleep," he began. "I thought you might be up here."

"I guess I needed to think. It's always easier for me to think up here." Feeling as awkward as he, she smoothed back her hair. It fell untamed, the color of the young sun, against the white shoulders of her robe. "Would you like to sit?"

"Yeah." He crossed the room and eased his aching muscles down onto the seat beside her. The silence dragged on, one minute, then two. "Some night," he said at length.

"Yes."

"Don't," he murmured when her eyes filled.

"No." She swallowed them back and stared out at the quiet dawn. "I thought he would kill you. It was like a nightmare—the dark, the heat, the blood."

"It's done now." He took her hand, curled strong fingers around hers. "You led him away from the garden.

You were trying to protect me, Lilah. I can't thank you for it."

Off guard, she looked back at him. "What was I supposed to do, let him jump out of the petunias and stab you in the dark?"

"You were supposed to let me take care of you."

She tried to jerk her hand free, but he held firm. "You did, didn't you? Whether I wanted you to or not. You came rushing out like a crazy man, jumping on a maniac with a knife and nearly—" She broke off, struggling for composure while he only sat watching her with those patient eyes. "You saved my life," she said more calmly.

"Then we're even, aren't we?" She shrugged and went back to watching the sky. "The oddest thing happened during those last few minutes I was fighting with Hawkins. I felt myself slipping, losing ground. Then I felt something else, something incredibly strong. I'd say it was simple adrenaline, but it didn't come from me. It was something—other," he said, studying her profile. "I suppose you could call it a force. And I knew that I wasn't meant to lose, that there were reasons I couldn't. I guess I'll always wonder if that force, if that feeling came from you, or from Bianca."

Her lips curved as she looked back at him. "Why, Professor, how illogical."

He didn't smile. "I was coming to your room, to make you listen to me, when I saw you go into the garden. Normally I would consider it only right—or logical—to back off and give you time to recover after what's happened. But things change, Lilah. You're going to listen now."

For a moment she leaned her brow on the cool glass. Then she nodded. "All right, you're entitled. But first

I'd like to say that I know I was angry earlier—about the book. It was the wrong reaction—"

"No, it wasn't. You trusted me with a great deal, and I didn't trust you. I was afraid you'd be kind."

"I don't understand."

"Writing's something I've wanted to do most of my life, but I...well, I'm not used to taking risks."

She had to laugh and, going with instinct, leaned over to kiss the bandage on his arm. "Max, what a thing to say now of all times."

"I haven't been used to taking risks," he corrected. "I thought if I told you about the book and got up the courage to show you a few pages, you'd see it as a pipe dream and be kind."

"It's stupid to be so insecure about something you have such talent for." Then she sighed. "And it was stupid for me to take it so personally. Take it from someone who isn't particularly kind. It's going to be a wonderful book, Max. Something you can be very proud of."

He cupped a hand behind her neck. "Let's see if you say that after I make you read several hundred more pages." He leaned toward her, touched his lips gently to hers. But when he started to deepen the kiss, she jumped up.

"I'll give you the first critique when it's published." Nerves humming, she began to pace.

"What is it, Lilah?"

"Nothing. So much has happened." She took a deep breath before she turned, smile firmly in place. "The promotion. I was so involved with myself before that I didn't even congratulate you."

"I wasn't keeping it from you."

"Max, let's not go over all of that again. The important thing is it's a wonderful honor. I think we should have a party to celebrate before you go."

A smile ghosted around his mouth. "Do you?"

"Of course. It isn't every day you get made head of your department. The next thing you know, you'll be dean. It's only a matter of time. And then—"

"Lilah, sit down. Please."

"All right." She clung to the desperate gaiety. "We'll have Aunt Coco bake a cake, and—"

"You're happy about the offer then?" he interrupted.

"I'm very proud of you," she said, and brushed the hair from his brow. "I like knowing that the powers that be appreciate how valuable you are."

"And you want me to accept?"

Her brows drew together. "Of course. How could you refuse? This is a wonderful opportunity for you, something you've worked for and earned."

"That's a pity." He shook his head and leaned back, still watching her. "I've already declined."

"You did what?"

"I declined, with appreciation. It's one of the reasons I never mentioned the whole business to you. I didn't see it as an issue."

"I don't understand. A career opportunity like this isn't something you casually turn aside."

"It depends on your career. I also tendered my resignation."

"You—you quit? But that's crazy."

"Yes, probably." And because it was, he had to grin. "But if I went back to Cornell to teach, the book would end up in a file somewhere gathering dust." He held out his hand, palm up. "You looked at this once and told me I'd have to make a choice. I've made it."

"I see," she said slowly.

"You only see part of it." He glanced around the tower. The light was pearly now, slowly going gold. There couldn't be a better time or a better place. He took both of her hands.

"I've loved you from the first moment I saw you. I couldn't believe that you could ever feel the same way, no matter how much I wanted it. Because I didn't, I made things more difficult than they might have been. No, don't say anything, not yet. Just listen." He pressed their joined hands to his lips. "You've changed me. Opened me. I know that I was meant to be with you, and if it took deceit and a necklace that's been lost the best part of a century, then that's what it had to take. Whether or not we'll ever find the emeralds, they brought you to me, and you're all the treasure I'll ever need."

He brought her close to kiss her mouth as morning rose and washed the last shadows from the room.

"I don't want this to be a dream," she murmured. "I've sat here before thinking of you, wishing for this."

"This is real." He framed her face then kissed her again to prove it.

"You're all I want, Max. I've been looking for you for such a long time." Gently she combed her fingers through the hair on his brow. "I was so afraid you wouldn't love me back, that you'd go away. That I'd have to let you go away."

"This has been home since the first night. I can't explain it."

"You don't have to."

"No." He turned his lips into her palm. "Not to you. One last thing." Again he took her hands. "I love you, Lilah, and I have to ask if you're willing to take the risk of marrying an unemployed former teacher who thinks he can write a book."

"No." She smiled and linked her arms around his neck. "But I'm going to marry a very talented and brilliant man who is writing a wonderful book."

With a laugh, he rested his brow on hers. "I like your way better."

"Max." She snuggled into the crook of his arm. "Let's go tell Aunt Coco. She'll be so thrilled she'll fix us blueberry pancakes for an engagement breakfast."

He eased her back against the pillows. "How about an engagement brunch?"

She laughed and flowed into the kiss. "This time I like your way better."

* * * * *

REQUEST YOUR
FREE BOOKS!

2 FREE NOVELS
FROM THE ROMANCE COLLECTION
PLUS 2 FREE GIFTS!

YES! Please send me 2 FREE novels from the Romance Collection and my 2 FREE gifts (gifts are worth about $10). After receiving them, if I don't wish to receive any more books, I can return the shipping statement marked "cancel." If I don't cancel, I will receive 4 brand-new novels every month and be billed just $6.24 per book in the U.S. or $6.74 per book in Canada. That's a savings of at least 22% off the cover price. It's quite a bargain! Shipping and handling is just 50¢ per book in the U.S. and 75¢ per book in Canada.* I understand that accepting the 2 free books and gifts places me under no obligation to buy anything. I can always return a shipment and cancel at any time. Even if I never buy another book, the two free books and gifts are mine to keep forever.

194/394 MDN F4XY

Name	(PLEASE PRINT)	

Address		Apt. #

City	State/Prov.	Zip/Postal Code

Signature (if under 18, a parent or guardian must sign)

Mail to the Harlequin® Reader Service:
IN U.S.A.: P.O. Box 1867, Buffalo, NY 14240-1867
IN CANADA: P.O. Box 609, Fort Erie, Ontario L2A 5X3

Want to try two free books from another line?
Call 1-800-873-8635 or visit www.ReaderService.com.

* Terms and prices subject to change without notice. Prices do not include applicable taxes. Sales tax applicable in N.Y. Canadian residents will be charged applicable taxes. Offer not valid in Quebec. This offer is limited to one order per household. Not valid for current subscribers to the Romance Collection or the Romance/Suspense Collection. All orders subject to credit approval. Credit or debit balances in a customer's account(s) may be offset by any other outstanding balance owed by or to the customer. Please allow 4 to 6 weeks for delivery. Offer available while quantities last.

Your Privacy—The Harlequin® Reader Service is committed to protecting your privacy. Our Privacy Policy is available online at www.ReaderService.com or upon request from the Harlequin Reader Service.

We make a portion of our mailing list available to reputable third parties that offer products we believe may interest you. If you prefer that we not exchange your name with third parties, or if you wish to clarify or modify your communication preferences, please visit us at www.ReaderService.com/consumerschoice or write to us at Harlequin Reader Service Preference Service, P.O. Box 9062, Buffalo, NY 14269. Include your complete name and address.

ROM13R

MARTA PERRY

introduces an enthralling new series set in not-so-peaceful Amish country.

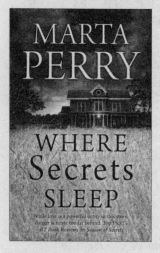

After suffering a terrible betrayal, Allison Standish flees Philadelphia for the small Amish village of Laurel Ridge. There, she comes into an unexpected inheritance—a mansion. Allison intends to sell Blackburn House, until one of her tenants, single father Nick Whiting, challenges everything she believes about her estranged grandmother and the Amish community.

When she discovers her grandmother's death may not have been accidental, and anonymous threats against her begin to escalate, Allison must face the truth that someone wants her gone…permanently.

Pick up your copy today!

Be sure to connect with us at:
Harlequin.com/Newsletters
Facebook.com/HarlequinBooks
Twitter.com/HQNBooks

NORA ROBERTS